"*Love, Lists, and Fancy Ships* is a delightful love story about setting and settling goals, about the journeys of the heart, and about how you have to let go of the past in order to move forward. You'll be rooting for Jo from the first page."

—Jodi Picoult, #1 *New York Times* bestselling author of *The Book of Two Ways*

"Sarah Grunder Ruiz's *Love, Lists, and Fancy Ships* is a book with enormous heart, and one that balances family grief with truly delightful witty banter. It made me laugh, it made me cry, and it made me swoon from all the delicious pining between Jo and Alex. It's a wonderful debut, and I can't wait to read more from her."

—Olivia Dade, author of *Spoiler Alert*

"Sometimes hilarious, sometimes devastating, and always heartwarming, *Love, Lists, and Fancy Ships* is an amazing debut about picking up the pieces after loss. With a complicated (but ultimately loving) family, fully realized friends, and a very handsome chef, this beautiful book shows how being generous with your heart can help mend it. I loved it!"

—Farah Heron, author of *Accidentally Engaged*

"This book is a love letter to letting yourself feel your feelings instead of pushing them away, or pushing away those who want to love you through it. Sweet, beachy, and emotional, you will want to read this one with a box of tissues." —Sarah Hogle, author of *Twice Shy*

"*Love, Lists, and Fancy Ships* is funny, touching, swoony, and brimming with heart. Sarah Grunder Ruiz writes characters you'll cheer for and fall in love with, and leaves you wanting more."

—Trish Doller, author of *Float Plan*

Love, Lists,

and

Fancy Ships

SARAH GRUNDER RUIZ

JOVE

New York

A JOVE BOOK
Published by Berkley
An imprint of Penguin Random House LLC
penguinrandomhouse.com

Library of Congress Cataloging-in-Publication Data

Names: Ruiz, Sarah Grunder, author.
Title: Love, lists, and fancy ships / Sarah Grunder Ruiz.
Description: First edition. | New York: Jove, 2021.
Identifiers: LCCN 2021001295 (print) | LCCN 2021001296 (ebook) |
ISBN 9780593335420 (trade paperback) | ISBN 9780593335437 (ebook)
Subjects: GSAFD: Love stories.
Classification: LCC PS3618.U55 L68 2021 (print) |
LCC PS3618.U55 (ebook) | DDC 813/.6—dc23
LC record available at https://lccn.loc.gov/2021001295
LC ebook record available at https://lccn.loc.gov/2021001296

First Edition: November 2021

Printed in the United States of America
1st Printing

Book design by George Towne

For my mother, Sophia Grunder,
whose fierce and generous love was the inspiration for this story.

In memory of Chad Jeffrey Moles (1982–1995)

Jo Walker's 30-by-30 List

1. Start a blog
2. Spend a week camping
3. Sing onstage
4. Meet a celebrity
5. Kiss a stranger
6. Go on a road trip
7. Start a garden
8. Get a tattoo
9. Go skinny-dipping
10. Buy an expensive dress
11. Attempt ballroom dancing
12. Go skydiving
13. Crash a party
14. Take surfing lessons
15. Run a marathon
16. Throw a surprise party
17. Develop a signature cocktail
18. Get a psychic reading
19. Go parasailing
20. Swim with sharks
21. Go zip-lining
22. Declutter the condo
23. Go free diving
24. Go horseback riding
25. Sleep in a castle
26. Stay out all night
27. Read 20 books
28. Host a dinner party
29. Go bungee jumping
30. Visit 10 countries

June

One

⚓

THE SUMMER I TURNED THIRTY STARTED TO UNRAVEL AS SOON as it began. It was the last day of charter season, and I was ironing a billionaire's underwear in the laundry room of the *Serendipity*, the superyacht I'd worked on for the last five years, when Nina called for me over the radio.

I set down the iron and unclipped my walkie-talkie from my shorts, kicking aside a pile of dirty sheets from last night's toga party. I'd been on laundry duty all morning, but I didn't mind, seeing as it had gotten me out of earlies—the first shift of the day.

"Jo?" the radio called again. "This is Nina. Do you copy?"

I rolled my eyes, glad she couldn't see me. I knew Nina was worried, given everything that had happened, but she could at least give me a second to respond.

"Go for Jo," I sang into the walkie-talkie.

"We need you in the galley."

"Copy that."

I clipped my radio to my shorts and turned off the iron. Off the boat, Nina was my best friend, but on it she was chief stewardess, aka my boss, meaning she made my life alternately fun and miserable. But over the last three months, ever since the accident, she'd been softer on me, letting me out of earlies because mornings were hardest, not complaining as much as she normally would when I missed a water spot on the faucet in the master bathroom. I was appreciative, but the special treatment made me uncomfortable, and I didn't like how she kept checking up on me. She'd corner me in the crew mess or pass me a drink in a Bahamian bar and ask how I was holding up. *Fine*, I always said, taking a long pull of whatever tropical concoction she'd ordered for me. Was I fine? Nope. Not even close. But that didn't mean I wanted to talk about it, not even with Nina.

Other than the week I'd gone to my sister's house in North Carolina, the last four months of my life had been back-to-back charters in the Bahamas. Every week the cycle repeated: pick up the guests, cater to their whims—including ironing their ridiculously expensive underwear (we'd googled the brand; who seriously spends $165 on a pair of briefs?!)—drop the guests back at port, flip the boat, enjoy a well-deserved night off, pick up the next guests. It was chaotic, and exhausting, and exactly what I needed. Out here in the middle of the ocean, I could pretend my real life, the one where I drove a car and wore shoes and lived alone, was on hold. But even I had to admit the cabin fever was starting to get to me.

Before Nina could radio me again, I raced up to the main deck and pushed through the galley doors where, as always, chaos was waiting for me.

"There you are!" Nina called, a wrinkle of concern on her brow. She sat at a small table, her fingers nimbly folding a mound of cloth napkins into little sailboats. "We have a beach picnic, remember?"

Beside the pantry stood Britt, third stewardess and my painfully messy bunkmate. Her curly hair shook as she dug through a plastic bin of decor, piling dried starfish, delicate sand dollars, and seashells at her feet. Once I'd asked her how she could be a stewardess and such a slob at the same time. We were essentially maids on fancy boats, after all. Britt replied that she spent so much time cleaning up after other people, she had no energy to pick up after herself.

"Fecking beach picnic," Ollie, the *Serendipity*'s chef, muttered. He whizzed around the galley like a pinball, his Irish accent rising above the hiss of pans on the stove.

"He's having a bad day," Nina said.

I glanced at Ollie, who was now hacking a watermelon to pieces. "When isn't he?"

"Touché." Nina tugged the sail of a napkin turned boat in her hands. Her dangling unicorn earrings, the ones she wore every day, swung back and forth as she looked me over. They were the only sign of the goofy Nina I knew outside of work, a stark contrast to her neat high ponytail and severe expression. Though she was tiny, and at five-two was a couple inches shorter than me, she carried herself with a confidence I doubted I'd ever have. We must have made an amusing pair: petite, dark-haired, intimidating Nina, and me, your nonconfrontational, average-everything blonde.

"What took you so long?" Nina said when I sat beside her. "Find skid marks in the primary's tighty-whities again?"

I swatted a napkin at her. "Why would you put that image in my mind?" Nina didn't usually joke about the primary—the guest who'd booked the charter—but this primary was . . . different.

Nina gave me a tight-lipped smile, then set a sailboat napkin on the table and handed me a checklist of everything we'd need to pack for the beach picnic. "Double- and triple-check it. I don't want another dessert spoon incident."

On my mental list of things that didn't belong on the beach (which included closed-toed shoes, reality TV weddings, and laptops), fancy silverware was one of them. "Because God forbid they eat dessert with any other type of spoon."

Ollie glared at me from where he stood over the sink, running watermelon purée through a strainer. "If I'm spending my entire morning spherizing watermelon, they'll eat it with a fecking dessert spoon now."

"All right, all right, I'll pack the dessert spoons." I held up my hands in surrender and backed away, joining Britt at the pantry, where her pile of seashells was growing larger by the second.

I prodded a seashell with my foot. "The picnic is on a beach, you know. That's why it's called a beach picnic."

Britt turned a conch shell over in her hands. "It's the last one of the season, so it has to be perfect." She sighed and clutched the shell to her chest. "Tell me again about your trip. I want to live vicariously through you. What's first?"

"Paris," I said, dragging a bin of silverware (including dessert spoons) onto the counter. Next month I'd be off to Europe to check off the last five countries for my thirty-by-thirty list—the list of thirty things I wanted to do before my thirtieth birthday at the end of the summer. I still had nine things to go, but hopefully I'd be able to complete them and get some great fodder for the blog I'd started to document my progress.

"And then Spain, right?"

"Barcelona and Madrid," I said. "Then Switzerland, Austria, and Scotland."

Nina joined us, dropping a handful of sailboat napkins onto the counter. "I'm horrified you're not going to Ibiza. That would've been my first port of call."

"I know," I said, inspecting a dessert spoon for water spots. She'd said as much every time I brought up my itinerary. If it weren't for the fact that one of us had to stay and work the day charters over the summer, I would've forced her to come with me.

"And why do you have to live vicariously through Jo?" Nina said to Britt. "Won't you be working Med season and making bank? I can't believe you're abandoning me. Honestly, I may never forgive you."

Britt rolled her eyes. "*Working* in the Mediterranean and vacationing there are two different things. I won't be sleeping in any castles."

Ollie banged a pot on the counter, making us jump. "Could you three shut it? I'm trying to prepare molecular gastronomy for a fecking beach picnic. That primary's a miserable little pox, and if I feck this up, I'm blaming you three for distracting me."

"Aren't chefs supposed to like cooking fancy shit?" Nina said. "Quit complaining and do your job."

Ollie gave her a look that could bleach coral. "Don't eat the head off me, Neen."

Nina dismissed him with a wave. "I swear, I hardly understand you sometimes."

Britt elbowed me and mimed sticking a finger down her throat, making me laugh. There was always some sort of tension between Nina and Ollie. We were never sure if they were about to murder each other or make out. My bet was on both.

"You'll text me if they hook up this summer, won't you? They've got way more drama than *The Bachelor*."

I raised my eyebrows at her. "Who's to say they haven't already?"

Britt gasped. "Josephine Walker, do you know something I don't?"

"Sorry." I zipped my hand across my mouth. "Solemn best friend duties. My lips are sealed."

Nina and Ollie leaned toward each other over the counter, tension sparking between them. (Sexual, or the kind that got you a special on Oxygen, who could say?) I had no idea if they'd hooked up or not. But whatever Nina felt about Ollie, it had to be serious, because she refused to talk about it, and Nina wasn't the sort of person to hold her tongue.

Though Ollie had a habit of complaining about everything, he was right about this: Molecular gastronomy and beach picnics did not go together. Everything about the food he was preparing depended on precise temperatures and chemical reactions, making sand and sun less than ideal. But on a superyacht, the primary got what the primary wanted. And I couldn't wait to get this one off the boat as soon as possible.

It wasn't that I didn't love my job, because I did. I loved the routine of it: stretching sheets taut on the beds, the thud of the lines as they hit the dock, the constant hum of the washer and dryer, planning theme parties and scavenger hunts. Most of our guests were fun and generous people. But our current guests made me wonder if I should've gone to college and found a job that required shoes, offered a 401(k), and had a regular schedule with weekends off.

Our current primary was a Silicon Valley type with a God complex. Last night, after spending the entire week working indoors in the Sky Lounge and complaining about spotty Wi-Fi, he'd chewed me out in front of everyone for not smiling enough during dinner service. *You're coming off a little bitchy, sweetie* were his exact words. What he didn't know was it had been three months to the day since Samson, my eleven-year-old nephew, was struck and killed by a car while riding his bike to a friend's house. I'd spent the entire morning crying—in the laundry room, while scrubbing toilets, as I collected leaves from a nearby island and hot glued them to construction paper to make laurel wreaths for the toga party. So yeah, my smile wasn't at full force. I'd wanted to tell him it takes a bitch to know one, but I liked being employed. Instead, I apologized and imagined all the offensive towel art I could make on his bed but wouldn't.

"Hey, hello? Jo?" Nina said, knocking on my forehead. "Can you check if the guests need a refill on drinks? They're on the sun deck."

I groaned. "Do I have to?"

Nina scowled, so I shut my mouth and marched up the spiral staircase without another word.

Though the laundry room was my true love, the sun deck was a close second. Known as the "party spot," the sun deck had a hot tub that could be converted into a dance floor, several oversized lounge chairs for sunbathing, and stunning panoramic views of the water. Another set of stairs led up to the highest point on the ship, a cushioned area called the bunny pad, where guests (or crew members looking for a moment alone) could escape for the best view on board. Mr. Silicon Valley didn't care about once-in-a-lifetime ocean vistas, however. I found him in the hot tub with his coworkers and their bored girlfriends, all of them staring at their phones.

"Anyone need a refill?" I asked, plastering my brightest smile on my face.

The primary unglued his eyes from his phone. "I'll have a gin fizz. And make sure you shake it long enough this time, Jen."

I almost said, *My name is Jo, jerk face*, but the rest of the crew would kill me if I put our tip in jeopardy, so I contented myself with a "You got it" and an eye roll once I turned away. Fussy drinks for fussy guests, go figure.

Nina and I used to play a game where we'd guess which drinks the guests would order based on our first impressions of them. After a few months, we got scary good at it. Vodka sodas were the favorite of youthful, weight-conscious girlfriends. Whiskey drinkers were contemplative types who stared silently out at the water, but when they did talk, they had the best stories. Winos, on the other hand, talked nonstop. They were the ones who inevitably ordered late-night snacks, meaning we had to shake Ollie awake to make them (we played rock, paper, scissors to see who got stuck with that unpleasant task). But they were also the guests who most frequently invited us to join the fun: dancing with us at theme parties, or requesting we go down the giant inflatable slide behind them or double-bounce them on the floating trampoline. Painkillers were for the flashy new-money types who squeezed every last perk from their trip. The margarita drinkers were my favorite, though. Fun, but not overly complicated, and I'm not only saying that because margaritas are my and Nina's drink of choice.

"Oh, and, sweetie," the primary called out. "These towels are a little damp. Mind getting fresh ones?"

And gin fizz drinkers were the worst of them all. After all that shaking and straining, they were never pleased. I shook his drink with extra vigor, imagining it were his head. I knew those towels were dry when I brought them up. What did a damp towel matter when he would get it soaked with his sopping-wet chest hair anyway?

When I finished making his drink, I stood near the hot tub and waited for his approval. All I got were smacked lips and a "Meh." But what did I expect, a thank-you?

I ran belowdeck to exchange the towels (aka went downstairs, refolded the towels, waited three minutes, and returned with the same towels), then stood behind the bar, watching the primary and his friends take business calls while their girlfriends took dozens of pouty photos. After what felt like an eternity, Nina appeared on the sun deck and joined me by the bar.

"Having fun, Jen?" she asked.

"So much fun," I said, wiping down the already-spotless bar with a damp rag.

Nina and I were peeking at the girlfriends' social media feeds (models, predictably) when my phone vibrated. At the sight of my sister's face on the screen, my chest tightened, and I stared at my phone, unable to move.

Nina squeezed my shoulder. "Take it. I can cover for you."

I nodded and stepped into the Sky Lounge, the phone still vibrating in my hands. Despite the five years between us, my sister and I had always been close. She was more than a sister to me, really. Beth had become the mother ours couldn't be after Dad died, taking me in when I was sixteen. I'd lived with her; her husband, Mark; and their kids for six years, until I moved to Florida at Beth's urging. She'd wanted me to go to college, but I'd ended up bartending instead. But now, my sister had experienced an unspeakable tragedy. We all had. And I had no idea what to do or say to be there for her.

"Joey," Beth said when I answered. "Are you ready?"

I sighed into a sleek white love seat, relieved Beth wasn't already crying. Half our phone calls started with her in tears these days. Out on the sun deck, the primary passed his empty glass to Nina with a grimace. No doubt about it, I was ready for charter season to end.

"I've never been more ready for anything in my life."

"Do you need me to send anything?"

Odd question, but then again, nothing had been normal with Beth lately. "I'd love it if you could send me some sanity. These guests are horrendous."

"I can't make any promises, but I'll see what I can do. I still can't believe he paid almost two hundred bucks for a pair of plain white briefs."

"You don't even want to know what the leopard-print ones cost."

Beth laughed, but it was thin and false, not the throaty cackle I'd always teased her for. I grabbed a nautical-themed pillow from beside me and hugged it to my chest. "How are you? Is everything okay?"

"Yes," Beth said, but her voice wavered. "No, actually. Things between me and Mark aren't great. That's why we need this break."

Break? I squeezed the pillow harder. Mark and Beth on a break? They'd been together since freshman English class in high school. Then Beth got pregnant their senior year, the year Dad died, and they got married right after graduation. Despite it all, they were the happiest couple I knew, at least until Samson died and the fighting started. But a break? I couldn't fathom it.

"I didn't know things were that bad," I said.

Beth sighed. "We wouldn't need this time alone if they weren't. I wanted to be the one to tell you, in case the girls bring it up."

I tried to imagine Beth's daughters—Mia, sixteen, and Kitty, thirteen—calling me to vent about their parents' marriage. The girls and I were close. Samson and I had been even closer. All three of them had visited me every summer since I'd moved to Florida. In between visits we video chatted and sent each other memes, but I wasn't sure we were vent-about-their-parents'-marriage close.

"I'm sorry, B." I snapped a loose thread from the white-embroidered anchor on the pillow. "I love you, no matter what happens. Mark too."

"I know," Beth sighed. "And thanks, Jo. You'll call if anything comes up?"

"Of course," I said, thinking she was talking about the girls reaching out to me about her and Mark.

"This will be hard, but I think it'll be good for all of us," she said.

I bit my lip, not so sure I agreed. How did she and Mark splitting up make an awful situation better? They'd lost so much already. But it wasn't my job to tell her what to do. My role was to be the supportive little sister.

A shadow fell across the room, and I looked up, spotting Nina in the doorway. She gave me an *everything good?* look, and I managed a weak smile.

"Listen, B. I've got to go. I love you." I hung up, taking my time to slip my phone in my pocket so I could avoid looking at Nina.

"How's Beth?" Nina asked when she sat down beside me.

"She's fine." I passed her the couch pillow and stood, crossing the room. "Just checking in."

"And everything's good?"

"Everything's fine."

"You don't look like everything's fine."

"Is it time for the beach picnic?" I turned to the sun deck. The guests milled around the hot tub, towels at their waists, their drink glasses filled. "Did the primary complain about your gin fizz–making skills too?" I tried to laugh, but my throat was thick with emotion, and I blinked back tears, angry with myself. I hadn't cried in front of anyone since the night my mother, whom I rarely spoke with, called to tell me about the accident. Shouldn't I be able to talk about this without falling apart by now? My pain over Beth's marriage, the loss of her son, it could be nothing compared to hers. Didn't I owe it to her to keep myself together?

Nina tilted her head, watching me. Why was she wasting time sitting there? What if the primary needed his underwear ironed again?

"I'm here to listen if you need to talk," she said. "I'm sure the guests can entertain themselves for a few minutes."

I turned away and adjusted a vase of flowers behind me. "I appreciate it, but I'm good."

"It's okay if you aren't, though. No matter what, I'm—"

"Nina," I said, my voice harsher than I'd meant it to be. I closed my eyes and let out a shaky breath. "Really, I'm fine. I just need a minute."

Nina went quiet, and for a moment I thought she'd left the room. But when I turned around, she was still sitting on the couch watching me.

"All right," she said. "Britt and I are doing the beach picnic. You're in charge of laundry while we're gone."

I eyed her, skeptical. Everyone hated beach picnics. They were hot, sandy affairs, and we spent most of it fanning away flies. Usually, we fought over who got to stay and do laundry. It was never this easy.

"This isn't some excuse to give me space, is it?"

Nina rolled her eyes and arranged the pillow tastefully on the love seat. "No. It's an excuse to get you to do your job. The sooner we get through lunch and flip the boat, the sooner we get to Palm Beach and drink margaritas at Mitch's."

This was best friend Nina talking, not boss Nina. And as much as I didn't like the special treatment, I was desperate to get out of this beach picnic.

"Fine," I said.

"Marvelous." Nina stood, squeezing my shoulder on her way out to the guests.

Once Nina left, I disappeared belowdeck, where the white noise of the washer and dryer, along with the tedium of folding and ironing clothes, took my mind off the conversation with my sister. The rest of the charter flew by, and before I knew it, the deckhands had docked the boat, and Captain Xav was calling us to the aft deck to send off the guests. I slipped out of my polo and tugged on my whites before sprinting up the steps and lining up with the rest of the crew.

"Don't look *too* happy to see them go," Nina said when I shuffled in line beside her. "It's not over until Cap has the tips."

The guests filed down the line, thanking us for making their stay memorable. I gave each of them, even the primary, one last *Serendipity* smile. When he reached the end of the line, the primary passed Captain Xav a thick white envelope. Britt wriggled in excitement beside me. We'd spent many nights post-charter counting out cash on our bunks and singing, *I like big tips and I cannot lie*, at the tops of our lungs, until Ollie, in the room next to ours, banged on the wall to get us to shut up, which only made us sing louder.

"We're free!" Britt shouted as soon as the guests were out of earshot. She did a dance Samson had taught me last summer, flossing or flossy, I could never remember. Captain Xav gave her a stern look. "Oh, relax, Cap," she said. "You hated them as much as we did."

Captain Xav shrugged, a smile visible beneath his beard. "Tell the deckhands we're meeting in the crew mess in five," he said, before leaving for the bridge with the tip envelope.

"What a season," Nina sighed. She shook her head, unicorn earrings sparkling in the sunlight.

"Yeah," I said. But I wasn't thinking about the guests or the crew drama; I was thinking about Samson.

Nina left with Ollie for the galley, which didn't go unnoticed by Britt, who suggested we spy on them before heading belowdeck.

I pushed her toward the stairs, away from Nina and Ollie. "Is there any particular reason you're so thirsty for drama?" I said.

"Oh, you're no fun." Britt's shoulders sagged as she reluctantly followed me down to the crew mess. We sat at the table where we'd eaten almost every meal for the last four months. One by one, the room filled with the expectant faces of my colleagues. And finally, Captain Xav arrived and smacked the tip envelope onto the table, banishing my thoughts of finding another career.

"I know this wasn't our best season," he began. "There were some hiccups." He eyed the deckhands, who'd nearly ruined our entire season when they didn't untie a spring line quick enough, causing the bow to bump against the dock. RJ, the bosun in charge of the deckhands, kept a straight face and didn't meet Captain Xav's eye. "We also had some personal tragedies," he added, and I looked down at my hands when he nodded to me. "But I'm really proud of all of you for sticking it out."

He held up the envelope. "These guests were a pain in the ass, but at least they showed their appreciation to the tune of . . ." He flipped through the cash. "Thirty large. That's three thousand for each of you." He slid our tips across the table, and I thumbed through my share with a little thrill.

After we counted our tips, Captain Xav dismissed us, saying that once we cleaned the boat and docked in Palm Beach, we could head home. Everyone left the crew mess to hurry through the last of their duties, and as I watched them go, the excitement of our big tip faded.

"You good, love?" Ollie said.

I blinked, taking in his and Nina's concerned faces from across the table. Nina was bad enough; I didn't need Ollie worrying about me too. I fanned myself with the wad of cash in my hand. "What could be wrong?"

Nina scowled. "Be serious, Josephine."

"I am serious!"

"Then I better not see you moping around Mitch's tonight. Don't wait until I'm drunk to have a heart-to-heart, okay?"

Ollie groaned. "Mitch's? Again? I hate that fecking place."

"Do not," Nina and I said.

"An Irish pub shouldn't have Mexican food."

"You love the tacos, so don't bullshit us," Nina said.

"Eff off, Neen." Ollie stood from the table, cursing under his breath as he left.

I ignored the look Nina was giving me and tried to seem excited, though I wasn't feeling entirely up for Mitch's. All season it had been hard to drag myself off the boat on our nights off. How could I go on drinking, and dancing, and laughing with friends when everything in my family's world was so wrong? But tonight, what was the alternative? Return home to my quiet condo and see that absolutely nothing, and yet everything, had changed?

"Come on," I said, pulling Nina to her feet. "If we don't hurry, we won't have time to look cute."

When we docked at the marina a few hours later, the sky was streaked in warm colors. I stared at the *Serendipity* as our ride left the parking lot, my heart in my throat. I'd be back for our first day charter of the summer in less than twenty-four hours, but off-season always had a different feel to it. I sank into my seat as the driver zipped past palm trees and high-rises, and turned my mind to happier thoughts: my trip to Europe, the Scottish castle I'd booked for two nights, the marathon I'd start training for—a gentler season, right around the corner.

Two

MITCH'S WASN'T THE MOST GLAMOROUS BAR IN PALM BEACH, but it boasted the most convenient location. Only three blocks from my condo, it was where Nina and I had celebrated every birthday, mourned every breakup, and toasted to every charter season for the last five years.

I followed Nina, Britt, and Ollie through the heavy wooden door and was hit by the familiar scent of stale beer and tacos as soon as I stepped inside. Mitch's was the opposite of the *Serendipity*, which was probably why we liked it so much. The *Serendipity* was chic and elegant, while Mitch's was decidedly not. Dim and wood-paneled, the bar wore its years proudly, with deep grooves etched into the tables and wobbly chairs with sunken seats. Hundreds of photographs and personal effects had been stapled or thumbtacked to the walls and exposed beams of the ceiling. I'd spent many nights drunkenly wandering and inspecting the tokens patrons had left behind.

Back by our usual spot—a table beside a dusty bookcase—was a photo of me, Nina, and Ollie. Nina had taken it a few years ago with an ancient Polaroid she'd found at a yard sale. Pulling a mini stapler from her purse, she'd stuck our photo beside one of a shirtless man with a snake draped around his shoulders. *There*, she'd said. *That ought to freshen up the place.*

Standing in Mitch's now, I wanted to find that picture and see myself from before. Before I'd met Shitty Peter, the ex-boyfriend who'd shattered my confidence, before the accident and the call from my mother, before every day felt like treading water. But it was Taco Tuesday, Mitch's was packed, and some college students wearing sweatpants occupied our table.

Nina bumped me with her shoulder. "Margarita? Yes? No?"

"Please tell me that's a rhetorical question," I said.

We joined the rest of the crew at the bar and ordered our drinks. I tried to look as happy as everyone else but didn't have the energy. Being there only reminded me of my list and the blog I'd been completely neglecting. Every now and then I'd get emails from concerned readers, which I deleted as soon as they arrived in my inbox. Not because they annoyed me, but because I knew there was nothing I could say. Many of them had been reading my posts from the very beginning. They thought they knew me. They were worried. But they didn't know me at all, not the real me anyway. And besides, my blog was a place for lighthearted adventure, which I hadn't had much of lately.

Nina and I had been drinking at Mitch's when we came up with the idea for the thirty-by-thirty list. It was my twenty-ninth birthday, almost a year ago now, and I'd spent most of the night moping at the bar, having recently broken up with Shitty Peter after discovering he'd cheated on me during charter season. Two margaritas in, Nina, who'd recently turned thirty herself, had tried to console me by explaining how I'd look back on my breakup with Shitty Peter one day and laugh.

"Thirtysomething is far superior to twentysomething," she'd said. "You stop caring what people think."

"I'm pretty sure you've never cared what people think." I'd set my drink on the bar and sighed. "Two years. I wasted two years on that douchebag, and for what? There was so much I didn't do because of him.

I missed my cousin's bachelorette party, the post-charter weekend away to Saint Thomas, Cap's anniversary—"

"Jo, Jo, Jo," Nina had said, pressing her hand over my mouth. "Listen to you! So you missed out on two years of stuff, you can still make up for it. Hell, I've been single for most of the last decade and still have things I wish I'd done in my twenties."

I'd pried her hand from my mouth. "Like what?"

"I don't know . . . like going to Burning Man or Coachella."

"Nina, you could still go to Burning Man."

"But it's different now. I can't survive the inevitable hangover. There's no way in hell I'm sleeping in a yurt. At twenty-five, maybe. But thirty? No way. What kind of word is 'yurt' anyway? It's like whoever named it wasn't even trying to make it sound appealing."

"I think it's Russian   "

Nina had smacked her open palms onto the bar. "I don't care if it's Russian! The point is, you've still got time. Why not make up for the last two years with this one? One year left to do all those twentysomething things."

"You're ridiculous," I'd said. But Nina had already grabbed a napkin and pen from the bartender and shoved them toward me.

I was maybe a little drunk by then, sad about the breakup, unsure what I wanted next, so I'd taken the pen and napkin from Nina and looked around the bar for inspiration. Thumbtacks dotted a faded world map behind the bar. There were photos of birthdays, and weddings, and runners crossing finish lines. Vibrant, well-lived lives.

"Thirty things?" Nina had said once I finished. "Don't you think that's a little ambitious?" I'd scowled, and she cleared her throat. "I mean, wow! Look at you being so ambitious! Though it's my duty as your best friend to inform you that blogs are very 2004." She'd read over the list again and gasped. "Josephine Walker, why is *decluttering* on here?"

I'd snatched the napkin from her hand. "It's very popular right now. I might become a minimalist."

"I don't get minimalism," Nina had said. "I'm a maximalist." She'd lifted up her drink. "I'll have one of everything, please. No! Two!" But she'd toasted to the list anyway.

Sitting at that same bar now, I realized Nina had been right. My breakup with Shitty Peter was laughable, but not for the reasons I'd hoped. Life had reminded me that there were worse heartbreaks.

An hour after we arrived at Mitch's, RJ and the deckhands left for another bar, and Britt pushed away her empty glass with a sigh. "It's been fun, but I've got an early flight tomorrow," she said.

I stood to hug her. "Stay out of trouble."

"Don't listen to her," Nina said. "Cause as much trouble as you can. You better bring good stories back next year."

Britt waved one last goodbye as she and the rest of the seasonal crew dragged their suitcases out the door, leaving me, Ollie, and Nina behind. Though Nina had told Britt to bring back stories, there was no guarantee we'd ever see her again. Charter season was a lot like being a camp counselor. The bonds you made with your coworkers were strong (positive or negative), and someone who'd been your closest friend one season could disappear from your life the next.

Once it was just the three of us again, Nina leaned her head on my shoulder. No matter what emotion I tried to hide, she homed in on it like a heart-to-heart-seeking missile.

"Sam would want you to have fun," she said.

"How would you know?"

Nina lifted her head and looked me straight on. "I loved him, too, remember?"

It was true. One of Mia, Kitty, and Samson's favorite South Florida attractions was Nina, who had the best ghost stories and bought strange vintage board games she found at thrift stores.

"You're right. Sorry."

"I know it's tough coming home after everything that's happened, but he wouldn't want you to be miserable."

I looked down into the watery dregs of my margarita, watching the ice at the bottom of my glass shift as it melted. Nina was right, of course. Last year I'd gone up to North Carolina for Thanksgiving, and Samson, who was an early riser like me, sat beside me on the couch as he devoured a Pop-Tart and watched cartoons while I edited a post for the blog. To my embarrassment, he'd noticed what I was working on and forced me to tell him all about the list.

"You have to finish all this by our birthday?" he'd said, his hands fidgeting in his lap like they always did. He'd been a boy in constant motion.

Samson had been born on my eighteenth birthday, back when I was still living with my sister. When I'd held him that first time, I knew we were made of the same stuff, that whatever we had would be special. Samson was the one who'd helped me with item number seven—start a garden. He'd been an enthusiastic member of his school's gardening club and a total plant nerd. He'd wanted to be both a botanist and a pro baseball player. He'd loved trees and plants and flowers, and didn't care that his sisters teased him about it. Whenever someone called his love of flowers girlie, he'd glare at them before continuing to inspect pistils and stamens. After he discovered my blog, we had spent the next hour ordering seeds for my garden: delicate hydrangeas, gaillardias the color of a sunset, waxy peperomias.

"And sword lilies," he'd said.

"Right, those."

"They're our birth month flower," Samson explained. "Gladiolus is the real name."

I'd typed it in, and a burst of color flooded my screen. They were beautiful, with funnel-shaped flowers that climbed vertically up stems, the leaves long and swordlike.

"Roman gladiators wore them around their necks to protect them from death when they fought."

"Sounds pretty badass," I'd replied, ruffling his hair until he groaned and scooted away from me.

The thought of seeing those plants again was like a black dart to my chest. How would I not think of him every time I saw them? How was I supposed to carry on watering and pruning them? And yet, not caring for them would be impossible.

I put my chin in my hands and looked at Nina. "Fine. But if you're forcing me to have fun, I need another drink."

"You got it, babe." She waved the bartender over and ordered two more margaritas.

Once our drinks arrived, Ollie captured Nina's attention again, and I looked around at the other patrons. Beside me sat a dark-haired man. His back was to me as he spoke to a blond woman on his other side. The woman's eyebrows crawled up her forehead, and I strained to hear their conversation. Whatever he'd said, the woman wasn't happy about it. She stood, swiped her purse from the bar, and left.

The man turned, watching her go with a weary expression. He caught my eye, and I couldn't help but notice he was handsome, with honey-colored eyes and tousled brown hair that was graying at the temples. He smiled at me, and I smiled back before turning away, ignoring how my heart fluttered like a sail in the wind. Not that I knew anything about sails, working on a motor yacht and all.

I sipped my drink, fighting the urge to sneak another glance at the man beside me. The margarita had me buzzy and warm. The ever-present knot in my stomach loosened, my shoulders relaxed, and I eased into the feeling. Everything around me seemed to glow as I listened to the murmur of voices in the bar without taking in their meaning.

At a hand on my shoulder I looked up, my heart skipping a beat, but it was only Ollie. With one hand on me, and the other on Nina, he leaned drunkenly between us.

"I'm off to the jacks. Save my seat?"

Nina said no at the same time I said sure, and Ollie smirked, pushing his hair off his forehead before ambling in the direction of the bathroom.

With Ollie gone, Nina turned back to me. "You really ought to start posting on your blog again. Your readers are worried about you, if the comments section is any indication. I expect a full-blown search party by the end of the week."

"And this coming from the woman who said blogs were so 2004?"

"I stand by that statement." Nina's eyes slid away from me, then flicked back, and a wicked smile came over her face. She patted my cheek. "I think I've got your next blog post lined up. How about you check off number five right now?"

Item number five—kiss a stranger—had been Nina's idea, of course. She'd been bugging me to do it ever since the night I made the list. I turned on my barstool, but Nina grabbed my arm. "Don't be obvious!" she hissed.

I followed her gaze, pulse racing when I realized she meant the dark-haired man beside me. "He's handsome, I'll give you that," I whispered.

"So kiss him!"

I shook my head. "I don't want to give him the wrong idea."

"Oh my God, Josephine, it's a kiss, not a proposal. And it's on the list, so you have to do it eventually. When are you going to find a hotter guy?"

I leaned closer, keeping my voice low. "He was obviously on a bad date. The woman practically sprinted out of here! What if he's a murderer?"

Nina gave me an exasperated look. "Who cares? You don't have to take him home. It's only a kiss. Maybe it will cheer him up."

"Absolutely not."

"Maybe it will cheer *you* up, then."

"Kissing a murderer would not cheer me up."

Nina raised an eyebrow and jabbed me in the shoulder with her index finger.

"Ouch! What the hell?"

"Do it." She jabbed me again. "Do it or I won't stop."

"Nina, I don't think—"

But then, instead of poking me, Nina lifted herself from her stool and hip-checked me, practically shoving me into the man's lap.

Mortified, I straightened myself up as quickly as I could, my face flaming. "I'm so sorry."

"No harm done," he said, and when he met my gaze, my breath caught in my chest. I froze, unable to look away. A bit older than I was—he looked about thirty-five or so—he was even more handsome up close, with warm eyes and lips that gently curved into an almost smile.

"Are you okay?" he asked, amusement in his expression.

I blinked, snapping back into the moment. "I . . . lost my balance. Not that I'm drunk or anything. This is only my second drink." I held up my half-empty glass.

The man's smile widened, and after settling back onto my stool, I pinned my elbows to my sides and held my drink close to my chest.

He stuck out his hand. "I'm Alex," he said.

I took a sip from my drink and snorted. I'd never had a man in a bar try to give me a handshake before. "So formal."

"What's that?" he said.

I nearly choked on my margarita. "I said, uh, you're so formal."

Alex laughed. He dropped his hand on the bar and drummed his fingers across the wood. "Well, how do you prefer to say hello?"

I stared at him, thinking of Samson and how Nina was right, time was running out, and he'd want me to have fun and finish my list—the list he'd helped me with.

"I kiss them," I said.

"Like on the cheek?"

"No. On the mouth."

Alex blinked. "Is that right?"

My cheeks grew hot again, but I couldn't chicken out now, not with Nina watching. "It's tradition. It's how we say hello in Florida."

He squinted at me. "Tradition, huh?"

"Yes," I said, sure this would go down as the most embarrassing moment of my life. "A very important tradition. Ancient, I've been told."

"How have I spent my entire life as a Floridian and not known this?"

"You're sure you're not a tourist?"

He tugged at his nondescript black T-shirt. "Thanks?"

"It's a compliment!"

"No one has ever called someone a tourist as a compliment."

"Until now."

Alex's eyes roamed my face. Any second now he'd push away his beer and run away from me.

But then he smiled. "Okay, sure."

"Sure . . . what?" I said, momentarily distracted when his eyes met mine again.

"You can kiss me," he said.

"I can?"

Alex shrugged. "I'm not sure I could live with the weight of ruining an obscure Floridian custom I've never heard of on my shoulders. So I'd better play it safe and let you kiss me, right?"

I glanced at his shoulders, which were quite nice, really. "Right."

Alex nudged his stool closer to mine and turned to face me. He set his hands in his lap and closed his eyes. "Okay, I'm ready."

If I hadn't been so nervous, I would've laughed. He looked like a man trying to meditate in the middle of all this noise. The upward curve of his mouth and the way he leaned slightly toward me were the only signs his mind was on sillier things.

"Well?" he said, eyes still closed. "Are you still there, Florida Girl? I'm going to be really disappointed if I open my eyes and discover you were a figment of my imagination."

Now or never, I thought. I closed my eyes and leaned in swiftly, kissing Alex before I could change my mind. His mouth softened, and he leaned in to deepen the kiss. He tasted like the bitter piney flavor of his beer, but the kiss itself was lingering and sweet. For a moment, the noise of the bar, my list, the aching sadness I couldn't seem to shake, it all faded as I got lost in the smell of him. Light and warm, it reminded me of days in the sun and hours on the water.

When we finally broke apart, my mind was spinning. Nina clapped, but I ignored her. Alex and I looked at each other, and I nearly kissed him again.

"Wow," he finally said. "I agree. This ancient and venerable tradition must be preserved. Do I get to know your name now, Florida Girl?"

"Jo," I said, stretching out my hand.

He smirked and took my hand in his. "So formal."

"Very funny," I said.

When he let go of my hand, I glanced at Nina, but she was absorbed in conversation with Ollie.

Alex watched me with a curious expression, his hands wrapped around his beer. He seemed friendly, but there was something sad about him too. Amid the happy throng of the bar, he felt like a kindred spirit.

"Rough night?" I asked, then shook my head. "Sorry, that was too personal. You don't have to answer that."

He raised his eyebrows. "More personal than a kiss?"

Point taken. "Okay, I'll give you that."

He took a sip of his beer, nodding as he lowered it back onto the bar. "But yeah, it hasn't exactly been my day. Until a minute ago anyway." He smiled, and that annoying fluttering returned to my chest. "Not a date," he added. "In case you were wondering."

"I wasn't," I lied, though my blush probably gave me away. Not that I was interested in him. I was just curious.

"Are you sure? Because I seem to remember you kissing me."

"You looked like you needed a pick-me-up. And like I said, it's tradition."

"Right. Consider me picked up, then." He nodded to my empty glass. "Can I buy you another? It's the least I can do considering you surely had to lower your standards to kiss me."

"Eh, it wasn't so bad."

"Oh, I didn't mean to imply I'm a bad kisser. Only that you are clearly out of my league."

"At least we're on the same page, then."

"About me not being a bad kisser, you mean."

I shrugged. "Whatever floats your boat."

Alex shook his head, that almost smile, which I guessed was his default expression, on his lips. "I've got to tell you, Florida Girl, you are—" But a swell of movement beside me cut him off. I turned just in time to catch Nina storming off toward the bathroom in a flurry of tears.

"Oh, for fuck's sake," Ollie said before running after her.

"Looks like someone's having a rougher night than I am," Alex said.

"My friends . . ." I was breathless, partly from talking to Alex and partly from worry. "I'm sorry. I better go check on them. It was nice to meet you. Thanks for the . . . uh . . ."

"Kiss?" he said.

"Yeah, that."

"Anytime, Florida Girl."

I stood, grabbing my and Nina's purses before pushing my way through the crowd to the women's restroom.

"Occupied!" Ollie called when I knocked.

"It's Jo!"

A moment later, the lock clicked, and the door eased open. Ollie stepped aside to let me past him, and I took in the scene of the bathroom slash storage closet. Nina perched on a cardboard box among the mop and broom and cleaning supplies, head in her hands. Ollie was at her side as soon as the door shut, his arm hooked around her shoulders. Nina glanced up at me with tear-filled eyes and smudged mascara.

"What's going on?" I said.

Nina buried her face in her hands again. "Ask him."

I glared at Ollie. "What did you do to her?"

Ollie's ears turned pink. "I think it's what I won't be doing to her that's the problem." Nina shoved his arm from her shoulders.

"What do you mean?"

Ollie sighed up at the ceiling. "I didn't want to say anything 'til to-morrow, but Neen got it out of me."

"Got what out of you?" I looked between Ollie and Nina, but neither met my gaze. Ollie wrung his hands in his lap, and my stomach plummeted with fear. Was he sick? Had someone died?

"I've got a job at a restaurant in Miami. Il Gabbiano." A smile touched his lips but disappeared as soon as Nina started crying again. "Tomorrow's my last shift on the *Serendipity*."

"You're leaving," I said.

"I am."

I leaned against the door, relieved. A sob escaped Nina, and I tried to see things from her point of view. Ollie leaving wasn't exactly a tragedy. No one in yachting expected to work with the same crew forever, and Il Gabbiano was one of the best restaurants in Miami. It was a big step up for Ollie. But it was also the end of an era. Other than Captain Xav and RJ, Ollie and Nina were the only ones who'd been on the *Serendipity* longer than I had, having started on the same charter season eight years ago. No wonder she was so upset. Not only was I certain the two of them were in love with each other, but the relationship between chief stewardess and chef was one of the most important on the boat. The guests' happiness depended on them understanding each other.

I'd met Ollie and Nina when I snuck onto the *Serendipity* in the middle of the night five years ago. I'd moved to Florida two years before and had found myself adrift and friendless. Old Gary, who lived two doors down from me, had a friend who owned a yacht in the marina. I'd known this because it was all he'd talk about whenever I ran into him at the pool or the shuffleboard court. It was all *Serendipity* this and *Serendipity* that. After a particularly bad night bartending, which had ended with a patron barfing down my shirt, I'd decided to cheer myself up by stealing a bottle of champagne and setting off for the marina, ready to sneak aboard the *Serendipity* and pretend I was someone else. Someone who didn't get barfed on in a bar.

Finding the yacht hadn't been hard. Sneaking onto it was easy. The trouble began when I couldn't pop the cork. Cursing myself, I'd snuck into the galley and grabbed a knife from the counter. But when I'd run the blade over the cork, it went flying, erupting in a bubbly mess on the floor. As soon as it had happened, Nina and Ollie burst into the galley, and I froze, not realizing anyone had been on the boat. They'd caught me standing over the sink, a champagne bottle cradled in my hands, the galley floor soaked.

"The fuck?" Ollie had said, bursting into laughter. Nina hadn't laughed. She'd narrowed her eyes at me, her expression searing. Not knowing what to do, I'd snapped up a damp towel from the counter and started wiping the floor without a word to either of them.

Eventually, I'd fessed up to why I was there and explained my connection to Old Gary, who they knew as Mr. Simmons; my shit day; and my trouble with the cork. Nina must've seen something in me—desperation, a good arm for cleaning up spills, or maybe she thought I'd be entertaining—because she told me they needed a new stewardess and wondered if I'd be interested, since I liked being on yachts so much. It turned out they'd needed someone to start that day, so I tugged on a spare polo and was trained well enough for my first shift under Nina's watchful gaze. A week later, I completed my required basic safety training. And the three of us had been friends ever since.

But now, Ollie was leaving.

"It's true, Jo. Time for bigger and better things," he said.

"You're an asshole," Nina said.

She stood, and I jumped out of her way, wincing when she raced from the bathroom and slammed the door shut behind her.

"Shit," I said. "You've broken her heart."

Ollie looked down at his shoes. "Let's hope the new fella's a charmer."

But I could tell he was heartbroken too. "I'm gonna head on," he said. "You'll take care of her?"

"You know I will." I squeezed Ollie's hand, and he strode out of sight, leaving me to wade through the crowd alone and find Nina.

My eyes darted back to where the three of us had been sitting by the bar. I hoped to catch a glimpse of Alex, wondering what he'd been about to say before Nina's outburst. *You are . . .* what? But he wasn't there, and so I shrugged it off. It wasn't as if I'd been planning to get his number. Our kiss was an item off the list and a bright spot in a long day, nothing else.

I wandered the bar in search of Nina, thinking about how I'd write about tonight as a blog entry. Focus on the excitement, the energy of the patrons, the music. Devote most of it to Alex, of course, since kissing him was the entire point of item number five. Write about that smile. His eyes. The flirty banter. The way I'd wanted to lean in and kiss him again as soon as we pulled apart. Leave out my numbing sadness, Nina and Ollie's outburst.

I found Nina at our usual table. When I took the seat across from her, she touched the photo of us with Ollie on the wall. "Still here."

"He's only going to Miami," I said. "We'll still see him."

"It won't be the same."

I grabbed Nina's hands in mine. "You're right, it won't."

Nina nodded, then her eyes darted around the room. "Your kiss! Hot Guy! Where did he go?"

"I think I might have scared him off," I said.

Nina sighed. "That was probably me."

"Probably. I was just trying to spare your feelings."

"Sorry, Jo."

"What do I care? It's not like I was going to fall in love with the guy. I'm done with romance, remember?"

Nina rolled her eyes. "Which is idiotic. I can't believe you let that douchebag turn you off men forever. I might not believe in relationships, but you're practically a doe-eyed Disney princess."

"I am not!" I cried. "And I'm perfectly happy on my own." What I couldn't tell Nina was that it wasn't only Shitty Peter who'd made me give up on love. It was a history of disappointment, not limited to the romantic kind. Yes, Shitty Peter was . . . well, shitty. He'd made me a lesser version of myself. When we were together, I'd stopped doing the things I loved most: going to Mitch's, thrifting with Nina, finding new hobbies to try out just because. But I'd learned that even people with the best intentions could disappear from your life whether they wanted to or not, and the wreckage wasn't worth it. I thought of Beth and Mark. If they couldn't make it, what chance did I have?

I sighed into my chair. My entire body ached with exhaustion—from the day, from charter season, from this entire year, and suddenly the only place I wanted to be was in my own bed.

I passed Nina her purse across the table. "Walk home with me and get a ride from there?"

"I thought you'd never ask."

We pressed our way through the bar and out into the night, humidity closing in on us from every side. It was strange not to feel the movement of the boat beneath my feet or the breeze off the ocean.

"Sure you're not mad I ruined things with your handsome stranger?" Nina asked.

"Positive."

"If you say so," Nina said, a mischievous look in her eyes.

"What?"

She shook her head. "Nothing, nothing."

I was too tired to press her. I probably didn't want to know what she was thinking anyway. I looped my arm through hers, and we leaned into each other as we made our way down the sidewalk. Neither of us spoke the whole way home, and I wondered what she was thinking about. Ollie, I guessed. But me? I was replaying that kiss with Alex, grateful to have something good to distract myself with when Nina left and I found myself alone for the first time in months.

Three

"YOU'RE HERE EARLY," NINA SAID WHEN I ARRIVED ON DECK THE
next morning. She sat at a table in the galley, polishing a knife with
alarming energy. I looked between her and Ollie, taking in his rigid
body language as he wiped down the counters. I'd missed either a fight
or a make-out session. Maybe both.

I set my purse on the counter. "I couldn't stand to be away from you,"
I said. Truthfully, my condo had been too quiet. All morning I'd moved
through my usual routine but found myself restless, fixating on the electricity humming through the walls, my pulse thudding in my ears. I'd
stepped onto the patio to make sure my plants were still alive. My
neighbor, Belva, took care of them during charter season, and I'd been
both relieved and angry to see they were even better than I'd left them.
The camellia shrub was heavy with blossoms, and the sword lilies were
tall and vibrant. Work, even with a pissed-off Nina, was better than letting my sadness and anger expand into the silence.

The guests for that day's charter were four college friends celebrating twenty years of friendship with a cruise down to Miami. They were
fun but high-maintenance. And not only was I adjusting to having one

less stewardess, but Nina and Ollie refused to speak to each other, leaving me to relay messages between them. Ollie's mood deteriorated even more when the guests asked if we could throw a "Boob Funeral," to mourn the perky breasts of their youth, and requested a breast-shaped cake.

"I didn't train at culinary school to make fecking boob cakes," he muttered, and I sprinted from the galley before he could direct his anger at me.

When I wasn't mixing drinks or trying to avoid being flashed by the guests, who, for being disappointed with their middle-aged breasts, sure didn't mind showing them off, I was busy crafting a boob-shaped piñata and filling it with miniature bottles of tequila.

After lunch, when RJ took the guests out on the Jet Skis, Nina finally radioed for me to take my break. I hadn't had a chance to catch my breath all morning and collapsed onto my bunk for a twenty-minute nap, then wandered into the crew mess for some food. Sitting at the counter with a peanut butter sandwich, I picked up my phone for the first time since arriving at work and noticed several notifications, all from one person—my niece Mia.

I scrolled through the messages, my anxiety growing with each one.

Landing!

Where are you?

JO!

WTF JO!

????????

I called Mia, leaving my half-eaten sandwich on the counter. Did she mean landing here, as in Palm Beach, here?

"What the hell?" Mia said, answering on the first ring. "We've been waiting for you for hours."

"Not hours," Kitty, her younger sister, said. "One hour and eleven minutes."

"Whatever. Too long."

"Waiting for me where?" I asked.

"At the airport, duh."

The airport? The girls and Samson had come down for a few weeks every summer since I'd moved to Florida, but I'd assumed that wasn't happening this year. The last time I'd seen them was the first week in March, when I'd come up for Samson's funeral.

"Is your mom there?" I asked. Maybe it was a surprise. Or perhaps a spur-of-the-moment family vacation.

"Uh, no," Mia said, sounding as if it were the dumbest thing she'd ever heard.

"Which airport?" I asked.

"The Palm Beach airport."

"It's the Palm Beach *International* Airport," Kitty said.

"Kitty, shut up."

I ran over the conversations I'd had with Beth lately. She hadn't said anything about the girls visiting this summer. And then our phone call from the day before came to mind. *Are you ready? Do you need me to send anything?* I'd thought she was talking about the end of charter season. But now, everything made sense. Beth and Mark were taking a break from the girls, not from each other. A small relief.

I tried to keep the panic from my voice. "How long are you down for?"

"All summer," Mia said. "So Mom and Dad can work things out. Which means they're definitely getting a divorce."

Divorce? My relief deflated in an instant.

"They are not getting a divorce! Stop lying!" Kitty whined.

"Are you coming to get us or what? I'm starving," Mia said.

Right. I looked out the window of the crew mess. We were in the middle of the ocean. No way Captain Xav would turn the boat around for a scheduling hiccup. "I'm sort of on the yacht right now. I don't know how to get you."

"Seriously, Jo?" Mia said. "Haven't you ever heard of Uber? Just text me your card info."

"I—"

"Do you have a key under the mat?"

"No, but Belva has a spare."

"Well, can you call her and have her let us in?"

An image of the girls getting kidnapped by a seedy Uber driver came to mind. "Can minors even use Uber?"

Ollie, who'd wandered into the crew mess, gave me a confused look, but I waved him off.

"Minors with fake IDs can," Mia said.

Oh God. "Listen, I'm going to send Belva to get you. She'll let you into the condo. And I'll text my card info so you can order some food," I added, thinking of my bare kitchen cabinets. I'd need to "borrow" provisions from the boat—milk, cereal, and maybe a bag of chips to bring home.

"Ugh, fine," Mia said, hanging up without so much as a goodbye.

I set my phone on the counter, staring at it until it vibrated again with another text from Mia.

Card info?

"Right." I dug my wallet from my purse and snapped a photo of my credit card. Then I called Belva, who was more than happy to pick up the girls.

"What was that about?" Ollie asked when I'd finished talking to Belva, but thankfully Nina's voice called for me over the radio.

"Go for Jo," I radioed back.

"The guests are in the Sky Lounge and very inebriated. Can you head up here?"

"On my way." I shoved my phone into my pocket and ignored Ollie's raised eyebrows as I headed for the stairs.

When I made it to the Sky Lounge, Nina took one look at my face and stopped me. "You good?"

"Family drama," I said. And before she could ask more, I stepped over to the bar and made some margaritas for the guests, who were topless again and snort-laughing over their college days.

Nina followed me behind the bar. "What's going on?"

I picked up a glass and avoided looking at her. "Mia and Kitty are at the airport right now waiting for me to pick them up."

Nina nearly dropped her radio. "Like *right now*, right now?"

"Yup." I kept my hands busy polishing some glasses. "Apparently, they're here for the entire summer, but I don't remember making plans with Beth. I don't know how, but I really fucked up."

"How are you supposed to get them? Doesn't Beth know you're supposed to go to Europe next month?"

"Belva is on her way to the airport now. As for my trip . . ." I shrugged. "I haven't told Beth about it. I'll cancel it. I can't just send them back."

Nina pried the cloth from my hands. "How can I help? Do you need a Xanax? A good travel agent? How about a houseplant?"

"A houseplant?"

"They reduce stress. I read it in *Psychology Today*."

"You read *Psychology Today*?"

"I'll have you know I'm an avid reader of many things," Nina said. "Just tell me how I can help."

I shook my head, unsure anyone could help. "You can help by taking your break."

"If you're deflecting, Jo, I—"

"Break," I repeated, snatching the cloth back. I steered Nina by the shoulders to the stairs, sending her belowdeck so I could be alone. As alone as one could be while hovering over topless drunken guests.

One of the guests called me over to see if they could change the flavor of the boob cake, and I stole from the room, checking my phone on my way down to the galley. I had two texts from Mia: one informing me that Belva's car smelled like cigarettes, and another saying they'd arrived at the condo safe and sound. Another from my credit card company notifying me of a thirty-dollar purchase from China Sky. And then I noticed a fourth text, this one from my sister, and my worry flamed into guilt.

are you at work

My thumbs hovered, hesitant, but then a slew of texts appeared on the screen, one after the other.

you were supposed to pick them up

are they with you

is everything okay

Was everything okay? I had no idea. Something had gotten lost in translation, and now I'd earned the title of worst sister ever. How had I missed something as big as the girls coming down for the entire summer? How had I dropped the ball when my sister needed me? She'd only just started going back to work, was only now talking to her friends and going to church again. *Everyone thinks I'm coping, but I'm not,* she'd told me after finishing her first week back at the hospital where she worked as a nurse. *I don't know how I'm supposed to do this, Joey. I'm only moving because I have to. I want it to get better, but it never does.* It scared me, my big sister feeling so out of control. I couldn't give her anything more to worry about.

Everything's fine, I replied. **Belva is getting them from the airport.**

ill call you after my shift 7pm, Beth's reply read. I imagined her walking the halls of the hospital, her sneakers squeaking across the floor. I mentally apologized to her patients, whose IVs she was likely placing with a little too much force.

I slipped my phone into my pocket, bracing for Ollie's inevitable freak-out when I told him he'd have to remake his cake, and returned to work, hoping I was prepared for whatever disaster might happen next.

THE CONDO HAD BEEN PART OF MY LIFE FOR AS LONG AS I could remember. Right on the beach, the Palm Beach White House Condominium Complex comprised two large white buildings austerely facing each other over the expanse of a blacktop parking lot. Beth and I had spent the summers of our childhood here, staying with our grandmother—my father's mother—until Dad died. Beth and I inherited her unit when she passed away seven years ago, and my sister insisted I take the place, seeing as she and Mark had their life with the kids in North Carolina. At first, I hadn't wanted to leave them, not when I owed them so much. But Beth had not so gently reminded me that I needed to get a life, and so I moved to Florida the very next month: without a job, without friends (other than the condo residents I'd known my whole life), without a plan. Somehow, the condo, with its saltwater pool, shuffleboard court, and bare-bones gym full of ancient equipment, was home.

When I eased open the door to my unit after work, I was struck by how quickly it had devolved from almost-thirty chic to something like a teenage girl's bedroom. The living room was a mess. Two pairs of tennis shoes were piled in a heap beside the shoe rack. Half-empty containers of Chinese food sat on the side table. And in the center of the living room, two exploding suitcases flopped open onto the white tile. I fought my yacht stewardess urge to tidy everything immediately and turned to the couch in front of the TV, where Mia and Kitty lounged with their legs outstretched.

Both girls were long and lean, but that was where their similarities ended. While Kitty had mousy brown hair that hung down her back, straight like mine, Mia's was dark and coarse, and she wore it in a messy topknot. Their eyes were different too. Mia's were dark and brooding, like her father's. Kitty had the same eyes as me and her mother. The Walker eyes, as my dad used to say. Moss green, with a sunburst of yellow ringing each pupil. Samson's eyes were that color, too, though his hair was the same dark blond as mine. Both he and Kitty reminded me of my sister, and Kitty resembled her more and more every year. They had the same delicate chin and nose, and looking at Kitty now gave me déjà vu, reminding me of the summers Beth and I had spent here as kids, especially since these were the same ivory couches we'd stretched out on when we would come to stay with our grandmother: one three-seater against the wall, and another one with a pullout bed before the TV. Mia looked a lot like I had as a teenager, with a chin she hadn't yet grown into and a splash of freckles over the bridge of her nose. You could tell, despite the differences, that they were sisters. They just had that sibling something, even if I couldn't name exactly what it was. As I looked at the two of them, a little of the tightness in my chest eased. I'd spent so much of my day worried that I hadn't thought about how good it would feel to see them.

Mia glanced up from her phone before her eyelashes fluttered back down to the screen. "Hey, Jo. Toss those chips over here." She reached out a hand and caught the bag without looking.

"Impressive," I said.

"I've got great peripheral vision."

I nodded to her phone. "No doubt because you spend so much time staring at that thing."

"Actually," Kitty said, "peripheral awareness is significantly lowered with cell phone use." She turned to Mia. "Didn't you read the article Dad sent us?"

Mia rolled her eyes. "Of course I didn't."

Kitty ignored Mia and stood to hug me. I held on tight, hoping to convey all the things I felt but couldn't say. *I've missed you. I love you. How are you so grown up? Are you okay?* When we finally released each other, I prodded Mia to move her legs and make room for me on the couch.

"FYI, Mom is majorly pissed at you," she said.

No surprise there. I sank deeper into the couch, wishing I could disappear completely. "Did she call?"

"She didn't have to." Mia crunched a chip between her teeth and tossed the bag to Kitty. "You know it's bad when she stops using punctuation in her texts."

Kitty sighed. "I tell her that improper grammar only weakens her argument, like Ms. Carter said, but she just gives me that look. You know the one." She screwed up her face, furrowing her brow and making her eyes smolder. Exactly like her mother.

I groaned and hung my head in my hands. "She's going to kill me."

Mia clapped me on the shoulder. "Yup."

"Anger may in time change to gladness; vexation may be succeeded by content," Kitty said, nodding soberly.

"Oh my God," Mia groaned. "If you're quoting that war book again, I swear I'm going to flush it down the toilet."

Kitty picked up a book from the side table. "It's from *The Art of War.*"

"Should you be reading that?" I took the book in my hands and flipped through the pages. Kitty had always had *unique* tastes in literature. She'd learned to read before Mia had, devouring words wherever she found them. I'd only been nineteen at the time and hadn't realized how unusual it was for a three-year-old to sound out the words on cereal boxes.

Kitty jutted her chin out. "Why shouldn't I be reading ancient Chinese military wisdom? It applies to many aspects of modern life."

"Because it's making you a total weirdo." Mia shifted her weight to drape her legs over my lap. "Isn't she, Jo?"

I already had one sister mad at me (mine); I didn't need to stoke the fire between these two. "I've been doing a lot of reading myself," I said, thinking of item number twenty-seven—read twenty books. "Ever heard of *Gone Girl?*"

"Who hasn't?" Kitty replied. "But I haven't read it. I prefer nonfiction and poetry."

She reminded me of my father in that way, who'd always had naval histories and poetry books on his nightstand. His copies of Whitman, Keats, and Dickinson now lived in my bedroom closet, though I'd pulled them out for Kitty to page through from time to time. "Have you read *The Life-Changing Magic of Tidying Up?*"

Kitty wrinkled her nose. "Not that kind of nonfiction."

"What should we have for dinner? Leftover Chinese food?" I asked.

Kitty clutched her stomach and groaned. "No way, I'll get indigestion if I eat any more."

I stalked off to the kitchen to put away the milk and cereal and stared into the refrigerator. Except for the days when Nina dragged me out to dinner, I microwaved a Lean Cuisine and called it a day. But I had a feeling my lazy dietary habits wouldn't work for this crowd. "Coffee and cereal," I said, returning to the living room. "That's all chez Jo has to offer you."

Mia stuck her hand into the pocket of her oversized tie-dyed hoodie and tossed me an envelope. I peeked inside and found a wad of cash. Written on the outside in Beth's neat handwriting: *Expenses.* How very Beth-like. She'd always been the organized one, but maybe that was because she'd had to grow up so quickly. When I moved in with her my junior year of high school, she'd stuck my class schedule on the refrigerator with an alphabet magnet, right beside the log sheets for Mia's naps and Kitty's feeding schedule. Each week she'd hand me an envelope with *Joey's Allowance* written on the outside. I'd told her she didn't need to do that. I was sixteen. I could get a job. But Beth wouldn't allow it. She'd said school was my job.

"Pizza?" I set the envelope on a side table. "What do you like?"

Not long after I'd placed our order, my phone rang. "It's your mom," I said to the girls.

"Nice knowing you, Jo!" Mia called as I made my way down the hall.

I closed my bedroom door behind me, then stepped onto the patio.

"What the hell is going on?" Beth said as soon as I answered.

I sank onto the step, watching the wind shake loose petals from my hydrangeas. "Are you getting a divorce?" It wasn't what I'd meant to say, but I needed to know. I picked up a tiny blue petal and rolled it between my fingers.

"Did Mia tell you that?"

"Are you?" I pressed.

"I don't know." Beth's voice was quiet. "We're trying to figure that

out. That's why we asked you to take the girls for the summer. We didn't
want them in the middle of all that."

"But I don't think you actually asked me."

"Yes, I did. I emailed you a month ago with dates and—"

"I don't have anything about dates. I'm supposed to go to Europe
next month."

"You're going to Europe?"

I went quiet, unsure what to say. I hadn't planned to tell Beth about
my trip until the day before my flight. Desperate for something to look
forward to, I'd booked the tickets as soon as I returned to the *Serendipity*
from Samson's funeral. But it felt wrong going on a big adventurous trip
when everything in my sister's life was falling apart.

"I asked you yesterday if everything was all set," Beth said.

"I thought you were talking about me coming home."

Beth didn't say anything. The wind picked up again, whistling
through the palms that separated my building from the next.

"Shit," Beth whispered. "The email I thought I sent you is still in my
drafts."

Relief washed over me. Thank God, this wasn't my fault. But then
Beth started crying, and all my relief dried up.

"Don't cry, B. It's all right. I'm happy the girls are here."

Beth let out a shuddering breath. "I can't keep things straight anymore. I'll think I've said or done something, then realize I haven't. Some
days it's so much I can't move. I lie in bed and think, *This has to be a
nightmare*, but I never wake up."

"I know." I stared down at my knees. I didn't know, though. Not really. My stern, organized, whip-smart sister could hardly function, and
I missed her. I didn't know how to bring her back. But maybe she didn't
want to come back. Mom hadn't after Dad died. I needed to be there for
Beth, and Mark, and Mia, and Kitty. For once in my life, I had to be the
strong one.

"I'm so sorry, Joey," Beth said. "Can you take the girls just until your trip?"

I held in a laugh. How could Beth think I wouldn't keep the girls for as long as she needed me to? In what world would I deny her anything? My trip, my list, my blog, what did that matter when my sister needed me? "Forget Europe. The tickets are refundable." (A lie, but a necessary one.) "And you know what they say, Florida is the Europe of the South."

"I'm pretty sure no one says that."

"Maybe they will now."

She paused. "Are you sure?"

"Of course I'm sure." I flicked the rolled hydrangea petal between my fingers onto the ground. "To be honest, I was disappointed when I thought they weren't coming."

Beth sighed. "Thank you, Jo. You have no idea what this means to me."

I squeezed my eyes shut, imagining Beth's face in my mind. The dimple on her cheek, her feathered eyebrows. Dad's eyebrows, she always complained. "I love you, B."

After hanging up, I lingered outside, allowing myself exactly one minute to mourn the carefree summer I'd planned.

BACK IN THE LIVING ROOM, I FOUND MIA AND KITTY HUNCHED before my computer.

"Why didn't you tell us you had a blog!" Kitty exclaimed.

"Why are you snooping through my stuff?" The blog wasn't a secret, exactly, but I was self-conscious about it, especially with my family. And while I'd told Beth about the list, I knew she'd find a way to make the blog evidence of why I should go to college. *If you can write a blog, you can write a paper!*

"I wasn't snooping," Kitty said. "I wanted to watch YouTube on a bigger screen, but Mia wouldn't let me use the TV. If you didn't want anyone to see it, why is it your homepage?"

"*XO, Jo?*" Mia snickered. "Is that like G.I. Joe for princesses?"

"No," I said defensively.

"I love it," Kitty said. She turned to Mia. "Remember when she went bungee jumping and called Mom after, crying? That was one of the things she had to do. The bungee jumping, not the crying." She squinted at the computer. "You haven't posted in forever, though."

True. Mia scanned the most recent post. It was from February, when Nina and I road-tripped across Abaco. Since then, I hadn't made a single post.

"You have to finish it by your birthday?" Mia asked.

"Yeah," I said, knowing we were thinking the same thing: by Sam's birthday. His first birthday without us.

"Samson's birthday," Kitty said. And I was reminded of how Beth called her Chatty Kathy for her habit of saying what didn't need to be said.

Silence fell over the three of us. It was the first time Samson's name had come up, and his absence seemed to move through the room.

When Samson died, every day felt like forever. Captain Xav and Nina had been kind enough to let me go to North Carolina for the funeral, operating a man down during one of the busiest weeks of the season. I'd booked the first flight I could, returning to the guest room I'd lived in a lifetime ago.

The door to Samson's room had remained closed until the day of the funeral. That night, as soon as everyone went to bed, I'd slipped down the hall and snuck inside. My heart had been in my throat as I'd looked around at the posters of baseball players and the dried-up Venus flytrap on his windowsill. Textbooks had been piled beside his desk, and I'd pulled the chain on the lamp, finding his agenda open to the week he'd died. The blocks for Monday, Tuesday, and Wednesday had homework and baseball practices written and crossed out in his awful handwriting.

He'd always pressed down too hard, the paper bending beneath the force of him. I'd passed my hand over the words and imagined him bent over a desk at school, his foot tapping as he scratched away, the ink staining his hand. Sam had been left-handed, which, according to him, explained his extraordinary talent in baseball.

Then there was the other side of the planner. Samson died on a Thursday afternoon. There'd been a Saturday baseball practice followed by three exclamation points. He'd never found out who the culprit was in *The Westing Game* or worked his way through chapter seven in his math textbook. *Impossible*, I'd thought, that he would never play baseball again or read another book or do another math problem. I'd shut the agenda, not wanting Beth or Mark or the girls to wander in and see it.

"Can we help?" Kitty asked, breaking the silence.

I thought through the remaining items. We could do some, but we'd never finish them all. I took in Mia's and Kitty's somber faces. I needed to keep their minds off Samson. Wasn't that the whole point of sending them to Aunt Jo's?

Fun, adventure, that was what these girls needed.

And honestly, I needed it too.

"You know what?" I said. "Why not? Let's do it."

Kitty leapt up from the chair. "Really? You'll let us help?"

"Really." I tried not to think about how this might come back to bite me when we inevitably failed to complete the list, and shooed the girls from the desk. I found the original list (which Mia noticed right away was on a bar napkin) and tacked it to the wall. "We need a plan. What's first?"

Mia begged me to book us flights to Europe, not knowing I'd already booked one for myself.

"Let's not worry about that one right now," I said. "We can do the easy ones first and figure out the rest later."

"Let's start with this one," Mia said, pointing at number nine—go skinny-dipping.

"Counterpoint. Let's start with this one." I pointed to number twenty-two—declutter the condo.

Mia rolled her eyes. "Thrilling."

I nudged her with my elbow. "New plan. Let's sleep on it and reconvene in the morning."

Mia flopped dramatically onto the couch, but Kitty wriggled in excitement as I helped them unfold the sofa bed. Once it was made, I wedged myself between them. Mia put on a show called *My Super Sweet 16*, a reality series about rich kids' birthday parties. I watched, equally intrigued and horrified as a girl in a sapphire ball gown screeched about getting the wrong color Lamborghini for her birthday.

I propped my chin in my hands and turned to Mia. "Why do you like this show anyway?"

Mia let out a puff of breath. It lifted the strands of hair that had fallen into her face. "I like knowing that these are the worst problems in some people's lives."

I didn't know what to say to that, and so I said nothing. As the next episode began, I listened to the sound of Mia's and Kitty's breathing. Their warm bodies on either side of me were like a sedative, and I closed my eyes, trying not to worry about what the summer would bring as I finally fell asleep.

XO, Jo: Blog Post #25

June 5

Hello, Hot Guy from the Bar

Hello, readers!

Charter season is finally over, meaning I've bid the Bahamas farewell and life has returned to its regularly scheduled South Florida programming. And let me tell you, it is thrilling to sleep in my own bed.

I'm sorry for my absence over the last few months. Seeing as I was stuck on a superyacht for the last four of them (I know, poor me), progress on the list has been slow. But never fear! My two nieces, Mia (16) and Kitty (13), are visiting for the summer and have agreed to help me finish the list. I'm sure they'll be invaluable as I try to do the impossible. But without further ado, let's get to the stats.

Of the thirty items on my original list, there are eight left, which is more than I'd hoped for this late in the game, but there's no use dwelling on it.

1. Sing onstage. *I am so ready to conquer my debilitating stage fright.*

2. Get a tattoo. *Did I think this would help me overcome my fear of needles? Because I doubt it.*

3. Go skinny-dipping. *I'll need a few Drunken Joeys for that* one . . . *Want the recipe? Check out Item #17—Develop a Signature Cocktail—the Drunken Joey.*

4. Run a marathon. *I may have been too ambitious when I added this one to the list.*

5. Declutter the condo. *Don't judge. I read that book about tidying up, and it was pretty inspiring, okay?*

6. Sleep in a castle. *BFF Nina says I'm already royalty to her, but I want the full princess experience.*

7. Host a dinner party. *My culinary skills peak at nuking a Lean Cuisine in the microwave.*

8. Visit 10 countries. *Luckily my job has taken care of some of these, but I've still got five to go.*

Now that we've gotten the housekeeping out of the way, let's move on to the fun stuff. Here it is: Item #5—Kiss a Stranger.

As I'm sure you can guess, this item was Nina's idea. But though I've sworn off love forever—no, I'm not being dramatic (okay, maybe a little)—I figured it couldn't hurt to take one for the team.

And let me tell you, it *so* did not hurt.

All right, enough teasing you.

This item began like almost every other, without any planning and with a lot of pressure from my so-called best friend. As soon as we docked in Palm Beach after our last charter of the season, Nina, the rest of the crew, and I found ourselves living it up at our favorite dive bar for a post-season celebration. It was Taco Tuesday, and the pub was packed to the gills with college students and poor souls with regular 9-to-5s meeting up for happy hour.

As luck would have it (or should I say habit?), after a few margaritas Nina and I were a little tipsy and sitting beside a sexy silver fox. Well, he wasn't quite silver, but I could tell that in another ten years he'd be a real George Clooney.

Let me paint a picture for you: honey eyes. Full lips. Stylishly tousled brown hair with a touch of silver at the temples.

BFF Nina and I agreed he was the perfect specimen for a random kiss. Tall, dark, handsome, and someone I'd never see again, just my type. It was spur of the moment, but was I going to come across a more handsome stranger in the next three months? Probably not.

I turned to him, he told me his name, and I somehow convinced him to let me kiss him after telling him he looked like a tourist. (He didn't. I would never kiss someone who wore socks with sandals.) Before I could think too much about it, I planted one right on those pillowy lips. The kiss went on a *little* longer than I'd planned, but only because he was very, very good at it. We had a nice conversation filled with flirty banter. He said I was out of his league, which I verbally agreed with, despite thoughts of wanting to be *in league* with him, if you catch my drift. He seemed like a nice guy, and I won't say I didn't think about kissing him again, but you'll be disappointed to know my stranger and I parted ways without so much as each other's phone numbers. Though I won't deny he's starred in my dreams ever since . . .

So there you have it. If you need me, I'll be hiding from your hate comments.

Just kidding. You know I'll be busy with the next item on the list. Fortunately, it won't involve surprising any strange men.

XO, Jo

Four

PAST SUMMERS WHEN THE KIDS VISITED, I'D WAKE BEFORE THEM and sit out on the patio drinking my coffee until Samson, always the first one awake, tumbled outside and begged for me to take him swimming. Afterward we'd go to the beach, and he and I would sit side by side in the sand, talking about baseball and poisonous plants as the world grew brighter around us. Mia and Kitty were usually still asleep when we'd return, their pillows dotted with drool. But as I peeked into the living room now, I was surprised to find Kitty and Mia wide awake. Mia sat cross-legged on the sofa bed, spooning cereal into her mouth as she stared at her phone with her headphones in her ears. Kitty's arm was draped over the back of the couch, and she appeared lost in thought as she prodded the succulents lined up on the windowsill.

I stepped into the kitchen before the girls could see me and scooped grounds into the coffee maker. When I turned around, I nearly jumped out of my skin at the sight of Kitty behind me, her long, tangled hair reminding me of an apparition from a horror film.

"Shit!" I held my hand over my racing heart. "Crap, I mean."

Kitty rolled her eyes. "Even Jonathan Swift used the word 'shit,' you know."

"He's the guy who wrote about eating babies, right?"

"Yup."

"Kitty, you're . . . thirteen. How have you read that?"

"Oh, I haven't," she said. "But I've read *about* it. Mia had to read it last year, and she told me about the baby eating, so I looked him up."

"Well, if 'shit' is all right with J. Swift, then it's all right with me." I took the milk from the fridge and set it on the counter. "Grab me a mug?"

A cabinet door creaked open, and then Kitty went quiet. Wondering what the holdup was, I turned to find her holding a souvenir mug with a map of the Bahamas I'd bought my first charter season. She stared down at it, running a finger along its side, where the handle used to be.

"Kitty?"

She passed the mug to me, her chin quivering. "Is that the one Sam broke?"

I looked down at the mug in my hands. Last summer, Kitty and Samson had trapped a caterpillar inside of it. Kitty had coaxed the caterpillar onto her finger, then jerked it into Samson's face with a laugh, and he'd dropped the mug, the handle cracking clear off. Embarrassed, Samson had refused to talk to Kitty for hours. That night, after emptying a glass jar and duct-taping mesh from an old pool skimmer around the top, Kitty and Mia sat watching the caterpillar, wondering what type of butterfly it would be. *That's a tent caterpillar,* Samson had said, breaking his silence. Kitty and Mia gave him blank stares. *It's a moth,* he explained. *You've caught a stupid ugly moth.* He then turned to me with a mischievous grin. *We should name him Peter,* he'd said, making me laugh. The three of them had spent their entire trip that summer trying to cheer me up post-breakup.

I looked at Kitty. "Yeah, I think it is."

She nodded, her eyelashes fluttering as tears raced down her cheeks. "I'm sorry," she said, pressing a hand over her mouth.

The broken mug in my hands anchored me in place. All I could hear was Samson's voice saying *stupid ugly moth,* and the memory of that fuzzy black caterpillar made it hard for me to see Kitty standing right in front of me.

Before I could find something to say, Kitty fled, and I heard the bathroom door slam shut.

Mia slid into the kitchen seconds later. "What happened?"

I held up the mug, hoping she'd understand.

She nodded, then darted to the bathroom. I set the mug on top of the fridge, where it would hopefully be forgotten, and followed her down the hall. Mia had her ear pressed to the bathroom door, her brows knit in concentration.

"Should I talk to her?" My hands were slick with sweat. What would I even say?

Mia ignored me. She knocked two, then three times on the door.

"What are you—"

Three sharp knocks sounded from the other side, and Mia sank to the floor, crossing her legs beneath her. "Three knocks means she needs to be alone," Mia explained. "Two means she wants to talk."

"Oh." I glanced at the door. How often did this happen for them to have a system in place?

"Grief support group thing," Mia said. "She'll be okay. She just needs a few minutes."

Grief support group? Beth hadn't told me about this. Was I supposed to be taking them to one down here? Was I supposed to know these "things" they taught at grief support groups? Our mother didn't believe in therapy, so when Dad died, we were left to deal with things on our own.

"You don't have to stand there, you know."

I took in Mia's oversized tie-dyed hoodie, the droopy topknot of her hair, her serious eyes. How had she grown up so fast? How could this be the same person I'd once potty trained by bribing her with Skittles?

"Let me know if there's anything I can do." I returned to the kitchen, my hands shaking as I poured coffee into a different mug—one that was part of a set, whole and unbroken, indistinguishable from the rest.

When Kitty emerged from the bathroom twenty minutes later, I tried to act normal.

"The surf report looks good," I said. "How do you feel about a little beach time?"

Kitty's eyes brightened at the suggestion. "I'll get my bathing suit."

I turned to Mia, who sat on the unmade sofa bed, frowning at her phone. "What about you, Mia?"

She yanked out a headphone. "Huh?"

"Beach day. Twenty minutes."

Mia gave me a thumbs-up and rolled off the bed to dig through her suitcase.

The emotional turmoil of Kitty's meltdown had me feeling unsure I could distract the girls on my own, so I texted the most distracting person I knew.

Beach day?

A message from Nina appeared seconds later. **Just say you need help babysitting.** Followed by **See you in thirty.**

KITTY, MIA, AND I DRAGGED LOUNGE CHAIRS BEHIND US, TRUDGing down the condo's private beach to the waterline. The sand warmed the soles of my feet, and the sight of the ocean loosened the tightness in my chest, allowing me to breathe deeply for the first time all morning. After setting up our chairs and putting on sunscreen, Mia spread out a towel and closed her eyes, while Kitty rushed into the waves with a boogie board under one arm.

I sank into my chair and wiggled my toes in the sand. Closing my eyes, I tilted my face to the sun. This beach was where I felt most at home. Many of my best memories had taken place here. I remembered leaning against my mother beneath the shade of the umbrella after a morning in the sun. I remembered my father adjusting my mask for the thousandth time, tugging on the strap and screwing up his face in the effort of it, but no matter what he did, water leaked in whenever I went snorkeling. I remembered Beth crouched beside me, examining a sand flea as it buried itself.

My phone vibrated. A text from Beth.

Everything okay?

I picked up my phone and took two pictures, one of Kitty out in the water, and one of Mia lying on the chair beside me, then sent them to my sister.

I'm glad they're having fun, Beth replied.

The text worried me. I wished she were here. But I also wanted her to work things out with Mark. Though I knew the statistics on divorce after the death of a child, I also knew the statistics on teenage parents staying together, and Beth and Mark had defied those odds. Why couldn't they overcome this? But I didn't know how to ask how they were doing, mostly because I feared the answer. I responded with a heart emoji and put my phone away.

"Jo!" I turned and spotted Nina dragging a beach chair behind her. Her bathing suit, like all her nonwork attire, was *creative*: a one-piece featuring a cat eating a slice of pizza.

"That bathing suit is hideous," I said when she stopped beside me.

Nina squinted in the sunlight, looking from Mia, next to me, to Kitty, who floated on her back in the water. "You call this a beach party?"

"I never said it was a beach party." But I could see what she meant. If my goal was to distract the girls, I wasn't doing a great job.

"Nina!" Kitty called. She paddled in, wrapping Nina in a wet hug when she reached us.

Kitty gasped. "I *love* your bathing suit. Mia, did you see?"

Mia cracked open an eyelid. "Hey, Nina. Cool bathing suit."

"See, Josephine?" Nina dropped into her chair. "I'm hip with Gen Z. Don't think I didn't hear you."

Kitty sat down on a towel in front of Nina. "Are you and Ollie to-gether yet? Mia owes me fifty bucks if you two get married."

Nina turned to me and wrinkled her nose. "This is unbelievable. Stop infecting your nieces with propaganda. Ollie is nobody to me."

Mia raised her eyebrows. "He sure doesn't *sound* like nobody."

"He is very much somebody," I said, ducking to avoid the towel Nina threw at me.

"You're driving now, right?" Nina said to Mia. "You'll have to take my convertible for a spin. Top down, wind in your hair, there's nothing better."

"Oh," Mia said. "I don't really . . . driving isn't really my thing." She turned to Kitty. "Come play shuffleboard with me."

"Okay, yeah," Kitty said, leaping to her feet and following her sister up the beach.

"That was weird," Nina said once the girls were out of earshot.

"Yeah, it was." I kept my gaze on the girls until they disappeared through the gate. Last summer, when Mia had her permit, she'd practically been my chauffeur.

Nina sighed into her chair. "How'd the first night go?"

I told her about everything that had happened since the girls arrived, including my call with Beth, Mia and Kitty's insistence they help with the list after discovering my blog, and Kitty's meltdown.

"Well that's not emotionally complicated at all. You'll have to think outside the box to finish the list, huh?"

"Looks like it." I buried my toes deeper in the sand. I didn't see how any sort of thinking could magic us into visiting five countries and sleeping in a castle. "Any intel on the new chef?"

"Zero. For the next twenty-four hours, work does not exist to me." Nina stretched out her legs, then bolted upright seconds later. "I almost forgot! I have a surprise for you."

I tensed. Nina's surprises weren't always the good kind.

She pulled out her phone. "Before my . . . incident . . . at the bar the other night, I managed to get Hot Guy's number."

"What?"

"Hot Guy from the Bar! While you two were talking, I snuck his phone from the bar and texted myself—not hard, seeing as his passcode was 1-2-3-4." She shook her head. "Then I deleted the text from his phone and put it back during your kiss—which was quite lengthy, by the way."

I stared at her in disbelief. "Nina, that's . . . outrageous. And maybe illegal."

Nina shrugged. She looked down at her phone, and a second later mine buzzed. "And now *you* have his number. You two are meant for each other. He has a shitty passcode. You have no passcode at all. You have a shared distaste for phone security." She turned to me, pushing her sunglasses on top of her head. "I wish you'd put even a shitty passcode on your phone. I worry about your identity getting stolen."

"I have nothing to hide. You know I don't like to waste precious time typing in a passcode. If a stranger really wants to hack my phone, they will."

"Who says it's a stranger trying to hack your phone? It could be someone you know. It could be me."

"You're welcome to hack my phone whenever you want."

"Josephine, I'm being serious."

I ignored her, opening the text and staring at the number. "What am I supposed to say? *Chick who kissed you at Mitch's here. I know you didn't give me your number, but my best friend stole it from your phone. How does dinner at eight sound?*"

"Sounds good to me."

"I'm not calling him." I slipped my phone into my beach bag. "I told you, I don't need anyone new in my life. All my relationship spots are filled."

"You're no fun, Jo."

I sighed back into my chair. "Why do people keep saying that?"

A few minutes later, Mia and Kitty returned, bringing with them a teenage girl I didn't recognize. Despite being a few inches taller than Kitty, she seemed to be about the same age. Her chin-length blond hair and bright blue eyes made her a stark contrast to Mia and Kitty. When the three of them reached us, the girl plopped down on a towel beside Kitty as if she'd known us all her life.

"Look, Aunt Jo, we found a friend," Kitty said.

"I see that."

The girl grinned at me. "I'm Greyson." She stuck her hand out for me to shake, then turned to Nina after I told her my name. "Wow. I love your bathing suit. I saw one like that on Instagram but couldn't get it because I once bought an industrial-sized box of glitter slime, and now my dad says I'm not allowed to buy things from Instagram anymore, not that they had my size anyway, but oh well." She shrugged.

"Are you visiting your grandparents?" I asked. I thought I'd met all my neighbors' grandchildren or at least seen them on Christmas cards.

"She just moved in with her dad," Kitty said.

"Not only old people live here, obviously," Mia said, gesturing to me. "Don't be so ageist, Jo."

"Yeah, Jo," Nina added.

Greyson rested her chin on her knees, her fingers twisting together around her legs. "My grandparents are hippies and travel all over in an RV playing music. I asked Dad if we could do that, but he said he's already spent enough of his life on wheels, so we moved here instead. I asked why we had to live like old people, when Marla and Tom were going around adventuring, and he told me to stop calling Grandma and Grandpa Marla and Tom and go do my homework. But it's not as bad as I thought. I like the pool, and the beach, and the exercise room has a rowing machine, and—" She paused, and her expression fell. "Am I talking too much? Katie Rose, this girl at my old school, said I talk too much and that's why no one likes me, but I can't help it. I think something, and it comes out my mouth. Well, I don't think, that's what my teachers say anyway."

I smiled at Greyson. Sure, she talked a lot, but there was something charming about it. The energy, her constant movement, it reminded me of Sam. "I think *more* people should say what they think."

"Katie Rose sounds like a real bitch," Mia said, and Nina leaned forward to give her a high five.

Greyson looked around at us, her face bright again. "Yeah, she kinda is."

The girls spent the next hour chatting as they stretched out in the sun.

Watching Mia and Kitty was like watching a home video of me and Beth, though when I was Kitty's age, we'd already been without Dad for a year.

After Dad died, I'd gone into isolation. I stopped answering the phone, sat by myself at lunch. For a few years I stopped putting myself out there. Beth, on the other hand, latched on to Mark and her friends. She went to more parties, drove recklessly, stopped coming home on weekend nights. Recklessness was how Mia had come into this world, so it wasn't all bad. And I marveled at how it was impossible for some of the best things in my life to exist without the worst.

A voice called out Greyson's name, and all of us turned in the direction of the pool, where a man stood waving his hands over his head.

"Phone's dead," Greyson said. "Dad's gonna kill me." She jumped to her feet and sprinted up the sand to the pool, hollering, "Nice to meet you!" over her shoulder.

"I didn't get a good look," Nina said when Greyson and her dad had disappeared, "but I *think* Greyson's dad might be hot. Let's call him Hot Single Dad, as a code name."

"How is that a good code name? It's longer than just calling him Greyson's dad."

"Yes, but 'Greyson's dad' doesn't have the same pizazz. You should get his number."

"Which is it, Nina? Do you want me to get with Hot Guy from the Bar or Hot Single Dad?"

"Why not both?"

I rolled my eyes and turned to Mia and Kitty. "At least you'll have someone your age to hang out with this summer."

"I like Greyson," Kitty said. She rolled onto her back, draping an arm over her eyes. "It'll be nice to hang out with someone who isn't Mia."

Mia kicked sand Kitty's way. "Please. Don't act like you don't follow me around twenty-four seven."

Five

AFTER NINA LEFT, I ORDERED WINGS AND SENT THE GIRLS
across the parking lot to the condo activities room to grab a board game.
When they returned, they plopped an ancient taped-up box of Sorry!
onto the table. Kitty lifted the top off the box, and Mia reached inside,
pulling out a small silver boot.

"This is a Monopoly piece."

"Oh, gimme!" Kitty said, nearly knocking over her chair as she
leaned over the table to swipe it from Mia's hand.

"Jesus," Mia said. "You didn't have to steal it from me. I was going to
give it to you anyway."

Kitty turned the silver boot over in her hands before placing it on
the green starting space.

"Here, Jo, you can be . . . what is this?" Mia said, holding a small
cardboard pawn depicting a leaping child.

"It's from Chutes and Ladders," I said. "You know, I'd bet anything
this came from the set your mom and I had when we were kids." Mia
handed me the piece, and I set it on the red starting space.

"Well, I guess that makes me yellow, since there's no blue piece,"

Mia said. "And just to buck the status quo I will choose . . ." She rummaged around in the box. "The yellow pawn that actually came with the game." She set down her piece with a snap, a smile breaking through her annoyed expression.

I rubbed my hands together. "All right. Let's begin."

"This game is really boring," Mia said after Kitty won the first game. She rested her cheek on her arm, a strand of hair flopping into her face.

"We should get one of those thousand-piece puzzles," Kitty said.

"Pass," Mia said.

"No offense, Kitty, but that doesn't exactly sound more fun than this," I said.

"Let's go looking for turtles," Mia said, and so we grabbed a flashlight and set off for the beach.

Mia bumped into me as she and Kitty raced down the walkway. It was a moonless night, growing darker around us with each step. I could hear the girls laughing as they walked side by side ahead of me. Instead of passing through the main gate to the beach, they turned left and raced past the shuffleboard court in the direction of the pool, and I found them standing beside the pool when I finally caught up to them. I looked from one girl to the other, confused. "You know turtles aren't going to be in the pool, right?"

Kitty giggled, and I caught the hint of a smile on Mia's face. And that was when I realized I was in trouble.

Mia held the flashlight beneath her chin. "Before we go turtle hunting, why don't you check off an item from the list?"

"I don't . . ." And then I looked at the pool, realizing the whole turtle scheme had been a trick. "You want me to go skinny-dipping right now?"

Mia and Kitty grinned.

I crossed my arms over my chest. "It's against the rules to swim after dark."

"Says the chick who snuck onto a yacht to go drinking," Mia said.

"That's not exactly—"

"Please, Aunt Jo?" Kitty pleaded. "It's the easiest item on the list! You said you'd do the easy ones first."

True. It *was* the easiest one, even easier than decluttering. When I'd come up with this item, I'd imagined skinny-dipping in the Caribbean or even the hot tub on the *Serendipity*. At no time had it crossed my mind to take a dip in the condo pool. What if Belva or Old Gary caught me?

"I don't have a towel, We can do another night." I turned to leave, but Mia cleared her throat.

"I thought you'd say something like that." Mia held out a phone, *my* phone, and dangled it in front of me. I patted the back of my shorts in disbelief. She must have snatched it from my pocket when she'd bumped into me on the walk here.

"Give that back," I said, giving her my best adult-in-control voice.

Mia held her thumbs poised for action over my phone. "What do you think we should text Hot Guy from the Bar, Kitty?"

Oh, no they didn't. I cursed myself for not having a passcode on my phone and made a mental note to murder Nina as soon as I arrived at work the next day. I lunged forward, trying to swipe my phone from Mia's hands, but she held it out of reach.

Kitty looked at me guiltily. "C'mon, Aunt Jo, it'll be quick."

I glared at them, weighing my options. The last thing I needed was Mia texting Hot Guy from the Bar, and him thinking I was some sort of stalker. Not that I cared what he thought of me, of course, I just didn't want him thinking he'd been kissed by a weirdo. And besides, if I did this now, I'd never have to do it again.

"Fine. But only for a second. And you promise I'll get my phone back after?"

Mia held my phone over her heart. "Promise."

I sighed, resigned to my fate. "Turn around and keep an eye out."

The girls obeyed, turning their backs to the pool. I scanned the balconies of the nearby condos and spotted no one. Stripping quickly, I peeled off my shirt and bra, then shimmied out of my shorts and underwear. A warm breeze blew in from the ocean, raising goose bumps on my skin. I raced down the steps into the glowing pool.

"I'm in the water. Can I get out now?"

"It doesn't count if you don't do a full lap there and back," Mia called.

"Says who?"

Mia put her hands on her hips. "Seriously, Jo. Where's your sense of adventure?"

I groaned, gripping the edge of the pool. I could do this quickly and get it over with. I launched myself off the wall with as much force as I could, the water blocking out all other sounds as my arms and legs propelled me forward. When I touched the opposite wall, I pushed off again, torpedoing back to where I'd started.

When I blinked the water from my eyes, I didn't notice anything out of the ordinary at first. But then I realized Mia and Kitty were nowhere in sight, and not only that, but my clothes were gone too. I'd been duped not once, but twice.

I looked wildly around the pool area. They were probably hiding behind the shower wall and waiting for me to freak out before they came back. But then a minute passed and another, and still no girls. I looked down at myself in the glowing water of the pool and cursed. How had I let the girls bully me into this?

The gate leading from the parking lot creaked open, and I whirled around. "What the hell was that?" I said, expecting to see Mia and Kitty. But to my great embarrassment, I was met not by my nieces, or even Old Gary with his whistle and a safety float, but by the silhouettes of a man and a teenage girl who didn't belong to me.

"Hey! You're Mia and Kitty's aunt, right? It's me, Greyson!"

So not only had I been caught naked in the pool, but I'd been caught by a teenager and her supposedly hot dad. "Hi, Greyson," I said, crossing my arms over my chest. I cast a hopeful look over my shoulder for Mia and Kitty. They'd be lucky if I didn't ship them back to North Carolina on the next flight.

"Where are they?" Greyson asked. "I was just telling Dad I wished my phone would've been charged, so I could've gotten their numbers."

"Uh, they went for a walk on the beach," I said, wishing it were Old Gary who'd caught me after all.

"Looks like we aren't the only rule breakers tonight. I knew you had good taste in friends," Greyson's dad said. He turned toward the pool. "It *is* against the rules to swim after dark, right?"

"Uh, yeah," I said.

"Dad, can I go find Mia and Kitty, please?" Greyson said. "I promise I'll use my head and won't do anything reckless."

"How about you wait until they come back?" he said, and Greyson groaned dramatically.

The two of them walked over to the table beside the pool. I was frozen in place, my brain moving slower than I would've liked. What was I supposed to do? If I said something, they'd know I was naked in the pool. But if they came any closer, they'd also know I was naked in the pool. Either way, they'd know I was naked in the pool, and I didn't want to flash Greyson or her dad, who was about to strip off his shirt.

"Wait!" I called out.

He let go of the hem of his shirt, and both he and Greyson turned to me expectantly.

I hesitated. I hadn't thought of what I was going to *say*. "Can I borrow a towel? I . . . lost my clothes."

"You lost your clothes?" Greyson's dad said.

"I lost a pair of shoes once," Greyson said. "I took them off in my room, and then they were just gone. Never did find them. Too bad, because they were really cool. They had these wheels on the bottom and I was always crashing into stuff. Dad hated them. Come to think of it, maybe they weren't lost." She turned to her dad. "Did you steal them?"

Greyson's dad didn't respond. He was looking at me. "Oh," he said, and it was clear from his tone he'd put things together. "I'm sorry . . . I didn't . . ." He shook his head and backed into the table.

"Do you have a towel?" I said again, blushing so fiercely I probably glowed like bioluminescent algae.

"Oh, right," he said. He grabbed his towel and started toward the pool, then hesitated. "Um, I won't look."

"What's . . ." Greyson started, but paused. "Wait, are you naked in there?" She turned to her dad again. "Is this one of those places Marla and Tom like to go to? A *naturalist* resort?"

"Of course we didn't move to a naturalist resort, Greyson," her dad said as he walked slowly over, eyes averted, the towel in his outstretched hand. When he got within a few feet of me, he tossed the towel to the side of the pool.

"Turn around, Grey," he said. He returned to the table, and both he and Greyson faced the parking lot.

I pulled myself out of the pool and hurriedly wrapped the towel around me. "All right, I'm . . . decent," I said, clutching the towel. *Decent* didn't seem like the right word. What was decent about getting caught skinny-dipping in the condo pool by a potentially hot stranger and his teenage daughter?

Just as Greyson and her dad turned back around, Mia and Kitty burst through the gate, their laughter ringing out into the pool area.

"How hard were you freaking out?" Mia said. But when she and Kitty realized I was out of the pool and *not* alone, they paused.

"You're back!" Greyson called, racing over to the girls and clearly undisturbed by the events that had transpired.

"I am going to *kill* you," I hissed at Mia.

Kitty's lip trembled. "I'm sorry, Aunt Jo. It was Mia's idea, and then we found a nest of turtles hatching and lost track of time."

"You found baby turtles?" Greyson said.

"Yeah." Kitty turned back to me. "You've got to come see, Aunt Jo, there's so many!"

"I can't exactly go look at baby turtles right now, Kitty."

"Oh, right."

Mia approached with my clothes, her barely contained smile infuriating me. I snatched them from her and strutted over to the pool shower, ducking behind the wall to get dressed as quickly as possible.

I combed my fingers through my wet hair, willing my pulse to slow. I needed to play this cool. Not because I cared what a possibly attractive stranger like Greyson's dad thought, but because he and Greyson were my neighbors, and I didn't want them thinking I was some sort of weirdo, which wasn't going so well at the moment. Greyson's dad was probably calling his landlord to get his deposit back right now.

When I emerged from behind the shower wall, Greyson perked her head up. "Can we go see the baby turtles now, please?" She whirled around to face her dad. "Can we? Please?"

Greyson's dad shrugged. "I don't see why not."

Before I could say anything to Mia and Kitty, they raced off with Greyson, probably trying to get away from me and my anger as quickly as possible. But maybe that was for the best, because I didn't want them to hear whatever lecture I was about to get from Greyson's dad. I turned around, an apology on my lips as I walked over to where he stood beside the pool. *Look apologetic*, I told myself, keeping my gaze on my feet until I stood right in front of him.

When I looked up, finally close enough to make out his face, I froze, realizing I'd *already* made out with his face. Two nights ago. At Mitch's.

"Alex?" I said before I could stop myself.

His eyes widened. "It's Jo, right?"

"That's me." Heat crept up my neck. How could Hot Guy from the Bar *be* Hot Single Dad? How could Alex be here? Beside my condo pool? Having caught me completely naked? Nina was going to love this. I tried not to stare at him, but it was impossible.

Alex looked like he was struggling not to laugh when I handed him the towel. This was not the face of an angry parent ready to call the cops on some creep in the condo pool.

"I don't usually do this," I said. "There's a whole story to it."

Alex slung the towel around his neck. "I'm sure there is."

"And the other night at the bar," I continued, "when, you know . . ."

"When you kissed me."

"Right. I have this list, you see, of thirty things to do before I turn thirty—"

"Like a bucket list."

"Basically. One of the items was to kiss a stranger, and the other was—"

"Skinny-dipping." He snapped his fingers. "I knew kissing strangers wasn't a real Floridian tradition, but a bucket-list item?" He shook his head. "And here I thought you kissed me because I'm irresistibly handsome."

"No!" I said, then realized I might have offended him. "Not that you aren't . . . or are . . ." I shook my head. "You know what? Forget the kissing. Tonight I only meant to get in and out of the pool, but my nieces grabbed my clothes and ran off, and then you and Greyson came along and . . ." Alex didn't say anything, waiting for me to finish my sentence. "And I don't want you to think I'm some kind of perv . . . Because we're neighbors," I added, just to be clear about my intentions.

Alex laughed. "Actually, I thought it was kind of cute."

Cute? "I don't date," I blurted out.

He raised his eyebrows. "I didn't say I thought *you* were cute."

"Oh." My blush returned with a vengeance. Was it possible to die of embarrassment?

I tried to read Alex's expression. Was this as awkward for him as it was for me? He clapped his hands together and nodded toward the beach, apparently not feeling awkward at all. "So about those baby turtles?"

Yes. Movement. That would be good.

We left the pool area for the beach, walking side by side in the sand. I kept glancing at him, expecting him to disappear, but there he was, as handsome as he'd been at Mitch's. Maybe I was having a stress-induced breakdown. Maybe he wasn't even real, and I'd made him up.

"I'm glad to see you," Alex said. His arm brushed against mine as we followed the sound of the girls' voices down the beach, and the sensation was definitely that of a real person and not an imaginary dream man my brain had cooked up to distract me from my problems. "Not because of . . . you know," he continued. "I was worried I'd be the only one under sixty in this place. How long have you lived here?"

"About seven years," I said, grateful to move on from both the kissing and pool incidents. "I inherited my unit from my grandmother."

"So you're a local."

"I grew up in North Carolina."

"Wow, so you're not even from Florida, Florida Girl?"

"You got me." I smiled down at the sand. "Greyson said you just moved here?"

"New job. We moved up here from Miami."

"Did you grow up there?"

"Sort of. I lived in an RV as a kid," Alex said. "We traveled all over the place, but Miami was home base."

"Greyson said your parents were hippies."

Alex laughed. "Yeah, I'd say that's accurate."

"You don't really seem like a hippie," I said. "You seem mostly normal."

"Mostly normal?" Alex looked at me, but I couldn't make out his expression. "That's because you don't know me yet."

Yet. I didn't know what Alex had in mind for the future of our neighborly relationship, but after tonight, there was no way I'd be getting to know him better. Whether he was devastatingly handsome or not, I refused to risk embarrassing myself again. It would be more than enough to admire him from afar.

Luckily, the conversation didn't last long, and we found Mia, Kitty, and Greyson sitting beside each other in the sand. I sank down beside Kitty. It had been years since I'd seen a nest hatch, and all of it—the turtles wriggling down the beach, their papery eggshells scattered in the sand—took my breath away.

"Isn't it beautiful, Aunt Jo?" Kitty said.

"Dad, can we keep one?" Greyson leapt up and pulled on Alex's arm.

"Absolutely not," he said, and at her disappointed face added, "It's illegal."

Greyson groaned and collapsed back down beside Kitty.

"Samson always wanted to see this," Kitty said.

Mia's face changed then, and she stared at the baby turtles as if she blamed them personally for Florida's beach erosion. Dread settled in my stomach. One moment, I had the girls happy and distracted, and the next, *wham*.

"Who's Samson?" Greyson asked, looking between Mia and Kitty.

No one answered her. It was cooler down here by the water, and I rubbed my arms to brush off the chill. Was I supposed to explain or let the moment pass? I glanced at Alex, who seemed to be purposefully keeping his eyes on the turtles and pretending he hadn't heard.

"This is boring," Mia said. Before I could stop her, she sprang to her feet and bolted in the direction of the condo. I watched her, unable to move. The sudden change in atmosphere made piecing my thoughts together like swimming against a current. My mind and body were too slow to call out or run after her.

The sound of the gate closing with a bang made me jump. Kitty and I exchanged looks, and I hoped she'd know what to do, like Mia had earlier.

"Did I say something wrong?" Greyson asked.

I gave her the best smile I could manage. "No, you didn't say anything wrong."

I turned to Alex, who had his eyes on Greyson. "I'm sorry, she . . ." I let the sentence trail off. How could I explain this to a stranger? What was I supposed to say? *Sorry she's being rude, her brother died*? I shook my head. "We'd better go after her." I helped Kitty to her feet and dusted the sand from the backs of my thighs. "Thanks for the towel."

"Anytime," Alex said, and I forced myself not to look back at him as Kitty and I trudged up the beach.

MIA WAS HUNKERED DOWN BENEATH THE BLANKETS ON THE sofa bed when we returned, music blaring through her headphones. I stared at the lump of her. Even if I could coax her out, what could I say that would make a difference? I couldn't bring her brother back.

Kitty crawled beside Mia on the bed and curled around her.

"Should I talk to her?" I asked.

"I don't know," Kitty whispered. "It's usually me."

"She probably wants to be alone, right?"

Kitty shrugged.

I sank into the chair at my desk and checked skinny-dipping off the list. "One down, seven to go," I muttered. I scanned the remaining items, starting to suspect my plan to distract the girls might not be as effective as I'd hoped.

"Sorry, Aunt Jo," Kitty said.

"For what?"

"For all the crying, I guess."

I joined her on the bed and rested one hand on her and the other on Mia. Kitty had always been sensitive, but this was different. And Mia, she was a different kid from the girl I'd snuck a sip of my champagne on New Year's—the last time I'd seen the kids before the accident. She had the same personality, the sarcasm and tough attitude, but now there was a current of anger beneath it that hadn't been there before.

"You're forgetting I lived with you when you were babies," I said. "I can handle a little crying."

"Do you think she's okay?" Kitty asked.

I looked at Mia, a girl who was pranking me one minute and having a meltdown the next. Obviously, she wasn't okay. None of us were. But I didn't want Kitty to worry. "I think she'll be fine. She just needs some sleep."

Kitty nodded and said she was going to bed. I tried not to worry about them as I changed into my pajamas and brushed my teeth, but did anyway. I'd been just like them once, a teenager wading through grief that seemed like it would never end. And it hadn't, not really. It only changed. But I knew that wouldn't help Mia or Kitty right now. I ran over the events of the day in my mind, amazed the girls had only been here for twenty-four hours. But if there was one good thing about this whole night, it was that after this, Alex would never want to speak to me again.

Which was perfect, seeing as I'd be avoiding him for the rest of my life.

Six

⚓

THE NEXT MORNING, BEFORE I LEFT FOR WORK, I BLOCKED THE
TV by standing between it and the couch, where Mia and Kitty lay head
to head, their legs draped over its arms. Mia's phone rested on her chest,
while Kitty had *The Art of War* open on hers. Their empty cereal bowls
were stacked on the side table, but at least they'd folded up the sofa bed.

"Move, Jo!" Mia sat up on her elbows, craning her neck to try to see
the TV. "I need to know if she's going to flip out when she sees her best
friend wearing the same dress as her!"

"What?" I turned over my shoulder to glance at the TV, where, sure
enough, a glossy-haired sixteen-year-old in a tiara and bubble-gum-
pink dress looked ready to burst into tears, and then whipped back
around. "You aren't supposed to watch without me!"

"She's right," Kitty said, and Mia clicked off the TV with a scowl.

"Thank you. I'm off to work and won't be home until six, so we need
to lay down some ground rules."

Mia and Kitty groaned in unison, burying their faces in the couch
pillows.

Usually, the kids came down for only two or three weeks. I'd take some well-deserved vacation time and spend every hour with them that I could. This was the first time I'd have to work while they were here, and I was looking forward to my two weeks off in July, even if I'd just be staying in Palm Beach.

"The rules won't be bad, I promise. I'm the *cool* aunt, remember?"

"You're our only aunt," Kitty said.

Mia lifted her face from the pillow, her expression stricken. "You sound like a . . . a . . . *mom.*"

"Oh, shut up." I grabbed one of the pillows they'd knocked to the floor and threw it at her face. "I'm serious. I'm going to be worried about you all day if you don't listen."

"All right, all right," Mia said. She and Kitty sat up and smoothed their wrinkled pajamas, looking as serious as chairwomen at a board meeting.

"We're ready for your presentation, Ms. Walker," Mia said with a nod.

"Thank you." I gave them a nod in return. "While I'm at work, there's no leaving the condo premises. Keep your phones *charged* at all times. Text me every two hours so I know you're okay. My credit card is in the desk drawer, for *emergencies* only. And no going into the water." Kitty opened her mouth, and I added, "Pool or ocean."

Mia broke from her mockingly serious demeanor. "What's the point of spending the summer in Florida if we can't go in the water? We're not little kids anymore."

She had a point, and if Samson hadn't died, I probably would've let the girls go in the pool without an adult so long as they were together and texted me every hour. But things were different now. I knew if I allowed it, I'd be sick with worry all day.

"You can go in the water, just not while I'm gone," I said, and the girls' expressions went from disappointed to sour. "I only work three or four days a week right now. I promise we'll make up for it on the days I have off. We'll swim until we're permanently pruney."

Kitty placed her chin in her hands. "So what are we supposed to do all day?"

I looked around the condo. It wasn't exactly the most teenager-friendly place. In truth, it was one Jo and Alex away from being a de facto nursing home, but that didn't mean there wasn't plenty to do.

"You can play games. I bet Old Gary would talk your ear off if you played shuffleboard with him. You can read a book." I nodded to Kitty's *The Art of War.* "I never said you couldn't go to the beach, just stay out of the water. And I'm sure Belva wouldn't mind a visit."

Mia stared blankly at me. "I take it back. You don't sound like a mom. You sound like a grandma. What has this place done to you?" She nudged Kitty. "Have you seen Jo's knitting basket anywhere? I want to make Mom a scarf."

I narrowed my eyes. If Mia was trying to make me feel guilty, it was working, but it wouldn't change my mind. "I'm serious. You can basically do whatever you want, except—"

"Have any fun."

I crossed my arms over my chest, not caring if I looked like a mom, or grandma, or school principal. Didn't they understand I was only do-ing what I had to in order to make sure they were safe? "If you want to see it that way, I can't stop you."

"Aunt Jo," Kitty said, her eyes lighting up with whatever idea had popped into her head. "Can we hang out with Greyson while you're gone?"

Last night's embarrassment leapt to the forefront of my mind, and I glanced out the window into the parking lot. Maybe I could avoid seeing Alex for long enough that he'd forget about the whole thing, and then we could be neighborly. "Yes. Just make sure she asks her dad. And I'd prefer if you three hung out either here or outside. At least until we get to know them better." Not that I was planning on it.

Mia smirked. "Greyson's dad sure knows *you* pretty well after last night."

"Which is *your* fault," I said, grabbing my purse and keys. "I'm off. Remember the rules. Text me every two hours."

"Bye, Grandma!" they called out after me.

AS SOON AS I ARRIVED ON DECK, NINA GRABBED ME BY THE ARM and pulled me into the laundry room, her expression so serious I thought Captain Xav had fallen overboard.

"What's wrong?" I asked, my heart racing at the sight of her. She looked wild, her unicorn earrings quivering as she kicked the door shut behind her.

"He's here!"

"Who's here?"

"The new *chef*." Nina threw herself onto a pile of dirty towels, looking as if all the joy had been drained out of her.

"Is that all?"

Nina's eyes narrowed. "What do you mean, *is that all*?"

I lowered myself onto the floor across from her. "I take it you don't like him."

"Of course I don't! He rearranged the drawers in the most nonsensical way and then had the nerve to ask *me* if I knew where the spiralizer was. Like *I* would know if we even had one!"

"But we do have a spiralizer, and you know exactly where it is." I tried not to laugh. I knew Ollie leaving would make Nina moodier than usual, but I hadn't prepared myself for how much she'd take it out on the new chef.

"That's beside the point! Also, I think I know him from somewhere. He's handsome but annoying, so he must be one of my Tinder dates gone bad. He hasn't said anything about it, though, so he—"

"*One* of your Tinder dates gone bad? How many bad Tinder dates have you had?"

Nina shrugged. "How many does the average person have?"

"Why would I know? You know I'm anti–app dating. It's too public."

"Says the blogger. Well, whatever that number is, double it." I stared at her. "What? This is Florida. We've got twice the bad eggs in the dating pool."

"I think you're just mad he's not *you know who.*"

Nina let out an exasperated sigh. "Come on. You'll see what I mean."

I allowed Nina to pull me out of the laundry room and up to the galley. The new chef, who was dressed in the traditional white chef coat and black slim-fit chef pants, stood at the sink, his back to us as he scrubbed carrots and lined them up on a cutting board.

"Look," Nina seethed. "Even the way he washes vegetables is annoying!"

I rolled my eyes. "Now you're really being dramatic. He's got a nice butt. You should be all over that."

"I am not being dramatic!" she hissed. "And I don't care how nice his ass is, he's irritating."

I shook my head. He could've been Jamie Oliver and Nina would've hated him. Deciding to nip this whole thing in the bud, I strode into the galley, giving Nina a wink before tapping him on the shoulder.

"Chef, I wanted to introduce myself. I'm . . ." But my voice trailed off when he turned around, and I took in the tousled hair, the honey eyes, the mouth that, every time I'd seen it, wore the hint of a smile.

Alex's eyes widened in surprise, and the hinted smile bloomed into a real one. "Jo. Hello again. I'm sorry, but I have to ask . . . are you stalking me?"

I stared at him. He couldn't be here. It was impossible. Too many coincidences. "Of course not, I—"

"Wait," Nina said, practically sprinting into the galley. She looked from me to Alex, then back to me again. "You know this guy?"

My cheeks grew hotter as I fumbled for something to say. "We—"

"Live in the same building," Alex said.

"Interesting." Nina tapped a finger to her pursed lips, and dread pooled in my stomach as I watched her fit all the pieces together. She snapped her fingers, her face gleeful. "I knew I recognized you! You're that guy from the bar!" She turned to me. "Jo, he's that guy from the bar!"

This was only getting worse by the second. "I know, Nina."

Nina grabbed my elbow, dragging me away from Alex and over to the far side of the galley. She dropped her voice to a whisper. "Josephine, he's the one you kissed!"

"I *know*!"

"And he lives in your building? Makes sense he'd be at Mitch's . . . Oh my God." Her eyes widened. "*He's* Hot Single Dad!" she said, then clapped a hand over her mouth when she realized how loudly she'd said it. She turned to Alex. "I'm so sorry. What I meant to say is you're *that* single dad."

Alex looked as if he were trying not to laugh as he chopped carrots. "No harm done. I can't deny I'm *that* single dad."

"Great. Marvelous. Sorry again for the . . . slip of the tongue." Nina turned to me, her voice a whisper again. "Jo," Nina said, practically shaking me by the shoulders. "*That* guy from the bar is Greyson's dad. He's *that* guy from the bar *and* that single dad!"

I pushed her away from me. "I know, Nina! Everyone knows!"

Nina paused, then laughed so intensely she had to brace herself against the counter. Alex glanced at me and then at Nina, and I tried to avoid looking at either of them, sure I was about to spontaneously combust.

"Wow," Nina said when she finally caught her breath. She patted my shoulder. "Guess they didn't name this yacht *Serendipity* for nothing. Since you already know Chef Alex, why don't you help him get settled." She turned to him. "I prefer to stay out of the chaos," she said. "And, uh, sorry again. For what I accidentally said."

I grabbed Nina's arm as she turned to leave. "Don't you think it would be better if I—"

"Nope." She pried my hand from her arm and winked before crossing the galley to the steps. "The guests requested a charcuterie board," she called to Alex. "You *do* know how to make one, don't you?"

"I'm sure I can google it," he replied, smiling to himself as he stored the chopped carrots in a Tupperware.

I lingered at the edge of the galley and watched Nina disappear, leaving me alone with Alex. I was afraid to turn around and face him. This had to be a dream. No, a nightmare. Why else would the very person I was avoiding have magically appeared in the galley?

"I get the feeling I'm not her favorite person," Alex said. I turned to find him leaning against the sink, watching me with that almost smile on his face.

I dragged myself from the edge of the galley and stood on the opposite side of the island counter. This didn't need to be awkward unless I made it awkward.

"It's nothing personal. She and the last chef were *close*." I raised my eyebrows, hoping he'd catch my drift.

"Ah." He nodded around the kitchen as if he could sense traces of Ollie in each appliance, then stepped away to rummage through the cabinets by the stove. I stared at him, blinking over and over, sure I really was having a breakdown this time and could snap myself back into reality. But every time I opened my eyes, he was still there.

Alex turned, catching me in the middle of a blink. "All right, I need to know what you're thinking." He leaned against the sink again, arms crossed casually over his chest.

"It's just . . . what are the chances, right? I see you at Mitch's, we live in the same building, and now you work *here*."

Alex stepped forward and rested his elbows on the island counter. "Do you believe in fate, Jo?"

I tensed. Where was this conversation going? "Of course not. But it seems like an awful lot of coincidences."

"Well, I do believe in fate. Blame the hippie parents, but I'm inclined to think everything happens for a reason."

My pulse raced, but I forced myself not to look away. "So what's the reason, then?"

Alex shrugged. "I don't know yet. Guess we'll have to wait to find out." His eyes finally left mine, and he disappeared for a moment, squatting down to dig through another cabinet. "Cheese board?" he called, and I directed him to a cabinet beside the stove. When he returned and set the cheese board on the island, he sighed. "If it makes you feel better, there's also a completely rational explanation for these coincidences."

That would definitely make me feel better, I thought. "And that explanation is?"

"Think about it." He turned to the refrigerator and piled various cheeses and slices of meats on the counter. "I'm guessing you went to Mitch's because it's the closest bar to the condo, right?"

I nodded.

"Which is exactly why I was there."

My eyes flitted to his mouth, and I remembered the events of our first coincidence. "Fair enough."

"You said you inherited the condo from your grandmother, but it's also the best place with two-bedrooms close to both the marina and Harper Middle School, which has the best special education program in the county. Greyson has some learning disabilities," he explained.

Also fair. "And working on the same boat?" I asked.

"Xav and my dad go way back. He helped me get my first yachting gig four years ago. So when I was looking for a good school to move Grey to and found Harper Middle, I reached out to Xav. I told him I was looking to move up to Palm Beach and to let me know if he heard of any open positions. He called a few weeks later to offer me a job, and here we are."

Alex stepped around the island on his way to the pantry, passing so close I could smell him again. The scent reminded me of a bakery— warm croissants and blueberry muffins. The thought was alarming. I did not need to be smelling this man or comparing his scent to various baked goods. I was probably just hungry. We were in a kitchen, after all.

"I should double-check what the guests want for today," I said, needing to put distance between us. I crossed the galley to look at the preference sheets, which our guests filled out so we'd know what they expected from us.

"I still think it's fate, though," he said. He set a box of artisan crackers beside the cheese board.

Nina believed in fate too. I wasn't looking forward to our next conversation. Knowing her, she'd probably steal my phone and look through the astrology app she'd forced me to download but that I never used. I flicked at a preference sheet with a finger, not acknowledging Alex's comment. We had wine drinkers today, which I should've guessed by the charcuterie board.

I thought about Mia and Kitty. I'd been here for only half an hour, and already I was anxious to get that first text from them. They'd get a kick out of this when they found out, though maybe they already had. I wondered if they were with Greyson right now and if the three of them would puzzle this coincidence out for themselves. Or would Alex and I not feature in their conversations at all?

I leaned against the side of the fridge and watched Alex work. What was it like to raise a teenage girl all on your own? How was it even possible with a job like ours? "How do you make it work?" I asked, curiosity getting the better of me. "Charter season, and parenting, and all. Does Greyson's mom have her when you're away?"

Alex arched a brow at me. "That's a very specific question."

I winced. What was it about this guy that brought out my inner weirdo? "Sorry, don't answer that. Too personal."

His almost smile lifted into a smirk. "I like that you skip the small talk." I blushed, thinking of how I'd *really* skipped the small talk the other night. "Every charter season for the last four years my parents have stayed at my place with Greyson." He set down his knife and stepped over to the fridge, grabbing a jar of olives. "This past season didn't go so well, though. Grey had a rough school year, and I should've been there." He seemed lost in thought for a moment, then sprang back to work and scooped olives from the jar. "So here I am, working off-season and hoping I can piece together enough private gigs once charter season starts up again. Working in restaurants, now that's not conducive to parenting." He caught my eye, and his joking expression returned. "That was probably more personal than you were looking for."

He picked up the box of crackers and held it out to me. Unable to resist food, I found myself standing right beside him at the counter. Damn my love of carbs.

"I think it's interesting." I bit into a cracker, and Alex gave me a skeptical look. "No, really. I always wonder how parents do it. My sister, she's a nurse and has three . . . It's cool how you manage it all. That's what I meant to say."

"I definitely don't manage it all. I have a lot of help. I'm sure your sister does too. She has you, right?"

"I guess." I nibbled the cracker and thought about Beth, not so sure I was much help to her. Was she at work? I knew she had a shift this morning, but what if today was one of her impossible days when she couldn't get out of bed? I felt helpless knowing that even if I were by her side, I couldn't take the pain away.

Alex swept his gaze around the galley. "Is there a speaker in here? The food tastes better if I listen to music."

I waltzed over to the pantry. "Bluetooth speakers. Just queue up the music on your phone. The password is right here." I tapped a small piece of paper taped beneath the panel for the sound system. "But don't play it too loud, or you'll give Captain a heart attack. He doesn't like it when the guests can hear us having real lives."

Alex glanced down at his phone. "How about the Weeknd?"

Was he really asking about my weekend plans? And here I thought we'd finally had a normal, non-embarrassing conversation for once. I kept my eyes on the speaker's panel. "I'm usually busy."

Alex laughed. "Hold on." He stepped over to the panel and con-
nected his phone to the speaker. A song I vaguely recognized from the
radio played, and Alex stared at me, singing along as if waiting for me
to pick up on something.

"Oh!" I said, understanding as soon as he got to the chorus. "The
Weeknd. The singer. I thought you were . . ."

"Asking you out?" He smiled, and I looked away. "You don't date,
though, right?"

"Uh, right."

"Well, there's another coincidence. Neither do I. You don't have to
worry about me. Though given past experience, I may have to worry
about you."

"No, I—"

"Teasing, Jo." He turned up the volume of the music and started
singing again, dancing his way across the galley. Alex was something
else, there was no doubt about it. Confident, but not in the blustery way
most men I'd met in bars were. There was something endearing in his
openness, even if he was sort of annoying.

When it was time to head up to the aft deck and greet the guests,
Alex paused on his way out of the galley. He ran a hand through his hair
and straightened his chef's jacket. For a moment I thought he was nervous. But then he turned to me, face serious, and said, "You think I can
become Hot Yacht Chef if I try hard enough?"

I rolled my eyes and pushed past him through the door. "I think you
mean *that* yacht chef." But what I was thinking was, *Become? You already
are*. And then: *Bad. This is very, very bad.*

WHEN I RETURNED HOME THAT EVENING, GIVING ALEX AN AWK-
ward wave when we pulled into the condo parking lot at the same time,
I found Mia and Kitty lying on their stomachs in the living room and
watching *Dr. Phil.*

"Jo, you've gotta see this," Mia said, waving me over. "This chick crochets sweaters out of her dog's fur. It's unbelievable."

"Mia says it's art," Kitty said, "but I think it's just disturbing."

I set my purse on the entryway table and slipped off my shoes, setting them on the shoe rack by the door. "Well, I've got an unbelievable story for you." I lowered myself onto the floor beside Kitty, crossing my legs beneath me. "You'll never believe who the new yacht chef is."

"If it's not Gordon Ramsay, then I don't care," Mia said.

"I do! I care!" Kitty said, turning to me with an eager face.

I leaned back on my elbows, tilting my face up to the TV. "Remember Greyson's dad?"

Kitty looked at me nervously, but Mia grinned. "Of course I remember. Seeing your panicked face after he caught you in the pool was only the best moment of my life."

"Well, he just happens to be my new *colleague*." I draped myself across Mia, mimicking one of her dramatic groans.

Mia pushed me off her and stared at me with wide eyes. "You're kidding."

"I wish I was kidding," I sighed.

Mia nodded, her expression unreadable as she fumbled for words. "That's . . . even *better* than Gordon Ramsay." And then she and Kitty burst into laughter. They laughed so hard that tears streamed down their cheeks. This seemed to go on for minutes, and every time they calmed, nearly catching their breath, they'd look at me and it would start all over again. It got to the point that even I was laughing along with them. The whole situation was ridiculous. Who would believe it? And by the time the three of us had finally calmed down enough to look at each other without dissolving into a fit of giggles, we were wheezing.

"Greyson is going to love this," Kitty said, shaking her head as she pulled out her phone.

"Did you three have fun today?" I asked.

"Yeah," Mia said. "Greyson is hilarious. We weren't bored at all, were we, Kitty?"

Kitty snorted as she looked at her phone, not hearing Mia's question. "Look." She showed us the string of brightly colored emojis filling the screen. "She's totally freaking out."

I was relieved. Mia and Kitty were happy, and Greyson seemed to be a good distraction. I thought about what Alex had said that morning about there being a reason for everything. I still didn't believe that. But maybe he was right about all our coincidences being fate, and maybe it had nothing to do with either of us.

Seven

⚓

TWO WEEKS AFTER THE GIRLS HAD ARRIVED, I WOKE UP EARLIER than usual, chugged a mug of coffee, and laced up my new running shoes, ready for my first day of marathon training. On my way out the door, I clicked off the TV, which Mia and Kitty had left on all night. *I just can't sleep without it*, Kitty had said that first night, and though it wouldn't do my electric bill any favors, I didn't push the issue. I could guess why she needed it.

I closed the door quietly behind me and eased into a jog, heading across the parking lot toward South Ocean Boulevard. My legs resisted me. Floating in the ocean was my preferred form of exercise, but I had a marathon to prepare for and no time to waste.

Since Mia and Kitty had arrived, I'd made minimal progress on the list. And by minimal, I mean none. The only thing I'd checked off was skinny-dipping, which hadn't exactly gone to plan. Something that *had* worked out like I'd hoped was Greyson, who'd become Mia and Kitty's greatest source of entertainment. She was a frequent visitor at the condo, joining us for beach days and dips in the pool. Almost every day when I arrived home from work, I found her on the couch between Mia and

Kitty, the three of them talking away as if they'd been friends forever. The only drawback of this was that wherever Greyson went, messes followed. A few days earlier she'd knocked over one of my grandmother's teapots while doing a cartwheel in the living room. Fortunately, I wasn't much of a tea drinker and was planning to get rid of it when I got to item number twenty-two—declutter the condo—but poor Greyson had tears in her eyes, apologizing as she scrambled to pick up the pieces. I didn't mind the messes much. Greyson had a way of lifting the energy in any room she stepped into, which was worth a hundred teapots, especially this summer.

Five minutes into my run, a stitch formed in my side, and my lungs burned with the effort of breathing. I wheezed past rows of condos and was nearly bowled over by a cluster of power-walking old ladies decked out in orthopedic sneakers and matching tracksuits. Twenty minutes in and I found myself doubled over in the middle of the sidewalk, nearly blinded by the mixture of sweat and sunscreen dripping into my eyes.

The night before, Greyson had told us about the *easy* seven-mile run she and Alex had done that morning. Twenty minutes later, Kitty had handed me her phone with a marathon-training plan that made me question why I'd put this on the list in the first place.

"This will have you ready in twelve weeks, which we don't have," Kitty had said. "So maybe skip the first few weeks. If you do the race on your birthday—"

"There's no way I'm running a marathon on my thirtieth birthday."

Kitty had narrowed her eyes at me. "Fine. Take off another day." She'd glanced at the phone. "Now you've only got to do four miles tomorrow."

Mia had cackled from the couch.

"Four miles isn't so bad," Greyson had said. "When I was running track at my old school, we had to do five miles every practice. Just make sure you breathe in through your nose." She'd demonstrated, lifting her hands toward her face as she breathed in. "And out through your mouth." She'd lowered her arms quickly, blowing hot air into my face.

"Four miles. I can do that." It wasn't like I was completely out of shape. I spent my days racing around a 150-foot superyacht, after all.

When I'd created the list that night in Mitch's, I'd wanted to challenge myself. I'd envisioned becoming one of those people with oval-shaped magnets on their car highlighting the miles they'd run. But now I realized I could've bought the magnet and put it on my car anyway.

I made it only two miles before I gave up and called an Uber to drop me off at the edge of the condo parking lot, hoping the girls wouldn't see me. Which, fortunately, they didn't. But as luck would have it, when I got out of the car and passed the mailboxes, wincing with each step, there was Alex with a stack of envelopes in his hand and looking like Colin Firth in that lake scene from *Pride and Prejudice* Nina had forced me to watch. Only Alex was drenched in sweat (likely from his own run) and wore a nylon shirt that stuck to his chest (instead of billowy white linen).

"Hey," he said, tugging his headphones from his ears and looking from me to the Uber that looped around the parking lot. "I see the marathon training is going well."

I leaned against the wall, still struggling to catch my breath. "Yeah, well. We can't all be Usain Bolt."

"You know he's a sprinter, right?" Alex said.

"I did not. Which only proves my point."

Alex laughed, and I wasn't sure if he was laughing with me or at me. He probably thought I was pathetic. *Who gets an Uber in the middle of a four-mile warm-up run?*

"I hate my past self," I said.

"I think a lot of people feel that way." Alex walked alongside me until I made it to my door. "But don't worry. I won't tell anyone about the Uber."

Alex and I had become fast friends in the two weeks we'd worked together. With him in the galley, there was always music, and dancing, and food like I'd never seen before. Duck hearts with mushroom floss and spiced broth. Deconstructed mackerel and wildflowers and ramp puree.

Every dish looked too pretty to eat, though that didn't keep me from drooling whenever I stepped into the galley. Because of the food, of course.

But as we stood before my door, an awkward silence passed between us. Unlike his daughter, Alex had made himself scarce outside of work. I caught occasional glimpses of him when he waved Greyson up from the pool, or in the mornings when they ran side by side from the parking lot. We left for work at the same time each morning and returned at the same time in the afternoon. But other than that, we didn't interact outside of work. It was odd speaking with him outside of the galley, and part of me wondered what he was like off the boat, not as Chef Alex but as the Alex I'd met at the bar.

"Well, it was nice seeing you," I said.

"Uh, Jo?"

"Yes?"

"Sorry about the teapot. Greyson told me. Let me know how we can replace it."

I waved him off. "Really, I was getting rid of it anyway. It wasn't worth anything." Not exactly true. It was worth at least a few hundred bucks according to my eBay search, but he didn't need to know that.

Alex sighed, seeming lighter. Had he really been that worried about Greyson breaking my teapot? "Thanks for letting her hang out with Mia and Kitty. Just let me know if she becomes too much. She, uh, has a lot of energy."

"Yeah, she does." The other morning she'd burst into the condo and convinced Mia and Kitty to follow along to old eighties Jazzercise videos on YouTube. I'd watched from the couch until Greyson started clapping and kicking in front of me, forcing me to join them. *C'mon, Jo! Elevate that heart rate! Swing it out!* "But she's a fun kid."

Alex smiled widely. "Yeah, she is. Sometimes a little too fun. The morning runs help, though."

"She reminds me a lot of my nephew." I looked away. I hadn't meant to bring up Samson. There was too much to explain, and I didn't want to do it now.

Alex nodded, and I could tell he already knew about Samson by how his mouth, always ready to smile, flattened. I wondered what the girls had told Greyson about Samson, and what Greyson had told him. Though the girls sometimes hung out with Greyson at Alex's place, so maybe they'd told him themselves.

"What was he like?" he asked.

"Oh." I fidgeted with my keys. "He was . . . great." *Great?* Like that did any justice to who Samson was.

"You don't have to talk about it." Alex ran a hand through his hair, and the silver at his temples caught the sunlight, not in an unappealing way. I dropped my gaze again, shaking the thought from my mind. Alex tapped the mail against his leg. Maybe he was as eager to escape this conversation as I was. "If you need a break from the teenagers, feel free to send them over. I'm sure I can whip up enough food to keep them occupied."

"If food is involved, I'm sending *myself* over," I said. "With the girls, I mean."

"Whenever you want. I'm happy to cook for everyone."

"That would be great." There was an awkward pause, and I was about to turn to my door when he spoke again.

"Oh, I meant to ask. I was wondering, seeing as we both live here and work on the boat, would you be interested in carpooling? You know, to save expenses and, uh, climate change. You can say no. I just feel a little silly watching you leave at the same time when we're going to the same place."

"Oh." The proposition took me by surprise. I didn't need to be spending more time with him than was necessary, and yet I couldn't think of a single excuse that wasn't *I can't spend too much time with you because I keep thinking about that time I kissed you,* and that obviously couldn't be spoken aloud. "Sure," I said before I could stop myself.

"Then what are you thinking?" Truthfully, movies weren't really my thing. Sitting still in the dark for two hours? No thanks. I was more of a TV show person. Short, sweet, and to the point. With TV I could tap out whenever I needed to. I could skip the episodes I didn't like, the ones that got too dark, or sad, or heavy, and not miss much.

"Maybe we don't do it based on the movies, but on the actor," Kitty suggested.

Mia propped herself up to look at her sister. "Like when Shia LaBeouf sat in a theater and filmed himself watching his entire filmography."

"That sounds . . . odd," I said.

"It was," Kitty said. "Mia made me watch it. *All* of it."

"It was *art*." Mia flopped back onto her pillow.

"So who should we have a movie marathon of?" I asked. "Chris Evans?"

"Gross," Mia and Kitty said.

"He's so *old*," Mia added.

"But he's hot."

"No way." Kitty crossed her arms, deciding the matter.

"Zac Efron," Mia said. "We should totally do that."

Kitty's eyes widened, and she jumped onto the bed, singing, "Mia loves Zac Efron! Mia loves Zac Efron!"

"I do not!" Mia cried. She chucked a pillow at her sister's head. "I like him in an *ironic* way."

"Oh, please. I remember a certain toddler who was *obsessed* with *High School Musical*," I said.

Mia rolled her eyes, the color rising in her cheeks. "I was a *kid*."

"No need to be embarrassed. Have you seen his abs?"

"It's decided," Kitty said, still standing on the sofa bed. She pounded a fist into her open palm. "The Zac Efron movie marathon is *on*."

Mia groaned, disappearing again beneath the blankets, but I could tell she was excited. And I was, too, not least of all because I could toss my running shoes to the back of my closet and never look at them again.

Eight

⚓

THE NEXT MORNING I SAT AT MY DESK AND RESPONDED TO BLOG comments while Mia and Kitty gnawed on strawberry Pop-Tarts and watched TV. It didn't take too long, seeing as I only had about thirty regular readers. Once I finished with comments on my "Kiss a Stranger" post, I clicked over to read the comments beneath my post about the skinny-dipping incident.

Boymom91: This is even better than The Bachelorette. I'm team Hot Single Dad!

XOJo: @Boymom91 Don't hold your breath waiting for me to pass out any roses!

XxSeaSunStylexx: Jo, take it from me, you do NOT want to hook up with your neighbor. Go find that handsome stranger from the bar!

XOJo: @XxSeaSunStylexx You're right about one thing: I won't be hooking up with my neighbor. But I won't be hooking up with Hot Guy from the Bar, either. Sorry, ladies!

Something I hadn't mentioned on the blog? That the men in these two incidents were the same guy, who was also my coworker.

UnicornStew: Why choose one, when you can have both? 😊

Nina, of course. Why she felt the need to comment on the blog, let alone read it, was beyond me. My reply?

XOJo: @UnicornStew Why choose one when I can have none? 😊

I shut my laptop with a sigh. Though I'd been blogging for almost a year now, I didn't promote the blog on social media or have a newsletter. I didn't even have a Facebook or Instagram account, which Nina said was ridiculous. She'd installed the apps on my phone and had logged into her accounts on it. Why? I had no idea. But it came in handy for stalking guests. I didn't hate social media, and I wasn't even an introvert, but I'd always kept my circle small and my feelings private. The only people I kept in contact with were the people I already talked to.

Writing on a public forum was different, though. Starting the blog had been a way to force myself out of my comfort zone and make my life into something worth documenting. I'd never imagined anyone would actually read it. What would my thirty regular followers—not including Nina—think if they saw me now? Hunched over my computer desk, reality TV blaring, my living room cluttered with Mia's and Kitty's dirty clothes. What did I want from blogging anyway? I'd never thought about what would happen once my thirtieth birthday came and went.

I went to the kitchen and grabbed the last Pop-Tart before plopping down on the couch between Mia and Kitty. All yesterday I'd thought about texting Alex to say I'd changed my mind about carpooling, but he didn't know I had his number, and I wasn't about to waltz over to his condo and bail on him in person. Anything I said now would make it seem like I was trying to avoid him (which I was), but I also didn't want to hurt his feelings. If he *knew* I was avoiding him, then he'd want to know why, and he might conclude that the very fact I was avoiding him was evidence I had some sort of attraction to him (which I didn't, beyond a natural pheromonal attraction, probably because he smelled so good). So really, the best course of action was to continue with the plan: both the carpooling and the not being attracted to him.

"Jo, chill out." Mia nudged my leg with her foot.

I set my feet firmly on the tile, not realizing I'd been bouncing my legs up and down.

Kitty set down one of my father's poetry books and gave me a sidelong glance. "Are you on cocaine?"

I nearly spit out my Pop-Tart. "What? Why would I be on cocaine? Why do you even *know* about cocaine?"

Kitty shrugged. "I had to do a project on Robert Louis Stevenson this year. Wanna know how he wrote *Dr. Jekyll and Mr. Hyde* in six days? Cocaine. That's how."

"Well, I'm not on drugs. But I am worried about what you're learning in school."

"Then why are you acting all weird?"

"I'm not acting weird." I took another bite of my Pop-Tart, and crumbs rained down on my shirt. "Probably too much caffeine and sugar. Do you know how awful these are for you? You shouldn't be eating them."

"I thought there was no such thing as too much caffeine," Mia said.

"And don't blame the Pop-Tarts on us. You're the one who bought them. Seriously, you eat like a fifth grader. It's concerning."

I eyed the time on my phone—8:40 a.m. I looked out the window into the parking lot. Alex's minivan (yes, the guy drove a minivan, and for some reason I'd agreed to ride to work in it) was in its usual spot. I turned back to the TV. The girls were watching a baking competition about long-distance couples who'd never met having to cook in their significant other's kitchen before meeting them IRL for the first time. It was amusing, but I had too many questions rolling around in my mind to focus on it. Was Alex the kind of guy who believed you were only on time if you were early? Or was he more of an *I'm five minutes away but actually haven't left my house yet* person? What were we supposed to talk about during the twenty-minute drive to the marina? Did he listen to podcasts? Was he a silent driver? Would he want to talk?

So maybe caffeine and sugar weren't my problem. Maybe I was nervous. But it *wasn't* because of any attraction I might or might not have felt toward him.

"So what are you girls up to today?" I asked, trying to direct my thoughts elsewhere.

"Kitty and I are throwing a kegger in the activities room with Belva and Old Gary," Mia said, her expression unnervingly serious.

"You said we'd be planning the decorations for the movie marathon!" Kitty exclaimed.

Mia rolled her eyes. "We're obviously still doing that, dingus. I was just messing with Jo."

Decorations? I didn't know there'd be more prep work than picking out which movies we'd watch and buying some popcorn.

"I know you're teasing me about the kegger, but I still don't like it." I took the last bite of my Pop-Tart, and a knock on the door startled the three of us.

I forgot all about the movie marathon at the sight of Alex's van running in the parking lot with no one in the driver's seat. I peeked past the plants on my windowsill, and sure enough, there he was, hands in his pockets as he stood before my condo door. So Alex was an eight-forty-five-means-eight-forty-five kind of guy.

"Is that Greyson's dad?" Mia's eyes widened. "Is he picking you up for work?" She grabbed me by the shoulders. "Is that why you've been a total weirdo all morning?"

"Don't," I said.

Kitty looked between the two of us. "Why would she be weird about that?"

I tugged myself from Mia's grasp and slipped on my shoes, getting as much distance between me and the girls as possible.

"Isn't it obvious?" Mia stretched her legs out on the couch, filling the space I'd left between her and Kitty.

Kitty shoved her sister's feet away. "Isn't what obvious?"

"You know what they say, Jo. First comes carpooling, then comes marriage, then comes—"

"Shh! What if he hears you?" How had I suddenly found myself in the middle of a CW teen drama?

"Jo likes Greyson's dad?" Kitty's eyes widened. She turned around on the couch and gawked at Alex through the window.

"No. I do not *like* Alex. Not in the way you're suggesting, anyway."

Mia smirked. "Then why do you care what he hears?"

I sighed, exasperated. This was very like Mia, who, even as a kid, was clear-eyed and perceptive. Not that she was *right* about everything, because she wasn't. But she always knew exactly what buttons to push—enough to get you annoyed but not angry.

"We're coworkers, and I don't want him thinking I like him because it could make things weird. We're just saving money and lowering our carbon footprint."

Mia nodded seriously. "The couple that cuts emissions together stays together."

"You're going to make me late!" I snatched up my purse and keys. "Don't say anything."

"Hi," Alex said, his face lighting up into a smile when I opened the door.

"Hi." There was that annoying fluttering in my chest again. Pheromonal chest fluttering, of course. Because he smelled good. Not that I could smell him right now. "Sorry I took so long. I didn't hear you." I hoped I sounded like a normal human being, and not an almost thirty-year-old who had just been bullied by two teenage girls.

"You have a nice door. I don't mind standing outside it. You ready?"

"Yup." I stepped outside and closed the door behind me. Mia and Kitty's laughter floated through the window.

"Sounds like a party in there."

"You have no idea." I followed him to the van, feeling like a girl being picked up for a date in the aforementioned CW teen drama. Though girls in CW teen dramas probably didn't get picked up for dates in minivans. I watched Alex as he walked ahead of me. He wore a variation of the same outfit he always did: a white tee and slim-fit chef pants. But there was something different about him today. *The hair*, I realized as he got into the driver's seat. His tousled waves were pushed off his forehead, slightly neater than usual. They wouldn't be that way for long, though. His hair had a habit of getting progressively messier as he cooked. By the end of the day he'd look like he'd been standing in tropical storm–force winds.

"You didn't have to come to the door."

Alex shrugged. "I didn't want to honk, and I don't have your number yet."

"Right. I can put it in your phone." The last thing I needed was him seeing I already had his, especially since the contact name was still Hot Guy from the Bar.

We got into the van, and I was relieved to hear the sounds of unfamiliar electropop. So he was a music person. That would lessen the pressure to fill the silence.

"Oh, I almost forgot." He took a stainless steel tumbler from the cup holder between us and passed it to me. "Extra cream, extra sugar, right? I think that's how you make it on the boat."

I took the coffee from him. Its warmth spread up my hands and through my arms. "Yeah, thanks."

Alex turned onto South Ocean Boulevard, and I looked out the window, watching Palm Beach pass in a blur. "So a minivan, huh? Interesting choice."

Alex raised his eyebrows. "What? Are you too cool for the van?"

"No, I only meant . . . I was just wondering."

He squinted at me a moment, then turned back to the road and nodded. "You are obviously the right amount of cool for the van. Grey calls it the man van, like a man purse, but a van."

That sounded exactly like something Greyson would say. "If I were you, I probably wouldn't go around advertising I drive a man van."

Alex patted the steering wheel. "I'll have you know I'm proud of my man van. This thing is top of the line. But if you really want to know, the van is great for catering gigs."

"I guess that makes sense." I turned over my shoulder. The van was kind of dorky, but with three rows and leather seats, it was way nicer than my beat-up Kia. "Do you do a lot of catering?"

"Not really, but I might. When Greyson's mom was still around, we lived in New York, and the restaurant I worked at catered occasionally."

Though we'd talked a lot about the girls, Greyson's mother had never come up. I turned over the words *still around* in my mind. What did he mean? But I didn't feel it was my place to ask. "But then you moved to Florida."

We made our way through a roundabout, and the ocean burst into view, sparkling beside us like a coin catching the morning light. Alex looked past me and out the window, the corners of his mouth turning down a fraction. "Things got a little out of control when it was just me and Grey. After a few years we needed a change of scenery, so I got my first yachting gig, thanks to Xav, and it's what I've been doing ever since."

"What do you like better, working at a restaurant or being a yachtie?"

Alex shot me that almost smile. "You and your tough questions."

"Sorry. You don't have to—"

"It's hard to say," he said. "I have a complicated history with the restaurant business, but I loved it. Yachting has its pros and cons too. What I'd really like to do is open a place on the beach—like Benny's, that brunch spot you told me about. You were right, they have the best chocolate chip waffles. Greyson loved it."

I imagined Alex and Greyson at Benny's, a stack of waffles between them as they watched seagulls out by the pier. "Why don't you open a restaurant now?" I knew Alex had money. The rent across the parking lot wasn't cheap, and the van looked brand-new.

"Don't have the time. Running a restaurant is like having three full-time jobs, and I don't want to miss out on being there for Greyson. Charter season is rough enough, but it makes it possible for me to only work twenty, twenty-five hours a week tops the rest of the year. In five years she'll hopefully be off to college, and maybe that will be the right time."

I imagined Alex running his own restaurant. It would probably be casual, like him, but a little quirky, perhaps with funky old Florida decor and an eclectic menu. "I envy your cooking skills. Mine are nonexistent. I'm a microwave enthusiast."

Alex gave me a skeptical look.

"No, really. I caught boiling water on fire once. I live off of microwaved dinners."

Alex shook his head. "That's a sad existence."

"I'm going to learn, though. I have to host a dinner party for my list."

"Now that I'd love to see."

"Consider yourself invited, but you aren't allowed to judge. You have to leave your chef's hat at the door."

"I wouldn't dream of judging."

I took a long sip of coffee and watched him as he drove, head bobbing to the music. "Did you always want to be a chef?" I asked.

"Pretty much. Growing up in the RV, I got to try food from everywhere. It was hard always being a stranger, but food made it easier."

"Greyson said your parents are musicians."

"Yeah, that's why we traveled so much. They play folk rock. They weren't big or anything, but they had a following. Sometimes they had me and my siblings play too."

"You play an instrument?"

"A few."

"Such as?"

"Mandolin, banjo, guitar. Not very well. I was always more into food."

He drummed his fingers on the steering wheel as the road pulled away from the ocean, and we slipped beneath a canopy of mangrove trees. Shadow and light danced across the dashboard. The silhouettes of leaves flickered over Alex's face, casting him in a green glow. I tried to imagine him as a little boy traveling the country in an RV with his musical hippie family. It explained a lot about him, really. It seemed like a life that would make a person relaxed, open to new people, and maybe a little weird too.

"And you?" Alex asked. "Did you always want to be a yacht stewardess?"

I laughed. "Not exactly. I didn't even know yacht stewardess was a thing until I got this job. But it's about as close as I can get to my childhood dream."

"Which was?"

I turned to him. "Promise you won't make fun of me?"

"Promise."

"My dad was in the Navy before I was born, and he used to tell me and my sister stories about all the places he'd seen." I smiled, thinking of Dad, who was soft-spoken and private, with the rigid habits of a military man. He'd had a love for opera and poetry and was a poet himself. The three of us, Mom, Beth, and me, adored him. Sometimes at dinner, he'd read poems he'd written for us, and we'd laugh ourselves silly. "When I was in kindergarten, I didn't really understand what the Navy was, and I thought my dad had been a pirate. I was always telling people I wanted to be in the Navy, but I really wanted to be a pirate."

"There are actual pirates, you know," Alex said. "You don't have to settle for being a yacht stewardess."

"You promised no teasing." Alex held up a hand in apology. "I just like being on the water," I continued. "My dad was always as close to it as he could get, so it makes me feel like I'm with him. He died when I was twelve. Brain aneurysm." There was more to it than that, of course. My guilt. How my mother gave up on everything, including me. Beth getting pregnant and moving in with Mark. "I like the job, though, even if I'm just a maid on a fancy ship."

"Hey, maids are great. And you aren't just a maid on a fancy ship. You're more a maid/bartender/waitress/party planner on a fancy ship."

"I guess you're right," I said. People tended to have one of two reactions when they heard about my job: they either thought it was super glamorous (as if *I* were the one enjoying all the amenities the yacht had to offer) or looked down on me for having a service job. It was hard to *get it* unless you were in the yachting world. Shitty Peter never seemed to understand how exhausting my job could be—the constant cleaning and serving and entertaining. Whenever I was too tired to go out, he'd say that if *anyone* should be tired, it was him. *You get to have fun all day, while I'm stuck at a desk making sales calls for eight hours.* Whenever I'd call him out on trying to guilt me, he'd tell me I was crazy and high-maintenance, which only made me more upset. I'd end up in tears, and he'd pull me to him and say something like *I just want to show off my beautiful girlfriend.* So I'd get dressed up and spend my Friday nights at whatever bar or club we were meeting his friends at, when all I really wanted to do was binge-watch the shows I'd missed during charter season or have a vintage board game night at Nina's.

After swapping celebrity guest stories (Alex had cooked for a Kardashian, though he wouldn't say which one, mine was JLo), we pulled into the marina. I was surprised how quickly the drive had flown by. It always seemed longer when I was by myself. But at least my fears of awkward silence had amounted to nothing.

"Regret being my carpool buddy yet?" Alex asked after he cut the engine.

Buddy, I thought, a safe, friendly term for what we were. That was what I'd tell Nina and the girls when they teased me. We were buddies! Or maybe buds? Bros? No, definitely not bros.

I squinted at Alex. "Too soon to tell. The coffee was a nice touch, though."

Alex grinned, but then his phone rang. He looked at the screen, all the humor draining from his face in an instant. "You go on ahead. I better take this."

"Sure." I wondered who could strike such a sudden change in him as I exited the van. At that moment, Nina stepped from her convertible a few spaces away. She spotted me, then glanced at the van. When I caught up to her, she pushed her sunglasses on top of her head and made a big show of looking around the parking lot.

"No car? What's this, Josephine?"

"It's nothing. We're carpool buddies."

Nina laughed as I dragged her over to the dock. "It sure doesn't look like nothing to me."

"YOU'RE HAVING A *WHAT*?" NINA SAID WHEN WE SET THE TABLE for lunch.

"A Zac Efron movie marathon," I repeated. I draped one of many colorful leis over a chair, decor for the luau-themed lunch we were throwing.

We'd pulled out grass skirts for ourselves and the guests and made Alex promise to wear one when he came up to check in with them after the meal.

"He's the guy from those singing basketball movies, right?"

"Yup." I was grateful Nina had latched on to the subject. She'd done nothing but tease me about carpooling with Alex all day, despite my insistence that we were buddies. *I know exactly what type of buddies you two are going to be,* she'd said with a wink.

"Oh, I am *so* in." Nina fanned out palm fronds on the center of the table. "He's as dreamy as they come. Though maybe he isn't your type. You're more into guys with minivans, right?"

I rolled my eyes. "No, and it's a man van, by the way. Why do you have to be such a horny old lady?"

"Who's a horny old lady?"

We turned to find Alex standing behind us, hands in his pockets.

"My nieces and I are hosting a Zac Efron movie marathon," I explained. "And where's the skirt? We've got ours on." I swished my hips, and the grass skirt rippled around me.

"Ah, yes, the Zefron-a-thon," Alex said. "Greyson told me. Still doesn't address the horny old lady thing. And I'll wear the skirt, I promise. But I don't think it'll be as good if I catch it on fire while I'm cooking."

"A Zefron-a-what?" Nina said.

"A Zefron-a-thon," Alex repeated. "Zac. Efron. Movie. Marathon. Zefron-a-thon."

Nina and I looked at each other, trying to hold in our laughter.

"I love that guy," Alex said. "I mean, *Greyson* loves that guy."

"Stop," Nina said, shooting Alex a glare that dissipated into laughter. "You are a public nuisance, Chef."

Alex turned to me. "If you wanted, I'd be happy to cook for everyone. You could have it at my place. Easier access to the fancy chef tools."

And more space, I thought. The units across the parking lot were all two-bedrooms with wide kitchens. That, and I wouldn't have to clean up Mia and Kitty's mess before the event.

"I'm going to take you up on that. I hadn't even thought about food. This . . . *Zefron-a-thon* has turned into a whole production. Your daughter and my nieces are making decor, and who knows what that will entail."

"Then it's a deal." Alex's eyes met mine, but then he stepped over to Nina and grabbed a lei from her hands, putting it over her head. "You're coming, too, right?"

"Uh, yeah," Nina said, uncharacteristically flustered. "I was planning on it. Wherever Jo goes, that's where you'll find me."

"Cool." He rapped the table with his knuckles. "The guests want lunch at one, right?" he asked Nina.

"Yup."

Alex flashed her a smile, then nodded to me before leaving for the galley.

I raised an eyebrow at Nina once he'd left. "What was *that*? Doesn't he know you hate him?"

Nina clutched a lei to her chest. "What? I love him! He's so easy to work with. Finally, a chef without an ego. I don't miss Ollie at all."

I snatched a palm frond from the table and fanned it in her face. "Oh, really? Because only a few weeks ago you hated Alex for simply existing."

Nina waved me away. "What are you doing?"

"Wafting away the smell of your bullshit."

"Am I sensing jealousy, Josephine Walker?"

"Not at all." I tried to keep my tone light, but Nina was starting to get on my nerves with all this Alex stuff. "I don't know how many times I have to tell you I'm not interested. Not in Alex. Not in anyone. He's just a flirt, and I'd be more than happy if he were interested in you. Then maybe you'd get off my case."

Nina pressed her lips together and looked toward the galley. "Maybe. But he doesn't really seem like a womanizer to me."

The voices of the guests floated over to us, cutting off our conversation. In an instant, our bickering was set aside, and with ready smiles and perfect posture, we transformed into our stew selves. I poured water and took drink orders, while Nina left to bring out the food from the galley.

I muddled mint and sugar for mojitos and wondered what she and Alex were talking about in the galley. Was Alex singing out the names of each dish as he passed them into her hands, like he did with me? Or maybe he was asking about her dream job as a kid? (Celebrity dolphin trainer.) Not that it mattered what they were talking about. Really, it would be a weight off my shoulders if there was something between them. My annoyance was more for Ollie than for anyone else. I looked down at the muddler. The mint leaves were crushed into too-tiny pieces that would stick in the guests' teeth and taste bitter. I sighed and dumped them into the trash before beginning again.

Nine

ON THE DAY OF THE ZEFRON-A-THON, MIA AND KITTY WERE ALready at Alex's when I knocked on his condo door. The *High School Musical* soundtrack blared from within, and I hugged the box of decorations I'd brought tighter to my chest as I waited.

The music quieted. "Coming!" Greyson's voice called, and a moment later she opened the door rosy cheeked and out of breath. She wore a Wildcats jersey and had her short hair pushed back in a red-and-white sweatband.

"You look festive," I said.

Greyson grinned. "Thanks. Marla and Tom took me to this mindfulness workshop for teens while Dad was on charter. It was really weird, but kind of fun, except the incense really bothered my nose and the group leader kept *glaring* at me during the meditation part. But anyway, we had to come up with a personal motto, and mine was 'Go big or go home.'" She frowned, her brow wrinkling beneath the sweatband. "She said our mottoes were supposed to be original, not clichés, but I figure everyone has to know it for a reason, right? So I just try to do that, go big or go home that is, though I guess that doesn't apply right now since I'm already home."

I opened my mouth to say something, but Greyson took the box of decorations from my arms and shouted over her shoulder, "Dad, Jo's here!"

I followed Greyson inside, shutting the door behind me. Though the girls had spent plenty of time at Alex's over the last few weeks, I'd never been over myself. For someone who could French-braid hair (which Nina and I had immediately put to the test), Alex was the typical bachelor dad when it came to interior decorating. Nothing matched, and there wasn't a single piece of decor that hadn't been made by Greyson: a rainbow-colored macaroni sculpture on the shelf beside the TV, a sickly green papier-mâché bowl on the coffee table, a large self-portrait hung on one wall (medium: crayon). On another wall hung a guitar, a banjo, and what I guessed was a mandolin. *Oh, Alex, we need to do something about this*, I thought. But at least his place was clean and smelled nice, like melting sugar and vanilla.

"Nice of you to finally show," Mia said. She was spread out beside Greyson and Kitty on an oriental rug that took over most of the living room. The red and white of the rug clashed with two lumpy forest-green couches. Was Alex colorblind? But at least the rug matched the color scheme for tonight.

Mia wore the same tie-dyed hoodie she always did, and Kitty had her hair pushed back in a sweatband that matched Greyson's. All three girls were red-faced and out of breath.

"What have you three been up to?"

"Dance routine," Kitty said. "Greyson knows the whole dance for 'Get'cha Head in the Game,' so she taught us."

"Fifth-grade talent show," Greyson said. "Dad knows it, too, I made him learn it with me."

"It's pretty impressive," Mia said.

"Hey, Jo." I looked toward the kitchen, where Alex stood drying his hands on a checkered dish towel.

Leaving the girls to their dance recovery, I met him in the dining room. "Great place," I said. Not a lie. Poorly decorated, but twice the size of mine.

"Thanks," he said. "I know it doesn't look like much, but I'm sure your and Nina's expertise in theme parties will get it up to par."

I took a longer look at Alex. It was rare that I saw him in anything but work clothes or his running attire. He wore the usual plain T-shirt, but instead of his chef pants he'd chosen dark-wash jeans. The outfit was simple but appealing. At least his fashion sense was better than his decorating skills.

Alex waved for me to follow him into the kitchen. "Hungry? Thirsty?"

"I'm all right." The kitchen, unlike everything else, was tastefully modern, with a granite island and sleek silver appliances. "What's that?" I asked, gesturing to the white ramekins Alex had lined up on the counter.

He set down the dish towel and plucked a raspberry from a small metal bowl. "Crème brûlée. You know, what Zeke makes for everyone in the first *High School Musical* movie." He bent over the counter, placing the raspberry on one of the ramekins of crème brûlée. "We *are* watching *High School Musical*, right?"

"All three. The girls tell me you've got some impressive Troy Bolton moves."

Alex plucked another raspberry from the bowl and shook his head. "Fatherhood. It changes a man."

"I have a feeling you would've learned Disney Channel dance routines anyway. I'm sad I missed it, though."

"Sorry to disappoint, but I don't bust out the choreographed dances until the third date." He paused, and his smile faded. I thought I saw his cheeks turn pink, but he cleared his throat and bent over the desserts again. "Not that I go on third dates. Or any dates, obviously. Since I don't date."

"Obviously," I said. That hadn't meant anything. Alex was just a flirt.

Silence fell between us, and I rested my elbows on the counter to watch him work. He always made the same face when he was really into a dish: scrunched eyebrows, mouth quirked on one side. It was fascinating how he cooked with such intensity, as if garnishing raspberries on these desserts were equivalent to disarming a bomb.

Despite Nina's and Mia's teasing, everything had been perfectly normal between me and Alex. I'd learned more about him in our time carpooling than I had about most people I'd known for years. His parents were vegetarians, but he wasn't. Even though he was "roadschooled," he'd made friends everywhere he went, though his best friends had been his older brother and sister. He would've liked more stability but was grateful for all the unique experiences his parents' lifestyle had provided. He'd gotten into running because it required no equipment and was the easiest sport to keep up with while traveling the country. *You took the term* cross-country *literally, huh?* I'd said, making him laugh. We never ran out of things to say, but sometimes we'd fall quiet, and the silences were comfortable too. It reminded me of the feeling I'd had when I met Nina. Right away she'd fit into my life, filling a Nina-shaped hole I hadn't known existed (though I hadn't had quite as many dreams about kissing her).

When I'd met Shitty Peter, there was romance from the beginning. Like Alex, I'd met him in a bar. But while Alex was . . . just Alex, even from that first night, Shitty Peter had been like a mystery to puzzle out. Before we got together there had been weeks of tension and anxiety. He wouldn't call or text for days, and then we'd talk all night and into the morning. It was confusing, but the kind of heart-pounding, sleep-deprived love you saw in movies. There was none of that with Alex. The only anxiety I'd felt around him had been caused by Mia's and Nina's overactive imaginations. Did he flirt with me? Sure. But he flirted with Nina too. Did I think about our kiss from time to time? Maybe. But who wouldn't think about a nice kiss? It wasn't like I'd done a lot of kissing lately.

I looked around Alex's kitchen. On the far counter I noticed a spread of different foods: shrimp and avocado over cucumber slices, tiny sliders stuck with toothpicks, prosciutto-wrapped breadsticks, and the fanciest nachos I'd ever seen.

"You really went all out, huh? I would've been happy with popcorn."

"We've got popcorn, too, don't worry. I make an excellent butter sauce." Alex arranged the last of the raspberries and shrugged. "Grey says I overdo things, but I can't help it. You should see Thanksgiving when it's just the two of us. We end up having Thanksgiving dinner for two weeks straight. Turkey sandwiches, turkey gumbo, turkey and stuffing tacos, turkey cake."

"Turkey cake?"

"All right, that one was a joke."

"Go big or go home," I said.

Alex smiled. "You've been spending time with Greyson, I see." He took a mixing bowl from the counter and two spoons from a drawer. "Try it."

He passed me a spoon. I had to lean against his shoulder to reach into the bowl. And it was comforting, the warm solidity of him, like I couldn't fall over if I tried. Alex watched me taste the custard with an annoyingly cocky smile on his face.

"So?" he asked when I pulled the spoon from my mouth.

I wrinkled my nose. "Are you sure you want my honest opinion?"

His smile faded, and he looked down into the bowl. "Did I miss something?"

"I doubt it," I said, and reached for another spoonful. "This tastes like heaven on a spoon."

Alex pulled the bowl up and out of my reach. "That was mean. I'm cutting you off."

"Hey!" I jumped and tried to grab the bowl from him, but he held it above his head. "You can't get me addicted and then take it away." I took my spoon and prodded him in the stomach. Alex, laughing, tried to back away from me and scooted around the island, but I cornered him by the stove and threatened him with my spoon again, laughing so hard I could hardly breathe.

Someone cleared their throat behind us, and we turned to the entrance to the kitchen, where Kitty, Mia, and Greyson stood with amused looks on their faces. I darted away from Alex, who lowered the mixing bowl from above his head. Kitty and Greyson giggled, and Mia gave me a knowing look that reminded me of Nina. Clearly, I wasn't doing myself any favors in the convince-the-teen-nieces-I'm-single-and-not-ready-to-mingle department.

"Can we help you?" Alex said.

Greyson twisted the hem of her shirt in her hands. "Dad, can I please have the key to the mailbox? Kitty's . . ." Her eyes darted to me. "*Thing* is here."

Alex raised his eyebrows. "If the thing you're talking about is the thing I think it is, then yes."

I looked between Alex and the girls. What were they talking about? Alex grabbed his keys from nearby, tossed them to Greyson, and the girls disappeared before I could question them.

"What thing?" I pointed my spoon at him again.

He passed me the bowl of custard and backed away. "No offense, but they're scarier than you, and I can't risk pissing them off."

A few minutes later, we met the girls in the living room. Kitty ripped open a large manila envelope and dumped a mess of colorful cardboard pieces onto the floor. I watched from the couch (where I sat with an entire cushion between me and Alex) as Kitty and Greyson fit one piece of cardboard into another, unsure what I was looking at. But a few minutes later, a life-sized cardboard cutout of Zac Efron as Troy Bolton stood before me. Kitty explained she'd gotten it from someone on Craigslist but hadn't wanted to tell me in case it didn't arrive on time.

"Wow." I stood to inspect the cardboard Zac. If I'd thought Alex had gone all out on the food, it was nothing compared to the girls and their decorating. Nina and Ollie were the only real guests, but the girls had wanted to make a big thing of it any way.

"We thought it would be great in your pictures for the blog," Kitty said.

"I love it," I said, and pulled Kitty into a hug. "You shouldn't be on Craigslist, you know." I was reminded of Nina's many Craigslist adventures. There'd been a year when, every Friday, Nina would respond to the most "unique" Craigslist ad she could find, just to see what would happen. She'd bought the ugliest bicycle I'd ever seen, become friends with a lonely old lady who wanted someone to see the new *Star Wars* movie with her, and had nearly gotten arrested rescuing black-market guinea pigs.

"You should be proud of me," Kitty said. "The seller wanted to meet in person, and I was like, *No way, you could be a murderer.*"

"She really did say that," Mia said.

Greyson jumped up and down as she spoke. "And the guy was totally offended and didn't want to sell it to us. So Dad had to *call him* on the phone and offer him *double* the money. And then—"

"Everything was completely normal, and I definitely didn't have to listen to him tell me about his bearded dragons for over an hour," Alex said.

"It's great," I said, moved that they had put so much thought into this. "Thanks, girls. And Alex." I scanned the living room. "Where should we put it?"

A timer went off, and Alex excused himself to the kitchen. Moments later, Nina stepped inside, decked out in a ringleader costume complete with a top hat.

"You know this isn't a costume party, right?" I asked. "Technically, it's not even a party."

Nina strode over to cardboard Zac. "It is now. I make a great P. T.

Barnum, and a girl has to look nice for her best friend's blog." She kissed cardboard Zac's cheek. "This is just as amazing as I expected."

"You knew about this too?"

"We needed her expertise," Mia said.

"I helped them find it. You know I'm always up for a Craigslist adventure."

I rolled my eyes and grabbed Nina by the shoulders, steering her in the direction of the box of decorations Greyson had set on the coffee table. "Make yourself useful at least."

"I've got more supplies in the car," she said, and sprinted out the door.

An excited buzz ran through the room as we set up various Zac Efron–inspired displays. There was the *High School Musical* station on the coffee table, with basketball napkins, plates, and a toy microphone. *The Greatest Showman* station on the side table had a deck of cards and a top hat along with animal figurines. The *Hairspray* station in the dining room had, well, a lot of different hairsprays. They weren't real hairsprays, but sprayable foods we decorated to look like hairspray: Cheez Whiz and whipped cream, mostly. The girls hung red and white streamers around the room, and by the time we were done, Alex's condo had become a literal shrine to Zac Efron, thanks to Nina, who'd printed photos and stuffed them into thrifted frames.

When Greyson called Alex out of the kitchen to see our work, he picked up one of the framed Zac photos Nina had put on the coffee table and examined it, his expression serious. For a moment I worried that this was all too much, that I'd let the girls get carried away, despite everything Alex had told me about his hippie parents and learning to go with the flow, but then he looked up at us with a grin.

"I love it so much I think I'll keep it up year-round." Our eyes met for what felt like a moment too long, and he looked away, turning to Nina. "You're a big thrifter, right?"

Nina blinked. "That would be correct."

"My parents sent me a box of some of their old clothes from the sixties and seventies. They want me to try to sell them, see if they're worth anything. I was wondering if you would lend me your expert knowledge and take a look?"

"Uh, sure." Her eyes darted to me as she followed Alex to what I assumed was his room. I sat on the couch and watched as Greyson taught Mia and Kitty one of the dance routines from *High School Musical*. Whenever Greyson paused the music, I could hear the tone of Alex and Nina's conversation through the open door. Nina said something, and Alex laughed, and I tried to ignore the flicker of disappointment beneath my ribs. Not disappointment for me, of course. I was sorry for Alex. For all his good qualities, there'd be no hope for him with Nina, not when Ollie was still coming around.

As if I'd summoned him, a voice outside mumbled curses and there was a knock on the door.

"You made it!" I said when I opened the door and found Ollie. I hadn't seen him since his last day, and though Alex was a good replacement (maybe too good), I missed my foulmouthed Irishman. Lurching forward, I wrapped him into a tight hug.

"I wouldn't miss your party," Ollie said.

"It's not a party."

Ollie followed me into the living room and took the seat beside me on the couch, waving to the girls, who greeted him back before immediately ducking their heads together to gossip.

Ollie scanned the condo. "She's in there." I pointed down the hall to Alex's bedroom, where Alex and Nina's laughter floated through the door. Ollie raised his eyebrows, bristling beside me.

Maybe inviting Ollie wasn't such a great idea after all. I cleared my throat. "How's Il Gabbiano?"

Ollie rubbed his chin. "It's . . . different. Grand. A lot more cooks in the kitchen, though."

Alex and Nina left the bedroom and sat at the dining room table.

Alex called us over, and Nina's expression soured as soon as she spotted Ollie.

"So that's the new fella," Ollie said as we stood from the couch. "He's pretty."

"Don't be jealous," I said, though maybe I was talking to myself too.

"What's Nina wearing? She's touched, isn't she?"

"That's why we love her."

After I introduced him to Alex, Ollie turned his attention to Nina. "Hey, Neen. You look good."

Nina ignored him and turned to me. "What is he doing here, Josephine?"

"Are Mia and Kitty calling me?" I cupped a hand around my ear and backed out of the dining room. Nina might act mad about Ollie being here, but I knew she'd thank me for it eventually.

Back in the living room, I pulled out my phone to take photos for the blog. This was definitely the strangest way I'd checked off an item, and I wondered what my readers would think of it. Weird? Funny? Both? I snapped photos of the decorations and the girls with cardboard Zac.

"You're up next." I looked behind me, and there was Alex with his hand outstretched.

"All right, all right." I handed him my phone and stood beside cardboard Zac.

"At least look like he's your celebrity crush," Alex said.

I put my arm around cardboard Zac's shoulders. "Chris Evans is my celebrity crush."

Alex shook his head. "Typical." He held up the phone. "On three say, *Damn, Chef Alex, you're a yachtie hottie.*"

I turned to cardboard Zac. "Did he just use the phrase 'yachtie hottie'?"

"Don't fight it, Jo. I'm going to earn the nickname Hot Yacht Chef, even if I have to dress as a sexy George Washington again for the Fourth of July charter."

"Dress up as a sexy George Washington *again?* What kind of yachts have you been sailing on, Chef Alex?"

Alex grinned from behind my phone. "Never mind that, Florida Girl. One, two . . ." Predictably he took the photo on two, as I was still laughing.

"You didn't give me time to rearrange my face!"

"I don't see why you'd want to rearrange it." He passed my phone back to me. The photo was better than I expected, even if my eyes were crinkly and my mouth was half-open. I looked happy. Real happy, not stew-smile happy.

I slipped my phone into my pocket and looked back at the dining room, where Nina and Ollie seemed to be in the middle of a heated discussion. "Did you need to escape the drama that is Nina and Ollie?"

Alex raised his eyebrows and let out a low whistle. "That is some . . . unresolved tension."

"See why she hated you so much?"

"Hard to say." Alex looked over at them. "I think hate and love look like the same thing with her."

Was he talking about Nina and Ollie, or how Nina had felt about him that first week? Maybe he really did have a thing for her. And why wouldn't he? She was exciting, gorgeous, creative. Maybe Nina sensed Alex's feelings for her. Maybe that was why she'd been so persistent in pushing him at me.

When we finally dimmed the lights and started the first movie, Nina waved me over to where she sat in between Ollie and Alex on the couch. She scooted closer to Ollie, leaving just enough space for me to squeeze in between her and Alex. *No, thank you.* I plopped down beside Mia, who was lying on her stomach next to Kitty and Greyson, a bowl of popcorn and several cans of sprayable food between them.

I stretched my legs out in front of me. Mia scooted closer and put her head on my leg, reminding me of my eighteenth birthday, the night Samson was born. Mia, then four, had curled up beside me on the couch as we watched *Tangled* for the thousandth time and waited for news of a baby brother. Beth and Mark had left for the hospital early in the day, leaving me in charge of the girls. Between contractions my sister had wheezed apologies for ruining my birthday, and I'd told her she was making my birthday even better. It was my mother who'd ruined everything, having invited herself over, much to my annoyance. I was still angry with her for how things had changed between us, and grew more upset with each glass of wine she poured herself as she complained over and over about how Dad had died on her, as if he'd done it on purpose. Mia, somehow sensing the tension, had been a quiet buffer at my side throughout the evening, and the only thing that kept me from snapping.

"Just one night," I'd said to myself after I'd put my mother to bed in my room. "I needed her to keep it together for one night." And Mia, thinking I'd been talking to her, patted my leg and said, "Don't worry, Jo, there's lots more nights."

When my father died, my mother had come unglued like the bottom of a cheap sandal. She drank more, talked to us less. She stopped cooking dinner and started sleeping in Dad's armchair. She was angry at him for dying. It was the only thing she could talk about. And that anger kept her from seeing what she still had: Beth, me, her grandchildren. I knew the pain of losing Dad had done this to her, but it was love too. Maybe if she hadn't loved him so much, she would've come back to me.

I blinked the memory away. The girls were happy and distracted, and I needed to keep them that way. I knew they were suffering. I could read the ache of it on their faces and sensed when it washed over them out of nowhere. Once you lived through it, it was easy to recognize, but I knew the pain would dull with time, like how the ocean smooths glass with every wave. There was nothing to do but tread water until your feet touched the bottom.

As I watched the movie, I brushed my fingers through Mia's hair like I had on the night Samson was born. It was easy to forget she was still a child. She was angry, unlike Kitty, which made it harder to know how to comfort her. But maybe in the dark with a Disney movie playing, she could be that little girl again.

"You just have a comfortable leg, okay," Mia said, but wedged herself closer to my side, nudging my arm when I let my hand drop from her hair. How did Beth do this? How could you make sense of a person when they said the exact opposite of what they wanted? There was something about Mia I didn't understand. Some days I'd catch her staring down at her phone, headphones shoved in her ears, a pained look on her face. Other times she'd deny herself something I knew she wanted: a second bowl of ice cream, a touristy flamingo-shaped keychain. She seemed to be punishing herself for something, but I wasn't sure what. Survivor's guilt, maybe? I'd need to find out if there were any grief support skills for that.

After the first film ended, Mia rejoined Greyson and Kitty in conversation. Ollie had moved to the other side of Alex to discuss the Miami restaurant scene, and so I took the seat Ollie had been in, as far away from Alex as possible. The girls sang at the tops of their lungs throughout the last *High School Musical* movie, during which Nina and Ollie got into an argument and left. I was pretty sure they hadn't gone to their respective apartments, though, seeing as Nina wasn't responding to any of my texts. As soon as they'd left, Alex moved from the couch to the floor. *See*, I mentally told Nina, *there's nothing going on between me and Alex. He's sitting as far from me as humanly possible.*

"Dad," Greyson called when *The Greatest Showman* began. "Why are you still on the floor like a weirdo? There's room on the couch."

"You're on the floor," Alex said.

"But I'm not an adult."

Alex sighed and took the empty space beside me.

Okay, so maybe he isn't sitting as far from me as humanly possible, I thought to Nina.

"Tough crowd," I said.

Alex rubbed his jaw. "No kidding. Everyone said it would get easier as she got older, but let me warn you, that is a lie." His smile faltered. "Not that you want kids. Or maybe you do. Not that you *should*, I mean."

I tried not to laugh at Alex getting flustered. "I don't, for the record. If they came out as teenagers, it would be a different story, but the baby stuff doesn't interest me. I got my fill of that when those two were little. I've changed enough diapers for a lifetime."

"You lived with your sister, right? Mia mentioned it."

"Yeah." I kept my gaze on the TV. Fortunately, Alex had a decent sound system, so the movie was loud enough to keep the girls from hearing us. "After my dad died, my sister got married and moved out. My mom, she . . ." I wasn't sure how to explain it. Typically I *didn't* explain it. Nina was the only friend I had who knew the details, but even she didn't know everything. Emotion needled its way out of me, the memories lining up like the crew at the end of a charter. "She was devastated, even more so after my sister left. It wasn't so bad when she was there."

Which wasn't entirely true. One night I'd made the mistake of wondering aloud what the last poem Dad wrote for us had been about. All I'd wanted was to remember the things I was already forgetting. But Beth had burst into tears and disappeared to her room. Mom had scolded me brutally. How could I ask such a thing? Was I trying to torture my sister? Her? I hadn't answered, and Mom left the room. I'd sat at the kitchen table and tried not to cry, realizing my broken pieces could hurt people. I didn't ask about Dad anymore after that.

"She started drinking," I continued, "and everything kind of spiraled out of control." The images flashed through my mind. Mom passed out by the time I came home from school. Mom, looking at me as if I were the last person on earth she wanted to see. She'd never said it, but I knew she blamed me for Dad's death because I was the only one home when it happened. I was sure Mom asked herself all the same questions I did. What had I been so preoccupied with when he died? What would've happened if I'd heard him fall? Could I have saved him if I'd gotten to him sooner?

"It got to the point that she couldn't take care of me anymore," I said. I could sense Alex watching me but didn't look at him. I knew I'd find pity in his face. I hated pity. It was the least productive emotion in the world. "When I was sixteen, my sister realized how bad things were. I moved in with her, and things got better."

Which was also not entirely true. I'd been a mess those first months at Beth and Mark's. Kitty was a newborn, and Mia was three, and now my sister had a grieving teenager to deal with. We'd told Mom I was moving in to help Beth with the girls, and Mom hadn't fought it. She'd let me go, as easy as that. Still, there were nights Beth sat up with me as I cried and begged to go back to Mom's. Not because I wanted to, but because the guilt was eating me from the inside out. What if something happened to her and I wasn't there? On one of those nights, Beth had grabbed my face in her hands as Kitty slept in a swing beside us. She'd forced me to look her in the eye and said, *You couldn't have known, Joey. You couldn't have saved him, and you can't save Mom. It's not your fault, and Dad would tell you that himself if he could.*

"It's hard to lose a parent young," Alex said. I prepared myself for the inevitable pitying look, but he wasn't looking at me anymore. His eyes were on Greyson, who was rolling around on the floor and laughing hysterically as Kitty sprayed Cheez Whiz into her mouth. There wasn't a trace of pity on his face, and I realized he understood.

Not for the first time I wondered what the story was with Greyson's mom. Neither Alex nor Greyson had talked about it. "Was it hard," I asked, "once her mom was, uh, gone?"

"It's even harder now that she's older. What do I know about being a teenage girl? You should've seen her face when we had *the talk*. And don't get me started on her first period. She practically murdered me when I brought five different kinds of pads home." I laughed at the image of Alex's arms filled with flowered boxes of pads. "No, seriously. I don't know how women do it. It's like rocket science. Wings? No wings? And why does each pack only have one size? That makes absolutely no sense."

"A man who knows the struggles of menstrual product shopping. How are you still single?" Alex raised an eyebrow at me. That had probably sounded like flirting. "I mean, *why* are you still single?" *Not a better question!* I clamped my mouth shut to keep from saying anything else.

Instead of the joking response I expected, Alex nodded slowly, quiet for a moment. "Greyson's mom and I were only dating when she got pregnant. We lived in New York at the time, and I was incredibly naive but made good money." He lowered his voice, and I held my breath as he leaned in closer. "I was only twenty-two, but I felt like I had it all: great job, happy family. But then the excitement wore off for Maggie. She'd never been the settling-down type, but we both thought that would change once Greyson arrived. We broke up right around her first birthday and had shared custody until Greyson was two, when Maggie just . . . disappeared. I was sure something awful had happened to her, but we tracked her down in Los Angeles a few days later. She said she needed to find herself and that we'd be better off without her, and it's been me and Grey ever since. Maggie gets the itch to see Greyson and visits every now and then, for a few days, sometimes a week. But she always disappears again without warning. I haven't dated anyone since Maggie because it's too complicated. Let's say I did meet someone. Someone I'm really into and who ticks all the right boxes. I can't just go for it. I'd have to think about how they'd fit into Greyson's life, if they'd even want to be in it at all. I'd have to consider how it would affect Greyson if things didn't work out. And if I can't trust Greyson's own mother to stick around, who can I trust?"

I stared at Alex. He was so easygoing that I'd assumed nothing could bother him. But there was a lot of hurt on his face as he talked about Maggie, and I realized there was more beneath that goofy exterior than I'd thought. "Greyson's lucky to have you. You're basically dad of the year."

Alex leaned back into the couch and shook his head. "That's nice of you to say, but you should've seen me four years ago. I didn't know how to be there for Greyson, so it was easier to put work first. When Maggie left, I was sous chef at this restaurant, Table. Great place. A year later I was recruited as executive chef at Mer Amère. Three years after that, the restaurant got its first Michelin star." He smiled at the memory. "I told myself I'd slow down, but there was always something to go after—another star, another award. I made *Food and Wine*'s thirty under thirty list. My career was taking off, but Greyson was miserable. She basically lived at our neighbor's place. I was miserable too. I just didn't know it. When you're running a restaurant like that, it's your whole life. Great money, horrible hours. Sometimes I'd work a hundred, a hundred and twenty hours a week easy."

Alex laughed at my surprise. "I'm not kidding. I hardly slept for years. It was like working charter season all the time. Anyway, I was so angry with Maggie for leaving that I refused to see the ways I was leaving Greyson too. Fortunately, my dad knocked some sense into me—almost literally, by the way."

"So what did you do?" I asked.

"In general? A lot of therapy. For me and for Greyson." Alex put his hands behind his head and sighed. "To be more specific, one day, my dad calls and says his buddy—that's Xav—knew a boat captain looking for a chef after theirs quit midseason. I was looking for a reason to leave New York and thought, *It's just a few weeks, why the hell not?* I quit the restaurant, rented a place in Miami, and my parents stayed in our apartment with Greyson while I was gone. It was only supposed to be a few weeks, but after charter season, the captain asked if I wanted to do the off-season too. I'd planned to find work in a more casual restaurant once charter season came around again, but Greyson wouldn't have it. She said she liked spending so much time with my parents and didn't want me taking a job I was too good for. Her words, not mine." He shook his head. "I've been working on yachts ever since, and my parents live with Greyson while I'm gone. I know it sounds unbelievable, but even being gone four months a year, I'm around more than when I worked at restaurants. Greyson's first now, like she should've been all along."

I thought about Greyson and how I'd liked her from the moment we met on the beach. We were similar, in a way, both abandoned by our mothers. But where I was closed off, Greyson was open. I was terrified to bring people into my life, but everyone was Greyson's friend. I'd spent my life trying to hide from others, where Greyson had no fear of standing out.

I hadn't had either parent, but Greyson had Alex, and despite his failings, it seemed to have made all the difference.

"Do you miss it? Running a restaurant?"

Alex looked at Greyson, who had Cheez Whiz dribbling down her chin. "Sometimes." He slung his arm over the back of the couch, pivoting to face me. "Your turn. Why are you single?"

I shook my head. "What is this, a middle school slumber party?"

"I told you my secrets," he said, eyes bright with mirth.

"Fine," I sighed. "Three years ago I started dating this guy, Shitty Peter—"

"His *name* was Shitty Peter?"

I glared at him. "Of course not."

Alex held up his hands. "Hey, there are some weird names out there. I need to make sure I have my facts straight. Please, continue."

"Anyway, as I was saying before I was *rudely* interrupted, we were together for two years. He cheated on me during charter season, and I dumped him." No need to mention how I'd allowed him to make me someone I wasn't, how he would make me feel like the most important person in the universe one day, only to tear me down the next. How he'd pushed everyone in my life away until he was the only one left. I was still ashamed of that, though Nina had told me a thousand times it wasn't my fault. How could I not have seen what was happening?

"It made me realize I like having only myself to worry about." Not entirely true. I didn't like eating TV dinners alone, or the days I only had my thoughts for company. But loneliness was better than the alternative. I couldn't take another heartbreak, and when you loved someone—

romantically, or otherwise—there was no such thing as a happy ending. It was better to keep my circle small and minimize the damage.

"Sounds like Shitty Peter really earned the nickname."

"He sure did." I turned my attention back to the movie. It was too serious in here. I needed to lighten things up. I nudged Alex and nodded to the screen, where Zac Efron twirled around on aerial silks with Zendaya. "Let's say I was interested in dating. Think I've got a shot?"

Alex squinted, looking me up and down for a moment. "Yeah," he said, that almost smile on his lips when he turned back to the screen. "I think you do."

July

Jen

ON THE NIGHT I DECLUTTERED THE CONDO, I'D JUST FINISHED sorting through the worst of my worn-out granny panties when Alex waltzed in holding the largest Tupperware I'd ever seen. Panicked, I grabbed all the underwear I had within reach, planning to shove them beneath my butt before he could see them. But I wasn't quick enough, and instead of one pair of underwear, Alex caught me clutching a fistful.

"Oh," he said, stopping short as soon as he stepped inside. "The door was open." He scanned the living room. "Where are the girls? I thought they were supposed to help you with the decluttering."

I hastily put the ugly underwear I was still holding into a nearby garbage bag. "They ditched me to have a shuffleboard tournament," I said. "I believe Mia's exact words were *Decluttering is boring AF*."

"And they thought shuffleboard would be any better?" He slipped off his shoes and held up the Tupperware. "Lasagna. Plate it or fridge it?"

"Fridge it," I said. "We had Pub subs for lunch, so I'll be hungry again in about . . . a thousand years."

He paused on his way to the kitchen. "Maybe I should order Pub subs for Thanksgiving this year and call it a day."

"The weird part of that scenario isn't the Pub subs. It's the thought of you *not* cooking on a holiday," I said.

"Hey, now. I'm more than happy to get takeout on Arbor Day." He stepped around a heap of books, and when he disappeared out of sight, I hid the sexier bras and underwear beneath the nearest couch.

Two weeks had passed since the movie marathon, and it seemed as if every time Alex or Greyson came over they had food with them: mini beef Wellington, chocolate chip cookies, enchiladas, half a duck, and other foods I didn't know the names of but that tasted like magic.

When Alex returned to the living room after putting the lasagna away, he found a clear spot on the floor and sat down opposite me. Between us was a pile of shoes, two cardboard boxes, and a collection of pens from various business offices around Palm Beach.

He picked up a pen from the pile. "Wow," he said. "I think you have a pen-hoarding problem. Should I have written one of those intervention letters?"

I balled up a bleach-stained T-shirt and threw it at his face. "Pens spark *joy*, Alex."

After throwing the T-shirt back at me, he inspected the pen in his hands. "*Little Smiles Dental*," he read. "Why do you have a pen from a pediatric dental office?"

I swiped the pen from his hands and tried to look offended. "You don't see me walking into your place and judging your . . . spatula collection."

"That's because I only own three spatulas."

I narrowed my eyes at him. "Your spice collection, then."

Alex clapped a hand over his chest. "Now that was personal, Florida Girl. A chef can't have too many spices."

"I wouldn't know. I've only got two."

"And they're salt and pepper. Essential, but not very creative." Alex leaned back on his hands and swept his gaze over the mess of my living room. "I can't believe you put decluttering on your list."

Why did everyone have a problem with decluttering? This would change my life; that was what the book promised, anyway. I wasn't sure exactly what was supposed to change, but whatever it was, I wanted it. "You sound like Nina."

"Who is conveniently not here," Alex said.

"Very convenient," I said.

Alex had that almost smile on his face, the one that made it look like he might burst into laughter at the slightest provocation. I turned my attention to the pile of shirts beside me, suddenly aware that outside of carpooling and work, we hadn't been alone together since the morning of my failed run.

"I need to ask you something serious," Alex said. I looked up at him to find that his almost smile had disappeared from his face.

"Yeah, sure." The possibilities of what he might ask filled my mind all at once. I held tighter to the shirt in my hands, unable to focus on whether it sparked joy or not.

Alex sat up straight, then leaned forward, and I held my breath as he drew nearer. His eyes were locked on mine again, and I felt I should look away, but couldn't. And then, Alex moved quickly, pulling something from the shoe pile and holding it up between our faces. "Where did you get a pair of bedazzled Crocs, and why haven't I seen you wear them before?"

I snatched the shoe from his hands and hugged it to my chest, feeling the rapid pace of my heart beneath it. "A Christmas present from Nina. She bedazzled them herself." I put the shoe on my foot and lifted my leg in the air. "And I don't wear them because Nina says these ooze sex appeal, and I don't think the world is ready for that."

"I see what you mean," Alex said.

I took off the bedazzled Croc and swatted him on the shoulder. "You had me worried you were actually going to ask me something serious."

Alex grinned at me as he rubbed his shoulder. "What did you think I was going to ask?"

I opened my mouth, fumbling for something to say that wasn't related to kissing, or being alone together, or how my heart had nearly stopped when his face was only a few inches from mine, but finally landed on "I thought you were going to ask which Pub sub is my favorite."

"That is a serious question," Alex said.

I stared down at the bedazzled Croc against my chest and closed my eyes. *Joy*. Definitely. When I opened my eyes, Alex was watching me with the same expression he made whenever he got lost in cooking, and I wondered what it could mean. That I was difficult? A problem to be solved? I tossed the Croc into the keep pile with its mate and glared at Alex's raised eyebrows. "They obviously spark joy. Just look at them," I said. "And my favorite Pub sub is the chicken tender one, by the way."

After explaining the ins and outs of the KonMari method, I put Alex in charge of maintaining the keep, donate, and trash piles. Whenever he passed me an item, he'd give me exactly two seconds to decide if it sparked joy or not. I'd toss the item back with my answer, and he'd set it in the appropriate pile. The clothing was easy enough, until he spotted the bras and underwear I'd stowed away under the couch, so I exiled him to the kitchen to make margaritas while I sorted through them.

"And make them fancy!" I called out after him.

"Oh, this will be the fanciest margarita you've ever had. By the time you've finished it, you'll feel like a guest on the *Serendipity*." He disappeared into the kitchen, then reappeared seconds later, hands on his hips. "Your provisions are disappointing. I need to run to my place."

When Alex returned, he had his shirt stretched out in front of him, using it to carry items I couldn't see but that clanged together with each step he took. I tried to ask about it, but Alex said a genius at work couldn't stop for conversation, so I continued deciding which of my bras and underwear sparked joy and which did not. A few minutes later, I told Alex it was safe for him to return, and he walked into the living room with two margarita glasses, each with an upturned beer sticking out of it.

"Seriously? A beer margarita?" I said, laughing as I took the glass. "Wow, I really feel like a Florida heiress now."

Alex clinked his glass to mine before sitting down. "The proper name is beergarita. And you're welcome. Try it."

I took a sip of the margarita and blinked in surprise. "What did you put in here?"

"If I told you, you'd have to make a blood oath," he said.

"Honestly, this is so good, I might be willing to do that." I took another sip. "Is that . . . Maggi seasoning?"

Alex tipped his head to the side. "Actually, yes. That's *one* of the secret ingredients."

"Don't look so surprised," I said. "Do you know how many drinks I make a year? Did you think I'd guess something ridiculous like nutmeg?"

Alex shook his head. "Why does everyone guess nutmeg as a secret ingredient?"

"Wait." I pointed down into the glass. "Is there Worcestershire in here too?"

Alex made to take my drink from me, but I pulled it out of his reach. "You know too much. Now we have to do the blood oath."

"I knew it!" I said, spilling some of the margarita on my shirt when I lowered my glass.

"Settle down, Heiress Jo. Shouldn't you be getting back to work? We haven't even gotten to the good stuff yet."

"What's the good stuff?"

Alex shrugged. "Yearbook photos. Secret diaries. Love poems."

"You're about to be sorely disappointed."

"No love poems?"

I shook my head and glanced at the two cardboard boxes.

Alex took out his phone, and Rihanna's "Work" rang out in the condo. "This is my cleaning playlist," he explained. He grabbed a garbage bag and danced along to the music, singing as he helped bag items, making me laugh so hard I had tears streaming down my face.

"That's quite the Rihanna impression," I said, handing him my copy of *Northanger Abbey* for the keep pile. "I thought you didn't bust out the dance moves until the third date."

"I said *choreographed* dance moves. This is pure improvised talent."

"That's one way to see it."

"And this is not a date. If I took you on a date, you'd know it. We wouldn't be decluttering. You sing the Drake part."

I looked down at the book in my hands. It was a coffee table book of North Carolina Beth had sent a few months after I'd moved here. What Alex had said was a hypothetical, of course. He wouldn't *really* think of taking me on a date. Though I wondered what sort of date he'd take me on if he were interested in dating or in me. He didn't seem like a dinner-and-drinks kind of guy. "No thanks. You can do both parts."

"Be careful what you wish for," he said.

Other than a brief slowdown when I paused to show Alex my father's poetry collection, the decluttering continued uneventfully. At some point the girls came by to eat lasagna. Greyson complained about Alex's dancing and singing, which only made him dance and sing more, and soon after they'd arrived, the girls left to watch something at Alex's condo. It wasn't until eleven o'clock that we'd gotten through everything but my two cardboard boxes. The only out-of-place items in my entire unit.

I knelt before the boxes and wiped the dust from the top of one with the hem of my shirt. This was the part of decluttering I'd been dreading. Clothes, books, papers, all the rest—it wasn't hard to decide what to keep and what to trash. But I knew that looking into these boxes would be like looking into my own heart, and I wasn't sure if I was ready for that, let alone with a guy I'd only met at the start of the summer.

Alex returned from taking the trash out to the dumpster. "Sorry that took so long. I ran into Sharon. You know, the retired hedge fund manager on the third floor? I'm pretty sure she just asked me out."

I snorted. Sharon was the fiercest cougar in the complex. I was surprised she hadn't cornered Alex before. "What did you tell her?"

Alex closed the door behind him. "Same thing I told you, I don't date."

"How'd she take it?"

"The same way most women do. She was devastated."

"Trust me, Sharon gets her fair share of younger men. I doubt you put a damper on her night." I eyed the boxes. "It's late," I sighed. "You don't have to stay. I can handle the rest."

Alex settled himself on the floor across from me. "And exile myself to the teen girl lair? No thanks. Besides, you still haven't eaten dinner, and I'm not leaving until you do. The only thing standing between you and the best lasagna you've ever had are those two boxes."

I took the top off the box I'd just wiped the dust from and peered inside. It was cluttered with souvenirs from the places I'd traveled while on charter: blank postcards, and museum ticket stubs, and business cards from restaurants and bars. I pulled one of the postcards from the box. It read *I'd rather go to Hell than to school. Hell, Grand Cayman Island B.W.I.* against a background of flames.

"I meant to send this to my sister," I said, passing it to Alex. "She wanted me to go to college, but I never did."

"Plenty of people have told me to go to Hell, but I've never actually been there," he said, then passed the postcard back to me. "Joy, or no joy?"

I closed my eyes. I had a hard time imagining letting the postcard go, letting any of these things go. To a stranger, maybe even to Alex, these things were junk. But for me, each postcard, brochure, and business card was a reminder I'd been out there in the world, living an adventurous life. It was proof I was making something of myself, even if I didn't know what the hell I was doing.

"Joy," I said, handing it back to Alex, who set it in the designated area.

After we spent far too long picking through my travel mementos, all that remained in the box were the remnants of my many on-again, off-again hobbies.

"Okay, I'm going to need you to explain this," Alex said, pulling a gallon-sized Ziploc bag filled with random metal odds and ends from the box.

I took the bag from him. Coins, rings, and pieces of metal I couldn't identify rattled against one another, glinting in the light. "I had a metal-detecting hobby a few years ago," I said.

"Buried treasure. There's that pirate side of you."

"Yeah, I guess you could say that." I opened the bag and found a tarnished silver ring with three small sapphires set into it. "This is probably the best thing we found."

"We?"

"Oh, well, I only got the metal detector because my nephew . . . When he came down with Mia and Kitty a few summers ago, he said he was sure someone could make a lot of money selling lost things they found on the beach. Nina found a metal detector on Craigslist, and I bought it the next day. We spent their entire trip metal detecting and geocaching."

Alex gave me a confused look. "What's geocaching?"

I looked down at my hands, realizing how dorky all this would sound. "There's this community of people who . . . hide things. And they give you coordinates. And you use those coordinates to find the hidden cache."

"More treasure hunting."

"Yeah, I guess." Sam had had us out and about for hours, with both the metal detecting and the geocaching. Sometimes we did both at the same time. It was one of the best summers we'd had, and I'd been just as caught up in the excitement as the kids. I handed the ring and bag to Alex. "Keep the ring, toss the rest."

"You're sure you don't want the rest of this?"

"I'm sure," I said. I looked back into the box. "I've had non-treasure-related hobbies too."

"Such as?"

"These are all for the donate or trash pile, by the way." I stuck my hand in the box and pulled out a ball of yarn. "Knitting."

"In Florida?"

"In Florida. But I only ever finished half of a hat."

"Impressive."

"Oh, here's a fun one." I handed him a ceramic coaster covered in blue sea glass. "A failed attempt at mosaic making. I found all the sea glass myself."

"We're not throwing this out. I'm keeping it," Alex said, setting it on the floor behind him. "You're a real Renaissance woman, huh?"

I shrugged. An assortment of paintbrushes, a baggie of buttons, and several origami cranes were the only things left inside. "I'm not like you. I don't have one thing I'm skilled at or passionate about. Beth says I don't have enough ambition."

"Ambition isn't as important as everyone makes it out to be," Alex said, setting the paintbrushes in the trash pile.

"Says the Michelin star–earning superchef."

"It wasn't as great as it sounds. Why would I want to be killing myself day and night at a restaurant, when I could be here with you decluttering your condo?"

I rolled my eyes and passed Alex the paper cranes one by one, not saying anything until the box was empty. "I don't know. I feel like I should've done more with my life by now."

Alex inspected one of the paper cranes, then set it beside the sea glass coaster. "I know your sister means well, but if you ask me, I think you've made a pretty good life for yourself. You've got a job you love. A best friend who would definitely murder someone for you, and who maybe already has. Great family. This stunningly organized condo. And you get to spend your days nursing a crush on a hot yacht chef."

I laughed. "I think you mean I spend my days being *annoyed* by a hot . . ." I paused, and Alex grinned. "A perfectly *average*-looking yacht chef."

Alex shook his head. "Damn. I was *this* close to getting you to admit I can be Hot Yacht Chef."

"*That's* what you wanted? I thought you were desperate to get me to admit I have a crush on you."

Alex shrugged. "Why state the obvious?"

I scanned the floor around me, my cheeks burning. "I've decluttered all the things I had to throw at you."

"One box left," Alex said. "Then food."

I pulled the box closer and took a deep breath before lifting the lid, knowing what I'd find inside. After the mug incident with Kitty that first week, I'd put away everything that might remind the girls of Samson. Right on top was a photograph that used to live on my fridge. In it, Samson and I stood on either side of a tiny bonsai tree, wide grins on our faces. That was the first time I'd taken him to the Morikami Museum and Japanese Gardens. He'd made me take him back every summer since.

"What's wrong?" Alex said. "Please tell me that's an embarrassing photo from high school."

Unable to speak, I handed Alex the photograph. When he looked at it, the humor disappeared from his face. "Samson, right? You have the same eyes."

I cleared my throat. "I think . . . maybe put that in the trash pile."

"What? Why?"

I sat back, wrapping my arms around my knees. "I don't feel particularly . . . joyful . . . looking at that. Whenever I run into something of his . . ." I shook my head. "I'd just rather not be reminded."

When I glanced at Alex again, he was staring at the photograph in his hands, his brows knit together. He caught me looking at him, and his expression softened. "How about I hold on to it, and when you're ready, I'll give it back," he said. "It'll probably be sooner than you think."

I sighed, feeling an ache in my chest. "Okay. Yeah. I guess that could work. You won't lose it, though, will you?"

Alex smiled. "See? You don't really want to get rid of it." He passed the photo back to me. "I told you it would be sooner than you thought."

The next moment Alex was on his feet.

"Where are you going?" I said.

"Two minutes," he said, and disappeared through the door.

I ran a finger around the edge of the photograph, trying to slip inside the memory of that day at the museum. It was hard to look back on it with joy, but maybe if I pretended to be the person in the photograph again, things would be different. I closed my eyes and thought I caught a spark.

When Alex returned, he had one of the framed photos of Zac Efron Nina had left at his place.

"I thought I was supposed to be getting rid of stuff," I said.

Alex undid the frame and took out the Zac Efron photo. "For your picture," he said, holding the frame out to me. "For whenever you're ready to put it back up."

I reached out, and my fingers brushed against Alex's as I took the frame and set it in my lap. "Is there a word for feeling joy and sorrow at the same time?"

"I don't know," he said.

I nodded to the Zac Efron photo Alex had set in the trash pile. "You sure you don't want to keep that photo in your living room?" I said.

"I have plenty. The guy who came to repair my AC the other day seemed a little disturbed by it. He couldn't get out of there quick enough."

I set the photo of me and Samson in the frame. "Thank you. I think I'll put it in my nightstand drawer," I said. "Just in case."

When I'd put away the last of my sentimental items, and Alex returned from one more dumpster run, he stood in the middle of my living room with his hands on his hips. "So did it change your life?" he asked.

"I'm an entirely new person," I said. "I think I can read minds now."

"Really?" He turned to face me, his eyes meeting mine. "Then what am I thinking right now?"

I tapped a finger against my chin, narrowing my eyes as I stared into his. "That you can't wait to get out of here and go to bed."

"Nope. I don't think I'm within range of your powers." A smile played on his lips as he came closer and stood directly in front of me. "Try again."

I racked my mind, again for something that wasn't about kissing or being alone together, but fortunately I was saved by Mia, who flung open the condo door. She looked at us, then called over her shoulder, "It's safe! They aren't making out!"

Alex laughed and took a step back. I busied myself straightening the already straight couch pillows.

"Dads aren't allowed to make out," Greyson said, following Mia inside. She eyed Alex and threw up her hands. "It's just the rules. I don't make 'em."

"It's ignorant to think adults don't engage in that sort of activity," Kitty said.

"Doesn't mean I want to know about it," Greyson replied.

"*If you know the enemy and know yourself, your victory will not stand in doubt*," Kitty said. She gave Greyson a curt nod.

Greyson stared at her. "I don't get it."

Mia grabbed Greyson by the elbow and tugged her in the direction of the kitchen. "Don't bother. There's nothing to get."

After pouring themselves bowls of cereal, the girls sat side by side on the couch, discussing a video they'd watched about Disney Channel child stars who'd become drug addicts.

"I thought you three were watching a movie," Alex said.

"I said we were going to watch *something*," Greyson said. "It's not my fault you assumed it was a movie. And anyway, it was basically a documentary and overall very educational. Right?" she added, glancing from Mia to Kitty.

"Right," the girls responded.

Alex and I looked at each other and shook our heads.

"Lasagna?" I asked him.

"Lasagna," he replied with a nod.

"Thank God we missed the decluttering," Mia said when I returned from the kitchen and sat beside Alex on the couch. "Wait. Where's all our stuff?"

"Trash pile," Alex said.

"It didn't spark joy," I added with a shrug.

Mia glared, and Kitty groaned, and Alex caught my eye right after I'd shoveled a forkful of lasagna into my mouth.

"You've got . . ." He leaned over and swiped his thumb along the corner of my mouth. "Sauce," he said, pulling away from me.

There was a moment of silence, and then a collective *oooooh* sounded from the other couch. Alex shook his head, I blushed, and we both ignored the girls. I stared down at the plate in my lap. That had meant nothing, of course. Just like all his flirting meant nothing. I was almost sure he would've done the same thing to Nina. We were good friends who spent a lot of time enclosed in small spaces together, nothing more.

Mia and Kitty giggled gleefully from across the living room. Greyson had her hands over her face and cried, "The rules, Dad! The rules!"

Alex leaned back into the couch. "I don't see how helping a friend is equivalent to making out. And I don't remember agreeing to these rules. I'm not sure I can abide by them."

Greyson pretended to gag, and I flicked my gaze over to Alex. *Friends.* That was all we were. He'd said it himself.

Then why had I thought, *Joy*, the moment he'd touched me, as if his thumb on my mouth were something I could keep?

Eleven

⚓

ONE MORNING, A FEW DAYS AFTER ALEX AND I HAD DECLUT-
tered my condo, I sank into a seat at the galley table and hung my head
in my hands, fighting off a wave of nausea.

"Good morning again," Alex, who stood before the open refrigerator, said.

When I didn't respond, the refrigerator door snapped shut and Alex
was suddenly beside me. "You okay?"

I let out a slow breath. "Forgot to eat breakfast. Probably too much
coffee on an empty stomach."

I'd been fine when Alex and I carpooled to work that morning. We'd
arrived a few minutes early, so I'd disappeared into one of the bunks and
called my sister. *Okay*, Beth had said when I asked how she and Mark
were doing. She'd changed the subject quickly and asked about the girls.
I'd told her they were great. I was keeping them distracted. And Beth
had asked if they were talking about Samson. After their meltdowns the
first week, I could count on one hand the times Samson's name had come
up. Whenever it had, I'd successfully steered the conversation to some-

thing lighter. The girls still had their moments, but they were quieter now, more private.

As much as I don't want them to be sad all the time, it doesn't seem right that they aren't talking about it either, Beth had said. And then she'd started crying, talking about how our mother had screwed things up with us after Dad died and how she didn't want to do that to Mia and Kitty. In the end, she'd made me promise to talk to Mia and Kitty and ask how they were feeling. The idea of a conversation like that (on top of not eating breakfast) had made me sick to my stomach.

Alex clapped his hands together. "Well, you're in luck, because I just happen to be a very talented chef. Chocolate chip waffles are your favorite, right?"

I tried to protest, but the motion only made me feel worse, and besides, Alex had already crossed the galley and was plugging in the waffle maker.

Ten minutes later, he placed a stack of waffles in front of me. "Eat up. We've got work to do."

"Thanks." I took small bites until my stomach settled and tried not to think about Beth, or Mia and Kitty, or Samson.

As I ate, Alex zipped around the kitchen. He pulled out the cutting board, his knife, and every fruit imaginable: a watermelon, a pineapple, kiwis, blueberries, strawberries. "I meant to ask," he said as he washed the blueberries and strawberries in the sink. "How's your list going? The picture of you from the Zefron-a-thon post was great, if I do say so myself. You must have had an excellent photographer."

I paused, a bite of waffle between my teeth. My blog. Alex had read *XO, Jo.* Of course he knew about it, in a casual sort of way. But the thought of him actually reading it had never crossed my mind. "You've read the blog," I said.

"My favorite is the kiss a stranger post, of course," Alex said. He carried the fruit over to the island and began nonchalantly slicing the pineapple. "It's good to know you don't really think I look like a tourist. The skinny-dipping post seemed to be missing crucial information, but I'll let it slide."

"I don't really dream about you," I said, my entire being burning in embarrassment.

"That surprises me," Alex said. "Because I'm very dreamy."

I stuffed another forkful of waffle into my mouth, because what else was there to do? The phrase *pillowy lips* popped into my mind, and I considered throwing myself overboard. I'd written that when Alex was basically a stranger. How was I supposed to know he'd become my buddy?

"Really, Jo, I like it," Alex said. "You don't have to be embarrassed. I know they're just blog posts and don't mean anything."

"Yeah, exactly," I said. "I didn't really mean any of that."

Alex continued slicing the pineapple, eyes on his knife. "How are you planning to go to five countries and sleep in a castle by the end of the summer?"

I prodded the waffles with my fork, happy to move on to a new subject. "I hadn't really thought about it. I keep telling the girls I don't see how it's possible, but anytime I bring it up, they insist we have to do *all* the items together. I didn't know they were coming for the summer. They sort of . . . surprised me. I had it all figured out before that."

"What was the original plan?"

I leaned back in my seat. "You know how I have the next two weeks off?" Alex nodded. "I had this big trip to Europe planned to knock out the last five countries. I even booked a room in a Scottish castle. But I canceled all that the day after Mia and Kitty showed up. As much as I'd like to finish the list, I can't imagine it happening."

"I see." Alex went quiet again. He'd finished the pineapple and moved on to the watermelon, staring down at it for so long I thought he'd forgotten I was there. Finally, he looked up at me and set down his knife. "Did you know there's a castle in Miami?"

"No," I said. I waited for him to explain himself, but he seemed lost in thought. "Care to explain, Chef Alex?"

He rapped the counter with his knuckles. "Coral Castle," he said, and picked up his knife again.

"Coral Castle," I repeated. Was this a joke? I'd spent the last seven years in South Florida. Surely, I'd know if there was a castle an hour and a half from my condo. "Sorry, but what is that?"

"It's a little sad, really. I need to preface this by saying it isn't a castle in the sense you're thinking. It's hard to describe. This Latvian immigrant single-handedly built the entire thing from limestone. And I mean giant slabs of it. No one knows how he did it."

I set my fork down, intrigued. "What's sad about that?"

"He built it as a monument to the love of his life, who left him one day before their wedding. The guy spent twenty-eight years building this thing, and she never even saw it."

"That is really sad."

Alex shrugged. "It's probably not the kind of castle you were looking for, but I know the event planner. I catered this psychic event when they were in a pinch, and I bet she'd let us stay on a night they don't have anything going on. If you wanted, that is."

I pulled out my phone to look up the place. Essentially, Coral Castle was a giant courtyard surrounded by towering limestone walls and filled with strange limestone sculptures. It was . . . weird. Florida weird in the truest sense. And Alex was right, it wasn't what I'd envisioned when I added this item. But then again, almost nothing this summer had turned out like I'd planned. It would certainly make for an interesting blog post.

"Why the hell not? It's not like I have a lot of options here."

Alex looked up from the cutting board. "Really? You'd be into that?"

I showed him the photo of Coral Castle on my phone. Giant limestone statues of moons and planets filled the frame. A creepy filter outlined each statue in a purple glow. "What woman in her right mind *wouldn't* want to spend a night here?" I said.

"I'll call the event planner, then." Alex nodded to my plate. "Feeling better?"

I closed my eyes for a moment, taking stock of my head, then my stomach. "Actually, I am. Thank you, Chef Alex."

"You're very welcome, Stewardess Jo."

"What's this?" a voice said. We turned to find Nina at the galley door, papers clutched in her hand. She gestured to my empty plate. "This is *work*, you know, not a diner."

"I wasn't feeling well."

"*Wasn't*, which means you *are* feeling well now. We've got a fun charter today, so there's a million and one things to do."

A *fun* charter could only mean one of two things. "Child or animal?" I asked.

"Animal."

"Pomeranian or bichon frise?"

"Bichon frise."

Alex and I groaned in unison.

Nina shot Alex a dirty look. "What are you complaining about? *You* only have to cook for it. *We* have to pretend to love it as much as the primaries do."

Nina placed three sheets of paper on the island counter. I stood to join her and Alex. At the top of one sheet of paper was a photo of a dog with a bow on its head. "This is Bitty," she explained.

"*Bitty is on a low-carb, grain-free diet,*" I read aloud. "*Her favorites include lavender-infused water, gluten-free biscuits with blueberry compote. Her owners request a special birthday lunch of foie gras.*" I looked up at Alex. "Can dogs even eat foie gras?"

Alex shook his head. "My plan is to make *faux* gras. With lentils. Fools them every time." He scanned the sheet again. "That is a definite no-go," he said, pointing to *beef carpaccio*. "No way I'm getting blamed if Mistress Bitty gets *E. coli*."

"You know a lot about what dogs can and cannot eat for someone who has never had a dog," Nina said.

Alex shrugged. "Comes with the job."

"And they want *us* to throw the dog a birthday party?" I said to Nina.

"Bitty is turning ten years old," Nina said. "Why wouldn't she have an extravagant birthday party with a price tag equivalent to an entire college education?" Nina pointed at Alex. "This will be the true test. Is Chef Alex as unflappable as he seems? Dog charters bring out the worst in everyone."

"I don't mind dogs," he said. "They can't complain about the cooking."

"Oh, Alex," Nina said. "You've got it all wrong. The dogs are never the problem. It's the *people*."

"You'll make a birthday cake, right?" I said to Alex.

"I'm thinking peanut butter and blueberry cupcakes."

"That sounds good, actually."

Alex's knife flashed in the light as he sliced through strawberries. "I'll be sure to save you one."

Alex grinned at me, but a moment later his face transformed into a wince of pain. He jumped back from the counter with a hiss, cradling his hand against his chest. Blood ran thick and fast over his white chef's coat, and I was on the other side of the island before I could think.

"Are you all right?" I took his hand in mine and examined the wound. The knife had sliced into his middle finger just above the first knuckle, but I couldn't tell how deep.

"I'll live," he said through gritted teeth.

"We need to wash this now." I grabbed him by the elbow and led him over to the sink. "Don't look at it."

Alex looked away as I rinsed his hand. I grabbed a clean dish towel from nearby and wrapped it around his finger, keeping pressure on the wound.

Nina, always calm in a crisis, called over her radio for RJ, who took care of any injuries we had on board. "Please tell me you can cook with one hand."

"How bad is it?" Alex winced.

I glanced at the bloody dish towel I held around his finger. "It's not ... great, but you've still got your fingertip."

"You're useless, Alex," Nina said, joining us beside the sink. "Don't you know how to hold a knife?"

"Jo distracted me."

"We were having a conversation!" I said.

"You are very distracting, Josephine," Nina said. "It's the knees—their beauty blinds me on a daily basis."

Alex looked down at my legs, that almost smile on his face even as he was clearly in pain. "They are pretty nice knees."

"I hate both of you. Here, hold your own damn finger." I pushed Alex's hand to his chest. "And you know what? I'm going to wear pants from now on, beautiful knees be damned!"

"You wouldn't dare," Nina said. "No one looks good in khaki pants. *No one.*"

"Just watch me!"

RJ arrived, looking both confused by the conversation he'd walked into and annoyed that he had to be there at all. I'd never heard RJ speak more than three words at a time, and those three words happened to be *Copy that, Captain.* He was silent as he examined Alex's finger. The ten minutes it took for him to stitch Alex up stretched on uncomfortably as Nina counted off all the ways khaki pants offended her, and RJ's eyebrows lifted themselves so high they eventually disappeared into his hair. In the end, Alex's hand was wrapped up and useless, and RJ left muttering under his breath. The three of us sat around the table, Alex with a sheepish look on his face.

"Thanks for nearly amputating yourself when we need you to cook, Alex," Nina said. "I can't believe you're leaving me to deal with his incompetence by myself for the next two weeks," she added to me.

I knew she was only half kidding. Nothing made her angrier than a charter going awry, and this one hadn't even started yet. But after Saturday, charters wouldn't be my problem for an entire two weeks. My only concern would be spending as much time with Mia and Kitty as possible.

"Should we just order food for the guests?" I asked.

"We're not serving takeout on a charter," Alex said. "Especially not for dog people. I can still cook. I just need a little help." He gave us a pleading smile.

"Not it." Nina touched her finger to her nose and gave me a pat on the shoulder. "Have at it, babe."

"If it means I'll be spending less time with the dog people, I'm in. Besides, I've always wanted to learn to cook."

"Liar," Alex and Nina said at the same time.

"We know you love your Lean Cuisines and microwavable popcorn," Nina said.

"Why do you think I'm always bringing over food?" Alex added.

After taking care of my usual morning duties (greeting the guests, making drinks, folding the ends of toilet paper into little triangles) and my not-so-usual duties (making lavender water for Bitty and crafting a tiny dog-sized sailor hat for her birthday party), Nina sent me to help Alex with lunch.

Alex didn't notice me when I walked into the galley. He was bent over a counter, his usual look of concentration more severe as he struggled to mix something with his good hand. He'd stripped off his bloody chef's coat, and I tried not to let my eyes linger on the way his white T-shirt clung to his broad shoulders.

I cleared my throat, and he looked up at me with a grin. "Am I glad to see you!"

I crossed the galley to wash my hands in the sink. "No offense, but *thank you* for injuring yourself. I needed to get away from those people. They treat that dog like actual royalty. It has its own tiny blow-dryer, and I had the pleasure of using it. I had to dry Bitty *in the direction of the fur*," I said, imitating the voice of Mrs. Daniels, the primary. "And let me tell you, that dog does *not* enjoy it." I paused in my tirade and dried my hands on a dish towel, noticing the hip-hop music Alex had on. "What is this playlist?"

"I believe the title of this playlist is *Songs That Make Me Feel Like a Bad Bitch*." I cocked an eyebrow at him. He threw up his hands. "I didn't make it. Nina added it. It's good, right?"

"It definitely sounds like a Nina playlist," I said, wondering when she and Alex had talked about it, not that it really mattered. I scanned the galley. "So, what are we making, Chef?"

"The dog food is already done, so we'll be cooking for the humans. For an appetizer, we're making beef vol-au-vents with a beet and marmalade chutney. Lunch will be red mullet with wild fennel, oven-dried tomatoes, and pickled eggplant."

I stared at the ingredients on the counter. "I think you are seriously overestimating me."

Alex passed me his knife with a laugh. "You're only the prep cook. Why don't you start by dicing the beets for the chutney, and I'll finish up these vol-au-vent cases."

I stepped up to the cutting board and beets. My back was to Alex, but I was aware of him across the galley, humming under his breath to the music. I looked down at the knife in my hands, feeling self-conscious. What did I know about cooking? I had zero skills, even for the basics. If I bought vegetables at the store, it was always the precut kind. Alex could halve and dice and chop like it was second nature. I set a beet in the center of the cutting board and pushed the knife into it, working slowly, the pieces not quite as uniform as I was sure Alex needed them to be.

I'd finished dicing the first of the beets when I felt Alex standing behind me, which made me more unsure of myself. I tried to work faster, but it only made my dicing sloppier.

"You'll chop your fingers off like that, and I don't want you ending up like me," he said. He stepped closer, his uninjured hand hovering over mine. "Can I show you something? Do you mind?"

"Oh. Uh, yeah. Go ahead."

Alex stepped closer and rested his hand on mine. "Make a claw with your left hand," he said. "It protects your fingers. That was my mistake earlier. Because you distracted me."

"I wasn't distracting you," I said. "*You* were talking to *me*."

"Talking to you was very distracting," he said, and his breath against my neck made the hair there stand on end. "Claw, please," he added.

I drew my fingers inward. "Claw, got it."

"Great. Now you've almost got the right grip." He squeezed my hand under his. "But you really ought to pinch the blade with your thumb and forefinger—it'll give you more control. And wrap your fingers around the handle." He shifted my hand forward and curled my fingers gently beneath his.

"Instead of chopping straight down like this," he said, lifting the knife (and our hands) straight up and down, "you should do a rocking motion." His chest pressed against my back, and he tipped the blade forward, rocking it back up in a single fluid motion. "Does that make sense?"

"Uh-huh." Was my hand sweaty? Could he tell it was sweating? What temperature had he set that damn oven to anyway? And why was this playlist so . . . provocative? I did not feel like a bad bitch with Alex standing behind me. I felt like I couldn't breathe.

With his hand wrapped around mine and his chest to my back, Alex guided me through one of the beets. The knife clicked against the cutting board as he murmured in my ear, "Make sure you've got a firm but relaxed grip. And use enough force. Most people don't use enough force."

"Firm and forceful," I said.

"But relaxed."

"But relaxed," I repeated. Our hands stilled, his resting on mine for what was probably only a few seconds but felt much longer. His breath was warm in my ear, and despite the rhythmic bass of the music, I thought I could feel his heart beating against my back. Alex passed his thumb over the top of my hand. (An accident? A caress?) For one wild second, I had the urge to drop the knife, turn around, and kiss him.

But then he cleared his throat, breaking the trance. He released my hand and jumped back as if he'd been burned.

"You're a natural," he said, standing there with his hands on his hips as if nothing had happened.

I blinked at him. Had he sensed that too? Or was it all in my head? The next moment he was across the galley, as far away from me as possible. He crouched beside the oven and looked in at the puff pastry, rubbing at the back of his neck with his good hand.

"Everything all right with those beets?" he called without turning to look at me.

"Just peachy. Or beety, I guess. Hey, do you think I should drop a *beet*?" I laughed, holding one up in my hand, but Alex either hadn't heard or hadn't thought the joke was funny. What the hell was wrong with me? Had I been single for so long that all it took to get me worked up was a touch on the hand and some hip-hop music? Had I suddenly wandered into a Jane Austen novel? If Jane Austen had somehow wandered into a nightclub? A nightclub that offered cooking lessons?

"I think I'm feeling like enough of a bad bitch for now," Alex said. He flicked through his phone, and "Cry Me a River" came on. "*High School Hits* playlist," he explained.

"Sounds like a middle school hits playlist to me," I said.

Alex narrowed his eyes. "Are you suggesting I'm old, Florida Girl who isn't even from Florida?"

"Maybe." I shrugged. "Older than me, anyway."

Alex shook his head. He sang along to the song but changed the words to be about his injured hand, Nina's wrath, my youth and newly acquired dicing skills. I smiled to myself as I continued dicing the beets, but it was hard to focus when I was expending so much energy trying not to think about how I'd felt with him standing so close. After a few verses, Alex's lyrics got stuck in my head, and I joined in at the chorus, the two of us singing at the tops of our lungs.

"Jo, Alex, this is Nina," our radios called.

I grabbed the radio and sang, "Go for Jo."

"Just wanted to let you know the guests can hear you," she snipped. "And I am *not* a vengeful sea goddess."

I held down the talk button to answer her, but Alex called out, "It was a compliment!" before I could say anything.

"Sorry," I added.

"Just get back to work, or *you'll* be crying a river," she replied.

I turned to Alex, and the two of us erupted into laughter I was positive the guests could hear too.

WE'D ALMOST SURVIVED THE DOG CHARTER WITHOUT FURTHER catastrophe. Lunch had gone well, and I'd been able to find another polo in my size after Bitty peed on me. And then everything went to shit at the birthday party. Bitty devoured the cupcake Alex had made her but immediately threw it up on the carpet of the Sky Lounge. Mrs. Daniels had started ranting and raving, convinced Alex had put something with gluten in it. Alex must have heard the commotion, because he appeared and calmly explained every ingredient he'd used, then asked if she would like him to prepare something else. Nina stayed out of the fray, keeping a watchful eye on Alex and Mrs. Daniels as she stood behind the bar to make drinks. Meanwhile, I noticed Bitty skittering over to another cupcake and raced to scoop her up. But the dog snapped at me, and I jumped away, a few choice words leaving my mouth. Mrs. Daniels turned her anger on me, claiming I'd provoked Bitty and was being a drama queen. Next thing I knew, *Alex* was the one shouting at Mrs. Daniels, telling her exactly where she could shove Bitty's blow-dryer.

Needless to say, the charter was awkward after that. Nina and I stared openmouthed at Alex as he stormed off in the direction of the galley. I'd never seen him so much as annoyed before, and yet he'd gone from accommodating to fed up in the span of a few seconds. Mrs. Daniels blanched, then whirled on her husband, demanding he do something. Mr. Daniels nodded and told her he'd speak to the captain, but his bored expression remained unchanged, which I guessed meant this behavior wasn't out of the norm—for Mrs. Daniels or for Bitty.

Once the guests had disembarked and the boat was clean, Alex, Nina, and I convened around the crew mess table, grumpy and exhausted. Alex said he knew the perfect way to blow off steam after a bad charter, but as soon as he started up the steps to the sun deck, Nina and me behind him, Nina called after us, saying she had a date and couldn't stay. I was halfway up the steps by then and glared down at her, but she only gave me a wave and a wicked grin before disappearing out of sight.

Now, as I stood beside Alex in front of the hot tub, I wasn't so sure Nina even had a date. Maybe she'd invented one in an attempt to force me into hanging out with Alex in a noncarpool/teenagerless situation.

"*This* is what you do after a bad charter? Stare at the hot tub?"

Alex gave me a sidelong glance. "Of course I don't stare at the hot tub. I get *in* the hot tub. I pretend to be a guest, which is what we're going to do."

"But the girls haven't eaten dinner."

"And are fully capable of microwaving leftovers," Alex said. He pulled his shirt over his head and dropped it on deck beside him.

"But I don't have a bathing—"

Alex unbuttoned his pants and slid them over his hips, and the words died in my mouth. I tried not to stare, but there he was, right in front of me, wearing nothing but black boxer briefs that clung tight to his ass.

"Bathing suit," I said. "I don't have a bathing suit."

"Neither do I," he said.

Yeah, I noticed, I thought.

"If we have to suffer on a yacht, we might as well enjoy it too," he added, turning to me with his hands on his hips.

I'd spent half the summer wondering what was underneath those neon-green running shorts, so focusing on the words coming from his mouth instead of everything below it was no easy task. "Enjoy it, yeah," I said.

"Good," Alex said, and then he got in the hot tub, making sure to keep his injured hand far from the water.

Had I made it sound like I was on board with this? I stared at Alex, then around at the other boats in the marina, and finally out at the ocean. The sun was only beginning to slip toward the horizon. And it really was nice to watch the sunset from up here. I glanced at Alex. Curse my love of sunsets and good butts. And curse Alex for having a good butt. Pheromones. Pheromones were responsible for this. I pulled my shirt over my head, telling myself that, really, this was *less* scandalous than when he'd found me skinny-dipping in the condo pool. I turned away and tugged off my shorts, kicking my clothes into a pile beside Alex's. Before I could change my mind, I raced into the hot tub and sat as far away from Alex as I could, submerging myself up to my armpits.

"This does feel pretty good," I said, adjusting myself so that a jet shot water right onto my back. "How's your hand?"

Alex looked beyond me and didn't answer. Maybe he hadn't heard me. Just when I was about to repeat myself, he turned to me, speaking so quickly it reminded me of Greyson. "I'm sorry for yelling at the primary. I know I should've let you handle it, and I probably only made things worse, but—and I'm not trying to excuse my behavior here— when she called you a drama queen, I just . . ." He shook his head. "Well, I stopped thinking."

I stared into the roiling water of the hot tub. "You probably shouldn't have done that, but I'm not going to lie. I thought it was pretty amazing."

"Then I'm glad I did it," Alex said, the worry disappearing from his expression. "I'd do it again, you know, though I hope I don't have to. I'm surprised I still have a job, to be honest."

"Cap hates dog charters as much as we do. He only had to yell at you to make a good show for the guests. Nothing drives him crazier than dog shit on the teak."

"You're missing the sunset sitting over there, you know," Alex said. "It's an important part of the guest experience."

"Right." I crossed the hot tub, sitting beside Alex.

He scanned the sun deck with an exaggerated frown. "Horrible service here," he said. "I ordered a gin martini almost thirty seconds ago!"

I tried to adopt a scowl of my own, but it was hard to stop giggling. "*I* was told the chef was very talented. Michelin-star earning. But I don't believe it. I still can't believe he made *chicken* for lunch. It was the best chicken I've ever had, but still. Chicken is what poor people eat."

Alex snorted, breaking character for only a moment before responding, "I know I didn't *put* foie gras on my preference sheet, but it's what I wanted. Why can't that idiot chef read my mind?"

"Well, *I* don't actually know what foie gras is, but I want it anyway."

Alex sighed and looked over his shoulder. "Really, where is that gin martini? If it weren't for the fact that the crew on this ship is stunningly attractive, I'd end this charter right now."

When we'd run out of ridiculous things to say, we fell quiet and looked out at the ocean. The tension of the day melted away with every inch the sun descended. It was nice to be off my feet, to do something relaxing and stare out at the water. It was nice to forget about the charter guests, my list, my worries about Mia, and Kitty, and Beth, and Mark. For a few minutes, it was as if the whole world were only this view and Alex beside me, making me laugh.

"Jo?" Alex said.

I turned to face him, momentarily distracted by how the warm colors of the sky lit up his face. We were nose to nose. Somehow over the last ten minutes, we'd drifted closer to each other, and I could feel his leg against mine. He'd slung an arm around the edge of the hot tub, and his skin grazed my shoulders. I thought about that moment in the galley—Alex's hand on mine, a pause, one I was almost sure meant something. Any more of this: the sunset, that almost smile, his arm against my shoulders, and I was sure the pheromones would win out over my common sense.

"Jo?" Alex said again. I snapped my eyes up to his, not realizing I'd been staring at his mouth.

"Yeah?"

"Who do you think Nina's going out with tonight?"

Or maybe that moment in the galley hadn't meant anything at all. "I don't know," I said. "She goes on a lot of dates, but I wouldn't entirely rule out Ollie." I didn't think she was actually out with Ollie tonight. But I didn't want Alex getting too invested in Nina if he *did* have feelings for her. It would only be a dead end.

"What happened between them?" Alex asked.

I sighed. "I have no idea. Nina won't say. All I know is *something* happened their first charter season. My guess is they're in love with each other, but too stubborn to do anything about it."

Alex nodded, looking thoughtful for a moment.

"You know what I like to do after a bad charter?" I said, wanting to change the subject.

"What?"

"Jump off the yacht," I said, scooting an inch away so that our legs were no longer touching. "It clears my head."

"Willingly facing possible death sounds like it would definitely clear your head," he said.

I stared at him. "Have you never jumped off a yacht before?"

Alex scratched his jaw with his good hand. "Will you think less of me if I say no?"

"Maybe."

"Then . . . maybe?"

I had a hard time imagining Alex scared of anything, especially after he'd had emergency stitches and taken on that primary today. "Are you scared of heights or something?"

"No," he said. "I'm scared of hitting the water wrong and breaking my neck."

"Alex, you won't die unless you jump off like a doofus."

"I'm a doofus sometimes," he said.

"That may be true, but I think you've got just enough sense to jump off a yacht safely." I stood from the hot tub, then remembered I was standing right beside him in only my bra and underwear and hurried out of it. "Come on, Chef Alex. We're doing this."

"You mean now?" Alex, still in the hot tub, looked as if I'd suggested bathing in jellyfish.

I snapped up two clean towels from beside the bar and wrapped one around myself before returning to the hot tub. I tried not to laugh at Alex's stricken face when I passed him the other. It was nice to be the one making *him* flustered for once. "Yes, now. No self-respecting yachtie *hasn't* jumped off a yacht."

"I have no self-respect," he said. "And my hand." He waved it in front of me. "I can't get it wet."

"Hold that thought," I said. I raced down to the crew mess and found a Ziploc bag and a roll of duct tape. Supplies in hand, I paused at the bar on the sun deck and poured out two shots of tequila.

Alex was sitting on a lounge chair when I returned, a towel wrapped around his waist. "We're all out of gin martinis," I said, and passed him the shot glass.

"What's this for?"

"Nerves."

"I don't see how a shot will make me less likely to break my neck."

I gave him a blank stare. "Are you going to get drunk off of one shot?" He shook his head. "Will this even make you tipsy?" He shook his head again. "Drink it or not, but I promise it'll be worth it if you jump off this ship."

Alex narrowed his eyes at me. "What do you get out of this?"

I shrugged. "The privilege of being the one to pop your yacht-jumping cherry."

"That is a coveted title," he replied, nodding seriously. "Okay, I'll do it. I can't deny you that."

I held out my shot, and Alex sighed, clinking his glass to mine. After downing the tequila, his eyes darted to the Ziploc bag and duct tape. "Are you . . . planning to murder me?"

"It's for your hand." I sat next to him on the lounge chair and reached for his arm, slipping the Ziploc bag gently over his hand and duct taping it until it was airtight.

I grabbed Alex's good hand and pulled him to his feet, dragging him to the best jumping spot on the aft deck.

"How far is it?" Alex asked, looking pale as we slipped beyond the railing.

"Twenty-five feet."

"The water in the marina . . . it's deep enough, right?"

"It's deep enough," I said. "I've done this a million times. We'll be fine." We dropped our towels behind us, and I took Alex's hand in mine again. "Don't chicken out, okay? If you don't jump and I end up pulling you off, we'll both hit the water wrong. It will definitely clear your head, but maybe not in the way you'd like. Hold your bad hand against your chest and just stay vertical. On three, okay?"

"I can't tell if you're trying to make me more or less nervous," Alex said, squeezing my hand tighter. He looked at me, then out at the water and nodded. "Okay," he said. "I can do this. See? My head feels clearer already. I've completely forgotten about the charter."

"Clearly not, since you just brought it up."

"But I won't be thinking about it soon," he said. "Not once we jump off this thing. Then we'll forget all about it."

I kept my eyes on the water below as he spoke. My pulse quickened with each second that passed. Why I suddenly felt nervous, I had no idea. I wasn't afraid of jumping. And it definitely wasn't because I was standing on the edge of a twenty-million-dollar yacht, in my underwear, holding the hand of my hot neighbor slash coworker, who was also in his underwear, and whom I did *not* have feelings for outside of a completely normal physical attraction.

"No offense, Alex, but I need you to stop talking," I said.

"No talking. Right. Shit, I'm still talking. Okay, I'm done talking . . . right . . . now."

"On three," I said again. "One, two—"

As soon as the word *three* left my mouth, we jumped. For a moment I felt weightless, and then we fell, and the thrill of it made me forget everything, even Alex. I'd jumped off this yacht more times than I could count last charter season. Every leap gave me a delicious moment of freedom, shoving me back into the world for a few blissful seconds. We plunged into the water too soon, and the world around me disappeared. I'd let go of Alex's hand as soon as the water swallowed us up, but when I resurfaced, he was already treading water in front of me.

"Holy shit," he said. He shook the water from his hair and swam closer. "Are you all right?" I thought I felt his fingers graze my waist, but the sensation was gone as quickly as I'd noticed it. A fish. It had to have been a fish.

"I told you we wouldn't die," I said. "How's your hand?"

"What?"

Adrenaline zipped through me, and I laughed at the awed look on his face. "Your hand, Alex."

"Oh." He pulled the Ziploc-bagged hand from the water. "It's fine. I forgot about it, honestly."

"See? Clears the head."

"I get it now," he said, still out of breath. "What the big deal is about yacht jumping. My heart . . ." He took my hand and pressed it to his chest. "It's racing."

I glanced at his hand holding mine against him. His skin was warm under my palm, and sure enough, I could feel his heart thudding away. "Mine too," I said, the nervousness I'd felt standing on the edge of the yacht coursing through me. "Still thinking about that charter?" I asked.

When he spoke, his voice was quieter than it had been a moment before. "No, I'm not," he said.

I looked up. The moment his eyes met mine the adrenaline faded, and all I felt was fear. But it wasn't the same fear I'd had the very first time I stood on the edge of the yacht, ready to jump. This was entirely different and exponentially more terrifying. More frightening than the bungee jumping, and skydiving, and zip-lining I'd done for my list. More frightening than suffering through twenty dog charters.

"It's getting dark," I said. I pulled my hand from his chest and looked up at the *Serendipity* towering beside us. "Maybe we should . . ."

"Go home," Alex said.

Right as I turned back to him, the sun slipped beneath the horizon. In the span of a few seconds, the sky softened into a solid wall of pink where before there had only been fire. It was still beautiful, but it reminded me the color would drain from the sky at a rapid pace now, daylight fading until there was nothing but night. "Yeah," I said. "We better go home."

THAT EVENING, MIA, KITTY, AND GREYSON CAME OUTSIDE WHILE I was watering the peperomias. Ever since I'd gotten home, I'd been trying to shake off that look Alex had given me when we were in the water and the feeling of his heart beneath my hand.

After the girls settled on the lounge chairs, I told them all about Alex's idea to spend the night at Coral Castle.

"That place is *so* weird," Greyson said. "I went there on a field trip once, and the tour guide was this super-creepy guy who kept talking about magnetic fields. Some people say the guy who made it levitated all the stones. But other people think it was aliens. I'd believe aliens before the levitating thing."

"Don't get too excited," I said when Greyson paused to take a breath. "Your dad has to talk to the event planner first. It might not even happen."

Greyson turned toward Kitty. "We should ask him if he's called yet, and if he hasn't, we should make him call *right now*."

I tried to stop Greyson and said there was no rush, but she'd already dragged Kitty back through the condo.

I moved on to the camellia shrub, hoping Alex wouldn't think I'd sent the girls over to rush him, when I noticed one person seemed decidedly unexcited about this plan. Mia had her knees drawn up to her chin, silent since coming outside. She stared out at the palm trees lining the back of the condo, picking absentmindedly at the leaves of my hibiscus bush.

"I know it's not the coolest thing in the world, but it might be fun," I said.

Mia shrugged. "I guess."

"You could drive us down there if you wanted. You haven't gotten any driving time in."

Mia's mouth parted, then snapped shut again. "No thanks. I don't really like driving."

What newly licensed sixteen-year-old didn't like to drive? I thought about the conversation I'd had with my sister that morning. Was this a moody teenager thing or a grief thing? *Just ask how they're feeling*, I heard Beth say.

Everything in me resisted Beth's request. I wasn't good at this sort of thing. What I wanted to do was suggest we watch an episode of *My Super Sweet 16*. That always cheered them up. But I couldn't let Beth down. Not when she'd specifically asked me to do this.

I sat at Mia's feet and spoke before I could chicken out. "How are you . . . feeling?"

Mia stared at me as if I'd sprouted gills. She searched my face, seeming to gather her thoughts, and I braced myself for whatever she had to say. I needed to be here for her, to listen, even though it was the last thing in the world I wanted to do. Not because I didn't care about Mia, but because I knew it would be painful for both of us. We'd had enough pain this year. How would talking about it make it better?

Just as I thought she was about to speak, Mia's expression hardened, and she shook her head. "I feel fine."

So this was going well. But I could feel Beth telling me to try again. *Fine, fine,* I thought to Beth.

"Do you . . . want to talk about anything?"

The muscles in Mia's jaw twitched. I tried to keep my face neutral, but inside I was withering. I hoped she couldn't see how uncomfortable this was for me.

"No." She plucked a petal from a hibiscus blossom and let it flutter to the ground. "I don't want to talk."

"Great . . . Not that you don't want to talk. Great that you don't have to . . . that you're fine, I mean."

Mia's expression was stony, and it was like looking in a mirror at my younger self. I remembered being sixteen and angry. And I'd been so angry. At myself, at Mom, at Dad too, sometimes. Most of the time I'd been able to keep it in, and after a few years that anger had cooled. But it frightened me, seeing it in Mia. I knew how anger like that could tear you up inside. *See?* I thought to Beth. *This is why I didn't want to do this. I'm supposed to be the distraction.*

I was relieved when Kitty and Greyson returned. They skipped around the patio humming the *X-Files* theme song.

"I take it your dad talked to the event planner," I said.

"Yes, he did," Greyson replied, stopping mid-skip. "And she said *of course* we could stay. I'm pretty sure she has a crush on my dad. There are a *lot* of women who look at him like this." She opened her mouth and fluttered her eyelashes as she pretended to drool, then clamped her mouth shut again. "Obviously I couldn't see her, but her voice sounded exactly like that."

I hoped my voice didn't sound like whatever the equivalent of that face was. "Are you sure these women aren't having strokes?"

"Maybe they're having strokes because they're in love with him," Kitty said, winking at me.

I ignored Kitty and turned to Greyson. "Did your dad say what day?"

Greyson scrunched her forehead. "Right. Sorry. I forgot. He wants to know if two weeks from tomorrow is all right. At least I think that's what he said. He wasn't sure if you wanted to do it during your staycation—well, he didn't call it a staycation, but I think he should've. Anyway, the castle doesn't have events that night, and Dad says there's no charter the next day."

It wasn't as if I had any plans besides hanging out with Mia and Kitty. "Two weeks from tomorrow it is, then."

Twelve

TWO WEEKS LATER, MIA, KITTY, AND GREYSON PILED INTO MY
car, and the four of us watched seagulls fight over a piece of bread in the
condo parking lot as we waited for Nina to arrive. Alex had already left
for Miami to get a drink with a friend (the flirty event planner?), so our
mini road trip down to Coral Castle was to be a girls-only affair. Kitty
and Greyson narrated the seagull fight as if they were sports announc-
ers, making Mia and me laugh so hard we were wheezing.

When Nina finally appeared, she yanked open the passenger door
and hurled herself into the seat. "You're not allowed to have fun without
me," she said.

"Only ten minutes late. That's pretty good for you," I said.

Nina sighed. "I am *so* ready to have you back at work, Josephine. I'm
tired of cleaning toilets all by myself."

I'd enjoyed the time off with Mia and Kitty, and Greyson too. The
girls and I had spent our days traipsing around South Florida. Inter-
spersed between beach days, we'd gone window-shopping on Worth
Avenue, visited the turtles at the Gumbo Limbo Nature Center, and
taken an airboat ride through the Everglades. Alex joined us on his days

off. But when he had to work, he'd find us as soon as he returned home and listen to the girls describe whatever adventure we'd had that day. The five of us—six if Nina dropped by—ate dinner together every night, sometimes at my place and sometimes at Alex's. Our evenings were loud, messy, and filled with laughter. I tried not to think about how this was temporary. How it would all go away once the girls were gone.

Nina rolled down her window and slapped the roof of my car. "Let's get this show on the road."

"You're the one who was late, and besides, we're eager to find out which of those seagulls will become the featherweight champion of the condo." My gaze dropped to Nina's waist, where something shiny caught my eye. "What is *that*?"

Nina grinned at me, looking even more hyped than she'd been a moment ago. "What, this?" She pointed to the pink-sequined fanny pack strapped around her waist. "It's my fun bag."

"Your fun bag."

"Yes, my fun bag."

"Do I even want to know what's in there?"

Nina rattled the contents of the fanny pack. "Tampons and Drama-mine. In case you can't fall asleep. The Dramamine, not the tampons."

Mia poked her head up beside Nina. "Did you bring it?"

I glanced at Mia as I backed out of the parking space. "Bring what?"

"Did I bring it? *Psh*. What kind of question is that?" Nina dug through her duffel bag and passed a shirt to Mia.

Mia squealed, a sound I hadn't heard her make all summer, and put the shirt on over her tank top. "This is epic. Thanks, Nina."

"I'm wearing one too." Nina turned to me. "Don't worry, Jo, I have a special shirt for you. And two extras for Kitty and Greyson. I even brought one for Alex."

"What kind of special shirt?" I wasn't sure I wanted to know, but since it involved me in some way, I had no choice but to ask. We stopped at a red light, and Nina stretched out what I'd thought was a normal gray

T-shirt. "*I'm just a good mom with a hood playlist*," I read aloud. "I don't get it."

"Yours is my favorite, Mia," Nina said.

"What does it say?" Kitty asked.

"*This mom runs on wine and Amazon Prime*." Mia sighed into her seat. "Friggin' perfect."

"Sorry, but I'm a little confused," I said. "Can someone enlighten me? And what's my shirt say?"

"Nina has a collection of sassy mom T-shirts," Mia explained.

"Whenever I see one, I just have to buy it," Nina said.

Of course she did. I should've known Nina wouldn't own a boring gray shirt. "Why?"

Nina shook her head, setting her unicorn earrings swirling. "That's the wrong question, babe. The question is why not?"

"You mean *wine* not," Mia said, earning herself a high five from Nina.

"To answer your second question," Nina said, "yours says *Tired as a mother*, because you need to sleep in a castle. I brought *Messy bun and getting stuff done* for Kitty and *Momming is my cardio* for Greyson. And for Alex *Boo boo healer, kiss stealer, snack dealer*, because he always has snacks, and, you know, the kissing thing."

"What kissing thing?" Greyson asked.

I shot Nina a glare.

"Because he's a chef," Nina said. "Chef's kiss." She brought her fingers to her lips and tossed them at me.

By the time we'd made it to I-95, everyone had their sassy mom tees on, including me (Nina had shoved it over my head at a red light). So far, everything was going according to plan: the packing, the extra twenty minutes I'd built in to account for Nina inevitably being late. Even the traffic was lighter than usual. The five of us sang girl power anthems with the windows down, letting the wind mess up our hair. And when we'd finished singing, Greyson talked nonstop, making us laugh with her stories of all the strange things she'd seen in Miami. But as soon as we pulled off the turnpike, she went quiet, and that was when the chaos began.

"Uh, Aunt Jo," Kitty said.

I turned onto US 1, less than two miles from our destination. "Yeah?"

"I think something's wrong with Greyson."

I glanced at Greyson through the rearview mirror. She had her eyes shut and her arms wrapped around her middle. Maybe it was nothing, but what if it wasn't? What if her appendix burst? What if it was a brain aneurysm? "Greyson, are you all right? Can you talk to me?"

"Carsick," she mumbled. "It happens . . . a lot."

My death grip on the steering wheel relaxed. Carsick, of course. Why did my mind always jump to the worst-case scenario? "We're almost there. Two minutes."

We were right at the turn into Coral Castle when we hit a red light. Greyson moaned, and Nina unzipped her fun bag. "Should I give her one of these?" She held up the bottle of Dramamine.

I shook my head. "Better ask Alex first. Aren't those the ones that make you drowsy?" I turned to Greyson. "We're right here. We've only got—"

But I didn't finish my sentence, because at that exact moment, Greyson projectile vomited and everyone screamed. It splattered onto my face, my hair, my shirt, and covered the center console of the car. Greyson lowered her face into her hands and started to cry. Nina opened my glove box and passed me a stack of napkins, and I wiped my face hurriedly.

"The light's green!" Nina cried.

I whipped into the empty gravel parking lot and braked with a jolt. Springing from my seat, I raced around to the back of the car. Mia and Kitty had already gotten out, and I looked in at Greyson, who had her face buried in her hands.

"Are you all right?" I asked.

She shook her head. "I'm . . . so sorry about your car and . . . your face. I didn't mean to."

"I know you didn't, and both my car and face are fine." I tried to ignore the massive amount of puke in my car, not to mention the smell of it all over me. "Come on, let's get you cleaned up."

Greyson slid over, and I helped her to her feet.

"I . . . I think I . . . ," she began, then clamped her mouth shut.

I pulled her to the bushes lining the parking lot and held her chin-length hair at the back of her head, steadying her as she threw up again, once, then twice, and then a third time.

"Think you got all of it?"

Greyson nodded, and I let go of her hair and tucked it behind her ears.

Greyson and I sat side by side on the curb. I scanned the parking lot, wiping as much of the puke from my hair as I could with the napkins from my glove box. Nina and the girls stood together at the back of my car, but there was no sign of Alex. He was supposed to meet us here right at seven. I had no problem taking care of Greyson, but I didn't know what Alex would do if he were here.

Just as I took out my phone to call him, headlights washed yellow light over us, and his minivan pulled into the parking lot. It was too dark to make out his face through the window, but he must have seen us, because as soon as the engine shut off, he was out of the van and jogging over.

"What's going on?" he asked. He sank into a crouch in front of Greyson, his eyes anxious when they met mine.

"Carsick," I said.

Alex nodded, then turned to Greyson. "How are you feeling, Grey?"

I backed away to give them some privacy, and Alex's eyes widened when he noticed the state of my appearance. "I see you were in the splash zone."

I stared down at myself. "Ah, yeah. Fortunately, I have another shirt. I do not have other hair, but it's nothing some water can't fix. Which I'm going to take care of right now."

Leaving Alex with Greyson, I met Mia, Kitty, and Nina at the back of my car.

"Is Greyson okay?" Kitty asked.

I stripped off my shirt, the one beneath it thankfully clean. "She'll be fine, but I think she's embarrassed. Maybe you two should go check on her. You can tell her about the time you tested the bounds of the word 'unlimited' at Olive Garden." The girls sprinted off, and I turned to Nina. "Sorry about the shirt."

Nina dismissed my apology with a wave of her hand. "Now it's officially a mom shirt. Nothing says 'mom' like getting puked on."

"I guess so." I ducked down to look into the back seat of my car and sighed. "This is . . . not good. How am I supposed to clean this?"

"There's a CVS down the street. It'll be quicker if we walk there. We can get water, trash bags, some paper towels. I'll tell Alex to keep an eye on the girls."

We set off for the CVS when Nina returned. Even at dusk the July heat was stifling, and as Nina and I waited at the crosswalk, I realized she hadn't spoken since we'd left the parking lot. She stood beside me, staring straight ahead and chewing on her lip. The Walk sign appeared, and I looped my arm through hers, hoping she'd loosen up, but when we made it to the sidewalk and she still hadn't said anything, I couldn't take the silence anymore.

"Nina, what is it?" I asked.

Nina opened her mouth, then hesitated. Strange. Nina never held back what she was thinking. "You're going to be upset."

Even stranger. "Seriously? You've never cared about upsetting me before."

She gave me a sidelong glance as we neared the glowing red sign of the CVS. "I've been . . . getting this feeling around Alex."

Here we go, I thought, sure my suspicions about her and Alex were about to be confirmed. I tried to keep it light and nudged her with my elbow. "Gross, Nina, I don't need to hear about your lady boner."

"God, Jo, not like that."

Now I was really worried. Since when did Nina not find boner jokes funny? "Okay. What kind of *feeling* do you get around him? Indigestion?"

We pushed through the doors of the CVS and stepped into searing fluorescent lights. Nina moved in the direction of the household items and pulled me into the aisle. She stopped, tucked a roll of paper towels under her arm, and faced me full on.

"I'm only going to bring this up once. And before I say anything, know I'm only doing this because I love you."

"Okay . . . ," I said, wondering what I'd done that Nina needed to have this big talk with me.

"I know I've teased you a lot about Alex," she said. "And it was a joke at first, but I think there may be something *more* between you two."

Nina paused, her eyes hesitant, and I examined the rolls of toilet paper on my right. "I don't know what you mean."

"Really, Jo? You have no idea?"

Of course I knew where she was going with this, she'd been teasing me about it all summer. But that was a joke, like she'd said. I didn't like this serious version of Nina. What did she expect me to say?

Nina looked me up and down, then grabbed a second roll of paper towels. "You're both clearly into each other."

"You're seeing things," I said. "He told us he doesn't date. And even if he did, you've got the wrong girl. If he's so into me, why was he so interested in you coming to the Zefron-a-thon, huh? Maybe you're projecting *your* feelings onto me."

"Don't be ridiculous. You know I'd never date someone who drives a minivan. I can't tell you why he cared so much about me tagging along. What I do know is he can't take his eyes off you. You know what he talks about when I'm on service? You. And I hate to break it to you, Jo, but you've been sending out some strong signals too. And I know—"

I laughed. "Now who's being ridiculous? The only *signals* I'm familiar with are the deckhands' arm signals for anchoring, not exactly seductive." I swung my arm right, then left, then above my head. "See? I'm not even good at them."

"Can you stop joking around for a minute and let me finish?"

I let my arm drop to my side. "Fine, go ahead."

"You say you're done with love. And if you truly want to be single forever, that's fine. I support that. It's me, after all. But I don't think you really want to be alone. I think you're scared. And I know Alex says he isn't into relationships, but I'm not so sure that's a hard-and-fast rule."

I stared at her. Okay, sure, I was *attracted* to Alex. According to Greyson, many women were. But that didn't change anything. "We're just *friends*," I said. "Good friends. And I'm not scared. Or alone. I have you, don't I?"

"You know what I mean." Nina grabbed my hand, her expression so sincere I had to look away. "I normally wouldn't butt into your love life, you know that. But Alex isn't like Peter. Whatever's between you two is . . . different."

"You're right. Because we're just *friends*. I don't know what's gotten into you, but this is ridiculous."

"Is it? Because every time you're around him you're laughing. I don't remember that with Peter. And if you *do* have feelings for Alex, I think you should give it a shot. I know it's scary to bring someone into your life when nothing's guaranteed. I know Peter really fucked you up, and you've lost so much already—your dad, Samson—"

"Nina, stop." I pulled my hand from hers. "Just leave me alone, okay?" Talking about Shitty Peter was bad enough, but she'd gone too far bringing up Dad and Samson. Blood rushed in my ears, drowning out the pop music playing softly overhead.

Between Nina's unicorn earrings, the sequined fanny pack, the sassy mom tee, and the smell of vomit in my hair, I wasn't sure if I wanted to laugh or scream. Nina nodded and walked down the aisle away from me and out of sight.

Fine, leave, then, I thought. I found the snack and beverage aisle, my breathing shallow and fast. Suddenly, everything in this CVS reminded me of Samson. The Mountain Dew Code Red Beth wouldn't let him drink, but which I kept stocked in my fridge whenever he came to visit. The sweet-chili-flavored Doritos the girls didn't like, but he did. Samson, who should be here tonight, jumping out from behind one of those ridiculous statues at Coral Castle to scare his sisters. I wrenched open a refrigerator door and grabbed as many water bottles as I could carry. I needed to get out of here as quickly as possible, whether or not Nina came with me.

I made my way to the registers, spotting Nina's dark ponytail flicking behind her. At the sight of her, my anger dissipated. How had my night gone from singing Beyoncé to fighting with my best friend in a CVS? She was only trying to help. And was she really wrong? About my feelings for Alex anyway?

Nina set the paper towels on the counter along with a car air freshener, some Lysol wipes, and a box of trash bags. When I caught up to her, I dumped the water bottles beside the other items. "I'm sorry."

Nina looked at me, and I was relieved to see she wasn't angry, only sad. "Me too."

We paid for our items, quiet until we left the CVS and started the walk back to Coral Castle. The night was growing darker around us. Streetlamps kicked on, flooding the sidewalk in yellow light.

"I'm sorry for getting so upset," I said.

"I shouldn't have pushed."

I kept my eyes on the sidewalk, counting the cracks as we walked. "It's only . . . I don't know how I feel about anything right now. Not really. I haven't let myself think about Alex in that way because it feels wrong. Not that *he* feels wrong. I can't go falling in love, or whatever, when Beth is . . ." I shook my head, unable to finish the thought. "I'm not making sense, am I?"

"You're making sense. But do you really think your sister would be upset about you having something good in your life?"

"I don't know."

"I think you do."

Nina was right that I couldn't imagine Beth being upset. But this wasn't about *Beth*. It was about me. How could I forgive myself for moving on with my life when Beth was stuck? How could I leave her behind?

We dropped the subject as we neared the entrance to Coral Castle. The girls sat on their bags and talked about alien conspiracy theories, and Alex stood nearby, expression serious as he stared at the limestone walls.

"Finally," Mia said when she saw us. "Alex won't let us go in without you guys. What took so long?"

"We needed supplies." I held up the bags on my arms.

"I'll clean your car," Alex said. He took the bag of cleaning supplies and walked away before I could get a word out.

Nina leaned in close to me and sniffed. "We need to deal with your hair situation."

I handed Nina two bottles of water and flipped my head down, yelping when she poured the frigid water over me. As she rinsed my hair, Mia and Kitty filled us in on everything we missed in the fifteen minutes we'd been gone, explaining how the event planner, a blond woman in an *I believe in aliens* T-shirt, had come to unlock the gate soon after we'd left.

"She did that forearm-touching thing to Greyson's dad," Mia said. "Which means she only wants one thing."

Greyson, back in her usual good humor, smacked Mia on the arm. "That's my *dad* you're talking about! You're gonna make me hurl again."

I was pretty sure she was joking, but took a step back, just in case.

Alex returned carrying a backpack on each shoulder and wheeling a cooler behind him.

"Yes!" Nina raised her hands to the sky. "I knew I could count on you to bring food."

"That's not all," Alex said. He let one bag drop from his shoulder and dug through the other, pulling out three thermoses. "Coffee." He passed one to me and one to Nina. "Yours is decaf, Jo. It's for psychological comfort only."

I took a sip and closed my eyes. "I'll give you this, you make a good cup of coffee."

Alex shook his head at me. "I'm a Michelin-starred chef who has cooked you literally dozens of meals, and you compliment me on my drip coffee?"

"What? I didn't say your other food wasn't good. I've just got priorities, and coffee is one of them."

We hauled our bags through the limestone gate of Coral Castle, which was even weirder in person than it had seemed online. Other than a small tower in one corner, Coral Castle was an open-air courtyard filled with bizarre statues and furniture, all made from limestone. We set our things in an area called the Grotto of the Three Bears, where limestone chairs circled a rock that had been hollowed out in the center. Nina turned on a camping lantern, and the rest of us unfurled our sleeping bags.

Kitty ran a hand over one of the limestone chairs. "This place is freaky."

Mia grinned at her sister. "I hear it's haunted."

"There's no scientific evidence of the paranormal," Kitty said, taking a step closer to me.

Nina pulled up a map of Coral Castle on her phone. "Ready to check out your castle, Josephine?" She led us around the courtyard, each limestone structure stranger than the last. They included a Florida-shaped table, a limestone barbecue, a bedroom with two beds and a bathtub, and something called the Polaris Telescope. Nina began a ghost story about Edward Leedskalnin, the guy who'd built this place, but I was almost certain the story was inspired by one of her bad Tinder dates. I tried to pay attention as we followed her around the courtyard, but I was worn out from the drive here, my conversation with Nina, and the thoughts about Alex I'd been ignoring for weeks. He and the girls followed Nina, fully immersed in her story, and I took the opportunity to slip away and walked back the way we'd come.

I walked past the Moon Fountain and the Sun Couch and stopped when I couldn't see or hear the others, finding myself in the "bedroom" again. I stretched out on one of the beds and put my arms behind my head to stare up at the sky, but there was too much light pollution to see any stars. Without Nina, Alex, and the girls around, I was ready to face the task of untangling the knot of thoughts cluttering my head.

I asked myself the question I'd been avoiding: Did I have feelings for Alex? I knew the answer. I'd known it for a long time but kept pushing it away because it would only make things more complicated. Yes, I did have feelings for him. Feelings that were not of the "buddy" variety. I couldn't deny it anymore, at least not to myself. What other explanation was there for the sparks that zipped through me whenever we touched? Or for how I couldn't stop thinking about our kiss from that night at Mitch's. I thought about our easy conversations each morning on the way to work and how he had the perfect playlist for any mood. I thought of the single-minded intensity of his work, and yet how he never took himself too seriously. I thought about how he made me laugh whenever he sang, how he made me laugh all the time. These were not feelings that could be explained away by pheromones.

Follow-up question: Did having feelings for Alex change anything? Just because I had feelings for him didn't mean I was willing to do anything about them, because Nina was right, I was terrified. I didn't want to be alone, but I also didn't want to get hurt. And hurt was the only way this ended—the only way anything ever ended. I wasn't convinced a little bit of happiness was worth the pain. I'd had moments of happiness with Shitty Peter, but being with him had been one of the biggest mistakes of my life. Even if I did want to pursue these feelings for Alex, it took two to tango. And so far, Alex didn't seem interested in dancing.

"There you are," a voice said, startling me from my thoughts. I sat up, spotting Alex with his hands in his pockets a few feet away. He looked unlike himself, with slumped shoulders and a serious demeanor. Did he know I'd been thinking about him? Was he a mind reader? He had catered a psychic event here, after all.

"Hi," I said, trying to get a better look at him, but the shadow of Coral Castle's walls fell over his face.

"You snuck off." He sat on the other limestone bed and stretched out with his hands beneath his head. The bottom of his shirt lifted, exposing a sliver of his lean stomach. I drew my eyes up to his face and settled on my back again. There was hardly any space between us. If we reached out, our hands would touch.

"I'm getting some practice in." I gave the limestone bed a pat.

"Sounds like a good idea," he said, but his tone was devoid of his usual humor.

Had Nina said something about our conversation in the CVS? I didn't think she'd betray me like that, but then again, she wasn't acting like her normal self. And here was Alex about to let me down gently. That would be the end of carpooling, and singing, and our easy friendship, probably. I looked up at the sky, not wanting to see his face when he told me what *great friends* we were. *It's me, not you,* I imagined him saying. Maybe it would even be good for me to hear. Then I could get over these feelings I'd dreamed up about him before they got too serious.

We lay in silence for a few minutes. I wondered why he'd come looking for me if he didn't have anything to say. I kept my breathing shallow and tried not to move. Maybe he'd taken my comment about practicing sleeping to heart.

"Thanks for taking care of Greyson," he said, breaking the silence. "And for not freaking out about the mess in your car and, uh . . . all over you."

I relaxed, though I didn't see why he'd gotten all weird only to thank me for helping his daughter puke in the bushes. "It was nothing, really."

"No." Alex's voice was insistent. "It wasn't."

I'd never heard Alex so serious before, not even when he'd nearly sliced his finger off. I rolled onto my side and traced the lines of his profile with my eyes: the slope of his forehead, the strong line of his nose, the angle of his chin. He turned to face me, his eyes on mine setting off that fluttering in my chest again.

"Greyson being sick makes me anxious. I freak out. Even when I know it's not a big deal."

This surprised me. I'd always thought of Alex as immune to anxiety. "Why?" I asked.

He went quiet. Maybe I'd stepped into overly personal territory again. I was about to apologize, when he spoke.

"I'm assuming you remember what I told you about Greyson's mom leaving."

"Yeah," I said. How could I forget?

Alex sighed and looked up at the sky again. "Greyson was sick when Maggie left. Just some childhood virus. High fever, vomiting, the usual. It was Maggie's week with Greyson, and one night, as I was unlocking my apartment after a long shift at the restaurant, my neighbor came out into the hallway with Greyson in her arms. I was shocked to see her. I wasn't supposed to have her back until the weekend. But Maggie just left her with my neighbor, saying there was some emergency she had to take care of. She didn't tell her where she was going or that Greyson was sick. She didn't even call me." His brow wrinkled as he spoke. I fought the urge to reach out and smooth it with my palm.

"I called Maggie over and over, but she didn't answer. You know the rest—we tracked her down, she said we'd be better off without her. Anyway, when I finally got in touch with her, I asked her what had happened. She said she'd been thinking about leaving for a long time, but when Greyson threw up on her carpet, she realized she was more worried about the carpet than Greyson. It terrified her. That was when she knew she didn't have it in her to be Greyson's mother." He turned his face toward mine, looking at me with an intensity I'd never seen before. "So what you did, it's not nothing to me."

I sat up, needing to move. "That sounds . . . hard." What more could you say to a story like that? "I'm just glad Greyson's okay."

We looked at each other for a long moment, and then Alex stood suddenly, closing the space between us. He sat beside me on the lime-stone bed, and the air between us reminded me of the heat lightning that moved over the ocean on warm summer nights. I tensed, unable to look away from him, wondering what he was about to say or do.

But I didn't get the chance to find out, because Greyson darted out from behind the Florida-shaped table and raced over, zapping all the electricity from the air as she wedged herself between us.

"Hi, Greyson," Alex said, his tone measured.

"I said we were going to the tower!" Nina called. She emerged from the darkness with Mia at her side and looked from me to Alex, no doubt calculating the distance between us. "I have no idea how you've survived the last month, Josephine. These girls are wild."

"But we totally forgot to give Dad his shirt!" Greyson said. "You're going to die laughing, Dad. I'm not sure it'll fit you, though. It might end up like a crop top, which is kind of gross."

"I'm not sure I want to know what you're talking about," Alex said.

I laughed. "Trust me, you don't."

When we returned to the grotto, Nina tossed Alex the shirt she'd brought him. He rolled his eyes when he read it but put it on anyway. He looked ridiculous, but weirdly good too. The shirt stretched over his arms, hugging tight to his torso. Greyson was right, though, it was basi-cally a crop top, not that I minded.

"Only for you would I wear this," Alex said, nudging me with his shoulder. He posed with Mia, Kitty, and Nina for a photo without too much pestering. *Only for you*, I thought, searching his face for a clue as to what he was thinking. But goofy Alex was back, and his face was impenetrable. He reached into the cooler and passed out gourmet s'mores he'd made earlier that day. Apple and chocolate s'mores. S'mores dipped in caramel or rainbow sprinkles. Some even had bacon layered beneath the marshmallow.

"Who knew s'mores could be so fancy?" I said after I'd devoured one of the bacon s'mores.

Mia stretched out on her back beside Greyson and Kitty. "It's kind of romantic, isn't it?"

"Fancy s'mores?" I said, though I knew *exactly* what she was doing.

Mia rolled her eyes. "This place, duh."

"Think about it," Kitty said. She rolled onto her stomach and propped her chin in her hands. "He loved that girl so much he built all this for her."

I unstuck a string of marshmallow that was hanging from my chin. "This place is creepy, and she never saw it. Not exactly romantic. He built all this for love and died alone, so what was the point?"

"I'm with the girls," Nina said. "It's a testament to the power of love. What do you think, Alex?"

I narrowed my eyes at Nina. Were she, Mia, and Kitty in on this together? Part of me hoped this place would awaken some latent psychic ability I didn't know I had so I could send her my annoyance telepathically.

Alex looked thoughtfully at the camping lantern. "It depends. Spending twenty-eight years building a monument for a woman who left you is a little out there. But who's to say his love for her didn't add something to his life even if she couldn't love him back?"

Alex's expression had that intensity again, and I thought about what he'd told me about Greyson's mom. Was that how he felt about her? I knew he didn't trust her, or anyone for that matter, but did a part of him still love her? Was that what he'd come so near me to say? Perhaps he hadn't wanted Greyson to hear. Maybe the real reason he'd been single all these years was because he was waiting for Maggie to come back and stay for good.

"Who gives a crap about love?" Greyson said. "*I* want to know more about the aliens. Do you think they were grays or reptilians? My vote is for reptilians. I saw this YouTube video once about how half our politicians are actually lizard people. At first, I didn't think that made sense, because wouldn't you see them? But the video says they're shapeshifters, so I guess it could happen."

Alex shook his head. "I think we need to reevaluate your internet privileges."

After that the subject of love was forgotten. Once the conversation moved on from debating whether or not reptilians were real, the girls argued over which list item I should tackle next and settled on number twenty-eight—host a dinner party.

Nina rubbed her hands together. "Now this is going to be good."

"Not just *any* dinner party," Kitty said. "A *fancy* dinner party."

"Everyone has to wear the fanciest outfit they can find from a thrift store," Mia added.

"A thrift store?" I said. "I was planning to wear the dress I bought for item ten."

"No." Nina sat up with a look of horror on her face. "Absolutely not. You've worn it to everything this year."

"Because it's a great dress!"

"You need to think about what you're *saying*," Nina insisted.

I shoved a caramel-dipped s'more into my mouth. "I'm saying I'm reliable."

"Nobody wants to attend a reliable dinner party. They want to go to an exciting one."

"Fine. Exciting, thrifty, fancy-pants dinner party it is. Does Saturday night work? Or is that too predictable? Maybe we should have it on a Wednesday! Now that's unexpected."

Nina rolled her eyes and turned to Alex. "Well, whenever it happens, Captain Lean Cuisine over here is going to need some help."

Alex looked behind him with a *who, me?* expression.

Yes, you! I thought.

He rubbed his chin and looked me over. "I don't know. I *guess* I could help you find some recipes, but what do I get out of it?"

"My undying gratitude," I said.

"Nah," he said. "I want a better nickname on the blog. Hot Yacht Chef will do."

I narrowed my eyes at him. "I'd rather use Pinterest. I bet there are better recipes there anyway."

Alex laughed, and I thought about the last time we'd worked together in a kitchen. One minute his hand had been on mine, and the next he'd fled as far away from me as possible. Tonight, it had happened again: a moment of closeness, his face so near mine I thought he'd kiss me, and now he was acting like nothing had happened. I couldn't make sense of him.

I didn't need Alex to find recipes for a dinner party. What I needed was to get Alex out of my head.

Because I knew *exactly* what this was: a recipe for getting my heart broken.

IT WAS PAST ONE IN THE MORNING WHEN THE SIX OF US FINALLY settled into our sleeping bags. The girls had whispered to each other for a long time, while Nina, Alex, and I traded yachtie horror stories. But one by one, the girls fell asleep. Soon, everything was quiet, except for the sounds of the occasional passing car and Nina's soft snores. All those charter seasons made it possible to sleep anywhere, which was usually true for me as well.

But of course I was having trouble falling asleep tonight. My mind wouldn't shut up. The pressure of *needing* to fall asleep to check this item off the list was one problem. But it wasn't the only one. My mind raced, replaying that moment on the limestone beds with Alex, my fight with Nina. I couldn't stop thinking about how she'd said Alex wasn't like Peter or how after tonight, there would only be four items left on the list. Two I was terrified of (getting a tattoo and singing onstage), one made me nervous (hosting a dinner party), and one was impossible (visiting five more countries). After what felt like hours, I sat up and grabbed Nina's fun bag. Maybe I really did need some Dramamine. I undid the zipper as quietly as I could and slipped out the bottle, inspecting it in the light of my phone, groaning when I realized the Dramamine was expired.

"Can't sleep?"

I looked over Nina and spotted Alex sitting on his sleeping bag.

"Yeah." Though we'd turned off the camping lantern, I could still make out his face in the light leaking in from the city around us. "You?"

Alex leaned back onto his hands. "Have you ever had to make a decision where you're pretty sure you know what the right thing is, but it doesn't feel like the right thing?"

Not what I'd expected him to say. I set the Dramamine back into Nina's bag and wrapped my arms around my knees. The question reminded me of the day I'd moved in with Beth and Mark. I'd known it was what I needed but still felt guilty for leaving my mother.

"Hasn't everyone?" I said.

Alex shrugged.

"Do you want to talk about it?"

Alex looked pained as he ran a hand through his hair. "Yes. But I can't. There are other people involved, and it wouldn't be right for me to tell you about it before I talk to them."

Now I was really intrigued. "I'm guessing this decision is why you can't sleep."

"Good guess."

"I'm sure you'll do the right thing."

Alex sighed. "I hope you're right. But what about you? Why can't you sleep?"

"I keep thinking about the list," I said, omitting the part where I was thinking about *him*.

"What about it?"

"It doesn't matter. It's irrational."

"We're yachties," Alex said. "We've both heard a lot of irrational things. I think I can handle it."

I looked down at my knees, trying to decide whether I should tell him or not. Maybe if I got it off my chest, I'd be able to fall asleep. If Nina were awake, I'd talk to her. But she continued snoring faintly between us.

"The items I have left are the hardest for me. They scare me. Almost everything I put on the list scares me, actually."

"Sleeping in a castle scares you?"

I laughed. "Of course not. I meant cooking, and singing on-stage, and—"

"Kissing a stranger."

"No." I looked up at him. "That one didn't scare me."

There was a beat of silence, and I thought I saw him smile. "Okay, so tell me about the fear."

I hesitated for a moment, wondering if what I was about to tell him would change his opinion of me. Alex was open and sure of himself, but I was none of those things, and the inspiration for my list was evidence of it. "Remember Shitty Peter?" I said.

"Who could forget someone with a name like that?"

I set my chin on my knees. "I kind of lost sight of myself when we were together. Things with Peter were either great or awful. When they were awful, he'd tell me I was crazy or overreacting, and I believed him because I was scared he'd leave. I guess I thought being in a bad relationship was better than being alone." My throat tightened, and I shook my head. "I don't think that anymore, though. I'd rather be alone. Like I said, it's irrational."

"You've lost a lot of people you care about. It makes perfect sense you'd feel that way, even if said person was shitty."

"Yeah, I guess," I said, grateful he could make the connection without my having to spell it out. "I'm sure you've noticed, but I don't let a lot of people into my life. It's why I don't have many friends. Peter charmed me. I still can't believe I fell for it."

"It's not your fault."

"You weren't there. You can't know that."

"But I know you. It could happen to anyone, Jo. Especially someone who cares so much about other people. It says everything about him and nothing about you."

"That's what Nina says."

"She's right," Alex said. "So what does Shitty Peter have to do with the nerves about your list?"

I sighed. "The whole point was to get back the time I'd wasted with Peter. I purposely put things on the list that scared me to make up for being so weak."

"You are the opposite of weak, Jo."

I kept my gaze on my feet, unable to look up at him. "I guess I thought the list would help me figure out what I want from life, or find myself again, as cliché as that sounds. I'm almost thirty. Shouldn't I know who I am by now? Or who I want to be?"

"I don't know," Alex said. "My life now is nothing like I expected it would be when I was twenty-nine. And thank God. I was kind of an asshole."

"You mean you didn't plan on wearing a crop top and sleeping in a creepy castle?"

Alex laughed. "No, that was absolutely in the plan."

I hugged my arms tighter around my knees. "I still don't believe you were an asshole."

"You can ask Greyson tomorrow, she'll tell you."

"No," I said. "I don't need to know the old Alex."

He didn't say anything, and I was reminded of the night we'd met and how I'd been drawn to him from the start. If I hadn't kissed him, would we still have found our way to this moment?

"Can I ask you something?" I said.

"Of course."

"The night we met at Mitch's, right before Nina ran off, you were in the middle of saying something. I wanted to know what you were going to say."

"Refresh my memory."

"You said something like *Florida Girl, you are* . . . and then you got cut off. I was just wondering what—"

"Unexpected," Alex said. "You're unexpected. Which I think turned out to be true. What did you think I was going to say?"

Unexpected. What did that mean? "I don't know," I said. "*Florida Girl, you're crazy* or something like that."

Alex shook his head. "No. I didn't think that."

We looked at each other in the dark, and just like when he had his hand on mine in the galley, the urge to kiss him swept over me, strong as a rip current.

And then Nina let out a loud snore. Alex fought to hold in a laugh and glanced at his phone. "It's late," he said. "You better try to get some sleep if you're going to check this one off the list."

"Hopefully the ghost of Edgar Leafskin will help me fall asleep."

"I think you mean Edward Leedskalnin."

"Whatever. You knew what I meant."

Alex settled down onto his sleeping bag, and I stretched out on mine. I closed my eyes and wrapped my mind around the flicker of happiness within me, the tug of sleep finally pulling me under.

Thirteen

꩜

WORLD THRIFT WAS THE LARGEST THRIFT STORE IN SOUTH
Florida, and therefore Nina's favorite. She'd dragged me around the giant warehouse to search through racks of used clothing more mornings
than I could count. Though the building was nondescript, the clothing
inside was arranged by color, rainbows as far as the eye could see. In the
middle of the open floor plan was the furniture section, and on the opposite wall from the entrance were shelves of seemingly random items.
A few years ago, Nina had found a meat slicer and insisted on buying it.
She kept it on a shelf in her living room, and when I'd asked her why she
never used it, she'd looked at me blankly and said, *It's a statement, Josephine.* Stating what, I hadn't bothered to ask.

Today we stood before a wall hung with formal wear: floor-length
evening gowns, puffy-skirted prom dresses, and one deflated-looking
wedding dress. Nina pinched the lace of the wedding dress between her
fingers and scowled.

"Absolutely not," she said, shoving it aside.

"You mean to tell me that Nina Lejeune, self-professed hater of love,
doesn't want to show up to my dinner party in a wedding dress?"

Nina inspected a mermaid-skirted dress and snorted. "Ha. Funny, Jo. If I remember correctly, you're a supposed love hater too."

"I don't hate love." I passed by a neon-green prom dress that reminded me of Alex's running shorts. "It's just easier to be single." After examining a sequined emerald dress from the rack, I held it out to Nina. It shimmered in the overhead lights. Floor-length and with a plunging neckline, it easily outshone everything I'd seen that morning.

"Your size?" Nina asked.

I checked the tag and nodded.

"Does it smell okay?"

I took a hesitant sniff. "It smells like a thrift store."

"Take it. Trust me, that's the best you can hope for. You don't want to know the smells I've had the misfortune of smelling in here." She wrinkled her nose and continued browsing through dresses.

I draped the emerald dress over my arm, relieved to have one less thing on the to-do list for the dinner party.

When we got to the end of the formal wear, Nina sighed. "I'm heading up front to see if Butch has anything special in the back. He knows what I like."

Dress in hand, I searched for Mia and Kitty and found them in the blue hues of the jacket aisle. Kitty held a yellow dress I was pretty sure was a Halloween costume. Mia didn't have a dress at all. When I reached them, she had one arm into the sleeve of a denim jacket.

"You're planning to wear a denim jacket to a fancy dinner party?"

Mia rolled her eyes. "It's not for the party, obviously."

"It looks good on you. You should get it."

Mia slipped out of the denim jacket and held it out in front of her. She bit her lip, and the excitement faded from her face. "Never mind. I don't want it after all."

"Are you sure?" It really did look good on her.

"Yeah, I'm sure." She put it back on the hanger.

I was tempted to ask her again but didn't want to press the issue. We were in public, and I didn't want to trigger a meltdown in case this was a grief thing.

"Well, don't forget to get something for the dinner party," I said. "Do you think we should find something for Greyson?" We'd planned on her tagging along, but Alex had texted late last night saying they had *a family thing to take care of*. Mia and Kitty shrugged, and I told them to pick something out, just in case.

Once Mia had chosen a black-fringed flapper dress for herself and a knee-length silver prom dress for Greyson, we brought our items to the front of the store and checked out. Nina waited for us by the entrance, her purchase hidden in an opaque garment bag.

I looked down at the grocery bags the cashier had given me and the girls. "Why do you get the nice bag?"

Nina shrugged. "Butch loves me."

"What did you get, Nina?" Kitty asked.

Nina clutched the bag to her chest. "It's a surprise, of course. I can't show up to a dinner party with everyone knowing what I'm wearing. Where's the fun in that?"

AN HOUR BEFORE THE DINNER PARTY, I OPENED THE CONDO door, and smoke poured out into the parking lot. I waved it away, my eyes watering, and spotted Alex.

"Thank God, you're here," I said. I grabbed his hand and pulled him after me into the kitchen, where Mia and Kitty fanned at the open oven with takeout menus.

Everything had been fine until about five minutes ago. I'd checked and double-checked each recipe, measuring ingredients with painstaking patience. I'd spent a good half hour standing around, trying to figure out which dish needed to go in the oven when. How did Alex do this every day? And so quickly? But after the initial stress, things had been going well. Near perfect, actually. I'd had a glass of wine and listened to a little music, feeling like Rachael Ray as I salted a pot of boiling water for deviled eggs. Everyone would be impressed by my cooking, I'd thought, even Alex and Ollie. But everything was ruined now. I'd burnt the main dish to a crisp and didn't have a plan B. I couldn't feed a party of nine on deviled eggs and a salad. The only thing Alex and Ollie would be impressed by was my incompetence.

Alex examined the still-smoking baking dish, but I couldn't look at the charred, inedible mess that was supposed to be truffle chicken and potato gratin.

"Think I can pass this off as blackened chicken?" I said.

Alex winced, prodding it with a fork. "You really weren't kidding when you said you couldn't cook."

Yup, I'd definitely impressed him with my incompetence. "I swear I set a timer. I don't know what happened."

"We can fix this," Alex said.

I nodded to the baking dish. "You can fix that?"

"No. That's beyond help. But we can still save the dinner party. I'll be right back." He clapped his hands together and sprinted from the condo.

"He's come to your rescue, Aunt Jo," Kitty said.

"How romantic," Mia added.

I turned to where the girls sat at the dining room table and looked from one mischievous face to another, realization dawning on me. "I did set the timer, didn't I? Did you two do this?"

"No," Mia and Kitty said at the same time. Mia held my stare, revealing nothing, but guilt twitched at Kitty's lips.

I closed my eyes, unable to look at either of them. The skinny-dipping was one thing, but this was out of hand. They could have burned my condo down, and for what? So Alex could come to my rescue? When I opened my eyes again, even Mia looked a little frightened. But Nina, Captain Xav, Ollie, and Belva would be here in fifty minutes. A brief lecture would have to do.

"I'll give you the benefit of the doubt and assume you were trying to help me. Help I have zero need for, by the way. Whatever fantasy you've cooked up about me and Alex needs to fall out of your heads. The only thing you've managed to do is make me look completely incompetent."

Kitty's face fell, and tears sprang to her eyes. I sighed, holding back everything else I wanted to say. I already had one mess on my hands; I didn't need another.

"Let's get ready at Greyson's," Mia said, bumping shoulders with her sister.

"I think that's a great idea." I pinched the bridge of my nose and watched them leave. These girls, whom I loved more than anything in the world, could be a real pain in the ass sometimes.

Alex returned a few minutes after Mia and Kitty left, and I did a double take when he walked in the door. He'd changed out of his usual shorts and T-shirt and into a tux that fit him perfectly. His hair was combed back, the tousled waves neat for once, and his face smooth, as if he'd shaved that morning.

"That definitely didn't come from a thrift store," I said.

Alex followed me to the kitchen. "You won't tell anyone, will you?"

"No," I said. I pulled at the hem of my T-shirt. Nina had bought it for me from a clearance rack in a Bonaire tourist shop a few years ago. On it was a shark in a Santa hat eating a scuba diver. A word bubble coming from its mouth read, *It's Beginning to taste a lot like Christmas! Bonaire, Dutch Antilles.* "But I feel a little scrubby now. Maybe I ought to change too."

"That's not what you're wearing tonight?" Alex said. "I'm a little disappointed. You'd make an excellent novelty T-shirt model." He flashed a grin and set a reusable shopping bag on the counter. Between the tux and the smoke, I could hardly breathe and considered fanning myself with one of the takeout menus.

"I won't have time to change," he explained. "Where's your apron?"

"I don't have one."

"Really?"

"Really."

"Well I know what I'm getting you for your birthday now. I'll just have to be extra careful not to spill anything." He pulled items from the bag and lined them up along the counter: salmon, pistachios, a lemon, spices, Parmesan, a box of orzo, a mound of asparagus.

I stared at the ingredients. This was already looking fancier than my failed chicken, and he'd come up with it on the spot. "What are we making?"

"*I'm* making pistachio-crusted salmon with Parmesan asparagus and lemon orzo. *You're* making deviled eggs and a salad."

"Fair."

He winked and set to work in the kitchen, fluttering through my cabinets and locating pans, bowls, and utensils. I'd seen him move around kitchens before—at his place, at work—but this was different, and not only because my kitchen was tiny, but because it was *my* kitchen, and he was here, in a tux, saving my dinner party. We worked together in silence, our arms grazing when we reached for an ingredient at the same time or swapped places: him to the stove, me to the sink. It was all very distracting, but somehow, I finished the deviled eggs and the salad.

I stood at the edge of the kitchen and watched Alex work, trying to be upset with Mia and Kitty. What was sexier than a man in a tux cooking a fancy dinner with you in a sardine can–sized kitchen?

"Jo?" Alex said, and I blinked.

"Huh?"

"You're doing that staring thing again."

"Oh." I released my lip, not realizing I'd been biting it. "I think I should get ready." I pointed down the hall to my room. "Thanks for saving me."

Alex kept his eyes on me as he sautéed the asparagus, flipping them in the pan without having to look. "I seem to remember you saving my cooking once. Did you really think I'd let you serve Lean Cuisines at a dinner party?"

I let out a breathy laugh. Alex's hair had grown messier as he cooked.

And in that moment, when his almost smile lifted into something real, my fingers ached to brush the hair from his eyes. Eyes that made me think of the first sip of coffee in the morning, or licking brownie batter off a spoon. *Oh God, I've lost it*, I thought, and forced myself to my room before I could say or do something I'd regret.

AFTER WE'D FINISHED COOKING AND SET THE TABLE (INCLUDING a few candles I'd hesitantly lit), Alex hooked his phone up to the TV, and jazz played softly in the living room.

"Artie Shaw," he said, as if I knew anything about it. He'd been quiet ever since I emerged from my bedroom dressed for the evening. *You look beautiful*, he'd said, but I wasn't sure he meant it, because when we stepped into the living room, he sat as far away from me as possible. With the lighting and the music, I kept daydreaming he'd cross the room and kiss me. But he only sat there bouncing his foot up and down as he rambled on about the differences between early jazz and swing music. He kept his eyes on his phone as he talked, hardly looking at me at all.

Captain Xav was the first to arrive, wearing the same suit he always did whenever the guests on the boat invited him to dinner. Belva came soon after, winking at me as she sat beside him on the couch and coyly adjusted the skirt of her jacket dress. How was it that Belva, a woman in her seventies, had more game than I did? Though based on some of her stories, I shouldn't have been surprised.

Mia, Kitty, and Greyson finally returned. They shouted hello, then disappeared onto the patio, probably trying to stay out of arm's reach of me. I scolded Ollie for his informal light-washed jeans and tuxedo shirt when he appeared. Nina showed up fifteen minutes late and barely fit through the door in a ball gown that, with its geometrically structured bodice and a rainbow chiffon skirt, looked like something off a runway and took up nearly half my living room. In each hand she carried a pitcher of Drunken Joeys, my signature cocktail.

I took the pitchers from her. "Not exactly fancy dinner party drinks, but thanks." She waved me away, her chest heaving, and I wondered how tight she'd tied herself into that dress.

The dinner began simply enough. I called everyone to the table, which was actually my kitchen table with a card table pushed against it. Ollie expressed his surprise at my wonderful cooking, and I admitted it was all Alex, except for the deviled eggs and salad. The Drunken Joeys disappeared quickly, so I brought out the wine I'd bought for the occasion. The conversation flowed easily, and even Captain Xav, usually silent at all social events, joined in, telling us about how he'd helped Alex get his first yachting gig. Captain Xav leaned back in his chair and sighed, rubbing at his beard with a hand.

"I took one look at his résumé and told my buddy he was the guy for the job. How could he not hire a guy named Ocean to be a yacht chef?"

"Ocean?" Nina said. "Have you had too much to drink, Cap?" She leaned over to grab his wineglass, but he pulled it from her reach.

"It's his name!"

Alex reddened and shook his head, looking down at his plate.

"It's true," Greyson said. "He thinks it's embarrassing, which it definitely is, so he goes by his middle name. Marla and Tom—"

"Grandma and Grandpa," Alex interrupted.

"*Marla and Tom*," Greyson repeated, "said something about naming all their kids after the magic that surrounded them when they were conceived, so—"

"All right," Alex said, dropping his fork onto his plate. "You are officially no longer allowed to talk to your grandparents without me present."

I pointed my fork at him. "Have you been lying to us about this very important information, Ocean Hayes?"

"Ocean *Alexander* Hayes," Greyson said.

"You knew my parents were hippies," he said. "When I told you there are some weird names out there, I was speaking from experience."

"I was at Woodstock, you know," Belva said, earning herself an impressed glance from Captain Xav.

"You were conceived on a boat, weren't you, bud?" Ollie said. "What're your siblings' names?"

"Summer and River," Greyson said.

"At least my name suits me better than my sister's," Alex said. "Summer is a skiing instructor in Colorado."

Nina held a hand over her heart. "You're kidding."

"One hundred percent serious. My brother, River, is an accountant. No good jokes there."

"I think Ocean is a wonderful name," Nina said. She turned to Ollie. "And Oliver is a perfectly good name too. I don't know why you don't use it."

"Lay off it, Neen."

Nina glared at him, and I sensed the tension between them getting into dangerous territory. I turned to Greyson, hoping to steer the conversation elsewhere. "We missed you at the thrift store this morning."

Greyson, who'd been giggling with Kitty, looked up at me. "Oh, yeah," she said, the laughter draining from her face. "I, uh, wish I could've gone."

Alex stilled and kept his eyes on his plate. So the family thing hadn't been for fun.

A hush fell over the table. Plates were empty, and the energy of the party was fading fast. "Dessert!" I cried, and left for the kitchen after telling Mia and Kitty to help clear the dishes. Fortunately, my guests rallied at the sight of key lime pie.

Alex took a bite and looked up at me. He pointed to the key lime pie with his fork. "Did you make this?"

Busted. "If by 'make this' you mean 'picked it up from the Publix bakery,' then yes."

Smaller conversations broke out around the table. Nina leaned against Ollie's shoulder, the two of them talking in hushed voices. Alex had Mia, Kitty, and Greyson enraptured as he told them about the time his parents had "accidentally" taken them camping at a naturalist resort. I couldn't hear what Belva and Captain Xav were talking about, but both were smiling.

I sat back in my chair, content to watch. Those first two years after leaving North Carolina, I'd fall into bed each night, achingly lonely and missing my family. I still missed my sister and Mark, and the girls when they weren't here, but things were different now. I thought about the trip to Europe I didn't take and was grateful for the screwup that had sent Mia and Kitty here for the summer. As I looked around the table, my heart was filled with more happiness than I'd had in months. My eyes settled on Alex, who was giving the finale to his story and had the girls doubled over in laughter. Maybe Nina was right. Maybe I didn't want to be alone after all.

WHEN OLLIE, NINA, BELVA, AND CAPTAIN XAV LEFT—NINA RATHER drunkenly on Ollie's arm and both tripping over the skirt of her dress— I stood at the doorway and watched them walk across the parking lot. Their laughter echoed back to me, and I rested my head against the doorframe, trying to etch this moment of perfect contentment in my mind. I wanted to remember the warmth spreading from my chest all the way to my fingers (though maybe that was the wine).

When their voices faded, I returned inside and kicked off my shoes, feeling silly in my floor-length gown now that the party was over. Marvin Gaye had replaced the jazz, and I danced my way through the condo. Candlelight cast a dreamy glow on the faces of Mia, Kitty, and Greyson, who dipped their fingers in the wax of an extinguished candle, tapping them along the table once the wax had hardened.

On my way to the kitchen I gave each of them a kiss on the head, Greyson included, counting them in my mind. One, two, three. I'd missed the cadence of that. Always, every summer, one, two, three.

When I took the kids to the store, or the beach, or the zoo. Each night before I went to bed: one, two, three. But this summer it had been one, two, one, two. Off rhythm, off beat, off balance.

I found Alex at the sink. He'd removed the jacket of his tux and loosened his bow tie. The sleeves of his shirt were rolled above the elbows as he washed dishes. His hair was fully disheveled now and had fallen into his eyes. He raised his gaze to mine, and when he smiled, the warmth in my chest spread right through me. So there was something sexier than a man in a tux cooking dinner.

Still dancing, I crossed the kitchen and stood beside him. "What do you think you're doing? Guests don't do dishes."

I tried to push him away from the sink, but he didn't budge.

Alex pulled a plate from the soapy water, watching me as he passed a dish towel over it. "Did you ever think that maybe I like doing dishes? Would you really rob me of one of the few joys I have in this life?"

I took the dry dish from his hands and danced over to the cabinet to put it away. "No one likes to do dishes, Alex. Or is this Ocean talking? I'm sure Ocean *loves* to do dishes."

"Oh no. Ocean hates doing dishes. He likes much more exciting things than Alex."

"Intriguing." I turned to face him. The kitchen was so narrow that when I leaned against the counter, we were barely a foot apart, giving me a marvelous view of his backside.

Alex dried his hands with the dish towel and turned to face me. He leaned against the counter on his side of the kitchen and crossed his arms over his chest, like he always did when he leaned against counters. He did a lot of counter leaning, come to think of it. I drew my eyes from his arms up to the dish towel, which he'd tossed casually over his shoulder. Was he doing this to me on purpose? How was it fair for him to be so easygoing and attractive at the same time? Could he hear how loud my heart was beating? It was practically drumming through my chest as he looked at me.

"You changed the music," I said when the first song ended and another Marvin Gaye song began.

"I did."

"Songs I actually know for once." I grabbed the empty wine bottle from beside me and lip-synched a few lines into it. "My mom loves Marvin Gaye," I explained. *Loved*, I thought. There wasn't much she loved anymore.

"So you like it?"

I shrugged, feeling a little light-headed. "Seems a little suggestive. It makes a person wonder what sort of exciting things Ocean might be into." I froze, clutching the wine bottle tighter. "Did I . . . say that out loud?"

"You did." Alex's eyes darted to the dining room before flicking back to me, and my face grew hot under his gaze. Damn those Drunken Joeys. And the wine. And that tux. All I could think about were my burning cheeks, and the silver in his hair, and how utterly screwed I was, because these feelings for Alex were more serious than I'd realized.

He pushed off the counter and stopped right in front of me. Ducking his head, he looked me in the eye. "Are you tipsy, Florida Girl?"

"N . . . no." I set the wine bottle on the counter, then glanced at the now clean wineglasses drying beside the sink with the pitchers Nina had left behind. "Maybe. Okay, a little."

Alex looked at me for a long moment during which I didn't breathe at all. "Good," he said with a nod. "It's your party. You should be tipsy if you want to be." He pulled the dish towel from his shoulder and dropped it into my hands, his eyes bright with amusement. "Here, you dry."

He stood at the sink again, hands back in the water. *Reel it in, Jo*, I told myself, and stood beside him. Shoulder to shoulder, we fell into a steady rhythm: wash, dry, put away. Neither of us spoke, though it was the loudest silence I'd experienced in a long time.

Mia, Kitty, and Greyson laughed, and Alex shot me a sideways smile as he passed me another plate. He didn't need to say anything, because

I knew exactly what he was thinking: there was no better sound in the whole world. I strained to hear the girls' voices. Their laughter made me want to be in on the joke, to have one more perfect moment.

"You know what I want?" Mia said when the laughter died down.

"What?" Greyson said.

"Red hair."

"Red hair? That's what you want?"

"Yup. But not the natural kind of red. Like fire-engine red."

"It's true," Kitty said. "In that video game, *The Sims,* she made herself with red hair. She also made her crush, Mason, and had them get married and—"

"Kitty! What did I tell you about playing my profiles?"

Alex's shoulders shook with barely contained laughter beside me, making it more difficult to hold in my own.

"You should totally do it," Greyson said. "Why haven't you?"

"Because Mom would kill her," Kitty said. The girls fell into silence, and Kitty spoke again, her voice quieter than before. "Red was Sam's favorite color."

"Duh. Why do you think I want red hair?" Mia said.

My stomach tightened at the mention of Samson. All the warmth of the evening left me. I looked down at the dish towel in my hands, willing myself to keep moving.

I could feel Alex watching me. His hands stilled in the sink, but I kept moving the dish towel in circles over the already-dry plate.

"Do you remember the night he died?" Kitty asked.

"Yeah, of course," Mia said, sounding annoyed.

"I don't remember," Kitty said. "That whole day, I don't remember it. And . . ." Her voice broke, and she paused. Why had Alex stopped washing the dishes? I turned away from him and put the plate in the cabinet. He could see I was fine, really, I was. "I'm starting to forget him too," Kitty continued. "I can't remember what his laugh sounds like. Is that normal?"

"Jo." Alex put his hand on my arm, but I pulled away.

"You don't have to remember it," Mia said. "Just watch his stupid YouTube channel."

"I forgot about that," Kitty said.

My entire body ran cold, and I froze, white-knuckling the counter. Samson had a YouTube channel? Beth had never mentioned it. Did she even know?

"It's just boring gaming stuff," Mia explained to Greyson. "You don't even see his face, but he laughs a lot on it. Here." I glanced at the table and saw Mia pull out her phone.

"Jo," Alex said again, and I shook my head, pressing my lips together to keep them from trembling.

Samson's voice suddenly, jarringly, filled the condo. I let go of the countertop, my chest so tight I could hardly breathe. "The mail. I have to . . . I really better go get it . . ."

I left the kitchen without looking back at Alex. Kitty and Greyson stared at Mia's phone. Mia looked up at me as I passed, but I couldn't make out her expression through the tears blurring my vision.

I pushed my way out of the condo and hiked up the bottom of my dress, running barefoot down the walkway and up the steps to the beach. I opened the gate with shaking hands and didn't stop running until my toes touched the water.

The sand was cool just beyond the ocean's reach, and I sat down near where the turtles had hatched on the night Alex caught me skinny-dipping in the condo pool, hoping the roar of the ocean would overwrite Samson's voice in my mind. But the tide was going out and would only get quieter as the water pulled away. I tried to keep from crying, but a sob broke loose, and once the tears started, I couldn't stop them. I cried harder than I had when Mom called to tell me what had happened, harder than I had at the funeral or when I'd snuck into his room. I cried because I'd been perfectly content standing in the kitchen with Alex. Because up until now, it had been one of the best nights of my life. But how could that be? How could it be possible for my life to become wonderful when he wasn't here?

At the sound of my name, I drew my knees up to my chest, wrapping my arms tightly around my legs. *Alex*. Why had he come here? Couldn't he see I wanted to be alone?

I kept my face turned away from him. "I'm fine," I said when he stopped beside me.

"You don't look fine."

I stretched out my legs and dug my toes into the wet sand, watching a wave flood in. It washed over my toes before falling back into the ocean again. "I needed some air."

"Do you want to talk about it?"

"No." Alex continued to stand there, not speaking. "Can I help you with something?"

"No," Alex said, voice gentle.

I pressed my hands to my temples and squeezed my eyes shut. "I'm sorry. Really, I'm fine. I'll be back inside in a . . ." My voice trailed off as Alex lowered himself into the sand beside me. "What are you doing? I said—"

"That you don't want to talk about it. I won't say a word. Just let me sit with you."

Alex rolled up his pant legs and stretched out his legs beside mine, getting his tux covered in sand. He looked out at the water, and I remembered how Samson and I used to sit like this and watch the sunrise, maybe in this very spot. Emotion caught in my throat again, and I tried to keep it in. I didn't want Alex, or anyone else, to see me like this. But then I heard music. Down the beach the bounce of a flashlight moved toward us—a runner with a radio strapped to their side. As the runner came closer, the music grew louder. The song ended and commercials played, harsh and obtrusive as they hawked Taco Tuesday specials and CoolSculpting fat loss procedures, louder and louder, until the runner passed, and the sound retreated. I started laughing: an uncontrollable, stomachache-inducing laughter. I buried my face in my hands, laughing so hard tears slipped down my cheeks, and in an instant, I went from laughing to weeping.

"It's not fucking fair," I said, my sadness turning to anger as I watched the runner's light fading in the direction of the pier. "It's . . . wrong. I don't understand, Alex. He was here, and then he wasn't. He was fine. He was riding his fucking bike! We were supposed to go to a fucking Marlins game this summer! My sister, she didn't deserve this. And Mia and Kitty, they loved him. They were all so close. Fuck!" I shouted, and closed my eyes, trying to push away the anger, but it wouldn't leave me. "I know I'm just his aunt. I should be getting better by now, right? I have to be there for everyone else. But he was family. Beth and Mark and the kids, they're the only family I have."

Alex hardly moved through the laughter and the crying and the rant-ing. I thought of the closeness that had grown between us and the strange combination of ease and tension I felt whenever he was around. I'd told Nina it was easier to be single. But there was more to it than that. Wasn't it obvious I was too much of a mess to love?

And then Alex wrapped his arms around me. I let him pull me to him, burying my face in his chest. "You're right," he said. "It's not fair. Of course you're still upset."

I cried, taking in the comforting, never-changing smell of him, which only made me cry even harder. If I let this smell and the reassuring sound of his voice shushing into my hair become familiar to me, that meant one day they would be gone, whether by choice or, as Alex would call it, fate. And then what would happen to me? Anyone could be taken in an instant. They could die, or leave, or change. You could spend eigh-teen years together, like Mark and Beth. You could do everything right and still not make it. I thought of my sister and the question I'd wanted to ask her ever since the night Samson died. *Was it worth it? If you'd known what would happen, would you do it again?*

When my breathing was even, I looked up at Alex. His face was inches from mine as he held me. His hands were firm against my back, and as I searched his eyes, full of warmth and kindness, all my excuses for why I couldn't have him fell away. All I could hear was the roar of the ocean, the quiet rhythm of his breath on my cheek. Before I could think, before I could change my mind, I leaned forward, drawing closer as if pulled by a magnet. Alex's arms tightened around me, but he didn't move. His lips were a mere breath away, one more moment, and we'd be—

"Jo," he breathed. He pulled back gently, the smallest of increments, and shook his head. "I don't—"

"Oh, oh my God," I said. I turned away from him. "I'm so sorry." I shrugged off his arms and stood. Alex reached out to grab my hand but only caught air. "I don't know what I was thinking. I'm just so . . ." I pressed my palms to my eyes. How had I read things so wrong? How had I let myself get so close?

"Jo, wait—"

"You've been such a good friend, Alex." I tried to keep my voice steady. "That was a mistake. I didn't mean . . ."

Alex got to his feet. He stepped closer, but I turned away and caught sight of the pool glowing softly up by the condo. If I looked at him, I'd start crying, and what if I said something I regretted? What if I embarrassed myself again?

"Jo, listen—"

I needed to leave before he could try to make me feel better. He'd say it was no big deal, or that he understood, which would only make me feel worse. I felt his hand on my shoulder and pulled away. "I have to go," I said, and ran back up the beach, the wind swallowing the sound of him calling my name.

Fourteen

MIA, KITTY, AND GREYSON WERE STILL IN THEIR DRESSES WHEN I
returned to the condo. The three of them stretched out on the sofa bed,
a bowl of popcorn between them as they watched TV.

"Hey, girls," I said, hoping I could sneak past them and into my room
before they noticed I'd been crying.

"Hey, Aunt Jo," Kitty said without looking up. Mia had lifted her
head as soon as I walked in, staring at me with that same hard look she'd
worn a few weeks ago when I'd asked how she was feeling.

Greyson, always the most energetic of the three, sat up and folded
her legs beneath her. "Where's your mail?"

"What?"

"Your mail. You went to check the mail."

Right. "Uh, it was all junk."

Fortunately, Greyson seemed appeased by this. "That's all we seem
to get too. Did you see my dad? He went to check the mail, too, but he
hasn't come back."

"No," I said. I bent down to put Mia's and Kitty's shoes on the shoe
rack, hoping it would keep the girls from getting a good look at me. "I
must've just missed him."

Greyson opened her mouth, but her phone dinged, and she looked down at it. "There he is." She read the message and rolled her eyes. "He says I have to come home now."

Once Greyson was gone, I excused myself to my room and stood before the mirrored doors of my closet: hair windblown, eyes puffy from crying, legs and dress covered in sand. It was a miracle the girls hadn't said anything about it.

I slipped the thin straps of the dress over my shoulders and looked away from my reflection. The dress fell into a puddle at my feet, and I kicked it beneath the bed. Maybe when I found it in a few months, I could look back on this night without cringing.

Jo, I don't— Don't what? The possibilities were endless. *Jo, I don't want to kiss you. Jo, I don't know what the hell you think you're doing. Jo, I don't like you. Jo, I don't want your face anywhere near mine. Jo, I don't date.* He'd said that before, but then again so had I. Either way, I didn't want to know the specifics of what he'd been about to say. I could guess the gist of it.

I grabbed the first pair of pajamas I could find from my closet, a ratty Navy T-shirt and a pair of faded rainbow-striped sleep shorts. I flopped facedown onto my bed, quieting the loop of Alex's voice saying, *Jo, I don't*, from my mind by staying as still as possible. It was a game I'd started playing after Dad died. Spreading out on my bed, I'd close my eyes and think of each body part one by one, telling it to still. Some days that was the only thing that dulled the constant guilt and ache of missing him. The only thing that kept all those broken pieces inside from puncturing straight through me.

I'd only gotten from my toes to my knees when my door creaked and jolted me back into being. Mia stood in the doorway with her hands jammed into the pocket of her hoodie.

"I need to talk to you," she said.

Now, at my most vulnerable, Mia wanted to talk? I didn't think I had it in me to talk about Samson right now, but what other choice did I have? I couldn't exactly say, *Sorry, I'm not in the mood to deal with your grief.*

"Sure." I patted the spot on the bed next to me.

Mia shook her head. "Outside."

I followed her onto the patio and shut the door behind me. She paced between my chairs with hunched shoulders, hands still in her pocket. I remained on the step and watched, waiting for her to gather her thoughts and say something. She turned and opened her mouth, then shook her head and stalked over to the other chair again.

At this rate we'd be out here forever unless I said something. "What did you want to talk about?"

Mia stopped beside my camellia shrub, drew one hand from her pocket, and flicked at a blossom with her finger. I wondered what argument she was having with me in her head, because she seemed to grow angrier by the second. I could trace it in her face: the downward curl of her mouth, the clench of her jaw. Kitty, she wore her emotions for what they were, but all of Mia's—sadness, guilt, anxiety—came out as anger. When she looked at me again, I realized this was different. This was true undiluted anger. Anger at me.

"Mia—"

"You can't do shit like that," she said, her face sharper than ever.

"Like what?" Did she know what had happened at the beach? And if so, why was she upset about it? Hadn't she and Kitty been pushing me and Alex together all summer?

Mia plucked a leaf from the bush and let it flutter to the ground. "You can't run away from Kitty when she's like that."

Run away from Kitty? "That's not why I left."

"Well that's what it looked like. She already thinks she's a buzzkill, even without your help. You know what she said? She said, *Did Aunt Jo leave because of me?* She was fucking falling apart, and even then, she was thinking about you."

All the breath whooshed out of me. I sank onto the step, too exhausted to hold myself up any longer. Kitty. Sweet, sensitive Kitty. Who'd always been emotional, even before. And who wouldn't be, in her shoes? Especially at thirteen. Suddenly, viscerally, I remembered the feeling of being thirteen, of carrying a grief so big I thought it would tear me in two.

"I'm sorry," I whispered. "I didn't think—"

"Yeah, no duh." Mia turned away from me again. The shadows deepened the angles of her face, making her look older than she was. "You only think about yourself."

I stiffened. How could Mia say that? I'd given up my living room, my entire summer for them. "That's not true, and you know it."

"Then why do you run away? Why did you take down all the pictures of him? Why do you flinch every time Samson comes up? See? There. You did it just now. Why do you always change the subject? How can you act like he never existed? Or do you want us all to forget him?" Her voice cracked, and she let out a frustrated groan, swiping at her tears with the sleeves of her hoodie.

The words stung, but at her tears my anger faded. I stood and took a step toward her, but she hugged her arms to her chest and backed away.

"I haven't forgotten. Of course I haven't." I thought of my garden, the one we were standing in right now, of the list, the one we needed to finish by his/my/our birthday. Didn't Mia see? I was doing everything I could to keep him alive, but there was only so much I could manage without unraveling. "I asked if you wanted to talk."

Mia laughed. "Yeah, and it was obvious you didn't want to. Why would I talk to someone I make so uncomfortable?"

"It's not that. It's only . . . I don't know how to make it okay."

"No shit you can't make it okay. Nothing is okay. Nothing will ever be okay again. And what I have to say, it would only . . ." She paused and shook her head.

I fumbled for words but only came up with the same ones. "I'm sorry."

When Mia stepped out of the shadows, her hands were back in the pocket of her hoodie. The hard lines of her face fell, and she looked like a kid again. "Aunt Jo," she said, her voice smaller than I'd ever heard it. "There's something I didn't say. Something about Samson."

I tried not to flinch at the sound of his name. I tried to keep my face smooth, to shove that urge to run somewhere else. But Mia saw it, of course she did.

The raw pain on her face hardened again. "You know what? Forget it. You wouldn't understand."

She stepped forward, and I hoped she would sit beside me and lay her head in my lap, letting me brush my fingers through her hair like she had a few weeks ago. I could comfort her without words. But instead she pushed past me through the door and into the condo.

I sat alone on the step, thinking of Beth at our father's funeral. She'd only been a year older than Mia was now, and her expression had been broken as we sat side by side in the church pew. At Samson's funeral Beth hadn't cried. She'd looked like Mia had tonight—sharp and dangerous. Afterward, Beth and I sat at her kitchen table. Talking to her that week was a delicate task, like ironing the silk sheets on the boat. "At least it's over," I'd said, referring to the funeral. "It's never over," Beth had said, anger in her face. "You know that." I hadn't bothered to say that wasn't what I'd meant. But there was nothing I could say to help her. My words could only hurt.

And now my silence had failed Mia and Kitty. How could I make them see that they weren't what made me uncomfortable? It was me, my words, always the wrong words. How could I explain that I'd only make things worse? Or that sometimes, all you could do was close your eyes and stay as still as possible. That the only thing that helped was tricking your mind into not existing for a while.

It was only when I crawled into bed and turned off the light that I thought about Alex again. And more specifically, that we had work the next day, which meant carpooling. No way in hell was I getting in his van and enduring twenty minutes of humiliation. I sent him a text saying I needed to go into work early and would drive myself. I knew he'd see through it, but I hoped he'd let it be.

I set my phone on the nightstand and turned to face the wall. If he texted me back, I didn't want to read it. Now I could see everything I'd gotten wrong. And not just about his feelings for me, but mine for him. They couldn't be real. They were only another distraction, like finishing the list. A distraction that had backfired in spectacular fashion. I closed my eyes, pushing away thoughts of him, and Mia, and Kitty, and Samson, and Beth. Instead, I thought my way into stillness from my toes up to my scalp, until finally, I fell asleep.

AS SOON AS NINA ARRIVED ON DECK THE NEXT MORNING, I dragged her into the master suite and collapsed onto the bed, covering my face with my hands.

"If you're trying to seduce me, it's working, but you could at least give me a heads-up first," she said.

I peeked between my fingers to glare at her.

Nina sank onto the bed beside me. "What's going on, babe?"

What wasn't going on? I'd gone from having one of the best nights of my life to one of the worst in a single hour. The confrontation with Mia . . . I couldn't tell Nina about that. If I did, I wouldn't make it through the day. But I had a more immediate situation to take care of, and Nina was the only one who could help.

"I have to quit."

Nina snorted. "Excuse me?"

"I can't show my face here ever again." I rolled away from her and crossed my arms over my chest. "And it's your fault, by the way."

Nina stretched out beside me on the bed. "I'm guessing this has something to do with Alex. Excuse me, *Ocean*."

I squeezed my eyes shut and nodded.

"All right, what happened? Which body part of his am I chopping off?"

I looked up at the ceiling, trying to get the image of Alex pulling away from me out of my head. "Last night after you left, I may have . . . tried to kiss him." Nina didn't need to know about everything that had happened: Samson's YouTube channel, the crying. That would open an entire part of me I couldn't deal with right now.

"You *tried* to kiss him?"

"And he rejected me."

"What?" The bed shook as Nina bolted upright. She paced the room with her hands on her hips, then halted, her unicorn earrings swinging against her cheeks as she faced me. "He did *what?*"

"Don't make me say it again."

She shook her head. "I don't understand. He's clearly in love with you."

"He's clearly not."

Nina sighed and sat at the foot of the bed. "Well, I hate him again. And you aren't quitting the boat. The obvious solution here is to duct tape him to a table covered in plastic wrap, stab him in the heart, stuff his body into a heavy-duty biodegradable trash bag, and dump it into the oceanic trench off the coast of the Bay Harbor Islands."

I stared at her. "That is oddly specific."

"I've watched a lot of *Dexter*," she said. I laughed, and the flicker of a smile appeared on Nina's face. "I know he's a chef and is good with knives, but I'm chief stew, and I'm good with party supplies."

"Stop trying to make me laugh."

"I'm serious! Curling ribbons isn't the only thing I can do with scissors." She mimed opening and closing a pair, then jabbed them at an invisible Alex.

I thought of all we had to do that day. Preparing the boat for the guests, greeting them, making drinks, ferrying food from the kitchen to the table, and cleaning, a lot of cleaning. "Don't be too hard on him. It isn't his fault."

Nina raised an eyebrow at me. "Uh, if he can't see what a catch you are, then yeah, it's his fault. If you weren't already filling the role of best friend, I'd be all over that."

I rolled my eyes. "Please, I'm totally not your type."

"Chop that beautiful blond hair of yours into a layered bob and maybe you would be."

"Just play nice. He told us he didn't date. I let you, and Mia, and Kitty, and pheromones get in my head. I'll be fine. It was only a teeny, tiny, totally not serious crush. A distraction."

Nina raised both eyebrows at me then. "If you say so." She took my hand, beaming at me like a proud parent. "I'm glad you took my advice, putting yourself out there and all."

"A lot of good that did me." I thought about our fight in CVS and how Nina had said I didn't really want to be alone. "I stand by what I said before."

"Which was?"

I squeezed her hand. "I'm not alone. I've got you."

Nina gave me one of her rare full-mouthed smiles. The boat was quiet, especially here on the main deck, and we sat together in silence, both aware the quiet wouldn't last for long.

"I can handle service on my own today," Nina said.

I didn't bother arguing with her. The last thing I needed was to be in another kitchen with Alex. "Don't be a jerk to him, okay?"

Nina stood from the bed and straightened her polo. "I can't make any promises."

EVEN ON A 150-FOOT SUPERYACHT, IT WAS HARD TO AVOID ALEX. As soon as I stepped into the crew mess, there he was, preference sheets spread out in front of him on the counter.

I took a deep breath and walked over to the coffee maker. I needed to act like everything was fine between us. Like nothing had happened. We were coworkers, and neighbors, and, hopefully, still friends.

I pulled a mug from the cabinet, and Alex perked his head up at the sound of it clinking against the counter.

"Oh, hey, Jo," he said. He tapped a preference sheet with a finger. "Captain says we've got picky eaters today. The devil's triangle: gluten-free, dairy-free, meat-free, and"—he glanced at the preference sheet again—"at least thirty-three grams of protein in each meal. Why thirty-three? Why not thirty or thirty-five?"

"You should season their food with protein powder," I said. I leaned against the counter and sipped my coffee, hoping I looked casual and not at all like someone whose heart was aching in her chest right this very minute. Distraction, my ass. Why was I constantly lying to myself?

Alex let out a laugh, looking more tired than I'd ever seen him. His hair, instead of stylishly messy, was an actual mess. Dark circles hung beneath his eyes, and there was no trace of that almost smile.

He drummed his fingers across the counter. "Can we talk?"

I watched as steam curled from my mug and pressed up toward the ceiling, then gave him my stew smile. I didn't want him thinking I was angry or hurt, even though I was a little bit of both. I'd told Nina not to be hard on him because it wasn't his fault. But I hadn't imagined everything, had I? Had I imagined the lingering gazes and flirty banter?

"Alex," I said, forcing myself to look at him. "There's nothing to talk about. It was a mistake. I didn't mean anything by it. I was in a weird place last night. I needed a distraction, and you were just . . . there. Too many drinks, I guess. Can we please forget it ever happened?"

Alex looked down at the preference sheets again. "That's what you want?"

I thought of how immediate the hurt and embarrassment had been when he pulled away last night. "Yes. That's what I want."

He rubbed a hand over his cheek, then met my gaze with a nod. "Okay, yeah. Let's forget it ever happened."

I stretched out my hand, like he had at Mitch's on the night we met, when he hadn't pulled back from my kiss. "Friends?"

Alex didn't say anything at first. He stared at my hand, as if weighing his options. Had I made things so awkward we couldn't even be friends? But then he put his hand in mine, that barely there, nearly imperceptible almost smile on his lips.

"Yeah," he said. "Friends."

August

Fifteen

⚓

"HAPPY BIRTHDAY MONTH!" NINA SANG WHEN SHE MET ME DOWN by the water. She plopped into a beach chair, wearing a gray one-piece with a floppy shark's fin between her shoulder blades. "Hydrate me," she said.

I passed Nina a water bottle from the cooler at my feet. It was the first day of August. Hot at ninety degrees, but a perfect beach day. The sky and ocean mirrored each other in color and stillness, blurring the boundary between them. Mia, Kitty, and I had decided to make a day of it. We had fruit and Pub subs in the cooler, a beach umbrella for shade, and plenty of sunscreen.

Nina may have been excited by my upcoming birthday, but everything inside of me shifted as soon as I'd woken up and realized August had arrived. Maybe I was imagining things, but I thought I noticed it in Mia and Kitty too. Since our conversation on the patio, things between Mia and me had gone back to normal again, but August meant a lot of things. My and Samson's birthday. The girls' return to an uncertain home life. Back to school, which I knew both girls were dreading. It meant returning to a clean and quiet condo, which wasn't as appealing as it sounded. I only had twenty-four days to finish the list. Just over three weeks to work up the nerve to sing on a stage, get a tattoo, and figure out how to visit five countries. The girls were still hopeful we'd figure it out, but I'd always known it was impossible.

"So you and Hot Asshole are officially no longer carpooling?" Nina asked.

"I've already told you that's an awful nickname. Just . . . gross. Why can't you call him Hot Work Friend or something? He isn't an asshole."

Nina shrugged. "I think he's pretty gross right now. But also hot. And also a total ass. It's very confusing for me, actually."

"Not reciprocating my feelings isn't grounds for being an asshole, Nina."

"It is in my book."

I ignored her, knowing I'd never change her mind on that one. "But to answer your question, you are correct, we are no longer carpool buddies." I closed my eyes and listened to the sure sound of the waves, trying to push away the embarrassment I still felt about the whole near-miss kiss with Alex. Things were mostly normal between us, but carpooling was one activity I couldn't even pretend to deal with, because what if he brought up *the incident*? I'd have no way to avoid the conversation except to bail out of the van at a red light, and that might ruin my knees, which Nina said were my best feature. *They're just so symmetrical*, she'd said. I didn't know what to make of my symmetrical knees being my best feature. What did that say about the rest of me?

Though I'd been the one to end the carpooling arrangement, part of me was hurt Alex had let it happen. Why didn't he corner me in some part of the boat and promise not to talk about *the incident*? Why couldn't he reassure me that nothing had changed between us? *What about the environment?* I wanted to say. *What about our carbon footprint?* I missed him and his stories of growing up in the RV with his hippie family, of life in New York's restaurant scene, of Greyson's childhood antics. I even missed his playlists, though I hardly knew any of the songs. Now all I had were the same five Top 40 hits on loop and my own thoughts for company. (Spoiler alert: they were not pleasant company.)

"Speaking of Hot Asshole," Nina said. I opened my eyes to find Alex (still hot, unfortunately) and Greyson making their way toward us with beach chairs strapped to their backs.

"Ugh." I slid down in my chair and pulled my wide-brimmed hat over my eyes.

"Pretend you're asleep," Nina whispered.

"It's awful, Nina. I want to be friends with him. I want to pretend nothing happened, but I can't look at him without replaying that moment in my mind."

Nina rested a hand on my shoulder. "You are a beautiful dove any human would be happy to kiss. Perhaps Alex is a Hot Alien? Greyson seems to know a lot about aliens for a human child, and it would explain a lot. Shh, stop talking." She forcibly closed my eyes by passing her hand over my face. "He's almost here. Keep your eyes closed."

I pulled her hand away. "I don't see how pretending to sleep would help."

After dumping her chair in the sand, Greyson whizzed past us on her way to the water.

"This seat taken?" Alex asked after slinging the chair from his back and opening it up beside me.

"It's *your* chair," Nina said.

I shot her a look I hoped said, *Hot Work Friend, not Hot Asshole.*

"You know, you're right." He stripped off his shirt and sat down with a sigh. I tried not to look, but not looking at Alex without his shirt on would be like ordering a salad instead of pasta at a restaurant (which I would never do).

When I turned away, Nina narrowed her eyes at me in disapproval, and I gave her a look that said, *Don't blame me, blame pheromones!*

"Hi, Jo." Alex gave me a grin that, for whatever reason, still made me melt a little.

"Hi." I tried not to sound like I was upset (because really, it wasn't his fault), but I couldn't come up with anything to talk about. The only conversation starters I had were *Can I borrow some sunscreen? Because you're making me hot,* and *Sorry I'm still painfully embarrassed about that time I tried to kiss you, but also why didn't you kiss me?*

We watched Mia, Kitty, and Greyson swim, their legs and the lines of their snorkels all we could see of them. I turned to Nina, hoping she could save me from having to come up with something to say. Why had Alex sat next to me? If he'd sat on the other side of Nina, at least there'd have been some space between us.

"So," Nina, my beautiful mind-reading best friend, said. "The girls say our next item is singing onstage."

Okay, not my favorite topic either. "Our next item? I think you mean *my* next item. And where do you find these things?" I gestured to her shark bathing suit.

"It's really . . . creative," Alex added.

"Quit changing the subject," Nina said. "But if you must know, it was a gift from a lover who said it suited my personality perfectly."

Whoever this mystery lover was, I was rooting for them. "Marry them, because they see you for who you really are."

Nina shook her head. "Oh, no. He's not marriage material."

"What is marriage material anyway?" Alex said. "Cotton? Spandex? A polyester blend?"

Nina looked him up and down, wrinkling her nose in disgust. "It's whatever you're made of, and I'm not interested."

"Don't look at me," he replied. "I've already told you I'm unavailable."

Nina rolled her eyes. Was he trying to make sure I got the picture? Because I definitely got the picture. My wallowing would have to wait, though, because Mia, Kitty, and Greyson returned, flopping onto their towels to devour grapes from the cooler.

"I can't believe it's August already," Greyson said, her usually sunny face touched by a frown. "You're so close to finishing the list, Jo, but I'm kinda sad about it too. School is coming, and you guys have to leave"— she nodded to Mia and Kitty—"and I'll only have Dad to hang out with, and did I mention school? I hate school."

"Wow, thanks, Grey," Alex said.

Greyson popped a grape in her mouth. "No offense, Dad. It's just that, you know, you're a dad."

"Really, Alex, she's explained it quite clearly," Nina said.

Greyson stared at the sand. No matter what ended up happening between me and Alex, it didn't have to change the friendship I'd struck up with Greyson. "You can still hang out with me when Mia and Kitty leave. If you wanted."

"Really?" Greyson looked up at me, her face bright once again.

"Of course. It's going to feel weird without any teenage girls around."

I glanced at Alex. He'd gone quiet, his eyes on Greyson. He seemed . . . upset. Did he not want me to spend time with her anymore?

"And we'll talk all the time," Kitty said. "Won't we, Mia?"

Mia punched a fist into her hand. "Yup. And if there are any Katie Roses at your new school, I'll be more than happy to give them a piece of my mind, virtually or in person."

Kitty sat up and faced me. "Jo, did you hear? We've decided you're singing onstage next."

"Yes, I've heard."

"We should go backstage at a concert," Mia said. "You can tell them about your list, and maybe they'll let you sing with them. Post Malone will be at the Coral Sky Amphitheatre this weekend, just saying."

I shook my head. "Who?"

"Are you sure you're a millennial? You know, like, zero things about pop culture," Mia said.

"I know Taylor Swift! And Rihanna! And Beyoncé!"

Mia rolled her eyes. "Everyone knows them. That's not impressive."

"Wait." Nina jumped up from her chair, setting her shark fin quivering. "I've got a tremendous idea."

"I don't want to know," I said.

Nina waved her hands in the air with each word, her unicorn earrings swinging along with the shark fin. "Karaoke night." She dropped back into her chair, a triumphant look on her face.

"No," I said as Mia, Kitty, and Greyson chorused, "Yes!"

Nina leaned forward in her chair. "There's this outstanding restaurant downtown that does karaoke on Friday nights. The girls can come too. It's got an actual stage, a legit DJ, strobe lights, and—"

"Can't we just go to Applebee's and call it a night?" I asked, feeling queasy.

"One," Nina said, "Applebee's doesn't have an actual stage, which is specifically mentioned in your list. And two, you know I would never set foot inside an Applebee's, Josephine."

I pulled my hat over my eyes again. "Good, fewer people to watch me."

Nina turned to the girls. "Are you in?"

And they were, which meant I had no choice. I knew I had to do it, and sooner rather than later. I'd only hoped the audience would be smaller and of the Applebee's variety.

After settling the details of the event, which was to take place the following Friday night, the girls goaded Nina into teaching them how to do handstands on the beach, leaving me to sit in awkward silence with Alex, as Mia, Kitty, and Greyson tumbled into the sand, trying to imitate Nina's graceful balance.

"Think I should sing the song about my injured hand for karaoke?" The thin white scar on his finger shone in the sunlight.

I knew he was trying to make me laugh, but I wasn't in the mood. "I don't think anyone would get it."

Alex turned his chair to face me. "You seem mad at me."

"I'm not."

"Then why can't you look at me?"

I pivoted my chair to face him, taking in the stubble on his jaw, the patches of silver along his temples that, even in the two months we'd known each other, had expanded. "See? I'm looking at you. I'm not mad."

"Upset, then."

I knew he wouldn't drop this unless I said something. "August is a hard month, okay? My nephew and I have the same birthday. It's got nothing to do with you." Mostly true.

"I didn't know."

"Well, now you know."

Alex looked as if he wanted to say something else, but I hopped from my chair to my feet before he could open his mouth. "I better go show them how it's done." I left him and joined Nina and the girls, who'd given up on handstands and were doing cartwheels instead.

"You look like you've just escaped Alcatraz," Nina said, putting her hands on her hips when she stepped out of a cartwheel.

"I feel like it." I glanced over to where Alex sat with two empty chairs beside him, then turned to the ocean. "What's with him?"

Nina raised an eyebrow at me as if to say, *Are you that oblivious?*

"It's not that. If it were, he would've kissed me."

"Maybe he's just confused."

"What does he have to be confused about?"

"Oh, I don't know. The strength of his feelings for you? I say we lock you two in a room and see how long it takes before you're all over each other."

"Be serious!"

"I am being serious. Maybe Alex likes you, but Ocean isn't sure. Or maybe it's the other way around. I hate him, but I kind of love Aloe as your couple name. No." She snapped her fingers. "Jocean! That's even better! It sounds like a boy band." She grinned at me, then ducked into another cartwheel before I could shove her.

"You are the worst best friend!" I called after her, even though we both knew it wasn't true.

THE NIGHT BEFORE MY KARAOKE DEBUT, NINA TOOK MIA AND Kitty for a walk down the beach to the pier. I'd stayed behind to catch up on the blog. I'd hardly looked at my website since posting about Coral Castle. After responding to comments and emails, I sat at my desk, a blank document on the screen. Every day it got harder and harder to tap into the positive persona I projected on the blog. I hadn't written my post for the dinner party yet because I wasn't sure how to start. I'd talk about my cooking disaster (it would be charming, relatable, funny). I'd omit that it had been Mia and Kitty's dastardly plan to get me and a certain someone closer together. I'd talk about the laughter, the conversation, everyone's fancy outfits, but the post would stop at dessert. No warm, buzzy feelings in the kitchen, no dishwashing with a disheveled Alex. No talk of Samson, no meltdown on the beach, no almost kiss and subsequent rejection.

I spun in my office chair, unsure how to start. My phone rang, and as soon as I looked at it and saw the word *Mom*, I set my feet onto the floor, braking hard mid-spin. Mom never called just to catch up, only to deliver bad news. I held my phone to my ear, answering before I could decide not to.

"Mom?"

"Jo?"

My mother's voice brought me back to the night Samson died. It had been past midnight when my phone rang, and I'd nearly bumped my head on Britt's bunk when I sat up, thinking it was morning and my alarm was going off. It had been disorienting, waking up in the middle of the night to the word *Mom* flashing on the screen.

Jo, my mother had said then, her voice thin and wavering. I hadn't heard her so broken since Dad died. For the last seventeen years she'd been nothing but angry.

When she'd told me about Samson, I hadn't felt anything. Not right away. Because it was impossible. I'd only seen him two months before, when I'd come up for New Year's Eve. We'd talked about going to a Marlins game. I'd watched him feed a spider to the Venus flytrap Kitty had gotten him for Christmas. At the time he died, I was throwing a black light party in the Sky Lounge. *That can't be right*, I'd thought.

"Jo?" my mother said again, bringing me back to the condo. I thought of Beth and Mark. Had something happened to one of them?

"Yes, Mom?"

"How are you?"

How are you? I breathed a sigh of relief—no one was in danger. But even so, I was on edge. "I'm . . . fine. Just work and spending time with Mia and Kitty. How are—"

"Have you talked to your sister lately?"

My stomach sank. As I'd predicted, Mom had bad news to bear. "Not for a few days."

"You might want to check on her. Mark moved out yesterday, and I know how close you two are."

A tinny buzzing started in my ears, making it hard for me to hear what she said next. Something about an apartment downtown, Beth looking for boxes. "Mark . . . moved out? But I thought they were working on things."

"Life isn't a fairy tale, Jo."

As if I didn't already know that. "Yeah, Mom. I'm aware."

"Well, call your sister."

"Okay, I will."

I waited for her to say something, anything. But after a few seconds of silence, she only said, "That's all I wanted to tell you. Love you," and hung up.

I lowered my phone, my hands shaking as I navigated to my favorites and tapped on my sister's name. I'd known Beth and Mark getting divorced was a possibility, of course I did. But this was Beth and Mark! And even though I'd told myself love only ends in hurt, I'd held on to a thread of optimism for them. Hadn't they been through enough already?

"Is it true?" I said as soon as she answered.

"Where are the girls?"

I leaned back into my office chair. "Walking to the pier with Nina."

Beth sighed, and the sound confirmed everything.

"So it is true."

"Did Mom call you? Because I told her—"

"What? To keep it a secret from me? I can't believe you'd tell Mom before me. I can't believe this is happening at all."

"This is why I didn't tell you. And I didn't tell Mom, she dropped by without warning, and it was obvious Mark was packing his stuff."

I leaned back into my chair and spun a lazy circle with my eyes closed. "But on the phone you two sounded so . . . good?" The last I'd spoken to them, Mark had called her Betty, the nickname he'd had for her since high school. I hadn't heard him say it in so long; I'd thought it was a good sign.

"It's not like we hate each other," Beth said. "It's mutual. Amicable."

"But you still love him, right?"

Beth sighed again. I could picture her sitting at the barstool in her kitchen with a hand against her forehead. She was probably still in her scrubs from work, ugly clogs on her feet, exasperated, as always, by her little sister. "Yes, but—"

"And he still loves you?"

"I think so, yes."

"Then I don't get it." I knew it wasn't my job to care so much about my sister's marriage. *Supportive little sister!* I reminded myself. But Mark had been family since we were kids. I knew he was a good man. He loved my sister. He loved the kids. He loved me. When I lived with them,

Mark had taken the time to help with my homework. When Beth worked evenings at the hospital, he'd insist he could put the kids to bed by himself. *Don't you have a paper due tomorrow?* he'd say. I knew it wasn't about the homework. He was just trying to make sure I didn't end up as a third parent. *You're still a kid, Jo,* he'd tell me whenever I tried to take on more responsibility at home.

Beth was quiet for a moment. "Sometimes love isn't enough, Joey."

The words hurt, though they shouldn't have. I knew it was true. Love and grief were dangerous, especially when they got caught up together. My mother's love for me—and I did believe she loved me—wasn't enough. My love for Dad and Samson wasn't enough to save them. My love for Alex—and yes, I had to admit that what I felt whenever I saw him, whenever I thought about him, whenever he touched me, was love—wasn't enough for him to love me back.

"Please don't tell Mia and Kitty," Beth said. "We want to tell them together."

Tears tracked quietly down my cheeks. I wiped them away, frustrated with myself. "Yeah, of course."

After we hung up, I closed my laptop and laid my head on my desk, and then a memory came, as strong and sudden as a Florida rainstorm. I could feel my sister's couch sagging beneath me. Samson, a few months old, asleep on my chest, his finger wrapped around my pinkie. I could see into the kitchen where Beth cooked dinner, singing off-key (neither of us had inherited our father's talent for singing). Mark was on the living room floor, Mia and Kitty climbing all over him with their toy ponies. The evening light slid through the window, dust suspended in its beams. An insignificant moment. A miracle I remembered at all. I'd felt the kind of peace you only had when everything in your life aligned, when the good outweighed the bad, which for me wasn't often. *If only I could remember this one moment,* I'd thought, taking a snapshot in my mind. And yet, I hadn't thought of it again until now.

I lifted my head, light bursting stars across my vision. The memory, which should have been sweet, left a bad taste in my mouth. The tile was cold against my feet. There was no singing. No music played. No beams of light fell through my window.

But there was Alex. His door eased open across the parking lot. I waited, tense. Would it be good to see him and know he simply existed? That he was safe, even if he didn't love me back?

But it wasn't Alex who stepped out of his unit. It was the blond woman from the bar, the one he'd been with the night we met. The "not date." Alex followed out after her. He leaned against the doorframe and folded his arms over his chest. I was too far away to make out their expressions, but when the woman put her hand on Alex's forearm, I remembered what the girls had said about the event planner from Coral Castle—blond, an old friend. They'd said she'd touched him like that and what it meant. But that couldn't be right. Alex said he hadn't dated anyone in years. He'd said it was too complicated.

As the woman talked, Alex stared at his feet and shook his head. Whatever was happening between them, I could read the tension from here. She stepped closer, and he looked up at her. He nodded, and then she leaned in and kissed him on the cheek. She placed her hands on his arms and embraced him. I waited for Alex to pull back. He'd tell her what he'd told me, *Event Planner, I don't*—

But instead he put his arms around her. They stood like that, holding each other, and for a moment I couldn't look away. This didn't look like the sort of hug you'd give a friend after they stopped by for a visit. It looked like it meant something.

They were still in each other's arms when I turned away. I didn't need to torture myself by seeing what happened next. As I stared down at the tile beneath my feet, everything clicked into place. Alex pulling back from me on the beach. Alex saying he was unavailable. It all pointed to one thing.

Nina had been right. Alex not being into relationships wasn't a hard-and-fast rule. But it turned out I wasn't the exception.

Sixteen

⚓

"THIS LOOKS REALLY BORING," I SAID, STANDING IN THE DOOR-
way of the karaoke restaurant. "Doesn't it look boring? Wouldn't you
rather go home and watch *My Super Sweet 16*?" All week I'd told myself
that karaoke would be fine. Maybe it would even be fun. What did I care
if I embarrassed myself in front of dozens of strangers? But as soon as I
peered inside the packed restaurant, my lifelong stage fright reared its
ugly head. I tried to back out of the doorway, but Mia and Kitty closed
ranks behind me and shoved me forward.

"You'll be fine, Aunt Jo," Kitty said. "You just have to think of your
anxiety as something that's trying to help you. That's what Dad said
when I was practicing for the school play, and it worked. It's science."

"You didn't get a part," Mia said.

"But I wasn't as nervous," Kitty said, shooting Mia a dirty look.

Mia ignored Kitty and turned to me. "If you can jump out of a plane,
you can sing karaoke. Even if you suck, it'll at least be entertaining," she
said, which didn't console me at all. She pushed me again and added,
"Will you hurry? You're making us look like weirdos."

The girls shoved me inside and led me through the restaurant. Karaoke hadn't started yet, but the place was filled with noise. All this time I'd imagined a dinky little stage, like the kind bars sometimes had for live music. But this was the stage of a grand production, complete with an array of lights that danced out across the room, making me feel as if I'd stepped into a rave, not a restaurant. It had a real party atmosphere, which shouldn't have surprised me, seeing as Nina chose it. I preferred the comfort of a dimly lit dive bar, but Nina would never allow me to check off this item somewhere unphotogenic. My stomach flipped at the thought of my performance being photographed, or even worse, recorded. But there had to be documentation for the blog, otherwise what was the point? And even if the blog hadn't been a factor, how likely was it I could convince my best friend to not record what would be my one and only foray into the performing arts?

It wasn't hard to find Nina, who, in a sparkly red minidress, looked like a bow on top of a present. Her hair was as over-the-top as the rest of her, transformed from its usual sleek high ponytail into a beehive, though she still wore the same dangling unicorn earrings. I felt too casual in the dress I'd bought for item number ten (short, tight, blue, expensive), though it wasn't casual at all. I could already predict Nina would complain about me wearing it again. But at least I hadn't left my hair in its usual limp curtain. Mia had curled both my and Kitty's hair into soft waves with a curling iron I hardly ever used. I'd taken a selfie with the girls and sent it to my sister, the first contact I'd had with her since she told me about Mark moving out. I pushed the thought of that away. I couldn't let the girls sense something was wrong. I'd promised Beth, and, besides, I wanted them to have as many happy moments as possible before finding out.

The table Nina had chosen was, predictably, beside the stage. Nina, surprisingly deft in stilettos for someone who spent most of her time barefoot, raced over when she spotted me.

"I can't believe you showed!" She squeezed me as if she hadn't seen me in weeks, though it had been less than twenty-four hours since she'd left the condo after returning from her walk with the girls.

"Of course I showed. It's for the list," I said, and at Nina's skeptical look added, "I tried to get out of it, but Mia and Kitty wouldn't let me."

Nina held me at arm's length and looked me up and down. "Trying to squeeze every last dollar out of that dress, huh?"

"It cost five hundred dollars!"

"So you're at what? A dollar per wear now?"

I flicked at one of her unicorn earrings. "Are you sure you want to fight about wearing something too often?"

Nina cupped the earrings in her hands. "These are different. One, they're accessories. And two, they're my signature item. It's impossible to overwear a signature item."

"This is my signature item!" I said, gesturing to the dress.

Nina sighed. "You're impossible, Josephine."

All week, me, Nina, and the girls had practiced songs by looking up the karaoke versions on YouTube and singing them in the condo activities room. I'd even chosen a song and practiced it a few times: "What Is Love?" Easy, accurate, no talent needed. But the lyrics fell out of my head at the sight of the stage looming before me. Not great, considering most of the lyrics were in the title.

I sat at the table, which was three tables pushed together. "Nina, I don't think we need this many seats. There's only six of us, right?" I looked up at her, but she examined her nails and pretended she hadn't heard me. "Nina!"

"What? I can't let your performance go unappreciated by those who love you!"

Oh God, I thought, wondering who she'd invited to this shindig. "You should've asked me!"

She pulled me to my feet. "We need to get a drink in you. Mia, Kitty, you watch the table."

At the bar, Nina ordered us each a rum and Coke. "Drink it!" she demanded, and shoved the glass into my hands.

"How many people did you invite?"

"Just a few friends."

"Define 'a few.'"

Nina stirred her drink with her straw. "Only us, Alex and Greyson, which you knew about. And Ollie—"

"*You* invited Ollie?"

Nina ignored the comment. "And Captain Xav . . . and maybe RJ."

"RJ? Since when are we friends with deckhands?"

"Speaking of." Nina waved toward the entrance, where Captain Xav and RJ walked through the door. Why hadn't I pushed harder for Applebee's?

Nina flicked at my rum and Coke with a finger. "Hurry up and finish that. You'll need it to get on that stage."

I finished my rum and Coke and set the glass on the bar top. I had no intention of getting onstage until well into the night. I needed all the time I could get to find my courage (and for everyone else to get a little drunk). When the DJ announced that karaoke would begin in half an hour, I turned back to the bar and ordered two tequila shots.

"Make that three," Nina said.

"Three?"

She booped my nose. "One for you, and two for me."

By the time we returned to the table, Ollie had arrived. I circled the table to greet everyone and took my seat beside Nina. Alex and Greyson were still missing, which was a relief. I didn't need to keep embarrassing myself in front of him. But as soon as we ordered appetizers, Greyson appeared at the table. I didn't recognize her at first. Not because her looks had changed, but because she seemed totally unlike herself. She kept her eyes on the floor and trudged past us before sitting beside Kitty, all without uttering a single word.

Nina and I gave each other a look that said, *Has Greyson been replaced by a reptilian?*

"Sorry we're late." Alex took the empty chair beside me, and though he wore a smile, a line of worry creased his forehead when he glanced down the table at Greyson.

"Is everything all right?" I asked.

"Huh?" Alex looked at me, seeming more anxious than when Greyson had gotten sick in the parking lot of Coral Castle.

"You seem . . . stressed," I said, wondering if this had something to do with the woman I'd seen at his apartment the night before.

Alex flashed a smile that didn't quite reach his eyes. "Oh, nothing. Tired."

Other than the day after my dinner party, I'd never seen Alex tired. Not even after a long shift on the boat. He had as much energy as Greyson did, though the vibe coming from her tonight was . . . concerning. I was tempted to push him but thought better of it. If he didn't want to tell me, maybe I didn't want to know.

Before long karaoke began, and Nina was right, I'd needed the shot and the rum and Coke. My stomach wound itself tighter as I watched person after person take the stage. Sure, I could sing in the galley or the man van with Alex, or in the condo with the girls, but this was different. I'd never been shy, but stage fright had plagued me ever since my kindergarten Halloween pageant, when, dressed as a pumpkin, I froze in the middle of my solo and threw up on the kid next to me. My anxiety wasn't helped at all by Alex, who drummed his fingers on the table as he stared vacantly at the stage and shot occasional glances Greyson's way.

Nina elbowed me after the first few performances. "Go put your name in!"

I shook my head. "Let me eat dinner first. I can't perform on an empty stomach." Though given my history with singing and puking, maybe I should. Nina rolled her eyes, then left to put her name in. Mia, Kitty, and even Greyson, who still looked miserable, followed her.

I busied myself by taking photos of the stage, the friends around me, the restaurant, my food. When the DJ called Nina's name, she strutted across the stage as if she owned it. She was no Whitney Houston, but she wasn't bad either. Her enthusiasm more than made up for any lack of talent. Ollie couldn't take his eyes off her.

I leaned over to Alex. "What is cake by the ocean? Is that a drug?"

"You're joking, right?" And when he realized I wasn't, he laughed for the first time all evening. "Uh, it's sex on the beach."

"Like the drink?"

Alex stirred his drink with his straw. "Kind of, but the song is about, uh, *actual* sex on the beach."

"Oh," I said. My cheeks felt hot all of a sudden, and I turned back to the stage, where Nina seemed to be singing directly to Ollie.

When Nina returned, Mia and Kitty took to the stage, singing a pop song I only vaguely recognized but that Alex and Nina knew all the words to, of course. I videoed their performance and sent it to my sister. **Wish I was there**, Beth responded, and my heart ached for her. I wanted nothing more than for her to be beside me so I could make her laugh, or let her cry on my shoulder. I'd get up onstage and sing a thousand songs if I thought it would make her feel better.

When the DJ called Greyson's name, she crossed to the center of the stage, a scowl on her face as she gripped the microphone and belted out the angriest rendition of Taylor Swift's "Bad Blood" I'd ever heard. Throughout the entire song she stood motionless, her eyes locked on Alex. I lowered my phone, realizing this was a message, not a karaoke performance. Alex was drumming on the table again, that line of worry deepening with each word Greyson sang.

As soon as Greyson's song ended, Alex was on his feet and crossed the room, meeting her at the bottom of the steps. He put his arm around her shoulders, but she pulled away and marched back to the table. Alex lingered by the stage for a moment, his face pained as he watched her walk away.

"Whoa," Nina said. "What was that about?"

"I have no idea."

Alex returned, taking the seat beside me again.

"Everything okay?"

He gave me a tight-lipped smile. "Teenagers."

I watched his face, but it was clear he didn't want to talk about it. I'd never seen Greyson like this. I'd never seen her mad at all, especially not with Alex. What had made her act out in such dramatic fashion? I didn't have long to think about it, though, because Mia and Kitty appeared on either side of me and pressed their faces to mine.

"Yes?" I mumbled through squished cheeks.

"It's been two hours, Jo," Mia said. "Go put your name in."

I looked at the stage. I didn't have Nina's confidence, or Mia's and Kitty's ability to carry a tune, or even Greyson's anger. "I'm still deciding what to sing."

Mia pulled away from me. "Seriously, Jo?"

"There's only an hour left of karaoke!" Kitty added. "If you don't get your name in soon, you won't get to sing."

"What about 'No Scrubs'?" Nina said. She sang the opening of the song, and Ollie nearly spat out his drink when he caught her glare, but I thought I saw her wink at him when she'd finished.

My eyes darted to the stage, the DJ, the lights circling above, and then to Alex, who looked down into his drink.

"I can't do this," I said.

"You have to do it; it's on the list," Nina said. "Don't disappoint us. You'll let everyone down if you don't sing." She gestured to the entire restaurant as if I'd be letting them *all* down.

"I can't." I brought my hand to my throat. "I think I'm losing my voice."

"Oh, give me a break," Mia said.

"*Never venture, never win,*" Kitty added, earning a glare from Mia.

"I need another drink." I pushed back my chair and left for the bar before anyone could stop me.

At the bar, I ordered a soda. More alcohol would make this situation worse, not better. The only thing I needed was space, which was hard to find in a packed restaurant. Why was it so crowded anyway? Was karaoke really this popular? My palms were sweating, and I hadn't even put my name in to sing yet. I scanned the restaurant and wondered if I could sneak out with no one noticing, but I knew I wouldn't. I thought about Samson, and how he would laugh at me and probably make me sing that "Whip/Nae Nae" song he'd taught me the dance to last summer. *It's stanky leg*, he'd say, *not stinky leg*. I took a long sip of my drink, and when I set it down, spotted Alex beside the stage in conversation with the DJ. The DJ nodded, and Alex filled out a karaoke slip before returning to the table. After Greyson's performance, I couldn't imagine he'd be in the mood for singing, even though he sang more than anyone I knew. Maybe he would sing a response to her. Another T-Swift song, "You Need to Calm Down," perhaps.

I remained at the bar for the next two performances and returned when an older man in a three-piece suit and one sequined glove sang "SexyBack" with impressive enthusiasm. I promised myself I'd put my name in at nine thirty, only twenty minutes from now. When the song ended, Nina leaned over and said, "At least you won't be as bad as that guy. Want to sing 'Shallow' with me?"

But before I could answer, the DJ's voice came over the sound system. "Next up, we have Alex and birthday girl Jo, singing 'I Believe in a Thing Called Love.' Happy dirty thirty to the birthday girl."

No, that couldn't be right. I turned to Alex. He shrugged, a mischievous smile on his face.

"It's not my birthday" was the only thing I could think to say.

Alex pushed his chair back and held out his hand to me. "White lie so you could skip ahead. It's almost your birthday, after all."

I stared at his hand, already feeling myself turn pink. "No."

Nina shook my shoulders. "Yes!"

Alex pulled me to my feet. "It'll be fine. I'm right with you."

Mia and Kitty started chanting my name, getting the rest of the table (except for Greyson) to chant along. I flushed all over, probably looking like a lobster in a tight blue dress about to be tossed into a pot of boiling water.

"I'm an awful singer," I said as Alex led me over to the DJ booth.

"I've heard you sing before."

"But that's different. I get nauseated onstage. I might puke on you."

"I'll live," he said. I looked back at the table, pleading for someone to rescue me, but they only kept chanting my name.

Alex took two microphones from the DJ and passed one to me. The microphone was slick in my sweating hands. Surely I couldn't keep a grip on this for an entire three minutes.

"I don't know the song," I said.

Alex raised an eyebrow at me. "Everyone knows this song," he said. "And I seem to remember you getting whiplash head-banging to this in the man van on the way to work."

I stared at him, unable to speak.

"Just pretend you're in the galley prepping for a beach picnic for an annoying primary," Alex said.

"A galley with strobe lights, a stage, and dozens of strangers," I said.

Alex's face softened. "If you won't do it for you, do it for me. I need a pick-me-up right now. And you owe me. I jumped off the yacht with you, you sing this song with me. Seems like a fair trade."

I thought of how hurt he'd looked when Greyson shrugged him off, and how terrified he'd been when we jumped off the yacht. "That's a dirty trick, you know." He smiled, and I let him pull me up the steps, even though every cell in my body wanted to leap off the stage and escape to my car.

We stopped in the center of the stage, and I realized with relief that the lights made it impossible to see the faces of the audience, though I could hear Nina and the girls whooping. Alex squeezed my hand, letting go when the strumming of electric guitars filled the room. I could feel myself sweating already and didn't know what to do with my body as the screen counted down to cue us in with the lyrics. When the first verse began, I held the microphone up to my mouth and moved my lips, but no sound came out.

Alex, however, sounded amazing. His voice was loud and clear, and he seemed completely comfortable up here. That was when I realized what a horrible mistake getting onstage with him had been. I'd known he could sing, but he sounded like a baby angel on Christmas. I should've known he'd be a born performer, he'd spent his whole life watching his parents do it, and so I gave up on singing as I listened to him.

Alex caught my eye and turned away from the audience, singing directly to me instead. I tried not to read too much into him singing about touching and being touched. Standing there only made me feel more awkward, so when the chorus began, I tried to sing along, though my voice was barely above a whisper.

"C'mon, Jo," Alex called to me at the instrumental break, "you know this."

When the next verse began, he grabbed my hand and pulled me closer. We were chest to chest, only a few inches separating us. He looked completely in character as he sang to me about kissing every minute, every hour, every day, and in that moment, I wasn't sure if he was singing to me, his karaoke buddy, or to *me*. His eyes were locked on mine, and it was impossible to be this close, to have him sing to me in front of everyone, and just stare back. The only thing I could do was sing louder. With each line my voice grew stronger, and Alex's facial expressions became more enthusiastic. By the time the chorus started up again, his smile had taken over his face, and I couldn't help it, it was contagious. I laughed as I sang with him, forgetting about the people watching us. He placed my hand on his chest, like he had that day we jumped off the yacht, and sang about the rhythm of his heart, but I could only feel mine beating wildly in my chest.

Alex let go of my hand and gave the best air guitar performance I'd ever seen. He nudged me with his shoulder until I joined in, and my fear

LOVE, LISTS, AND FANCY SHIPS   237

turned to pure adrenaline. All the stress and tension of the last few months escaped me in the form of enthusiastic air-guitaring. My hair flew around my face as we head-banged to the music. We sang to each other and danced wildly. By the final rendition of the chorus, I was doing my best to match Alex's over-the-top acting, which was impossible to beat. During the final instrumental break, he spun me toward him and held me close doing a two-step as if we were dancing in a ballroom, odd for a song like this, but somehow it seemed to fit (and I was grateful I'd already checked off item number eleven—attempt ballroom dancing— and had taken a few lessons).

Alex lowered me into a dip as the sound wound down, and I felt light-headed when he set me on my feet again. We faced each other, grinning and giddy, fighting to catch our breath, but then the sound of the audience broke me from the dream of it all. The lights onstage dimmed, and I looked out at the restaurant, the faces of Nina and the girls coming into focus. Alex dropped my hand, and I turned to tell him that I got it now, what the big deal was about karaoke, but he was no longer beside me. He'd already crossed the stage, leaving me behind. I watched him fly down the steps and pass his microphone back to the DJ before disappearing into the crowd without so much as a backward glance.

Hurt and confused, I left the stage. When I made it to the table, I realized Alex wasn't there, and I spotted him making his way through the crowd toward the exit. I moved to follow him, but Nina bear-hugged me, stopping me in my tracks.

"You're awful, babe, but that was amazing. And Alex!" She laughed. "What a riot!"

"I told you you'd be entertaining," Mia said.

I tried to make sense of everyone talking to me all at once, but the heat and noise of the crowd grated on my nerves. All I could think about was Alex, and how sudden that change between us had been. Had what I felt between us onstage really been just acting?

"I need to get some air," I said, and pulled away from Nina, pushing my way through the restaurant before anyone could offer to come with me. It was warm when I stepped out into the night, but it was a relief from the heat of the crowd within the restaurant.

I scanned the parking lot for Alex, and my confusion turned to anger at the sight of him crossing the parking lot in the direction of his van. I set off after him, no longer caring that what I was about to say would put my feelings for him out in the open. He would know it wasn't a mistake when I tried to kiss him. And maybe it would ruin our friendship, but I wasn't sure I could be friends with him when he was constantly drawing me close, only to push me away again.

"Hey!" I called when I had nearly caught up to him. Alex turned at the sound of my voice, stopping a few feet from his van.

"Hey, Jo," he said, not meeting my eye.

This was not the same man who'd just serenaded me in front of a room full of strangers. "*Hey, Jo?* That's all you have to say to me right now? What the hell is wrong with you?"

Alex shrugged and looked out at the parking lot. "I needed to get away," he said.

"From me?"

"I'm not sure what you want me to say." But the strained look on his face gave me my answer.

"Oh, I don't know, maybe something like *Jo, I'm sorry for singing you a love song in front of an entire restaurant, then running away.* I know you aren't interested in me. I know we're just friends. But you can't do things like that. Not after you pushed me away. Not when I'm trying to get over you."

Alex's eyes darted to mine. "What do you mean?"

"Come on, Alex. Can we please stop pretending—"

But before I could finish my sentence, Alex's hands were on my waist. My breath caught in my chest when he pulled me to him, walking me backward until I was pressed up against the side of his van.

"Alex—"

"What do you mean *get over me?*" he said. He dipped his face close to mine, our noses nearly touching as he looked at me with the same intensity he'd worn that night at Coral Castle.

With his hands on me it was hard to think, and when I found my voice, it was barely above a whisper. "I don't think the phrase has that many interpretations."

"I see." His eyes searched mine, and for a moment we were completely still. All I could do was stare back at him, dizzy at the closeness. I couldn't think straight, confusion and wanting knotted together in my mind. And then Alex let go of my waist. I stood frozen as he looked down at my mouth, brushing a thumb over my lips before holding my face in his hands. His fingers were warm against the back of my neck, setting off a wave of goose bumps over my skin. And even though I knew what would happen, even though we'd kissed before, I was unprepared for the way his mouth on mine would feel like the first time.

But unlike the sweet, slow kiss from the night we met, this kiss was urgent, a release of the pressure I'd felt building between us all summer. My surprise gave way to hunger, and I wrapped my arms around his neck, pulling him closer, tangling my fingers in his hair. One kiss became two, then three, and then I lost count. I breathed him in, the smell and taste of him more intoxicating than I'd remembered. His hands left my face, finding my hips, and he leaned into me, his body warm along the length of mine. As he kissed me, everything was only Alex—his hands, his hair in my fingers, his mouth, which left mine to trail down my neck, starting from just beneath my ear all the way to my collarbone.

A car horn sounded nearby, pulling me from the stupor of kissing him, and I remembered my anger, and the woman at his apartment, and how he'd stopped me from doing just this on the beach less than two weeks ago.

"Alex," I said, hardly able to breathe as he kissed my shoulder. "What are you doing?"

He paused, his breath hot against my skin, and part of me (approximately ninety-nine percent) wished I'd said nothing. He looked dazed when he pulled back. His face was flushed, his hair a mess.

"I'm . . . kissing you? If that wasn't clear, then I'm doing something wrong."

"That's not what I mean." Without his mouth to distract me, I could think again. My hands fell from around his neck, and I moved out from beneath him. "It's only . . . one second you're pushing me away, and the next you're all over me. It feels like a trick or a game."

Alex rubbed at the back of his neck with one hand. "You think this is a game to me? You really see me as that sort of man?"

I didn't, but my history in trusting men wasn't so great. I covered my face in my hands. "No? Maybe? I don't know."

"Jo, look at me." He held my wrists and gently tugged them from my face.

I met his gaze, wanting to believe the way he looked at me, like I was something he wanted, maybe the only thing. "I saw that woman leaving your condo last night," I said. "New girlfriend?"

"You know I'm not seeing anyone."

"It sure didn't look that way."

"Why would I lie about that?"

"I don't know, Alex. Nothing you do makes sense. What am I supposed to think when you've got some woman leaving your apartment after saying you're *unavailable*? All summer you've flirted with me one minute, then Nina the next. Who else are you flirting with, Belva?"

Alex laughed. "Not that Belva isn't a catch, but no, I haven't been flirting with Belva. And yeah, I flirted with Nina, too, but not because I was attracted to her."

"So you were flirting with her because . . . ?"

He took a step forward, then hesitated and turned away, running a hand through his hair. "Why are you making me do this?" he said.

"Do what?" I asked, but he continued pacing the parking lot in front of me and didn't answer.

"Alex—"

He spun around to face me. "Everything with Nina was because I'm obsessed with *you*, Jo! Anytime I caught myself paying extra attention to you, I'd shift my attention to her, so it wouldn't be so obvious. I told myself I'd get over it, but you were always there—at work, at home. I tried to avoid you whenever I could, but then I had the brilliant idea to invite you to carpool with me." He laughed, rubbing his face. "It seems ridiculous now, but I told myself you'd shoot me down, and then I'd see you weren't interested, and could move on. But then you said yes! So that plan backfired."

I stared at him, frozen in place. His avoidance of me at the beginning of the summer, the interest in Nina, I'd interpreted it all wrong. "But you said . . . when you caught me skinny-dipping in the pool, you said you didn't think I was cute."

He shook his head and took a step closer. "That's not what I said. I said I didn't *say* I thought you were cute. Don't you remember the night we met? I thought I made it pretty clear I was attracted to you. And for the record, you are more than cute."

I fumbled for something to say. The distance between us was closing again. I wanted to give in and lose myself in kissing him, but things still didn't add up. "If you're so into me, why did you push me away on the beach?"

Alex sighed. "I didn't push you away. I pressed pause. You were so upset . . . it didn't feel like the right moment. Which is what I would've told you if you hadn't run away. But the next day you said it was a mistake and to forget it, so I figured you meant it when you said it didn't mean anything."

"You wanted to kiss me then?"

"I've been trying *not* to kiss you all summer long. I almost did, more than once. I thought that was obvious."

"I thought . . . well, I wasn't sure. I couldn't read you."

Alex closed the distance between us, threading his arms around my waist. My hands were on his chest, the steady rhythm of his heart beneath my palms like an anchor tethering me to him.

"I swore I'd never fall in love again, you know," he said.

"Love?"

Alex pulled back, and there was only his heart beneath my hands and him, so close, that if I tipped forward, we'd be kissing again.

"Yes, Jo. I love you. You are frustratingly beautiful, and kind, and funny, and it's making things very complicated."

"How is that complicated?" I said, as that word, *love*, drumming in my mind, caught through me like wildfire.

Alex turned his face away from me. "Why are you making me do this?" he said again.

"Do what?"

He looked at me, and I recognized the sadness I'd seen in his eyes that night at Mitch's. "I don't want to hurt you."

"What are you talking about?"

"Ah, fuck," he whispered. He placed his hands over mine, and I could feel his heart beating faster. "Things are complicated because of the woman you saw leaving my place last night."

The heat spreading through me cooled. I moved to drop my hands, but he held them beneath his. "But you said you weren't seeing anyone," I said. "The event planner, what does she—"

"The event planner? What do you mean?"

"The event planner . . . from Coral Castle."

Alex looked bewildered. "You thought I was dating her? She's . . . nice, but I have a rule against dating conspiracy theorists. That wasn't who you saw."

"Then who was she?"

Alex pulled my hands from his chest, holding them tight in his. "That was Maggie."

Greyson's mom? I took a step back, and this time Alex let me go. "I don't understand."

"We've been talking every week for the last year," he said. "She wanted to prove she's ready to be in Greyson's life again. I didn't tell anyone, because I wasn't sure what would happen. Do you remember the woman who walked out on me at Mitch's?" I nodded. "That was her. She just . . . showed up at the beginning of the summer. I wasn't ready to let her see Greyson, which really ticked her off. But when she showed up the night before your dinner party, I let her see Greyson, and she really did seem like a changed person."

"And what? You're getting back together?"

An indignant look flashed over Alex's face. "Are you kidding? I can forgive her, but I can't forget. We were always wrong for each other. The only good thing to come out of that relationship was Greyson."

"Then I don't understand what this has to do with us."

Alex tipped his face up to the sky, quiet for a moment before he looked at me again. "Maggie lives in California. She's a casting director at a film studio. She can't get a job just anywhere, and—not to sound conceited—I can. We decided it would make the most sense for me and Greyson to move to L.A. We're leaving at the end of September."

Leaving. I thought about the way Alex had looked when I told Greyson she could still hang out with me after Mia and Kitty were gone. It hadn't been about me at all. He'd known they were leaving. I thought about Greyson and her anger as she'd stood in the center of the stage. "Does Greyson know?"

"We told her last night. That's why you saw Maggie leaving my place. Greyson was upset. She wouldn't talk to either of us. I told Maggie I'd talk to Greyson and try to make her understand. That's what you saw."

How could I have gotten things so wrong? Looking back, nothing I'd seen was overtly romantic. It wasn't like he and Maggie were enemies. They were Greyson's parents. "How long have you known you were moving?"

"We made the decision not long after your dinner party, but I'd known it was a possibility all summer. It's why I didn't kiss you sooner," he said. "Or try harder to keep you from pulling away. I didn't want to be just another person who left. But if this is Greyson's shot to have her mother in her life, for real, then—"

"You can't take that away from her," I said, thinking of my own mother. I'd have given anything at Greyson's age for her to come back into my life.

"I knew you would understand," Alex said. "Which is only making this harder." He pulled me to him again, and I rested my head on his shoulder, trying to imprint into my memory the feeling of his arms around me.

"If it were just me, it would be easy, but—"

"Greyson's first," I said.

"Yeah," he sighed. "Greyson's first."

We stood there for a long time, neither of us speaking. I tried to fold the hurt within me, like one of the cloth napkins on the boat, smaller and smaller until it took up the least amount of space possible. I'd known from the very beginning, from the moment I walked onto the boat and saw him in the galley, that this would end badly, and still I'd allowed it to happen.

It was only when Alex wiped the tears from my cheeks that I realized I was crying. "Talk to me."

I leaned into him so he couldn't see my face. Why had he done this? Kissed me, told me he loved me, made me love him, when he knew he'd be leaving. "I hate you for making me love you."

"You love me, too, huh?"

"You need me to say it?"

"I did just declare my love for you in the parking lot of a karaoke restaurant, so yeah, I think some confirmation would be nice."

I laughed and looked up at him, thinking about the night he'd helped declutter my condo and hadn't let me toss my photo of Samson. I still hadn't found a word to describe feeling joy and sorrow at the same time. I didn't think there was one. "Fine, if you need me to say it, I'll say it. I love you, Alex. And I guess I love Ocean too. And I wish neither of you had kissed me."

"You kissed me first, Florida Girl," he said. "And I prefer to go by Hot Yacht Chef."

"That's still not happening."

Alex kissed me again, but this time it was gentle, as if whatever was between us could break at any moment. It was hard to pull away, but eventually I did.

"We should probably keep our distance," I said, after kissing him one last time. "We can't do this again, or let it go anywhere. It'll only make it worse when you leave."

He pressed his lips together, grimacing slightly. I hoped he'd argue with me, but he only sighed. "If that's what you want," he said.

When we walked across the parking lot, he put his arm around me, and I leaned into him, stealing as much of his touch as I could before going inside, where we'd spend the rest of the evening pretending nothing had happened at all.

Seventeen

AS SOON AS WE RETURNED FROM KARAOKE, MIA, KITTY, AND I collapsed onto the sofa bed, planning to melt our brains with as many episodes of *My Super Sweet 16* as we could stand. I settled between them like I had the first night they'd arrived, and tried to focus on the TV. We still had four seasons to get through before the girls returned home to North Carolina, but I couldn't pay attention to bratty teens' birthday parties because Alex was the only thing on my mind.

"Are you having a stroke or something?" Mia asked.

I turned away from the train wreck of a birthday party on the screen. Mia eyed me with suspicion, the blue light of the television flickering over her face. "What are you talking about?"

Kitty sat up and leaned over me. "Do you feel any numbness? Tingling?" She pinched my cheek. "Did you feel that?"

"Ouch! Yes, Kitty, I felt that."

"I don't mean a literal stroke," Mia said.

Kitty dropped back onto the bed. "Oh."

"If I'm having a literal or figurative stroke, it's because the people in this episode are even more outrageous than usual." I nodded to the screen, where a father and his teenage son interviewed models to jump out of the son's birthday cake, assigning each one a chili pepper on a ten-pepper hotness scale.

Mia pursed her lips. "I don't think so. You keep doing this." She grinned, then furrowed her brow, then dropped her mouth into a frown before springing into a smile again.

Probably an accurate representation of both my face and my inner turmoil. Since my kisses with Alex in the parking lot, I'd thought of little else. Except for the part where he and Greyson were leaving. "Haven't you ever heard of facial yoga?" I said. "I do this every night. It's a natural anti-aging treatment."

"Yeah, sure," Mia said. She set her chin on her hands, and the three of us returned to watching TV.

"There!" she said a few minutes later, jolting upright on the bed. "You're doing it again!"

"That's just my face, Mia. I don't know what you want me to say."

She gnawed on her lip as she studied me, and I tried not to think about Alex, in case she could read my mind. Though she probably wouldn't need to read my mind with how bad of a liar I was.

"Where did you and Alex go after your song?" she asked. "You were gone for a loooooong time."

Damn it. "I went outside for some air. It was hot in there."

"And Alex?"

"May or may not have been there." There was no use lying about that. They'd seen us come in together.

"And what were you two *doing* outside?" Mia pressed.

"Talking." Not a lie. We'd talked.

"Uh-huh, just talking. Really."

"Yes, really." The corner of my mouth twitched, and I fought off a smile.

Mia clutched a hand to her chest. "Oh my God! Kitty, something definitely happened."

Kitty pretended to swoon onto the bed.

"Nothing happened!" I cried.

Mia raised an eyebrow. "Sure, because both of you got your hair messed up on your own."

"There was a lot of head-banging happening onstage," I said.

"Yeah, I'm sure there was a lot of banging," she replied with a smirk.

I smacked her on the shoulder. "Mia!"

"You kept looking at each other like this all night." She fluttered her eyelashes and gave me a hurried glance.

"That's not—"

She gasped. "Did you guys do it in his van? Oh, gross!"

Kitty bolted upright, then swooned onto the bed again.

"We didn't do anything in his van! Get your mind out of the gutter."

"Third row folds down, just saying."

I threw a pillow at her face, but she caught it in her hands before it hit her. "I refuse to accept you're old enough to think about sex in cars."

"You've been deflowered!" Kitty cried, swooning so hard she tumbled from the bed to the floor.

Mia crossed her arms over her chest. "Why not? Mom does. She says it's important to have open conversations about sex."

I cursed my sister's open communication with her daughters. "Yeah, well, she's your mother. And she probably wants to talk about it because that's how you got here. Either way, we are not discussing my sex life."

"So you did do it!" Mia jumped to her feet on the sofa bed. "I don't know if I should be impressed or throw up in my mouth." She pointed at her sister. "Kitty, you owe me twenty bucks."

"No!" I said. "We did not have sex in his van or anywhere else! And will you sit down? You'll ruin the sofa bed."

Mia grinned at me. "What? Planning to ruin it some other way when we're gone?"

"Oh my God, what is wrong with you?" I buried my face in the blanket.

"Then what did you do, huh?" Mia asked. I didn't answer her. Maybe if I pretended to have a literal stroke, she would leave me alone. Mia jabbed my cheek with her finger. "What did you do, huh? Huh? Tell me!"

"Fine! Fine!" I grabbed her finger, unable to take another jab to the face. Next summer I wouldn't let her spend so much time with Nina. I turned onto my back and stared up at the ceiling. "We may have kissed, that's all."

Mia and Kitty went quiet. I kept my gaze on the ceiling. The quiet only lasted a moment, however, because they began shrieking like the best friends in a rom-com.

"When? Where? How?" Mia said. "Paint a picture for me."

Kitty climbed back onto the bed, propping her chin in her hands. "Tongue or no tongue? That's French kissing, right? I saw Mia and this boy from her—"

Mia gave Kitty a dangerous look. "You saw nothing!"

"This is ridiculous," I said. For all Mia and Kitty's interest, I was pretty sure they didn't actually want the nitty-gritty details of their aunt making out with their friend's dad against the side of his van. "I'm not telling you anything. And it's a little disturbing you want to know."

"You're no fun!" Mia said at the same time Kitty shouted, "Tongue or no tongue?!"

"You know, I'm getting tired of hearing about how un-fun I am."

"Does this mean Greyson will be related to us?" Kitty asked.

"Don't be a doofus, Kitty," Mia said.

I grabbed back the pillow I'd thrown at Mia and hugged it to my chest. "As great as Alex is, I don't think it will work out."

Mia stretched out beside me with a grimace. "That bad of a kisser, huh?"

I raised an eyebrow at her. "Do you really want to know?"

"Yeah, no thanks. I don't want that visual after all."

The three of us stared up at the ceiling, the only sound the party music on the TV.

"It's because they're leaving, right?" Kitty said.

So they knew. I wondered what Greyson had told them. "Yeah," I said. Kitty scooted closer to me, and I tucked her head beneath my chin.

"So what?" Mia said. "You could do long-distance or something."

It wasn't like I hadn't thought about it. "I don't know. That sort of thing only works if there's an end date in mind." And if the man in question wasn't moving to be closer to his ex.

"Bad excuse," she said. "If you love someone, you don't give up on them. You try."

I let out a slow breath, thinking of Beth and Mark. As far as I could tell, the girls knew nothing about their dad moving out. What would they think when Beth and Mark told them? "Sometimes love isn't enough," I said.

"Then what is?" Mia asked.

"If you figure it out, let me know."

"*If fighting is reasonably sure to result in victory, then you must fight, even though the ruler forbid it; if fighting promises not to result in victory, then you must not fight, even at the ruler's bidding,*" Kitty said.

Mia's eyes darkened. She lunged over me to grab at her sister. "Where's the book? That quote doesn't even apply to the situation!"

Kitty squealed and leapt from the bed, racing to hide *The Art of War* somewhere in the condo. Mia chased after her, and I paused the TV, trying not to laugh as the girls shouted at each other. When they finally returned, Kitty having stowed *The Art of War* safely somewhere in my room, I hit play, and we continued watching our episode.

"How is Greyson taking it, by the way?" I asked.

"You saw her. What do you think?" Mia said.

"It's sad to think we might never see her again," Kitty said.

"Yeah." I didn't want to think about that. Poor Greyson. I could sympathize with her. Even though I'd been angry with my mother for how she'd pulled away from me, I'd wanted nothing more than to have her back. "It's . . . complicated. I think she'll feel differently about it when she's actually there."

Mia and Kitty looked at each other but said nothing. We returned our attention to the TV, and I watched until I couldn't keep my eyes open any longer. Not that I could pay much attention to the show. I kept running over that kiss with Alex in the parking lot, the words *Yes, Jo. I love you* followed by *We're leaving at the end of September* on repeat. My emotions cycled from exhilaration to despair at impressive speed. Part of me wondered if I should take back what I'd said about keeping our distance. But getting closer to Alex would only make it worse when he left.

When I said I was off to bed, Mia leaned her head on my shoulder. "Sorry I pushed you at him. I didn't mean for anyone to get hurt."

"Don't be sorry," I said, running a hand over her hair. "I think it would've happened anyway. There are worse problems to have."

On my way to my room I paused at the entrance to the living room, watching Mia and Kitty burrow beneath the blankets and trying not to think about how, in a few short weeks, they'd be leaving me too.

THAT NIGHT, I JERKED AWAKE TO THE SOUND OF MY PHONE ringing. I fumbled for it on the nightstand, my heart in my throat when I saw it was almost two in the morning. The memory of my mother calling to tell me about Samson sharpened in my mind, and my hands shook as I answered the unfamiliar number.

"Is this Jo Walker?" The voice was the deep baritone of an older man. I didn't recognize it. Could this be about Beth? My mother? Had something happened to one of them?

"Yes, that's me," I said.

"This is Officer Thomas with security at the Palm Beach Yacht Club and Marina." My anxieties left my mother and sister and landed on Nina and Captain Xav. I clutched the phone with both hands, pressing it harder against my ear. "I have two teenage girls that say they're your nieces. Mia and Kitty Taylor. They're staying with you for the summer?"

"What?" I flicked on the lamp, wincing as my eyes adjusted to the brightness of the room.

"Ma'am?"

I covered my eyes with a hand. "Yes, they're my nieces."

"Right. I caught them with their friend in a hot tub on one of the yachts down here. They say you work on the boat."

Three girls could only mean one thing: Greyson was there too. Had Alex already gotten this call? "Yes, I'm a stewardess on the *Serendipity*."

"That'd be the boat, then. Listen, they seem harmless enough, so as long as you can come get them, I think a warning will do."

"Yes, of course, thank you." I hung up and swung my legs from the bed, still only half-awake. I slid on my shoes, pausing on my way out the door to look at the empty sofa bed, anger flaring within me at the sight. Once in my car, I crossed the parking lot and stopped in front of Alex's unit. But before I could call him, he stepped outside, van keys in hand and looking as tired and confused as I was.

"I'm guessing you got the same call I did," Alex said when I waved him over.

"Yup." I patted the passenger seat. "Get in."

"This isn't what I thought we'd be doing together in the middle of the night," he said once he'd closed the car door after him. I raised my eyebrows at him, and he rapped against the window with his knuckles. "Distance. Right. Just trying to lighten the mood."

I shook my head, flexing my fingers around the steering wheel as I drove. "Sneaking onto the boat to use the hot tub? What were they thinking?"

"They weren't thinking."

"I don't understand." I kept my eyes on the empty road ahead, taking the same route Alex and I had on all those morning commutes. "They were acting perfectly normal all night. They were half-asleep when I went to bed." Had they been planning this even then? How could they be so deceitful?

Alex stared out the window when the ocean came into view. "Sounds better than my night. Greyson went straight to her room. She hasn't spoken a word to me."

"You okay?"

Alex shook his head. "I'm doing what I think is best for her, but we're both miserable."

Then stay, I wanted to tell him. But that would be selfish, so I let us fall into silence. My thoughts turned to Mia and Kitty, my anger growing with every mile. That phone call had scared me out of my mind. Anything could have happened to them. Didn't they know better by now? Hadn't losing Samson taught them anything?

By the time we arrived at the marina, I was shaking again. Alex didn't look any better off, fuming beside me as we walked to the security office. The girls sat against the wall outside, staring at their knees. Beside them was a big guy in a security guard uniform. Officer Thomas, presumably.

"I believe these three belong to you," he said when Alex and I stopped in front of him.

"Yes. I'm so sorry." I shot Mia and Kitty a glare, but they avoided my gaze.

After a few minutes of polite conversation and a warning to the girls, Officer Thomas disappeared inside, leaving Alex and me alone with our delinquents.

"Car," Alex said to Greyson. I pointed the girls in the same direction, too angry to speak.

The girls slid silently into the back seat, and I was glad to be driving. It gave me something to do. The atmosphere was tense as I pulled out of the marina, and I glanced in the rearview mirror. Kitty looked down at her feet, Greyson had her face to the window, and Mia stared straight ahead, tugging on the strings of her tie-dyed hoodie, face expressionless.

After a few minutes of silence, Alex turned in his seat to look at Greyson. "Why were you there?"

Greyson didn't respond.

"Greyson, answer me," Alex said.

Through the rearview mirror I could see Kitty looking between Mia and Greyson, her lip trembling. "We only wanted to cheer her up," she said. "Like you and Aunt Jo did after that charter with the dog people."

"Thank you, Kitty," Alex said before turning to Greyson again. "The silent treatment ends now, Grey. I'd like *you* to tell me why you were there."

Greyson turned to him, talking so fast and so loud, it made me flinch. "Because I'm tired of listening to you! Why should I when you don't even care what I think? You're always giving up things I never asked you to give up! I don't want to go to L.A.—"

"I don't see what this has to do with you sneaking onto the—"

"Ugh!" Greyson groaned, knocking the back of my seat with her knees. "You always decide what's best for us without even asking me. You don't want to leave, either, so I don't understand why we're going when neither of us wants to go."

"Because your mom—"

"I don't have a mom! She didn't want me, and now she does? Why? What changed? She came to see me twice and now we're supposed to just pack up our life and fit into hers?"

"It's more complicated than—"

"We literally just moved here, which you didn't ask my opinion about either. Or when you quit the restaurant and we left New York. How about Maggie fits into our life if she wants to be in it so bad?"

"It's not that simple, Greyson." Alex's eyes flitted over to me, but I stared straight ahead. "Your mom, she—"

"I told you. I don't have a mom. Maggie can pretend she's my mom all she likes, but she isn't, and she never will be, and I don't even need a mom, because I have you." Her voice broke, strangled as she forced the words from her mouth. "I know you think you have to give up every-thing for me, or fix things, or whatever. But there's nothing to fix. She left, and you didn't, and I don't want anyone else, even though you make me so mad sometimes!"

Alex looked at her for a long moment, and I wished I could know what he was thinking. "We'll talk about this at home," he said, then turned back around in his seat and stared out the window.

Quiet overtook the car again. I'd intended to keep silent until we were back at the condo, but then I caught Mia making a face at Kitty when I glanced in the rearview mirror, and couldn't hold it in any longer.

"Wipe that look off your face, Mia," I snapped. "I can't believe you would do this. Do you know how sick I was with worry? To get a phone call in the middle of the night? How did you get there? And don't tell me you walked."

"Nothing happened," Mia said, and I remembered her comment on the day they'd arrived about minors with fake IDs being able to use Uber.

"Let me guess, you called an Uber, right? And you're lucky nothing happened. Two thirteen-year-olds and a sixteen-year-old getting in a stranger's car in the middle of the night? It would've been better if you'd stolen *my* car! Do you have any idea what could've happened? You could've been kidnapped! Or fallen overboard or gotten hurt. The boat isn't a toy. And don't even get me started on the trespassing. Alex and I will be lucky if the owners don't find out about this, because if they do, Captain will have our heads. We could lose our jobs for this."

"It's not a big deal," Mia said. "You got this job by trespassing."

I gripped the steering wheel tighter. "It is a big deal, Mia. And that was different. I was an adult, and yeah, looking back on it, it was a ter-rible idea. Your mother entrusted me with the two of you for the sum-mer, and if something happened to you—" I shook my head. "I have to keep you safe."

"But you can't keep us safe!" she said. "Haven't you figured that out yet? No one can keep anyone safe! It's all random. People die and there's nothing anyone can do about it, so why try?"

I forced myself to keep my eyes on the road ahead, too angry to look at her. "You're right, Mia. I can't guarantee your safety, but that doesn't mean you should go out of your way to be reckless."

The car went silent again, and no one spoke the rest of the way home. All I could think about was what Mia had said. *Safe.* I turned the word over in my mind like a stone. It was as if Mia were looking for trouble, like she was daring it to follow her. If anything happened to her or Kitty . . . I couldn't even think about it. What would it do to me? To Beth?

"Thanks, Jo," Alex said when I stopped in front of his unit. I gave him a sympathetic smile, our eyes meeting before he shut the door. I watched him disappear inside his condo, our kisses in the karaoke restaurant's parking lot feeling as if they had happened forever ago.

The girls didn't move or speak when I parked the car, and their silence only made me angrier. I clicked out of my seat belt and turned to face them. Didn't they have anything to say for themselves?

"Do you have any idea what I gave up this summer to be with you? I had a whole trip planned. I was going to go to Europe, actually finish my list, but instead I'm getting calls in the middle of the night because my nieces thought it would be fun to take an Uber to party on the yacht!"

Mia remained still, but tears shone in Kitty's eyes. "After everything we've gone through, you should know better than to put yourselves in danger like that. Don't you think your mother's been through enough? Haven't you seen what losing your brother has done to her? If you don't care about yourselves, at least think about her."

Mia glanced up at me with that guilty look I'd seen pass over her face from time to time, the one I'd tried to make sense of but hadn't figured out. She shook her head, tears running down her cheeks as she stared at me. "I ruin everything," she said, her voice breaking. She undid her seat belt and swung open the car door, slamming it behind her before running inside. Kitty, still in the back seat, looked at me with wide eyes, and I turned away. Moments later, she got out of the car, and I saw her run into the condo after her sister.

My first instinct was to chase after them and explain that nothing was ruined, but I couldn't move. I sat in my car, thinking again of how, in a few weeks, I would walk into that condo and be alone. How I would look across the street, and there'd be no Greyson or Alex passing by in their running clothes. I told myself I should go inside and make up with the girls. I should enjoy the time I had left with them. But I didn't want them to see me falling apart like I was now, angry and crying in my car. I was supposed to be the one keeping things together. I stared out the windshield, watching the glow of the TV from my condo until my breathing was even again. When I finally slipped into the living room, both girls were asleep on the sofa bed, Kitty with her arm thrown around Mia.

I watched their sleeping faces, filled with regret for what I'd said. I'd been too harsh. They were just kids. They'd lost their brother, and nothing made sense anymore. Of course they were acting out. Of course they were seeking out good memories. Hadn't I been doing the same thing? I wanted to wake them and apologize. But it was almost four in the morning, and I'd need to leave for work in a few hours. Sleep. That was what all of us needed.

Mia's eyelashes fluttered. For a moment, I thought she might wake up and we could step outside and talk. But she turned away from me, facing her sister in her sleep. I kissed them each on the top of the head before I left for my room, feeling a rush of tenderness toward them. Things would be better tomorrow. Everything looked so different in the light of day.

Eighteen

⚓

WHEN I PASSED INTO THE LIVING ROOM A FEW HOURS LATER, I'D hoped to find the girls as I did most days, perched side by side with bowls of cereal on their laps as they watched TV. Mia would tease me about Alex, Kitty would spout off a random Chinese military proverb, and no one would have to say anything about last night.

But the living room was quiet. The TV flickered in the early-morning light. I glanced at Mia and Kitty, who'd buried themselves deep beneath the blankets, either asleep or pretending to be. I wanted to shake them awake and tell them I was sorry. But maybe it would be better to wait. Things might even resolve themselves, like my argument with Mia after the dinner party. By the time I returned home from work today, everything would be back to normal.

I was eating cereal in the kitchen when my phone buzzed with a text from Alex. **I know this goes against the whole distance thing, but do you want a ride to work?**

Yes, I replied. Because one, I didn't want to fall asleep at the wheel, and two, even though our romantic relationship couldn't go anywhere, that didn't mean we couldn't resume being carpool buddies.

I showered and dressed as quietly as I could, and when Alex's van appeared outside, I paused by my desk and took a sheet of paper from the drawer. I didn't need to leave a note to tell the girls when I'd be home. They knew the rhythm of my days. But it felt wrong to leave without saying something, so I wrote, *Be home at 6, order food with my card*.

"Rough night?" Alex asked, handing me a coffee when I shut the passenger door behind me.

"Ha." I stifled a yawn. "That was . . . not great."

"You mean you didn't enjoy listening to my daughter tell me what a horrible father I am?"

"I think Greyson was saying the opposite of that, actually."

Alex nodded, staring out at the road ahead. "Mia and Kitty okay?"

I squeezed the coffee in my hands. "I wish I knew. They're still asleep."

He set his hand palm up on the center console. I saw the gesture for the invitation it was and placed my hand in his. *He's leaving*, I thought. But carpool buddies could hold hands, right? Surely a little hand-holding wouldn't put me in danger of heartbreak and van sex.

"Should I put on the *Pissed-Off Bad Bitch* playlist?" Alex asked.

"Nina?"

"How'd you know?" he said, shooting me a smile.

"I think it's her most listened-to playlist during charter season."

Alex rolled down the windows and played the music as loud as we could stand. We shouted along to the lyrics, and by the time we pulled into the marina, I was feeling a little better about everything that had happened.

Once he'd parked, Alex turned in his seat to face me. "I'm going to miss you when we go," he said.

I looked down at my hand in his. "Don't start saying goodbye yet."

"Hey," Alex said. I glanced up at him, catching the hesitation that flickered over his face. "We could try it. Long-distance. We could visit each other every month or something."

When he looked at me like that, I wanted to say yes. It sounded romantic, getting on a plane and crossing the country to see each other. But what kind of relationship would that be? If Beth and Mark couldn't make it when they lived under the same roof, what chance did Alex and I stand thousands of miles apart? I shook my head. "It's too complicated."

"We don't have to have it all figured out right now," he said.

I closed my eyes, a wave of sadness passing over me. "Please, Alex. It's just easier this way. A relationship like that wouldn't be worth it."

"You don't think something is better than nothing? We can figure it out."

I sighed. "We'll only hurt each other."

"You can't know that."

Alex's sincerity needled me. Why did he have to make this harder than it already was? Didn't he understand I was only trying to protect both of us? "You already *are* hurting me," I said, pulling my hand from his to press my fingers to my temples. "I get it. You're this happy-go-lucky guy who believes in fate and destiny. But life isn't a fairy tale, Alex. There is no happily ever after."

Alex laughed, but there was no humor to it. "I hate to wreck whatever image you have of me, but I don't exactly see my life as a fairy tale."

So much had happened over the last twelve hours that I couldn't think straight. I was tired, and confused, and didn't want to talk about this. Not now. Not ever. If this conversation continued, I'd end up doing what I always did: lash out, say things I didn't mean, push him away. I grabbed the door handle. "Let's just go inside."

"Hold on, Jo," Alex said. "Say it, whatever it is you want to say to me."

I turned to him, my annoyance flaring into the anger I'd felt last night in the car with Mia and Kitty. "This is what you do, right? You decide what's best for everyone, but you don't actually know what you're doing. Any opportunity to turn your life upside down and you go for it. It's so easy for you to leave, because none of it really matters to you, does it? You're so busy being a martyr that you end up hurting people."

"That's not fair," he said.

"You're right, it's not. I think Greyson would agree with me."

Alex's expression darkened. "Yes, I've given up a lot. You don't even know the half of it, but I don't expect you to understand. How can you when you're so busy protecting yourself?"

"That's not—"

"You're so afraid of getting hurt that you make yourself miserable. Isn't keeping everyone at arm's length exhausting? Aren't you tired of it?"

I turned away, unable to look at him. The *Serendipity* sat prettily on the water, stark white against a cloudless blue sky. At least on deck I knew what to expect: when the guests would arrive, what they wanted from me, when they would leave. "Yes, Alex, it is exhausting. But it's better than the alternative. You can dream up ways for this to work, but when it comes down to it, you're leaving, and I'm tired of being left." I didn't look back at him as I swung open the door. "Don't wait for me after work, I'll have Nina give me a ride home."

Alex didn't say anything when I got out of the van. I walked as fast as I could across the parking lot, telling myself I wouldn't cry. Not for a guy I'd only known for a summer. Not for someone who would end up as a blip in my life, even if we had loved each other. With every step I took toward the dock, it became harder and harder to blink back the tears, and by the time I boarded the boat, they were falling faster than I could wipe them away.

"YOU LOOK LIKE SHIT," NINA SAID WHEN I WALKED INTO THE CREW mess. She looked at me with raised eyebrows and set her mug onto the counter.

"Thanks, Nina." I pushed past her and headed for the laundry room, not wanting to be in here when Alex came inside. "I don't really want to talk," I called at the sound of her footsteps behind me.

Nina followed me into the laundry room and shut the door behind her. I ignored her, starting on a bird-of-paradise fold with a cloth napkin I'd grabbed from a pile on top of the dryer.

"Are you going to tell me what's going on or what?" she said, hopping onto the washing machine.

"Or what."

"Fine, I'll talk until you decide to, then." She folded her hands in her lap. "That was some show you and Alex put on last night, and I'm not talking about the karaoke. Don't think I didn't notice the lipstick on his face after your little rendezvous in the parking lot."

I folded the napkin in half diagonally and didn't respond.

"I thought you'd be happier, though," Nina continued. "I told you he was just confused about his feelings for you. Those kneecaps, really, who can resist them? So is he still a good kisser now that you know him? Yes or no? My guess is yes, given his refined palate and how wrinkled your dress was. Though you look miserable, so maybe no?"

I kept my eyes on the napkin in my hands, folding it until I had a sloppy-looking diamond.

"It's the minivan, isn't it?" Nina continued. "You know I have a thing for soccer moms—the mom jeans, the bob haircuts, the whole Target aesthetic really gets me going. But it's the minivans. I just can't do it. I get that sliding doors are very appealing, but wouldn't an SUV—"

My fingers were jittery as I tugged the last fold of the napkin, and my bird-of-paradise looked more like a bat out of hell. "Oh my God, Nina, please shut up!"

Nina snatched the napkin from my hands, her fingers flying as she refolded it with more skill than I possessed even on my best days. "I'll think about it, if you'll tell me what's going on."

"All right, all right! We made out in the parking lot and he told me he loves me. And yes, he's still an excellent kisser. And no, I'm not happy, because none of it matters. He and Greyson are moving across the country, and who knows if we'll ever see each other again. Oh, and then there's the fact that Mia, Kitty, and Greyson got caught in the yacht's hot tub last night. And Alex and I just got into a fight, and I said some horrible things I didn't mean, and I'm still too pissed at him to do anything about it."

"Whoa, JoJo." Nina hopped off the washer and set the bird-of-paradise onto it. "Deep breath, now," she said, pressing her hands onto my shoulders.

I sucked in a breath through my nose and exhaled in one big whoosh out of my mouth, like Greyson had shown me.

Nina patted my cheek. "First, bravo on the kissing. You needed a good spit swap. Second, I guess we know what Greyson's deal was last night. And finally, I am very sorry to hear he's leaving. That's the butts."

"The butts?"

"It sucks ass! Is that what you want me to say? I was trying to be polite. And I'm sure Alex knows things are . . . difficult right now. Just apologize later."

Nina pulled me into a hug, and I leaned my head on her shoulder as she rubbed my back in big circles.

"I can't imagine he'll want to talk to me after this morning. But you're right. This is the butts," I said.

"I really wish you'd say that more often."

"The butts?"

"Sure, but I meant the part about me being right."

I rolled my eyes.

"And I may have heard about the hot tub incident already."

I pulled away from her. "You did?" Had the owners found out? I'd only met them the few times they'd taken out the yacht themselves. Mr. and Mrs. Green were nice, but they expected nothing less than perfection. I didn't think they'd have any second thoughts about firing me if they felt I deserved it. Would I be losing my job on top of everything else today?

"Officer T told me," Nina said. "I made him promise not to tell Cap or the Greens."

Relief flooded through me, and I wrapped my arms around her, picking her up off the floor. "Nina Lejeune, you are the best human being."

"That's what you think. Maybe I'm a reptilian."

I set Nina back on her feet. "Wait, how do you know Officer Thomas?" It wasn't like we interacted with security much. I'd never heard Nina mention him before.

"Remember that year I answered those Craigslist ads?"

"Never mind, I don't want to know," I said, and tossed a napkin at her.

Nina snatched the napkin from the air and shrugged. "Suit yourself. You wouldn't believe what he does in his free time anyway."

WHEN NINA DROPPED ME OFF THAT EVENING, THE TV WAS STILL glowing through the window. On the way home we'd stopped by the grocery store, where I bought three pints of ice cream and the biggest tub of cheese balls I could find.

"You sure you don't want me to come in with you?" Nina said.

"Yeah, I'm sure," I said, looping my arms through the grocery bags. "I think tonight should be an aunt-nieces only thing."

I thanked Nina for the ride and stepped out of the car. Mia, Kitty, and I would deal with our feelings the way thousands of women before us had, by eating junk food and watching reality TV. No talking required.

"Hey!" Nina called, and I turned back to her. She nodded across the parking lot in the direction of Alex's van. "Promise me you'll think about going over there to kiss and make up. Or maybe make up and make out. I like that better."

"No promises," I said. Though my anger with Alex had faded, I was still embarrassed about what I'd said and ashamed I'd brought Greyson into it. Alex and I hadn't spoken a word to each other the entire charter. Who knew if he'd ever want to speak to me again?

When the condo door swung open, I expected to see Mia and Kitty on the couch watching TV with Greyson. But the girls were nowhere to be found. The sofa bed was put away. The linens were folded in a neat pile beside the couch. As I walked through the condo, I couldn't find so much as a stray phone charger or half-empty glass of water abandoned on a table.

Maybe they'd cleaned to apologize for last night, I thought, and walked to my bedroom. Perhaps they were out on the patio with Greyson. Just last week, I'd found them spread out on lounge chairs and holding magazines before their faces, their freshly painted toes shining in the sunlight.

"This is what teenage girls do in the movies," Greyson had explained, making me laugh.

"Ugh," Mia had groaned, covering her face with the magazine in her hands. "Now you've made it sound uncool."

But when I opened the door and stepped onto the patio now, I was alone. There were no giggling teenage girls. No bottles of nail polish left open and drying in the sun. No long, lanky bodies stretched out on my chairs and holding magazines. No half-empty chip bags gone soggy from a passing rain shower.

I circled the patio, looking one way, then another down the stretch of grass that ran behind the building, but the girls were nowhere in sight. *Relax*, I told myself. Maybe they were up on the beach or at Alex's place. There were plenty of explanations. But as I looked around my garden, flowers withering in the August sun, I knew the girls weren't off having another adventure with Greyson. I'd known it as soon as I didn't see their exploding suitcases in the living room.

I returned inside and scanned the condo for anything belonging to Mia and Kitty. I passed by my desk and spotted the note I'd left the girls that morning. Something caught my eye, and I picked it up. Scrawled at the bottom in Mia's loopy artistic handwriting, the girls had left a note of their own, the only trace they'd been here at all.

Sorry for ruining your summer.
XO, M&K

Nineteen

AS SOON AS I READ THE NOTE, I GRABBED MY PHONE FROM where I'd left it beside the grocery bags, swiping away a notification from my credit card company before calling Mia. Sent to voice mail. I called Kitty, hoping for better luck, but she didn't answer either.

"Shit," I said to my empty condo. "Shit, shit, shit!"

I thought of how Mia had looked before leaving the car last night. Why hadn't I immediately gone after her? Or woken them up when I went inside? Why had I left without saying something? I should've confiscated Mia's fake ID at least. I covered my face with my hands, struggling to keep the panic from clouding my mind. Beth had trusted me to take care of Mia and Kitty, but less than twenty-four hours after their escapade on the yacht with Greyson, I'd lost them again.

Greyson. I shoved my phone into my pocket and left the condo, not bothering to slip on my shoes before racing across the parking lot, the asphalt burning my bare feet. I hesitated in front of Alex's door, worried about what he might say when he saw me, but if anyone would know where Mia and Kitty had gone, it was Greyson.

I knocked on the door, then stilled, listening for movement from within. Maybe Alex was ignoring me. I lifted my hand to knock again, but the door swung open. Alex stood before me, a dish towel tossed maddeningly over his shoulder. I wanted to reach out to him, to say how sorry I was, but there wasn't time for that now.

"Jo. Hi," Alex said. He looked me up and down, his guarded expression giving way to concern. "Are you all right?"

"Is Greyson home?" I lifted onto my toes and looked past him into the living room but didn't see anyone. Could Greyson be missing too?

"Yeah, she's here. Do you . . . want to come in?"

"Yes." I stepped inside, grateful at least one teen was accounted for.

I scanned Alex's couches, but they were empty. Part of me had hoped this was one of Mia and Kitty's pranks and I'd find them here watching TV. But the TV was off. There was no giddy laughter, only the sound of whatever playlist Alex had on. I walked to the kitchen, but the girls weren't around the table eating Alex's gourmet junk food like I sometimes found them.

Alex followed me with his hands in his pockets. "Are you looking for something?"

I scanned the hall, then turned to him, trying not to let the way he looked now—hurt, upset, confused—distract me. "Mia and Kitty. I can't find them. Have they been here?"

"No," Alex said. "Not since I've been home at least. When did you last talk to them?"

"Last night in the car. Right after we dropped you off. All their stuff was gone when I came home. They didn't text me to check in today, but I figured it was because they were still upset."

Alex took me by the shoulders and steered me to the kitchen table. "We'll figure it out. Here, sit." He turned away, and seconds later pushed a plate of lemon cake in front of me.

"I'll be right back." He left down the hall and knocked on Greyson's door, pausing for a moment before poking his head inside.

I stared down at the lemon cake. At least Alex didn't completely hate me after what I'd said. But then again, maybe he did. He seemed like the type of person who'd bake his mortal enemy a cake.

Greyson appeared moments later with Alex at her heels.

"Hey, Jo," she said, taking the seat across from me. Alex stood behind her, bracing the back of her chair with his hands.

Greyson chewed on the string of her hoodie—no, it was *Mia's* hoodie. The one I'd seen her wearing last night. "Have you seen Mia and Kitty today?" I asked.

Greyson tugged the sleeves of the hoodie over her hands. "They didn't come over today."

Maybe that was true, but she'd definitely seen them. How else had she gotten Mia's hoodie? "But did you see them today? Maybe at my place? Or the beach?"

Greyson shook her head.

I didn't believe that for a second. Since they'd met, there hadn't been a single day the girls didn't see each other.

"They left this," I said, and passed the note Mia had written across the table.

I watched Greyson's face carefully. She looked down at the note, the hoodie string still in her mouth.

Alex bent over her shoulder to read it, then took the chair beside her. "You don't know anything about this?"

Greyson shook her head, and her hands grew still as she stared at the note in front of her.

I leaned toward her, hoping I looked as desperate as I felt. "I've called them, but their phones are off. I don't know where they are, or where they're going. I just need to know they're safe."

Greyson shifted uncomfortably in her seat. She pushed the note back to me and let the hoodie string drop from her mouth. "Okay, I saw them, but they made me promise I wouldn't say anything, and I pinkie promised, and you can't break a pinkie promise. Only . . . I don't want anything bad to happen to them, and if you haven't heard from them . . .

Well, I thought they'd call you, or at least text. They came to say good-bye, and I said I thought they weren't leaving for another three weeks, but they said they had to go right now because they'd messed up your summer enough. I said I didn't think that was true. I begged them to stay, but they wouldn't."

Alex went rigid in his seat. "And you didn't think to tell me or Jo about this?"

Greyson shrugged. "They made me promise."

"Do you know where they are?" I asked.

"They wouldn't say." Greyson looked up at me with tear-filled eyes. "They said it was a secret. I asked them, and Kitty wanted to tell me, but Mia said not to because she knew I'd tell. I would, you know. I'd tell you if I knew where they were."

"When did you see them?"

"I don't know, like, four hours ago."

Four hours! They could be anywhere by now. I hung my head in my hands.

"I'm sorry," Greyson squeaked. "I didn't know—"

"You know better than to keep a secret like that," Alex said sharply.

Greyson kept her eyes on the table.

I felt a twinge of sympathy for her. She'd only done what Mia and Kitty had asked. Greyson and Mia were only a few years closer in age than me and Beth. At thirteen, I would've done anything Beth asked of me. I groaned at the thought of her. "What am I supposed to tell my sister?"

"You haven't called her yet?" Alex said.

I shook my head, then looked up at him. "Maybe she already knows. Maybe she knows where they are." I walked into the living room, hands shaking as I called her.

"Beth," I said, relieved she'd picked up. "Have you—"

"I was just about to call you," she said.

"So you've heard from the girls?"

"Mia texted me a few minutes ago."

I was so relieved I thought I'd swoon onto the floor, like Kitty had last night. "Do you know where they are? They left a note but didn't say."

"Look." Beth's tone was as angry as it had been the day the girls had arrived and she thought I'd abandoned them at the airport. "They're safe at a hotel. They booked flights home for tomorrow morning. I don't know how they did all this or what happened between the three of you, but they made me promise not to tell you which hotel they're at."

"Beth, I didn't mean for—"

"I shouldn't have sent them. It was too much, too soon." Too much for them or for me? I didn't want to know. "They're fine. No one's hurt. They promised not to leave the hotel and will go directly to the airport."

"I can explain—"

"I can't talk about this right now," she said. "I'll text you when they get here."

"I'm so sorry," I said, but Beth had already hung up.

"Your sister's heard from them?" Alex said when I took my seat at the table again. "What did she say?"

"They're at a hotel." The icing on my untouched slice of lemon cake had melted, making a sticky puddle on the plate. I thought of Kitty, who loved lemon everything—lemonade, Lemonheads, the lemon-flavored Girl Scout cookies—she would've devoured it whole. "They made her promise not to tell me which one, but they're safe. They have flights home in the morning."

"I'm sorry," Alex said.

I shook my head. How could he feel sorry for me about anything after what I'd said to him that morning? "It's my fault."

"I'm sure that's not true."

"No, it is. You didn't hear what I said to them after you left. I went too far."

"How can we help?"

What was there to help with? They'd left, and it was my fault. "I don't think there's anything you can do."

I stood to go, and Alex walked me to the door. We lingered awk-
wardly on either side of the threshold, our fight from the morning hanging between us.

He drummed his fingers along the doorframe. "You'll tell me if you
need anything?" he said. "If you hear from them?"

"Yeah, I will," I said. I avoided looking him in the eye. I wanted to
tell him I was sorry, but what could I say that would be enough? My
words had already hurt him. And so I left, crossing the parking lot to
my empty condo, where three pints of melted ice cream were waiting
for me.

I WAS HALF-ASLEEP ON THE COUCH WHEN A KNOCK ON MY
door roused me. I sat up, disoriented when I realized it was dark outside.
As soon as I'd come back from Alex's, I fell onto the couch and watched
episode after episode of *My Super Sweet 16*.

Mia and Kitty. I moved the blinds aside but didn't see the girls or their
oversized suitcases. Instead, there was Greyson, still wearing Mia's tie-
dyed hoodie, though it was over eighty degrees out. Greyson perked her
head up when I opened the door, and I felt a surge of hope. Maybe she'd
heard from them.

"Dad thought you might be hungry," she said, and held out a Tupperware to me.

"Oh, thanks." I took the Tupperware from her hands, its warmth
spreading through my fingertips. "Good leftovers?"

Greyson shook her head. "It's pizza night, but Dad said you looked
like you needed comfort food."

I peeled back one corner of the lid. Inside was some sort of casserole
topped with breadcrumbs.

"It's good," Greyson said. "It's got like three fancy cheeses I can't
pronounce. He always makes it on report card day. Not as a reward or
anything. I just hate report card day."

"Today definitely feels like a report card day," I said, tapping my fingers against the lid of the Tupperware, my heart full at the thought of Alex in his kitchen cooking for me, even after everything that had happened between us. "Will you tell him I said thanks?"

"Sure." I expected her to sprint off toward her unit, but she only stood there, gnawing on the hoodie string again.

I set the Tupperware on the entryway table. "Do you want to come in? You can have some."

Greyson shook her head, dropping her eyes to her shoes. "I'm sorry I didn't tell you when Kitty and Mia came to say goodbye."

"You were just trying to be a good friend."

"Yeah." I thought she would go then, but she lingered at my door. "Have they called you yet?" she asked.

"No. You?"

She shook her head, and I could see the hurt on her face. Her only friends had up and left, refusing to tell her where they were.

"You're sure you don't want to come in?"

"Yeah, I'm sure." She let the hoodie string fall from her mouth and started speaking so fast that I had a hard time keeping up. "Speaking of being a good friend, Mia made me promise I wouldn't tell anyone. But I don't know, I think you should probably know about it. And Dad's basically drilled into my head that we aren't supposed to keep secrets, especially harmful ones, but please don't tell her you heard it from me, because she'd kill me, and I don't want her to hate me, even if we never see each other again."

A secret? A harmful one? What secret could Mia possibly have? "Slow down, Greyson. Mia made you promise not to tell anyone what?"

Greyson scanned the walkway, one direction, then the other. I leaned forward in anticipation. What had Mia said to make Greyson act this paranoid?

"Greyson, what—"

"Mia said it's her fault Samson's dead."

Greyson stuck the hoodie string back in her mouth, and I stared at her. "But Samson was hit by a car. Mia was home when it happened."

"I know. That's what Kitty and I said. But she said it was her fault because Samson asked her for a ride to his friend's house, and she said no, and so he took his bike and . . . and . . ." She shook her head. "She hates herself."

I gripped the doorframe, glad I'd set down the Tupperware. Moments from the summer flitted through my mind. Mia's words from last night *I ruin everything*. Her distaste for driving. The guilt I sometimes found on her face. That night on the patio—*Aunt Jo. There's something I didn't say. Something about Samson*.

Aunt Jo. Mia had never called me that, not even when she was a kid. It was always Jo this and Jo that. Was this what she'd been about to tell me? I'd suspected something was going on, and yet I hadn't pushed. I'd been so closed off that Mia felt she couldn't come to me. Instead, I'd spent all summer trying to distract her and Kitty. I hadn't wanted to talk about Samson at all. And so they'd turned to someone who would listen—Greyson. How had I failed so miserably at being there when they needed me most?

"Jo?" Greyson said.

"Thank you for telling me." I sighed, taking in Greyson before me, who'd been kind, and open, and loyal when I couldn't be. "They're lucky to have you as a friend."

She dropped her eyes to her shoes again. "It's awful, and I . . . I feel bad for how much I complained about moving. They must think I'm so annoying. It's not like anyone's died."

"You're allowed to be sad," I said. "Mia and Kitty understand. They don't think you're annoying, and neither do I, and neither does your dad."

Greyson's lip trembled. She looked up at me, then jolted forward and wrapped me in a hug. "He really likes you," she said. "I do too."

I hugged her back, not knowing what to say. It was obvious I'd miss Alex, but I knew I'd miss Greyson just as much.

She pulled away from me and wiped at her eyes with the sleeve of

Mia's hoodie. "Dad's probably wondering where I am," she said with a sniff. "He's going to think I got kidnapped by aliens or something. Well, he probably wouldn't think that. But he might think I got kidnapped, so I better go home."

I watched her bound off across the parking lot, only closing my door when I saw her disappear through hers. Then I went to the kitchen and leaned against the counter, shoveling the casserole straight from the Tupperware and into my mouth until I thought I'd be sick if I took another bite. I opened the refrigerator, pushing around cartons and containers to make room for one more. There was a pizza box, a jug of milk, a carton of half-and-half, three Chinese takeout boxes, a pile of candy bars, and about five containers of food Alex had sent over with Greyson this week that I hadn't returned yet. It was the fullest my fridge had been in years, and I thought of the day the girls had arrived—the cereal and milk I'd stolen from the boat, my refrigerator bare. I pulled out the pizza box and set it on the counter, wedging the casserole into a space on the top shelf.

The refrigerator beeped, and I shut the door, wondering what Kitty and Mia were doing right now. Probably watching TV in their hotel room. I flopped onto the couch and covered myself with a blanket they'd left folded nearby. Closing my eyes, I tried to still each part of my body one by one, but it didn't work. I gave up and turned the TV back on, resuming the episode of *My Super Sweet 16* I'd been in the middle of before Greyson came over. The main conflict was about the mother surprising her daughter with matching outfits (silvery minidresses even Nina would deem inappropriate), and I cried as I watched it. The episodes with parents trying to act like teenagers were Mia and Kitty's favorites. I cried all throughout the episode and into the start of the next one. For Kitty, who couldn't remember Samson's laughter. For Mia, who blamed herself for his death. For my sister and Mark, who'd lost their son and their marriage. And for myself, not because I deserved any pity, but because in trying to protect myself, I'd pushed away the people I loved the most. And to what end? The distance hadn't made their leaving hurt any less.

WHEN I WOKE UP THE NEXT MORNING, THE TV DISPLAYED A MES-sage asking if I was still watching *My Super Sweet 16*. I rubbed my hands over my face, smoothing the welts the couch pillow had left on my cheek. My body was stiffer than when we'd slept at Coral Castle, but at least I had the day off. There was no way I would have been able to put on my stew smile. I checked my phone, hoping for something, anything, from Mia and Kitty, but there was nothing. Not even a punctuation-free angry text from Beth.

It was still early, night fading into gray. I went into the bathroom, where my bathing suit hung over the rail of the shower curtain. Shedding my work clothes from the day before, I pulled it on, avoiding my reflection in the mirror.

I left my condo and walked down to the pool. All night I'd dreamed of my father and Samson. The dreams had been memories of things I'd forgotten or had wanted to forget. I'd come early enough that I had the pool to myself. The water raised goose bumps on my skin as I descended each step, and once I adjusted to the temperature, I did laps back and forth, the memories looping through my mind again as I swam. My father stretched out beside me on my bed, the two of us listening to songs from an opera I didn't understand. I'd never cared what they were about. It was the sound of my father humming along that was beautiful to me. The day Samson lost his first tooth, and how I'd tried not to laugh when he cried because he was terrified of the tooth fairy. My father teaching me to ride a bike, how he'd promised not to let go without telling me, a promise he'd kept.

I lifted myself from the pool when I was too tired to swim any longer, and watched as the sky shifted and changed. Florida was famous for its beaches, but Florida skies were what I loved most about living here.

Every morning looked like a miracle. Light flooded above the horizon, threading gold through the towering clouds strung overhead. I thought about Samson again, who'd sometimes joined me for my morning swims. We'd go down to the beach when we were done, the two of us watching the sunrise while his sisters slept. I couldn't remember the last sunrise we'd watched together. There were too many identical insignificant mornings like that one. Only they weren't insignificant, even if they weren't memorable. I would have forced myself into memorizing every second if I'd known we'd never watch another sunrise together again.

"There you are, Jo Jo." Startled, I turned around. Beside the gate to the pool stood Nina, looking exactly herself in an oversized Hawaiian shirt and mom jeans.

"What are you doing here?" I asked.

Nina sat beside me on the ledge of the pool. She rolled up the bottoms of her jeans and let her feet dangle in the water. "Alex called. He said you might need me."

"Did he tell you what happened?"

Nina nodded. She put her arm around my shoulders. "Do you want to talk about it?"

"No," I said. "But I think I need to."

She rubbed my arm. "All right, then. Hit me."

I kept my eyes on the water and told Nina all about my fight with Mia and Kitty. Mia's secret. How I'd refused to talk about Samson all summer, pushing the girls away. How I knew exactly what Mia was going through, because I'd felt the same way when my father died. I told her about the note the girls had left and how they thought they'd ruined my summer.

"I really fucked up, Nina. If I hadn't been so bent on trying to make them happy, maybe Mia would have told me, and I could have helped."

"They probably haven't left yet," she said.

"It's too late. They won't answer their phones, and Beth won't talk to me." I watched ripples of sunlight web their way across the pool and thought of what Mia had said last night: *If you love someone, you don't give up on them. You try.* Maybe it wasn't too late. Maybe I could find them. I was sick of waiting, sick of pushing people away. I was so damn tired of being afraid and defensive. I'd thought my list and my job meant I was adventurous, a risk taker. But I wasn't, not with anything that mattered. I couldn't take the easy way out. Not with this. A phone call once they returned home wouldn't be enough. I had to find them before they left. I at least had to try.

I hopped to my feet and wrapped my towel around my waist. I could find the girls and explain they hadn't ruined anything. I could talk to Mia like Beth had talked to me on that long-ago night in her kitchen. I could show her I understood. I could convince them to stay and save what was left of the summer.

"We need to hurry," I said.

Nina jumped to her feet beside me and hurriedly rolled down the bottoms of her jeans. "Yes! I love a good airport run."

"How many have you done?"

"How many has the average person done?" Nina asked, following me through the pool gate and into the parking lot.

"I don't know, probably zero."

"Double that, then."

"That's . . . still zero. And besides, I'm hoping a hotel run will be enough."

Instead of going left to my condo, I went right and stopped in front of Alex's door. I knocked, and Nina turned to me. "Why are we—"

Alex opened the door, and my heart stuttered at the sight of him in his plaid pajama pants and a white T-shirt, his hair messy from sleep. Ordinary in the best way. His eyes widened in surprise, probably confused at the sight of me standing there in my bathing suit and towel, and Nina dressed as she always was. "Jo. Nina. Good morning."

"Remember how you told me to let you know if I needed anything?" I said.

Alex stepped aside without hesitation. "Come on in."

Twenty

⚓

"IS IT RINGING?" I ASKED.

Greyson set her phone on the table. "Yes, but it keeps ringing and ringing and ringing. It doesn't even go to voice mail now."

"And there wasn't anything on their social media accounts?" I asked.

Greyson shook her head.

"And you're sure they didn't mention where they were staying?" Alex said.

"All they said was they were leaving. They didn't tell me anything."

"You're sure?"

Greyson slumped in her chair. "Yes, Dad, I'm sure. I think I'd remember if Mia and Kitty had told me the name of the hotel they were staying at." Alex raised an eyebrow at her. "Okay, so maybe I wouldn't remember the *name*, but I'd remember if they'd told me a name, and they didn't. They didn't even tell me they were staying at a hotel."

Nina leaned against the kitchen island, crumbs falling onto her shirt as she ate a slice of Alex's lemon cake. "Don't you teens use location-tracking on Snapchat? I do. That's how I always know where my enemies are."

"Dad won't let me have Snapchat." Greyson said.

"That's not true. I said you could have it as long as you were my friend, and I believe you said, *Then what's the point?*" He turned to me and Nina. "Which I found quite offensive. I think my snapchats would be very interesting."

Greyson rolled her eyes. "Snaps, not snapchats. And they'd probably all be of food or you singing or both." She shuddered. "And besides, TikTok is cooler than Snapchat now."

"Oh God," Nina said, covering her face in her hands. "Am I getting old?"

As entertaining as it was to mull over Alex's potential Snapchat habits and Nina's aging crisis, I had more-pressing concerns. I'd hoped the girls would've said something to Greyson by now. Or that she'd have come up with a way to locate them. But both turned out to be dead ends. "Did you try texting them again?"

Greyson stared at her phone on the table. "They haven't responded to any of my texts, but I know they've read them. Mia has her read receipts on. She says she likes people to know when she's ignoring them." Greyson frowned. "Not that I think she's doing it to me to be mean. She probably just forgot to turn it off."

I buried my face in my arms. My grand gesture was going nowhere fast. "I guess I'll just have to call them when they get home."

"Would they have used your laptop to book a hotel or buy their flights?" Alex asked.

"I doubt it. Those two are glued to their phones." And then I remembered Beth saying she didn't know how they'd done it. Which meant she hadn't paid for the hotel or flights. I had all the cash she'd sent down with the girls, which wasn't much at this point. I couldn't imagine either of them had enough money for a hotel and two tickets back home.

I jolted upright, remembering the notification from my credit card company I'd ignored the day before. I hadn't thought anything of it because I'd set up alerts for any purchase over ten dollars after a thief nabbed my credit card in Nassau years ago. Could the girls have used my card? I'd sent Mia the info on the day they arrived. I'd told them to use it yesterday. They knew I kept it in the desk drawer in case they needed it for an emergency. It would explain how they'd done it, and I bet I could figure out where they were staying if they had. I only hoped I wouldn't be too late.

"I'll be right back," I said, ignoring the confused looks of the others as I raced out the door to my condo.

I tossed my towel onto the couch and grabbed my phone from where I'd left it on the table. Scrolling through my messages I found two texts from my credit card company. The first, from yesterday, was to notify me of a purchase from an airline. The second, sent that morning, was a charge from a hotel. I slipped on my shoes, grabbed my purse and keys, and raced back to Alex's condo.

"I know where they are," I said as soon as I stepped inside. "But I can't stay. I've got to—"

The look on Alex's and Nina's faces stopped me.

"What? What is it?"

"You, uh, want something to wear?" Alex said.

I looked down and realized I was still in my bathing suit. In my excitement over the texts from the credit card company, I'd forgotten to toss on some clothes.

"I know I have some bold fashion choices, but wearing that into a hotel lobby is next level," Nina said.

"I can just—" I pointed across the parking lot, but stopped when Alex, who'd changed out of his pajamas, slipped on his shoes and grabbed the keys to his van. "You don't have to come with me."

"Are you kidding?" He knotted his laces and stood from the couch. "One second."

He disappeared into his bedroom and returned moments later with a T-shirt and the neon-green running shorts I'd admired all summer for the blessed view of his legs they'd provided. "No time to waste," he said, tossing them to me. I slipped them on over my bathing suit, reminded of the night he'd lent me his towel.

Which Nina was apparently thinking about too. "You've really got to stop meeting Alex barely clothed, Josephine."

WHEN WE ARRIVED AT THE HOTEL, A DAYS INN ONLY A MILE FROM the airport, Alex and Greyson kept watch by the entrance, while Nina and I marched up to the front desk attendant, a woman with bright orange lipstick and matching cat-eye glasses.

She scanned my and Nina's outfits with skepticism. "Checking in?"

"Did two teenage girls get a room here yesterday?" I asked.

The woman gave me a glassy stare. "We don't allow minors to book rooms, ma'am."

"One of them has a fake ID. Please, they're my nieces. They were staying with me for the summer, but they ran off."

The woman pursed her lips, unmoved. "I told you, we don't allow minors to book rooms."

Apparently appealing to this woman's sympathies wouldn't work. "They used my card. Their names are Mia and Catherine Taylor, but the card they used was under my name, Josephine Walker. That's fraud, right?" I showed her my ID, but still the woman didn't move.

Nina shoved me aside and stood on her toes to lean over the counter, eyeing the woman's name tag. "All right, Brenda. I'm going to level with you."

Brenda raised her eyebrows, unimpressed.

Nina jerked her thumb in my direction. "This gorgeous human butterfly needs to get to her nieces, and you're going to help her because, one, I'd hate to call corporate and tell them you don't have proper security. Seriously, letting minors rent rooms? And two, I know exactly what goes down in room 24 on Wednesday nights. I'm sure the local news would love a good story on—"

"One moment," Brenda said, cutting Nina off.

I turned to Nina as Brenda typed on her computer. "Is this another Craigslist thing I don't want to know about?"

Nina winked. "I've got blackmail on half of Palm Beach."

Brenda cleared her throat. "It seems they checked out about an hour ago."

My heart sank. I'd finally tracked the girls down, and we'd missed them. It had been a ridiculous idea thinking I could get to them in time. Deflated, I thanked Brenda and turned to go, but she called out after us.

"They booked the shuttle to the airport. It says they had a ten fifteen flight."

I turned to her, adrenaline coursing through me again. They weren't gone yet. There was still time. "Thank you. Thank you so much." Breathless, Nina and I joined Alex and Greyson at the entrance.

"They already left the hotel." I walked past them and out the hotel door without stopping. I checked my phone; it was already nine thirty. We had to get to the airport and find them before they boarded their flight.

"Looks like I'm getting my airport run after all," Nina said once we were in the van again.

"You were amazing in there," I said to Nina. "And for what it's worth, I think you're a gorgeous human butterfly too."

Nina waved me off. "Nah. I'm much more exotic. Like a gorgeous human flamingo."

WHEN WE TUMBLED OUT OF THE VAN AND INTO THE AIRPORT parking garage, Alex shoved his keys into his pocket and turned to me. "What's the plan?"

I stared at him. Wasn't the plan obvious? We'd race through the airport, getting to Mia and Kitty just as their flight was about to board. They'd run into my arms when they saw me. Right now, they were probably sitting in those fake leather chairs, Mia with her headphones in, Kitty reading *The Art of War*.

"I'll march in there, ask for the cheapest flight I can buy, and hope I find them before their flight boards," I said.

Nina and Greyson looked ready to sprint toward the terminal.

But Alex looked less than enthused. "I don't think that will work."

"Why not?"

"You can't just waltz in there and start asking for the next flight. It'll look suspicious. And don't take this the wrong way, but you look kind of suspicious right now."

I looked down at myself, remembering I was wearing Alex's baggy running clothes over my bathing suit. My tangled, damp hair stuck to the back of my neck. Alex was right, I didn't exactly look like someone who'd been planning on air travel today.

"Right." I looked at my phone. "And I have no idea what gate they're at. The airport is small, but none of it matters if I can't get past security."

Alex started typing on his phone. Had he given up already? As if sensing my disappointment, he looked up and gave me that almost smile. "Don't look like that." He held up his phone. "I know which flight they're on. It's the only flight to Raleigh at that time. They'll be at gate C11." He looked back down at his phone. "And I'm buying you a plane ticket now, so you won't cause any suspicion at the counter. Their flight is full, so it looks like you're going to Atlanta tonight."

"You don't have to—"

"Too late, I'm already putting in your information. I obviously know your birthday."

I dug through my purse for my debit card, but Alex pushed it away.

"It'll take too long to type out your card info when mine's already in here. Consider it an early birthday present. You're checked in and everything. You've got a middle seat, though."

"You keep your credit card info in there with that shitty passcode?" Nina said.

"How do you know my passcode?" Alex replied. "What are you all standing around for?" He set off toward the terminal, and Greyson raced ahead, taking long strides across the concrete.

"Fine, I give in," Nina said as she jogged beside me. "He can be Hot Guy from the Bar slash Hot Single Dad again."

"I really prefer Hot Yacht Chef," he called over his shoulder.

PALM BEACH INTERNATIONAL AIRPORT WAS NOT LARGE BY ANY means, but today it was packed with people. As Alex, Greyson, Nina, and I passed through the automatic doors and into the air-conditioning, my hopes of finding Mia and Kitty faded at the sight of the crowded check-in counters. Lines from almost every airline snaked across a gleaming white floor. Tired moms bounced babies on their hips, dads wrangled toddlers, and groups of college students with gigantic backpacks looked around impatiently as they waited to check their bags.

I scanned the room for Mia and Kitty, hoping to find their faces in the crowd. They were most likely at their gate already, waiting for the boarding process to begin, but maybe they'd gotten caught in the chaos out here. After circling the check-in counters and finding no sign of either of them, I made my way to the back of the security line. Alex, Nina, and Greyson stood beside me. The line stretched far ahead, the roped-off area signaling the start of security seeming an impossible distance away.

"Are you going to make it?" Greyson asked as the line shuffled forward. "We've only got twenty-five minutes."

Alex's eyes met mine. "You have to try, right?"

"Yeah. I've got to try." This wasn't only about Mia and Kitty. It was about me too. I needed them to be with me on my first birthday without Samson. I needed to tell Mia how I felt about him so she would know I hadn't forgotten. I needed to tell her about what I'd gone through after my dad died so she'd know she wasn't alone.

"Oh, she is absolutely doing this," Nina said. "I was told there'd be an airport run, and I demand nothing less."

The line kept moving, but it took forever to get to the first check-in point. Nina, Alex, and Greyson stepped out of the line and wished me luck, and then I was on my own. The TSA agent glanced at the ticket Alex had sent to my phone, and then waved me through. The line to the body scanners zigzagged ahead of me, inching forward. I only had fifteen minutes until Mia and Kitty's flight boarded. I searched the crowd, hoping to find anyone who could help. Not the agent at the first checkpoint. She'd seen my ticket, so I couldn't claim I was running late. Then I saw her, another TSA agent heading in my direction, just beyond the roped-off edges of the line.

I leaned over the barrier to catch her attention as she walked past. "Excuse me!"

The agent turned to me with a blank expression.

"Please, I'm going to miss my flight," I lied. "Can I skip ahead?"

The woman squinted at me, no doubt taking in my wet hair and baggy clothes. "Sorry, but if we do it for you, we have to do it for everyone who's running late."

Why hadn't I asked Nina to come with me? Maybe she had blackmail on this random TSA agent. If this woman didn't help me, I'd never get to Mia and Kitty in time. I'd done everything I could, and it still wasn't enough.

But maybe I hadn't done everything I could. If lying didn't work, there was always another option: the truth. "Fine. I'm not running late," I said. The woman shook her head and turned to go, and I started speaking as quickly as I could, the story spilling out of me. I told her about Samson and how Mia and Kitty had shown up at my condo without warning. I told her how they thought they'd ruined my summer, and how Mia thought it was her fault her brother had died, and how I had to get to her before she left.

"Please, I can't let them go. Not like this."

At the TSA agent's unchanged expression, I figured I was about to get a one-way ticket to extra security. But then she rolled her eyes and lifted the barrier. "Oh, come on."

"This is as far as I can take you," she said, leading me to the end of a much shorter priority line. I thanked her and watched her walk away, wondering if she had nieces she loved too.

I slipped off my shoes at the body scanners. Anxious, I waited as the people in front of me took out laptops and tablets, unclasped watches, and dumped loose change into bins, all of it slower than the *Serendipity* leaving port. A man set off the scanner when he forgot to take off his belt, wasting precious time. Each second was agony.

Finally, it was my turn, and I breezed through the body scanner without incident. I snatched up my purse and shoved my feet into my shoes, finally in the terminal. I looked at my phone, and my pulse quickened. I only had three minutes.

Gate C11 was one of the farthest from security, of course. I broke into a run, earning scornful looks from travelers as I ran down the terminal, narrowly avoiding crashing into a few of them. Before long a stitch nagged at my side, making me wish I'd kept up the marathon training.

Just when I thought I could run no more, I arrived at the gate, frantically searching the crowd for Mia and Kitty. The boarding process had already begun, and I hoped they weren't among the passengers already on the plane. Even though I'd know Mia and Kitty in an instant, I gave any teenage girl a double take. But it was no use. I was too late. They'd already boarded the plane.

I sank into an empty seat at the gate. All this trouble, the money Alex had spent on my ticket, and nothing. The girls would leave without even knowing I'd tried to get to them. They'd think I didn't want them to stay. I'd have to take off work and book a flight to Raleigh. And how long would that take? How many more hours would Mia walk around thinking Samson's death was her fault? How many days would Mia and Kitty spend thinking they'd ruined my summer?

And then I heard Mia's voice.

I looked up, and sure enough there they were, racing to the gate with iced coffee in their hands. They didn't see me at first. Out of breath, they stepped into the crowd beside the gate.

"I told you we didn't have time to get coffee, Kitty."

"Obviously we did have time, because—" Kitty caught sight of me as I approached. "Aunt Jo," she said, her eyes immediately welling up with tears.

Mia's face went through the same ripple of surprise as Kitty's. "Jo? What are you—"

"I texted you," I said. "I called a million times."

"I didn't want to talk," Mia said. She glanced at the line of passengers boarding the plane, many of them staring at us, and tugged Kitty's sleeve. "We have to go."

"Don't go," I said. "Please. This is all my fault." I thought of all the times Mia and Kitty had tried to talk to me about Samson, and every time I'd deflected them. "I'm sorry I didn't—"

"No," Mia said. "I ruined everything. Your summer, your—"

"Are you kidding? You didn't ruin my summer. This summer would've been the worst of my life if you hadn't shown up."

Mia looked down at her shoes. Kitty, who'd started crying as soon as she saw me, cried even harder.

"But your list," Kitty said. "We ruined it. You had to cancel your trip."

"The list, the blog, it doesn't matter. Look at all we did! There are only two items left, and I promise, if you'll forget about getting on this plane and come with me, I'll walk into the first tattoo shop we pass on the way home. I'll get one right now. Twenty-nine items out of thirty is an A-plus. And are you really going to make me celebrate my birthday alone?"

"You won't be alone," Mia said.

"But if you leave, I won't have you. I won't have any family with me on Samson's birthday."

Only a few passengers waited to board the plane now, and Mia glanced at the line again. "Kitty, you should stay," she said. "But I can't." Tears slipped down her cheeks, and she gave me a watery smile. "Thanks for everything, Jo, really. But I . . ." Her voice trailed off as the tears came faster, and she shook her head, unable to speak. She turned to go, but I caught her by the arm.

"Mia, it's not your fault Samson died."

Mia turned to me, her face pale. Kitty's eyes widened as she looked between the two of us.

"I know it feels that way, but—"

Mia's expression clouded over. "How can you know? You can't possibly know."

"Has your mom ever told you about the day our dad died?"

"Of course," Mia said, swiping at her tears. "But I don't see how—"

"Did she tell you I was the one who found him?"

Mia stilled. "No."

"I was twelve," I said. "Your mom and grandma weren't home. He asked if I wanted to watch a movie with him—some opera he'd shown me a million times. I said no and went to my room. I don't even remember what I was doing. I found him when I went downstairs. Do you know how many times I asked myself what would've happened if I'd just watched that opera one more time? I'd give anything to watch it again. I didn't kill him, but I always felt it was my fault."

Mia pressed her lips together and looked away. "That's different. When Sam asked me for a ride, I told him to take his bike. He said it would rain, and I told him . . . I told him to fuck off." She whimpered, blinking back tears. "That's the last thing I said to him."

Kitty leaned her head onto Mia's shoulder, and neither girl resisted me when I pulled them into a hug. I stroked Mia's hair as she dissolved into sobs. The two of them were nearly as tall as I was. And though Mia was right on the cusp of adulthood, as she cried on my shoulder, she was that little girl who used to lay her head in my lap again.

"We all say things we don't mean," I said. "You can't blame yourself, Mia. I blamed myself for a long time, and it was a mistake. I stopped talking to people. I didn't sleep or eat . . . I had no one, except your mom. And she told me the same thing I'm going to tell you. It didn't fix anything, but it helped me start to forgive myself."

"What did she say?" Mia asked.

"You couldn't have known, Mia," I whispered. "It's not your fault, and Samson would tell you that himself if he could. It was an accident, a horrible accident." I was crying now, too, as I held Mia and her guilt and Kitty and her sadness in my arms. "Samson knew you loved him. I know I don't talk about it, but I miss him too. And if you stay, we can talk about it. I want to talk about it. Please, stay."

The three of us stood there, crying in each other's arms for a long time, but if people were staring, I didn't notice. I didn't care. When the girls finally pulled away, Mia looked around at the terminal in a daze. Her eyes landed on the gate for their flight, and she let out a hiccupping laugh. The flight was closed. The plane had already pushed back.

"Guess we don't really have a . . ." Mia paused, a look of horror crossing her face. "Our suitcases! They're on the plane! No offense, Jo, but there's no way I'm wearing your clothes for three weeks."

"Come on," I said, pulling them to my sides. "We'll pick a few things up from Target and go home. I'll call the airline when we get there."

Mia hesitated. For a moment I thought she'd changed her mind, but then I caught the hint of a smile.

"I believe you promised us a trip to the tattoo shop first," she said.

"I was hoping you'd forget about that."

"Not in a million years."

Twenty-One

AN HOUR LATER I SAT ON A CUSHIONED CHAIR IN A TATTOO SHOP and tried not to throw up.

"Are we sure I need to do this right now?" Mia and Kitty glared at me from the spinning stools they perched on nearby. "Fine, fine. I'm doing it."

"It's not so bad," the tattoo artist, a woman around my age with electric-green hair and gorgeous floral tattoo sleeves, said.

I looked over at the tattoo machine. "Needles make me queasy."

Mia nudged a wastebasket closer to me with her foot.

Alex, Nina, and Greyson remained at the front of the tattoo shop, giving me and the girls some privacy. From what I could hear of their conversation, it seemed they were arguing over Greyson getting a cartilage piercing.

When we'd arrived, Mia, Kitty, and I flipped through a binder of colorful designs, but I'd already known what I wanted. The truth was I'd known it all along, ever since I'd returned home from charter season and stood in my garden.

The tattoo artist sketched out the design and placed it above the crease in my right arm. I stepped over to the mirror and held my breath, moving from side to side, examining it from every angle.

"Do you like it?" Mia asked.

My eyes met theirs in the mirror. "Yeah. Do you?"

The girls nodded, and for once I didn't get a snarky remark.

I let out a breath and turned to the tattoo artist. "All right. Let's do this."

I lowered myself into the chair again and squeezed Kitty's hand, gritting my teeth as the tattoo artist leaned forward. The needle buzzed to life and bit into my skin, but the sting was more bearable than I'd imagined, and my grip on Kitty loosened.

"You know what they say, Jo," Mia said.

"What do they say?"

"It only takes one tattoo to get addicted."

"Have you ever seen a yacht stewardess covered in tattoos?"

Mia spun in a slow circle on her stool. "No. But you and Nina are the only ones I've met." She paused in her spinning. "We could've gotten one together."

"Yeah right, your mom would love that. As if she needs another reason to be mad at me right now." I'd had Mia and Kitty call Beth as soon as they'd gotten in the van and tell her they were staying. *Seriously?* she'd said. *I switched my shift to pick you up. Now my sleep schedule will be off.* But she sounded relieved.

When the outline of the tattoo was almost finished, Kitty said she was bored, though I suspected the sight of ink and blood had gotten to her. She joined Greyson and Nina at the front to look through displays of jeweled earrings, belly button rings, and nose rings. Alex caught my eye and shot me a small smile that I returned, reminding me of the first time I saw him. My heart fluttered like a sail again—no, *again* wasn't right. It just kept on fluttering. I don't think it ever really stopped.

Mia nodded to my arm. "What's it mean?"

We were alone with the tattoo artist, our voices muffled by the buzzing. I looked in the mirror and watched the progress unfold. It felt like scratching at a sunburn, but it was more uncomfortable than painful. The tattoo artist had finished the outline and began filling it in with bursts of red. A sword lily, or, as Samson had called it, a gladiolus. Our birthday flower.

"It's for Samson."

"Obviously." Mia rolled her chair closer to me. "But why that one?"

I told Mia about the morning Samson had discovered my blog. How he'd helped me pick out flowers for my garden and answered every question I had about taking care of them. I told her what he'd said about Roman gladiators wearing them around their necks for protection. How whenever I saw them in my garden, I took a picture for him, even though I couldn't send it. I told her how I imagined the most beautiful ones were ones he'd sent for me.

Mia stared at her hands in her lap. The hard lines that had taken over her face this summer softened. "I can't stop thinking it's my fault."

"I know," I said. "But it's not your fault. And I wish I could've told you that sooner. I spent all summer trying to distract you—and myself, I guess—from thinking about what had happened. But all along we should've been facing this together."

Mia laughed. "You come up with pretty good distractions."

"I do, don't I?" I winced as the tattoo artist passed over a sensitive part of my arm. "Though maybe this wasn't my best idea. I'm only trading one type of pain for another."

"Which hurts worse?"

"I think you know."

Mia nodded. "Yeah, I do."

"You'll be okay," I said. "Not all the time, not every day. But you will be. And I know you can't forgive yourself right now, but eventually you will. I promise."

Tears ran down Mia's cheeks again, and she pressed her hands to her face. "Ugh, what are you doing to me?"

"What I should've done all along," I said, reaching out with the arm that wasn't currently being jabbed by a needle to take her hand.

WHEN WE RETURNED TO THE CONDO AFTER GETTING THE GIRLS clothes at Target and stopping to pick up pizza, the six of us piled into my living room to watch *My Super Sweet 16*. Nina sat on one side of me, and Alex on the other. The girls spread out on the floor in front of the TV. With everyone here, safe, I relaxed for the first time all day.

"My first charter season I had a primary whose kid was on this show," Nina said. "That kid thought he could get away with murder."

"He probably could," Alex said. "I don't get the appeal of this. It makes me scared for the future."

I took the last bite of my pizza and leaned over Alex to set my plate on the side table. "You don't have to worry. For every kid like that, there's three like them." I nodded to Mia, Kitty, and Greyson.

"You mean for every entitled brat, there are three trespassing delinquents?"

I elbowed him in the side. "You know what I mean."

When Nina went home, Alex and I left the girls to another episode and escaped to the patio. We each took a lounge chair and leaned it as far back as it could go. After the chaos of the morning, Alex had been quieter than usual all afternoon. I wondered what he was thinking about as he sat there, so near to me, and yet not near enough.

"Alex?"

He turned his head to me. "Hm?"

"I'm sorry about what I said yesterday. I didn't mean it. I don't really think you're a . . . a martyr or anything. Greyson's lucky to have you. And I understand if you never want to speak to me again. I shouldn't have brought her into it."

Alex shook his head. "How could you think I'd never want to speak to you again? I was mad, but it doesn't change how I feel about you. You can't get rid of me that easy. And I shouldn't have said what I did either."

Relief flooded through me. At least I hadn't pushed him away completely. "No," I said, holding back a laugh. What he'd said about me was true. Ever since Shitty Peter and I broke up, I'd said I wanted to be alone, and that was exactly what I'd gotten. "You were right about me."

Alex held my gaze. "Maybe you were right about me too."

"I'm serious about paying you back for that flight I didn't take."

Alex put his arms behind his head and looked up at the sky. "I told you, it was an early birthday present."

Which was what I figured he'd say, so I let it go.

"Remember when you asked me what Samson was like?"

Alex turned his face to me. "Yes."

"And I said he was great."

"You did."

I watched the palm trees sway in the breeze. "Will you ask me that question again?"

Alex sat up. No almost smile touched his lips, but his expression was kind. "What was he like?"

I closed my eyes, picturing Samson as he'd been the last time I saw him. He'd come with Mark to drop me off at the airport. Before wheeling my suitcase inside, I'd turned back to wave, and Samson was already hanging out the window, waving back with both hands, laughter in his eyes. "He was . . . busy, for one. Energetic like Greyson." I laughed, remembering how I'd once told Samson he'd probably found every good climbing tree in Palm Beach. "He was crawling, and I mean full-on crawling, not army crawling, at six months. Walking at nine. I caught him climbing a windowsill when he was two. He was always climbing things."

"What else?"

"He loved baseball, plants, and video games. He never cared what anyone thought, even when they said he was girlie for liking flowers. He was kind, but you'd regret it if you made him mad. You can ask Kitty about that. They were always at each other's throats. The last few years we'd, uh . . ." I took a slow breath, the memory sharp and painful. "We'd call each other right at midnight on our birthday, so we'd be the first ones to say happy birthday to each other. My sister didn't know about that, she's strict with bedtimes."

I tried not to cry, but it was impossible, because I missed him. What was I supposed to do at midnight on my birthday this year when my phone didn't ring? "I know I'm not supposed to have favorites," I said. "And I love Mia and Kitty so much it hurts, but Samson was my favorite. We just had this . . . bond." I wiped my eyes with Alex's shirt I hadn't yet changed out of. "That's what I meant to say when I told you he was great."

"You must miss him a lot."

"Yeah, I do."

Neither of us spoke for a while. All morning as we'd raced from place to place in pursuit of Mia and Kitty, I thought about what Alex had said about trying long-distance. I loved being around him, listening to him sing, watching him cook, having him close. I loved *him*. But the events of the last two days had only made me more certain long-distance wasn't what I wanted.

"Alex?"

"Yeah?"

"I can't do long-distance."

"I know."

I sat up in my chair, pivoting to face him. We were only inches apart, which was too far for me. I crossed the space between us and sat beside him, feeling the warmth of his thigh against mine. He watched me, silent, and I ran a hand through his hair, unable to keep myself from touching him any longer.

"But I don't want to keep my distance either," I said. "I want to be together until you leave, even if it makes things harder when you go."

His eyes searched mine, and he tucked a loose strand of hair behind my ear. "You're sure?"

"Yes." I stared at him, wanting to keep him forever in my mind exactly how he was now. I memorized the way his hair curled at the nape of his neck, the precise angle of that almost smile, the exact shade of his eyes, more amber than honey, really. He took my face gently in his hands, that intense look in his eyes again, and I was sure I'd die if he didn't kiss me right then.

Fortunately, I didn't have to wait, because the next moment he leaned in, brushing his lips against mine. The kiss was intimate, unlike our kiss at the bar when we were strangers. Tender, unlike the desperate kisses in the parking lot of the karaoke restaurant. My hands found his shoulders and I tugged him down on top of me, kissing him until I forgot where I was. When he pulled away, I felt light-headed in the best possible way. But already, the distance between us was too much, and I tried not to think about how much I'd miss him when he left.

He hovered over me, out of breath, eyes all mischief. "Friends?"

"Absolutely not," I said, the two of us laughing as I pulled him to me once more.

Twenty-Two

THE FOLLOWING SATURDAY I SHOOK MIA AND KITTY AWAKE BE-
fore the sun rose and prodded them into the parking lot, where Alex and
his minivan were waiting for us. The side door slid open, revealing
Greyson and Nina, both blinking groggily.

"Why did you make me get up this early?" Nina complained.

"You invited yourself, remember?" Alex said.

"At least you know where we're going." I climbed into the passenger
seat and fluttered my eyelashes at Alex. "Can I know now?"

"Nope." He took my hand and kissed it. "It's a surprise."

Three days earlier, Alex had stopped by my condo after dinner and
told me to clear my schedule for Saturday but wouldn't tell me where we
were going. To my annoyance, he'd told Mia and Kitty, and their excited
yelps had reached me from where I sat on the patio. *You're a genius*, Mia
had told him. Whatever we were doing, it had to be good.

Alex drove north on the turnpike, which did nothing to narrow
down the possibilities. Almost everything was north of us. It wasn't until we passed into Orlando and Alex put on a Disney playlist that I put
things together. His rendition of "I'll Make a Man Out of You" (in which

he sang all the parts, even Mulan's) earned a round of applause from all
of us, while Nina's "Poor Unfortunate Souls" was so spot-on I was
slightly worried for my own soul.

And me? I was confused. Sure, I'd watched all three *High School Musical* movies at the Zefron-a-thon, but I wasn't one of those Florida residents with a season pass. I'd been to Disney only a few times. One of
those was the summer after I'd moved to Florida. Mia was nine, and Kitty
was six. Both girls had been infected with a severe case of *Frozen* fever, so
Beth flew down with all three kids and met me in Orlando. It had been a
weekend full of walking, and princesses, and a crabby four-year-old who
couldn't care less about Queen Elsa or Mickey Mouse. He'd loved It's a
Small World, though, and forced me to take him on it a dozen times.

Alex glanced over at me. I smiled at him, unsure how to react. What
about this had made Mia call him a genius? Disney would be fun, but
why did it have to be a secret?

"Just wait," Alex said. "You'll understand."

"There it is!" Greyson shouted when we arrived, not at Magic King-
dom, but at Epcot. Ahead of us, the silvery golf ball–like structure of
Spaceship Earth rose above the park. Alex pulled into a space, and I could
sense everyone in the van staring at me, waiting for me to puzzle it out.

I shook my head. "I'm sorry, but I'm not sure what I'm supposed
to get."

Alex grinned. "How do you feel about finishing your list today?"

I blinked. "But the last item is . . ." I looked at Alex, then out at Spaceship Earth. "Oh!" I turned back to him, my smile matching his. All this
time I'd been looking at flights and hotels, desperate to figure out how
to visit five more countries before my birthday, when all I'd needed to
do was look at my own state, where there were eleven "countries" less
than four hours from my house.

"This is . . ." Emotion caught in my chest. I'd said I was okay with not
finishing the list, but I wasn't. I'd gotten so close, which only made missing the mark worse. "Thank you," I said.

I leaned over to kiss him, and shouts of "Gross!" rang out from the back seat.

I whipped around. "Really, Nina?"

"What?" She elbowed Greyson beside her. "Peer pressure."

CANADA WAS OUR FIRST COUNTRY OF THE DAY. WE PASSED INTO Victoria Gardens, flowers in every color blooming all around us. Alex and I slowed, letting Nina and the girls pull ahead.

"It's almost your birthday," he said. "How are you feeling?"

He put his arm around my shoulders, and I sighed into him. "Sad. And happy. And confused."

"Makes sense."

I looked ahead to where Greyson skipped alongside Mia and Kitty. "Greyson seems like she's doing better. How'd it go with the family psychologist?" After Greyson's outburst the night she'd snuck onto the yacht, Alex had called her psychologist and started going to weekly appointments with her.

"I wanted to talk to you about that." Alex stopped walking and turned me to him. "Greyson and I have been talking." My pulse picked up, worried he was about to ask me to come with them to L.A. It wasn't something I expected, but I'd thought about what to say if he asked. And when it came down to it, I just couldn't leave. Florida, my condo, Nina, the *Serendipity*—they were home.

"And Greyson's right," he continued. "If Maggie wants to be her mother, then she needs to fit into Greyson's life. Not the other way around."

I stared at him in disbelief. "You're staying?"

"We're staying."

"Really?"

"Really."

I threw myself at him, nearly knocking him into a tree. I grabbed his face in my hands and couldn't stop kissing him, so happy I thought I'd float away.

"Dad! How many times do I have to remind you of the rules? What I wouldn't *give* to be abducted by aliens right now."

I let go of Alex, finding Greyson and the others a few feet away. "I told you I couldn't abide by the rules, Grey," Alex said, and pulled me to his side.

Greyson rolled her eyes, but she was smiling too.

We spent the day traveling through each of the countries Epcot had to offer, stopping for photos in front of each pavilion and eating our way around the world. We had macarons in France and baklava in Morocco. In Japan, Nina, Alex, and I had sake, while the girls slurped down rainbow shaved ice. By the time we stopped to eat lunch, I was so full I swore I'd never eat again.

"This is it!" Kitty said, skipping ahead as we passed the border between China and Norway, the last of the countries I needed to get to ten and check the final item off the list.

"Here," Alex said. He pulled out his phone as the rest of us stood in front of a replica of the Gol Stave church.

"How do you say 'cheese' in Dutch?" I asked.

"We're in Norway," Kitty said. "They speak Norwegian."

"Right. I knew that."

As the sun set, we squeezed into the crowd of tourists around the World Showcase Lagoon, finding the perfect spot to view the fireworks moments before they began. Nina pulled out a selfie stick from her fun bag and took pictures with the girls, who murmured excitedly with each shimmer of light. A rainbow glow shone on Mia's and Kitty's faces, and I was grateful for this one moment in which their pain was dulled completely. Another firework cracked to life above the water, and as I turned to watch it burst and fizzle in the sky, my eyes fell on Alex beside me, who was looking not at the girls or the fireworks, but back at me. He pressed a kiss to my hair, and I rested my weight against him, my heart thundering in time with each explosion of color above us.

XO, Jo: Blog Post #31

August 24

Happy Birthday (Eve) to me, confessions, and the future of *XO, Jo*

Hello, readers!

Tomorrow is the day you've all been following me for—my thirtieth birthday! Last you heard, I only had two items left: get a tattoo and visit ten countries. I can practically hear you asking, *Did you do it? Did you check off every item on the list?*

I have a confession to make, dear readers. I've been keeping a secret from you (many secrets, actually). Despite the optimism you've seen on this blog, I was 100% certain I wouldn't be able to finish the list when I returned home from charter season in June. I was heartbroken, but not because of the blog or my personal #lifegoals. I was heartbroken because of my nephew, Samson.

And here's my biggest confession: I lied to you about the reason I disappeared during charter season. I didn't want to talk about it, because I thought it was too sad. You come here for lighthearted adventure, right? And besides, I wasn't able to talk to my family and friends about what had happened, let alone the internet.

Some of you may remember my nephew from my post on Item #7—Start a garden. You may remember how he busted me for my blog and gave me a crash course in Gardening 101. But you didn't know Samson loved baseball and adored his older sisters. You didn't know he had so much energy he drove his parents to exhaustion. You didn't know he and I shared the same birthday.

One month into charter season, Samson passed away unexpectedly. The loss devastated me, and I didn't have the energy to blog or check off items on the list. Not until my nieces arrived. Mia and Kitty begged to help finish the list, and though none of us said it, we knew we were doing this for Samson, who was as gentle as he was energetic, as adventurous as he was kind. All summer as I worked on the list, I kept thinking, *What would I have to show him on this first birthday without him? What could be a better gift than making the most of my time, time he didn't get?*

But it turns out finishing the list wasn't the best gift I could give him on what would've been his twelfth birthday. The best gift was something that took me all summer to figure out: letting others in, being as open with my heart as he'd been with his, talking about him and how much he meant to me, even though it hurts. So that's what I'm doing now. Happy birthday, Sam. I love you and miss you more than you could ever know.

But to answer your question. Yes, I finished the list, just not in the way I'd planned.

To explain, I need to divulge my last secret. Deep breath, everyone.

I'm dating both Hot Guy from the Bar *and* Hot Single Dad. Now, before you accuse me (or congratulate me) on my sudden influx of boyfriends, I have to confess that Hot Guy from the Bar and Hot Single Dad are the same guy. Oh, and he's also my coworker. He's asked to go by Hot Yacht Chef from now on (feel free to eye roll), and yes, he's the guy who was wearing the sassy mom shirt in my post on Item #25—Sleep in a castle. (Don't think I didn't read your comments objectifying him in his crop top.)

I'd gotten my tattoo (be on the lookout for that post soon), but with two weeks to go before my birthday, I'd lost all hope of checking off those final five countries. But last Saturday, Hot Yacht Chef forced me to get up at an ungodly hour and pile into his man van (yes, he drives a van) with BFF Nina, my nieces, and his daughter. I had no clue where we were going, but four hours later, I found myself at Epcot and checked off not five, but eight new countries. Goal. Smashed. (I'll have the full details for you as soon as I finish celebrating.)

What's next for *XO, Jo* now that my journey to thirty is at an end? My nieces think I should turn this into a travel blog. Hot Yacht Chef thinks a blog in which I chronicle my attempts at cooking would be hilarious. (I disagree. It would be sad.) BFF Nina suggested a decade-long forty-by-forty list, but just thinking about it stresses me out. All I can tell you is I'm not sure what the next chapter of my internet life or real life holds. But I know that no matter what, I won't be alone through any of it.

Thank you, dear readers, for accompanying me on this journey, and I'll see you soon for whatever's next.

XO, Jo

Twenty-Three

ON THE MORNING OF MY THIRTIETH BIRTHDAY, MIA AND KITTY woke me with an enthusiastic round of "Happy Birthday," then pinned me down and wrangled a sleep mask over my face.

"Don't look so scared, Aunt Jo," Kitty said.

"It's not like we'll strand you somewhere," Mia said, grabbing me by both hands and lifting me to my feet.

I rolled my eyes, which the girls didn't see, thanks to the sleep mask. "It wouldn't be the first time you've ditched me."

"Which turned out great," Mia said. "You should thank us."

"Can I at least put on shoes?"

"You don't need them," Kitty said.

When we stepped outside, I recognized the grit of the concrete walkway, the five steps up to the beach, and the squeak of the gate, so it didn't surprise me when the ground turned to sand beneath me.

"Okay," Mia said. She released her grip on me after we'd walked down the beach a few hundred feet, the ocean growing louder with each step. "Mask off."

I lifted the mask from my face. The sunrise stretched out like a halo above the horizon, and when my eyes adjusted to the light, I spotted a long table draped in heavy seafoam-green cloth: a breakfast buffet of all my favorite things, including chocolate chip waffles, pitchers of orange juice (Drunken Joeys, too, from the looks of it), and a birthday cake in the middle of the table, the frosting blush pink. A beach picnic of my very own.

"Wow," I said, taking in the food and the people standing around it: Nina, Ollie, Alex, and Greyson. Alex and Greyson shouted, "Happy birthday!" while Nina and Ollie shouted, "Happy birthday, bitch!" and, "Happy fucking birthday!" respectively.

I pulled Mia and Kitty into a hug. "You did all this for me?"

"There's still one more surprise," Kitty said.

I turned at a tap on my shoulder, my breath catching in my chest at the sight of my sister standing before me. I barreled into her, the two of us nearly toppling into the sand. "You're here!" I said, bursting into tears and not caring who heard.

"Happy birthday, Jo," Beth said. She held me tight, and the two of us cried into each other's hair, rocking from side to side.

There was so much I wanted to say, but I could hardly speak. "You're here!" was all I could say, over and over, unable to let go of her.

"Okay, okay," Mia grumbled. "Enough of the lovefest, I'm hungry."

Beth put her arm through mine and sat beside me at the table. With my sister on my left, and Alex to my right, so many of the people I loved surrounding me, I couldn't stop smiling. If only Mr. Silicon Valley could see me now.

Beth gestured to the table. "This is beautiful," she said. "I knew my daughters were crafty, but I didn't know they were *this* crafty."

"We're not," Kitty said. "Nina and Alex are."

"You girls have always been great at delegating," Beth said.

"'Delegating' is a nice word for it. Those two are bossy," Nina said.

Beth laughed. "I can't argue with that. You two bossed poor Samson all over the place."

Samson's name was a prick of pain, especially today. But instead of dulling the sting of it by steering the conversation elsewhere, I let it flood through me until it dissolved like sugar under the tongue, no longer solid, but still there.

"It's true," I said. "Kitty, remember when you tricked him into putting your laundry away by telling him you'd left a twenty-dollar bill in your pocket and he could keep it if he found it?"

"You were so upset when he wised up to that one," Beth said to Kitty.

"Yeah," Kitty said. "But it was nice while it lasted."

Beth looked around me to Alex. "Thank you for taking such wonderful care of my sister on her birthday, Chef Alex."

"Mia and Kitty promised me fifty bucks," he said. "But I'm guessing that's not happening."

I nudged him with my shoulder. "I'm teasing," he said. "I'd cook you a birthday breakfast for only twenty dollars."

I swept my gaze around the table, the same glow of happiness I'd felt at my dinner party washing over me, only stronger. I rolled my eyes at Nina and Ollie's bickering and the apron Alex gifted me, then shook with laughter at the birthday song and dance written, choreographed, and performed by Mia, Kitty, and Greyson. Alex made Beth and me cry when he brought out a second cake for Samson, decorated in ferns, and flowers, and even a Venus flytrap. After singing a tearful "Happy Birthday" to him, Mia, Kitty, Beth, and I shared our favorite Samson memories.

When we'd finished eating cake, Beth took my arm in hers. "Walk with me?"

"There's nothing I'd rather do," I said. We left everyone behind, heading toward the pier like we had when we were kids.

"I still can't believe you're here," I said. "And Mark?"

Beth sighed. "We're still figuring things out. I don't know what will happen."

We walked in silence, and I remembered the dozens of walks I'd taken with her over the years. When we were kids, the distance had seemed eternal. Two whole miles. One there, one back. "I miss Samson," I said.

Beth squeezed my arm. "Me too."

Our feet disappeared and reappeared in the water, and I let my courage build with each wave until I was ready to ask her the question that had rolled around in my mind all summer. "If you'd known what was going to happen, would you do it all over again? Was it worth it?"

"Are you kidding?" She stopped and made me look back the way we'd come. Mia, Kitty, and Greyson were doing handstands with Nina again. I wondered if Beth and I were imagining the same thing: summers past, what it would be like if Samson were here. He'd probably do a better handstand than all the girls. "How could it not be worth it?" she said. "I'd do it a thousand times if I could."

Nina, Greyson, and Mia burst into cheers after Kitty successfully held a handstand for a good five seconds. The good, the bad, how could you untangle it? It was impossible. So why not take the good where you could get it? "Yeah," I said. "I think you're right."

AFTER THE BEACH PICNIC ENDED, BETH, ALEX, AND I SAT ON THE beach with the girls, facing the water.

Kitty rested her head on my shoulder. "I wish we didn't have to go."

"I wish you didn't, either, but your mom wouldn't listen when I told her you were too cool for school."

"It's true," Beth said. "You're not."

Mia rolled her eyes, then put her arm through mine. "We'll be back soon."

"Thank God," Greyson said. She flopped onto her back in the sand. "I think you should all move down here. Can you imagine if we were in the same class, Kitty? But either way, I guess we'll see a lot of each other from now on."

The girls convinced Beth to take them to the pool one last time, leaving Alex and me alone on the beach.

"You know what's funny?" he said.

"What?"

"I haven't actually taken you on a real date yet."

I leaned away from him. "You're telling me all those times we carted around a van full of teenagers weren't dates?"

Alex grinned. "I know it isn't the way most guys do it, but I prefer not to have my thirteen-year-old daughter with me when I take a woman out."

"And why's that?"

He shrugged. "I have a feeling it would kill the making-out-at-the-drive-in vibe I'm going for."

"So that's what we're doing? I figured you'd want to cook a romantic dinner together."

He laughed. "Don't take this the wrong way, but that sounds a little too stressful for a first date. Maybe after you've had a few cooking lessons."

"Oh, do you know a good chef or something?"

"I might."

I eyed him. "I'll think about it."

"Think about what?"

"Going out with you."

"You'll think about it?" Alex said. "I haven't even asked you."

He leaned back on his hands and turned away from me to stare out at the water again. I watched him, waiting. After a full minute of silence, I bumped his shoulder with mine. "Well, are you going to do it?"

He turned to me as if he'd only just noticed I was there. "Going to do what?"

I rolled my eyes, and that almost smile lit up his face. "Are you free tomorrow night?" he said.

I shrugged. "I might be."

"How would you like to see a movie and make out in my van?"

I mirrored his posture, leaning back on my hands. "I guess that sounds all right."

We fell silent, and as I looked at Alex, I marveled at how twelve weeks ago he'd been a stranger. Nothing more than a man I'd kissed in a bar and told myself I never wanted to see again. But what amazed me more than the thought of how quickly he'd become part of my life was the thought of him ever having been a stranger at all.

"What?" Alex said, catching me staring at him.

"Close your eyes," I said.

"Why?" Alex asked, but he closed them anyway.

Instead of answering, I leaned in and kissed him, exactly as I had the night we met.

"Wow," Alex said when I pulled away. "If this is the reaction I get by *asking* you on a date, I'm really excited for the actual date."

I moved closer, resting my head against his chest. "Don't get too excited. That's just how I say hello, remember?"

He wrapped his arms around me and pulled me close. "Do you say hello to everyone like that?"

"Nope. Just you."

"Well, then," Alex said. He pressed a kiss to my temple. "I hope there are a lot more hellos where that came from."

"Me too," I said.

I hoped for more than I could count.

Acknowledgments

Many thanks to my literary agent, Wendy Sherman, for believing in me from the beginning. To my editor, Kerry Donovan, thank you for loving this story and making it better.

Thank you to the many publishing professionals who had a role in the making of this book: Callie Deitrick, Mary Geren, Jessica Mangicaro, Natalie Sellars, Michelle Kasper, Alaina Christensen, Angelina Krahn, George Towne, Jessica Brock, and the entire team at Berkley. Thank you to Emily Osborne and Janelle Barone for a beautiful cover.

To Carly Gates, Stace Budzko, and Belle Boggs, thank you for mentoring me. My thanks to all the folks at NC State University's MFA program. To Therese Anne Fowler, thank you for your advice and support.

To anyone I interacted with while writing this book: Thank you, and I'm sorry. Special thanks to the friends who lift me up: the MIMs, Joanna Anderson, Katie Morris, Viktorija Girton, Giedre Sidrys, and Kelsey Godfrey.

To Krystal Beaumont, Melinda Benbrahim, Kelly Herman, Laurel Hostetter, Sasha Frinzl, and Maria Putzke: Thank you for reading this book at its worst and helping it become its best.

My deepest gratitude to the friends of my heart: Danielle Gillette, Emelia Attridge, and Raven Heroux. Thank you for listening to countless voice notes, talking out every story idea, reading draft after draft after draft. You are the readers I hold in my heart when I write.

Thank you to TISWIT, the Berkletes, and the Sprint Team, for making me feel seen. My thanks to the online spaces that have become my home, especially during this last year: r/RomanceBooks, the Romance Author's Writing Group Discord, and the bookstagram and writing communities on Instagram.

To my family, for making me a little weird and teaching me to always find joy. To my parents, Sophia, Chris, Camencha, and Neto: Thank you for loving me and supporting me in every way. Thanks to my sister, Michelle, for having a cool job and introducing me to *Below Deck*.

To my children, Carolina and Nicolas: My world is brighter with you in it. Thank you for inspiring me, for loving me, and for your endless patience.

To my husband and greatest champion, Marco Ruiz: Thank you for always saying yes to my wildest dreams and for being my partner in every way. I could write a million romance heroes, but none would live up to you.

Above all, I give thanks to God, whose goodness and faithfulness sustains me through all things.

CONTINUE READING FOR A PREVIEW OF

Luck and Last Resorts

BY SARAH GRUNDER RUIZ,
COMING IN AUGUST 2022!

JUNE

RETURNING HOME FROM MONTHS AT SEA IS LIKE WAKING UP from one dream right into another. Charter season is four months of sunshine, the bluest water that ever existed, and lots and lots of money. But it's also sixteen-hour shifts, sleep deprivation, and late nights scrubbing the vomit of hungover billionaires from white carpet. Yet at the end of the season, we always come to Mitch's, an Irish pub that puts the "dive" in "dive bar." Mitch's is dirtier than someone who cleans a twenty-million-dollar yacht for a living would like, and the dust on the bookcase beside our table is likely a health violation, but seeing as it's the first mess in months that isn't my responsibility to clean, I couldn't care less.

Some people never experience déjà vu, but I feel it all the time. More and more as the years pass. Every time I slip into this booth at Mitch's, for instance. Jo, the *Serendipity*'s second stew and my soon-to-be *former* best friend, says I'm just bored. But I disagree. How can I be bored when I work on a giant boat and run away to the Caribbean four months a year? How can I be bored when I get paid to see the places most people only dream of? As Jo's nieces would say, I am *living the dream*. Usually, I don't disagree.

Usually.

But as I stare across the table at Jo, *nightmare* is the word that comes to mind. I can see her mouth moving, but I don't hear a word. I'm distracted by the sudden ache in my bad knee, which, after the last four months working barefoot, is aggravated by even the lowest of low-heeled wedges. In a few days, my knee will adjust to life on land along with the rest of me. All I have to do is ignore the pain until it fades. But what Jo's just told me? I won't adjust to it. I refuse.

"Nina?" Jo's voice comes back into focus, the feeling of déjà vu slipping away. Her gaze darts from me to her fiancé, Alex, beside her.

"It's an awful idea," I say. It's all I can manage, because this is the most ridiculous thing I've ever heard. Jo quitting the yacht? To help Alex run a restaurant?

Jo frowns into her drink. "That's all you have to say?"

"You can't even cook, Josephine. They don't pass out Michelin stars for knowing how to operate a microwave." I gesture to Alex. "How are you going to help this man run a restaurant? Sure, he makes a great cheese Danish, but the sex can't be that good."

"I'm trying to focus on the part where you compliment my cooking," Alex says.

"Don't." I shoot him a glare.

"I won't be cooking," Jo says, twirling the straw in her margarita glass as she speaks. "I'll help manage the place."

Alex puts an arm around Jo's shoulders, and though I love him for loving Jo, I also want to punch him in the ribs. Not hard enough to break one, but enough for him to understand how all of this is making me feel. Enough to make breathing difficult. I haven't set foot on a balance beam in years, but the thought of Jo quitting the *Serendipity* knocks the wind out of me, reminding me of when I busted my knee during Olympic team trials, ending my athletic career with one poorly timed dismount.

A better friend would smile, buy a round of shots, celebrate this new phase of her friend's life. But I am not Jo's better friend, I'm her *best* friend. And as such, I can't help but think of all the things I'm losing. *You're upset because she's choosing him over you*, the bitchy voice in my head says. The voice isn't wrong. Of course Jo is choosing Alex over me. He's the fiancé. I'm the best friend. That's what happens when people get engaged, or land their dream job, or find something else they can't resist.

"This is worse than a secret fetus," I whisper into my drink.

Alex tenses in his seat. "A what?"

I wave a hand at Jo. "I thought you may have impregnated her. She's been acting weird all week."

Alex looks at Jo, beer dribbling down his chin.

"I'm not pregnant," she says. "You've seen me drinking all season. We shared a fishbowl at that weird pirate bar—"

"Davy Jones's Locker is *festive*, not weird." I fiddle with one of the dangling unicorn earrings I only take off to shower and sleep. "You could've been pregnant. I don't know your life. How am I supposed to know if you adhere to the CDC guidelines for pregnancy?"

"You *do* know my life," Jo says. "Which means you also know I never planned to work in yachting forever. I never planned to work in yachting at all."

The three of us fall silent. Mitch's walls are littered with photographs and ticket stubs and dollar bills, making me feel as if I've stepped into a stripper's scrapbook. I glance at the wall beside us, my heart cartwheeling in my chest when I spot the Polaroid of me, Jo, and Ollie, the *Serendipity*'s chef before Alex. I decide that our current chef, Amir, is my new favorite. His food isn't as good as Ollie's or Alex's, but at least Amir has never broken my heart.

Ollie and I started on the *Serendipity* the same year, when both of us were new to yachting. We'd worked together for eight charter seasons, and it was in this very bar, almost two years ago to the day, I'd found out he was leaving to become sous-chef at Miami's illustrious Il Gabbiano.

Don't think about him, the bitchy voice in my head chides. But how can I avoid it when he's staring right at me from that damn Polaroid? I lean over and grab the photo, yanking it free from the wall with one sure pull.

"Nina," Jo says. "What're you—"

"Souvenir." I shove the photo into my bra. I'm not sure what I'll do with it: burn it, tuck it into a book, sneak back here in a week and staple it to the wall again.

"Shots!" a voice sings out.

Beside the table is Britt, the annoying little sister I never had, and the *Serendipity*'s third stew. She grins at us, completely oblivious to the tension at the table, four shot glasses crowded in her hands.

I take two of the shot glasses and glare at Jo. "None for you, traitor," I say, tipping Jo's shot down my throat before chasing it with mine.

Britt scoots into the booth energetically, nudging me against the wall and blocking me into this hellscape.

"Lord help me, sitting next to you all night," I say, shoving Britt over until half her ass hangs out of the booth. "Where's RJ? He'd let a girl have some peace of mind."

Britt snorts. "I doubt it."

I've never heard RJ, the *Serendipity*'s bosun, string more than a sentence together at a time, and I've known him for as long as I've been in yachting. Jo and I exchange a look that says *What's that supposed to mean?* But I look away when I remember she is now my *former* best friend.

"Shouldn't you be somewhere mooning over Amir anyway?" I ask Britt. Their love affair had done nothing positive for the efficiency of the interior crew this season.

"I'm letting him miss me," Britt says. Her gaze is unfocused, and I wonder how many shots she's had already. "What is it with stewardesses and chefs?" she muses. "Is it the knives? I mean, it's got to be more than a coincidence. Me and Amir, Jo and Alex, you and—" I raise an eyebrow at her. She mimics my expression, realizing her mistake. "Uh, Chrissy Teigen."

"Is Chrissy technically a chef?" I ask, twirling the two empty shot

Excerpt from LUCK AND LAST RESORTS 319

glasses on the table before me. "There was an enthusiastic debate about it on Twitter a few weeks ago, and I don't remember what the consensus was." Alex opens his mouth to answer, but I cut him off. "Rhetorical question, Alex. I don't want to hear anything from you. It's bad enough you've stolen away my former best friend."

Jo looks stricken. "Former?"

Britt sighs unsteadily against the table, nearly toppling out of the booth. "They told you, huh."

Impossible. "You knew about this?"

"Britt!" Jo hisses.

"Surprise!" Britt says, flashing drunken jazz hands at me.

"She's taking over for me," Jo explains.

Which means Xav, our captain, already knows about this too. "Next you'll tell me RJ found out before me."

"That may be my fault," Britt slurs. She grabs Jo's unfinished margarita, but I pry it from her hands, passing her my water instead.

"She wasn't supposed to tell anyone," Jo says.

"RJ made me tell him," Britt says. She leans forward, trying to catch the straw for the water in her mouth and missing.

I ignore the revelation that RJ actually speaks to someone and turn to Jo. "When?"

"When did Britt tell RJ?"

"When are you leaving me?"

Jo bites her lip but doesn't answer.

"*When*, Josephine?"

"Two weeks," Alex says, putting Jo out of her misery.

Two weeks? No, no. Clearly, she hasn't thought this through. "Britt can't take over for Jo. She always does Med season." Almost every photo Britt posts is either of her on the *Serendipity* or the *Talisman*, the super-yacht she works on in the Mediterranean Sea after we finish charter season in the Caribbean. The woman only lives on land October through January. I elbow Britt. "Tell them."

"Screw Med season," Britt says, her cheek pressed to the table.

I look between my two colluding stewardesses, the cartwheels in my chest becoming Tsuk vaults and back handsprings.

"I need another drink," I announce, forcing Britt to sit up and move out of my way so I can escape.

"Now, now, girls, let's just talk this through," Britt slurs.

"You're drunk," I tell her. "You're all drunk!" I add, waving to Jo and Alex. "But she's the drunkest," I say, pointing to Britt. "So keep an eye on her." I'm more than a little tipsy myself, but I can't be trapped here in this booth, not right now, or I'll say something I regret.

"Nina, don't go," Jo says.

"I'm just going to the bar for another drink, like I said." I shoot her a smile I don't feel, because I know my hysterics will only hurt her, and Jo is the last person in the world I want to hurt, even when I'm angry with her. "I'll only be a minute."

Instead of going to the bar, I prowl the perimeter of Mitch's, running a hand over the dozens of dollar bills that jump out at me, crowded by the photographs and refuse of people's lives. A shame to leave all this money here, still valuable but stuck. What could a person buy with it all? After making sure no one is watching me, I pry a dollar from the wall, the paper so worn it feels like fabric in my fingers. I stuff it into my bra beside the photograph.

Drunk on tequila and greed, I reach for another dollar. Instead of returning to the table, I'll go down the street to the gas station and buy a pack of cigarettes. I'll spend the evening chain smoking in the parking lot. I'll inhale the whole pack, one after another, until I throw up. It probably wouldn't take long. I haven't smoked in years.

"One charter season without me, and you turn to a life of crime?" a familiar Irish accent says, startling me as I pull the dollar from the wall.

I didn't know he'd be here, but a part of me had hoped. Even so, I won't give him the satisfaction of turning around to face him. "What are you doing here? You aren't part of the crew," I say, folding the dollar and tucking it into my bra.

"Alex invited me. He's not crew anymore, either. Besides, Mitch's is open to the public, is it not?"

I should've known this was Alex's doing. He and Ollie have become *buds* over the last year. They even have matching T-shirts with Gordon Ramsay's face on them that say, *Where's the lamb sauce?* I don't get the joke, and I don't want to. All I know is Ollie talks to Alex about me, and I don't like it.

"What's the craic?" Ollie says, pronouncing *craic* like "crack."

His breath is warm against my skin, and he smells like the mint tea he drinks obsessively. My instinct is to lean into him, but I'm not sure if being around him will make tonight better or worse, so I try not to move.

"I don't know *where the crack is*, Oliver. Do I look like I buy drugs on street corners?" I know that's not the "crack" he's talking about. I've picked up more Irish slang over the years than I let on. This is just part of the game we play.

"You know I don't like being called Oliver," he says, like he always does when I use his full name.

"And you know I don't care," I reply, like I have hundreds of times. Thousands, maybe. Same old barbs. Same old reactions. I like to think of them as the grooves of our relationship. We settle into them when we're around each other just to remind ourselves they exist. If we stick to the lines, we can play this game for as long as we like. If we follow the rules, no one gets hurt.

Ollie wraps his arms around me, resting his chin on my shoulder. I hate how I don't mind it. How I can't help but rest my weight against his chest. Before Jo, it was just me and Ollie. A whole lifetime ago, it seems. He and I have more history than I care to admit. And though Jo is my best friend, my relationship with Ollie means just as much, albeit in a vastly different and infinitely more complicated way.

Ollie's barely-there stubble scratches my cheek when he speaks. "You good, Neen?"

"Why wouldn't I be?" I say, keeping my eyes on the wall ahead of me. *Better*, I think. *Being around him will make tonight better.*

"Heard you might've got some bad news," he says.

I stiffen in his arms. So even he found out about Jo and Alex's betrayal before me. *Worse*, I decide. *Being around him will make tonight worse.* "I'm marvelous."

Ollie's nose nudges my neck, and I try to ignore the way it makes me weak in the knees, and not just the bad one. "I've missed you," he says, not at all the way you tell your ex-coworker you miss them.

I want to put some space between us, but Ollie is comfortable, and warm, and familiar. "Where's your girlfriend?" I ask. Sondra? Samantha? Tall. Redhead. I like her.

"Don't have one anymore."

No surprise there. The man goes through girlfriends faster than I can snap up a pair of vintage Levi's off the rack. "What was wrong with this one?"

"She wasn't you," he says, his breath raising goose bumps on my neck. So he wants to play *that* version of our game.

"Not tonight," I say, pulling his arms off me with a sigh.

"It's true."

I turn, getting the first good look at him I've had since I left for charter season. He's unchanged, everything about him as in-between as ever. His hair, between blond and brown, between straight and curly, the sides short and longer on top. He isn't tall, but he isn't short either. Even his outfit—a navy button-down, light-wash jeans, and white sneakers—falls somewhere between formal and informal. That's not to say Ollie is plain, because he isn't. There's something striking about the balance of him. Beautiful, really.

The only out-of-balance feature on Oliver Dunne are his eyes. Blue, but not like the sky or the ocean. They're an intense, impossible blue that reminds me of the blue raspberry Slurpees I shared with my father after gymnastics practice when I was a kid. We'd stop by the 7-Eleven, and I'd stay in the truck while my father disappeared inside. He kept a lucky penny in the cupholder between our seats, and I'd warm it between my palms while I waited for him. When he returned, I'd pass him the penny for his scratch-off ticket in exchange for the Slurpee. Every now and then the smell of copper and scratch-off dust washes over me, making me sick. I'd thought my father and I were playing a game. I suppose we were. But that didn't mean there weren't consequences.

I've encountered many attractive people in my life, ones who wanted exactly what I did—no feelings, no strings attached—but none of them drives me crazy like Ollie does. At first, I thought it was the accent. But even with his mouth shut I want to kiss him. I tell Jo I don't love him. I tell *him* I don't love him. But of course I do. If soul mates exist, Oliver Dunne is the closest thing I have to one. That doesn't mean we're good for each other. It doesn't make either of us immune to the damage we can inflict on one another. It doesn't change the rules.

Ollie looks me up and down. "Nice dress," he says. It is nice. A knee-length color-block dress with matching buttons down the front. Vintage Liz Claiborne. One hundred percent silk. He catches the hem between his fingers, and his knuckles brush against my thigh. "Where'd you get it?"

"Do you really care?" I should take a step back, but my muscles are frozen. I blame the bad knee.

"Maybe I do," Ollie says, his eyes on the fabric between his fingers.

"Butch, of course." Butch, the owner of my favorite thrift store, knows exactly what I like.

"Aye, the one and only Butch. You make me jealous when you talk about him."

When he lifts his gaze to mine, I force myself not to look away. I hate when he does that—makes me feel stark naked when I'm obviously overdressed.

"You *should* be jealous. Butch is the man of my heart, and—"

"Jo is the woman, aye, I know."

"Not anymore." I look beyond Ollie. Amir, RJ, and some of the other deckhands have joined Jo, Alex, and Britt at the table. Amir says something that makes everyone but RJ laugh. The look RJ gives him could fillet him alive. At least I'm not the only one who's miserable tonight.

Ollie doesn't say anything else. When I look up at him again, I catch the soft smile he saves only for me. Being near him is like sighing into my couch when I first get home from charter season. We haven't spent much time together since Jo and Alex got engaged. The restaurant keeps Ollie busy, and I've avoided driving down to see him ever since the last time I ended up in his bed.

Lately, my friendship with Ollie has consisted of phone calls on his drive home from work. Most nights he calls just as I've gotten into bed. I always put the phone on speaker and close my eyes as we talk, mostly about nothing. The restaurant, the yacht, weird Craigslist listings. By the time Ollie unlocks his apartment door, I'm usually half asleep, lulled there by the sound of his voice.

It sounds like a capital "R" Relationship, but it's not. I don't know what to call it. The phone calls and occasional hookups are all I can give. They're enough for me. But this phase, the one in which we can be friends, only lasts so long before Ollie is itching for more, something with a label. And when I refuse, he'll pull away from me again. We won't talk for months, maybe a year. He always says he's done, and sometimes he finds someone else, someone he really likes. But it's no use. We always find ourselves back here, walking this in-between place like a balance beam.

"Did you miss me?" he asks.

Yes. But I'd never tell him that. "We spoke yesterday. Though you failed to mention you'd be here."

"Wasn't sure I'd come. But I like to see the faces you make when you're teasing me."

"Teasing? Me? Never."

I rest my hands on his shoulders. "You're built like a hunky fridge," I say, my hands sliding down to give his biceps a squeeze. He laughs, and I shoot him a glare. "What? You're frigid, and bulky, and occasionally provide food." I'm making quite the spectacle of myself tonight. Maybe it's time to give up the tequila.

"That face. Right there," Ollie says. He presses his thumb to my lips. "And you say you don't tease me."

The moves my heart are doing now would be physically impossible for anyone but Simone Biles. If he wants to play this version of our little game, then that's what we'll do. Screw the consequences. I take Ollie's hand in mine, tracing my fingers over the back of his hand before flipping it over to squint at his palm like a fortune-teller. I know the callous at the base of his forefinger, could map out the small scars and discolored burns that run up his hands and arms. Even when I don't want to, I think of them whenever someone else touches me. It's a real mood killer.

"No new injuries, I see."

"Not on this hand, no."

"And the other?"

He puts his other hand in mine, and I spot a new burn right away, just behind the knuckle of his pinkie finger. "New line cook who doesn't look where he's fecking going," he says.

"I wish you'd be more careful," I say, regretting it as soon as I look at Ollie and see his smile has become a smirk.

"So you did miss me."

"I didn't say that."

"You seem to care an awful lot about what happens to me."

"Because I plan on being the one to kill you."

"Oh, you'll be the death of me, all right," he says.

"Good. We agree. Follow me."

"Yes, ma'am."

I drop one of Ollie's hands, keeping a tight grip on the other as I pull him through Mitch's and toward the door that leads to the back parking lot. This will only make me feel better for a little while. I know that. But I'm not very good at taking advice, especially my own.

As soon as we step outside, I press my hands to Ollie's chest, pushing him against the brick exterior of Mitch's.

"You smell like a tin of Altoids," I say.

"Probably taste like them too," he says.

"This means nothing."

"Sure thing, Neen."

I lift myself onto my toes, Jo's news and the ache in my bad knee all but forgotten. At first the kiss is soft, almost sweet. Kissing Ollie is like working a charter—familiar, but never boring. He tastes exactly as I remember. I'd bet all my tips he has a still-warm tumbler of peppermint tea in his car. Ollie's fingers slide into my hair and he pulls me closer, deepening the kiss. My hands find his shoulders again. Really, does the man do anything besides swear, and cook, and work out?

When we pull apart, Ollie drags a hand over his mouth. "This is a little fucked-up, Neen."

I ignore the comment and lean in to kiss him again, but Ollie catches my shoulders, holding me back. "You want to tell me what this is really about?"

A flame of annoyance licks through me. This is not part of the game. We don't talk about *why* we do things. We just do them. "I've been at sea for four months, what else could it be about?"

Ollie pushes my hair, down from its usual high ponytail for once, over one shoulder. He tugs gently at one of my unicorn earrings. "These give a man false hope, you know."

My eyes leave his to run over his gently sloping nose, to his mouth, the full bottom lip, bowed on top. "Please, don't," I say, surprised to find myself blinking back tears.

How do I always end up kissing Oliver Dunne in secret? Despite what he says about missing me and breaking up with his girlfriend, this thing between us is not serious. We shouldn't be anyway. And as Ollie said, this is fucked-up. I should be inside celebrating the next chapter of my best friend's life. But instead I'm in a bar parking lot making out with the ex Jo doesn't even know is an ex so I can forget about it.

Ollie's hand drops from my ear. He pulls me closer, and I think he's going to kiss me, but instead he tucks my head beneath his chin, holding me to his chest. "It's all right," he whispers, one hand rubbing my back in big circles. "Nothin' has to change. You and Jo will be the same as ever."

I want to believe him, but Ollie is wrong. I can feel it. My entire universe is being reordered, just like when he quit the boat last year. Things between us changed, and now we hardly see each other. My bad knee is throbbing now. It's the same feeling I get when I'm on the *Serendipity* and know a storm is coming. The sky may be cloudless and blue, and RJ and Xav can tell me there's nothing on the radar until they're red in the face, but I'm never wrong about storms. It's like they're a part of me.

Ollie can pretend he doesn't feel it, but I know he does.

Everything is about to change.

Photo by Joanna Sue Photography

Sarah Grunder Ruiz is a writer, educator, and karaoke enthusiast. Originally from South Florida, she now lives in Raleigh, North Carolina, with her husband and two children. She holds an MFA in creative writing from North Carolina State University, where she now teaches First-Year Writing.

CONNECT ONLINE

SarahRuizWrites.com

SarahGrunderRuiz